Sweet Passions at Bayside

Sweet with Heat: Bayside Summers Series

Addison Cole

ISBN-13: 978-1-941480-63-2
ISBN-10: 1-941480-63-2

SWEET PASSIONS AT BAYSIDE

Cover Design: Elizabeth Mackey Designs
Cover Photographer: Elvind Lunde Tellefsen
Cover Models: Stian Bjørnes and Vibeke Rose Johansen

PRINTED IN THE UNITED STATES OF AMERICA

A Note to Readers

Every time I create a story set on Cape Cod my world gets a little bit brighter. Emery and Dean's story is one of love, laughter, and of course, a sweet happily ever after. I hope you enjoy their love story as much as I do! If this is your first Sweet with Heat book, you might also enjoy reading Sweet with Heat: Seaside Summers, another fun series featuring a group of friends who gather each summer at their Cape Cod cottages. You may enjoy starting with *Read, Write, Love at Seaside* (free in digital format at the time of this publication).

Not all of my future releases will have preorders. Please be sure to sign up for my newsletter and follow me on Facebook so you don't miss them.

www.AddisonCole.com/Newsletter
www.facebook.com/AddisonColeAuthor

About Sweet with Heat Novels

Addison Cole is the sweet-romance pen name of *New York Times* bestselling author Melissa Foster. Sweet with Heat books are the sweet editions of Melissa's award-winning, steamy romance collection Love in Bloom. The storylines and characters remain significantly the same as the original titles, with minor repositioning of secondary characters. Within the Sweet with Heat series you'll find fiercely loyal heroes and smart, empowered women on their search for true love. They're flawed, funny, and easy to relate to. These emotional romances portray all the passion two people in love convey without any graphic love scenes and little or no harsh language (with the exception of an occasional "damn" or "hell"). Characters from each series appear in future Sweet with Heat books.

Bayside Summers is just one of the series in the Sweet with Heat romance collection. All Sweet with Heat books may be enjoyed as stand-alone novels or as part of the larger series. There are no cliffhangers or unresolved issues, and characters from each series make appearances in future books, so you never miss an engagement, wedding, or birth.

For more information on Sweet with Heat titles visit www.AddisonCole.com

Chapter One

THERE WERE A few things worse than being stuck in traffic and needing to pee, but after driving since the crack of dawn and sitting on the same stretch of highway for the past forty minutes—which was about thirty minutes longer than her bladder could handle—Emery Andrews couldn't think of a single one. Her back teeth were floating, and if she didn't find a bathroom soon, her car would become a swimming pool. She should have thought about weekend traffic *before* hightailing it out of Oak Falls, Virginia, and heading for her new home and workplace, Summer House Inn, in Wellfleet, Massachusetts. But thinking things through wasn't Emery's forte. She was more of a just-do-it-and-worry-about-things-later type of girl, as evident in her move to the Cape.

Now, if she could only get there.

She gazed out at the long line of brake lights in front of her and picked up her phone to call her best friend, Desiree Cleary. Desiree had been like a sister to her since they were five years old, and last summer, she had fallen in love, reconnected with her half sister, Violet, *and* decided to move to the Cape and open the inn, all in the space of a few short weeks. Desiree's excitement was contagious. Every time they spoke on the

1

phone, she raved about her new life with her fiancé, Rick Savage, and her plans for the inn, and it had sparked introspection in Emery. She realized *she* wasn't living a life she was excited by in Oak Falls—and she had no one to blame but herself. After making a poor decision right before the holidays and going out with her boss at the Oak Falls Back Care and Rehabilitation Center, where she had worked full-time as a yoga back-care specialist, she'd ended up leaving the practice. Unfortunately, she'd signed a non-compete specifically for providing the one thing that brought her the most fulfillment and could no longer practice yoga back care within a fifty-mile radius of the rehabilitation center. In the small rural town of Oak Falls, her career, and her personal life, seemed to have stalled.

She'd needed a fresh start, and when Desiree had invited her up to Wellfleet to teach yoga at the inn, she'd jumped at the chance.

Desiree answered the phone on the second ring. "Hey, Em. I can't talk. It's changeover day. I have three customers waiting to be checked in and two on hold. Call you later?"

"Wait! I'm in Orleans, trying to get there. But—"

"Orleans? Really?" There was no missing the excitement, or the hesitation, in Desiree's voice. "I thought you were coming next week. I don't have an open room until this Wednesday. Why didn't you call and let me know you were coming early?"

"Because after quitting my job and packing up my apartment, the emptiness freaked me out and I was excited to get the heck out of Oak Falls and see you!"

Emery had always been the adventurous one, while Desiree had been cautious, thinking things through to the nth degree. But along with Emery's boxed-up belongings came a big *what if.* What if she couldn't find enough clients to make a living? And as she'd sat in her empty apartment contemplating that worry, she'd realized that leaving the only place she'd ever lived, and leaving her family, wasn't going to be as easy as she'd imagined. But although she'd been sad about leaving them, her three older brothers had called her several times during her long ride up, making her glad to be moving out from under their watchful eyes. She knew if she had stayed in town for another week, they, and her other worries, would have driven her batty. She had never let *anything* stop her from doing things in the past, and she knew the only way to get over those fears was to plow full speed ahead—and plow she did!

"But with this traffic," Emery said, "I'll never get there. I'm stuck on the highway right before the rotary. Should I get a motel room until you have a vacancy?"

"Oh, Em, you'll never get one. It's peak season. Everyone's booked. But don't worry. I'm sure Vi will let you stay in her cottage." Desiree and Violet had renovated the old Victorian and the four cottages that had once been owned by their grandparents. "I'll mention it to Vi, but you might as well find someplace to hang out for a few hours until the traffic eases up. Maybe you can do some shopping in Orleans," Desiree suggested. "I'm so sorry, but I really can't talk right now. Will you be okay for a few hours on your own?" Before Emery could respond Desiree said, "*Of course* you will be. You love new adventures! We'll catch up when you get here. And if you hang out in Orleans, be sure to bring me something from the Chocolate Sparrow!" Desiree blew a kiss into the phone and the line went dead.

The decadent chocolate shop had been closed when Emery had visited over the holidays, and the way Desiree talked about it, their chocolates sounded practically *orgasmic.*

I could use a few orgasms—chocolate inspired or otherwise.

She mulled over the idea of trying to make it to the chocolate shop as the cars ahead of her crawled into the rotary. Traffic was at a standstill getting off the rotary and onto the main drag in either direction—toward the Summer House Inn *and* toward the orgasmic chocolates in Orleans. She squeezed her thighs together. She'd worn her new bikini beneath her tank dress and had hoped to be lying out on the beach by now. The last thing she needed was to pee all over it. She spotted an exit on the opposite side of the rotary.

The heck with it. Desiree was always telling her about back roads the tourists didn't know about. It was time for her first Wellfleet adventure.

She squeezed by the line of cars waiting to get onto the main drag and drove halfway around the rotary to a side road. As she pulled onto it, she realized it ran in the wrong direction, back the way she'd come. She scrolled through her contacts and called the man who had become her *second* best friend, Dean Masters. She'd met Dean when Rick, who was Dean's business partner and one of his closest friends, had flown Emery in over the holidays to surprise Desiree the night he proposed. They'd hit it off right away, and they'd kept in touch after she'd returned home to Virginia. What had started as a storm of daily teasing texts about a big red ribbon she'd had tied around her body the night they'd met had turned into evening phone calls and morning wake-up messages, and eventually, into a friendship she'd come to trust and rely on.

"Hi, doll. How's it going?"

Dean's deep voice, and the endearment he'd used since the day they'd met, brought a smile, and just like that, the knot in her stomach eased. Dean had seamlessly filled the gap Desiree had left behind, binge-watching shows with Emery while they Skyped and talking until the wee hours of the morning about everything and nothing at all. They were so different, they shouldn't have clicked. While Emery barreled into situations with little thought about repercussions, Dean was a thinker, careful and methodical, like Desiree. And, like Desiree, he'd become the yang to her yin.

"Hey, big guy. *Please* tell me you can get me to the inn from"—she glanced at the road sign—"Rock Harbor Road." At the next corner, she turned off the main road and onto a residential street, hoping to find a back way to the inn or maybe one of those small-town shops Desiree was always talking about, so she could use their bathroom.

"You're in town?"

"Yes! *Please* get me to someplace with a bathroom fast. Traffic is a nightmare, and I've got to pee so bad I swear I'm going to knock on the next door I see."

"Okay, slow down," he said with a serious tone. "Before you make some stranger's day, follow my directions. Turn right onto Bridge Road."

"Um…" She looked for road signs. "I turned off the main road already, and I have no idea what street I'm on now."

"Of course you don't."

She rolled her eyes at the smirk in his voice.

"Why don't you use your GPS?"

Two weeks ago, she'd called him when she'd gotten lost coming home from a concert and he'd walked her through how to use the GPS. Even with his careful instructions, she'd gotten frustrated and nearly thrown the darn thing out the window. "You *know* I hate that thing. The stupid voice tells me what to do way too late, and I can't hear it with the radio on, and I *really* think it should have a male voice option anyway."

He laughed.

She tried to concentrate on the narrow, windy road and not on her near-bursting bladder. "Don't do that!"

"What?" He chuckled again.

She squeezed her thighs together. "*Don't laugh!* If I laugh I'll wet my pants."

He was silent for so long she checked her phone for a signal. "Hello? Dean? Are you there?"

"Sorry. I muted you."

"Why?"

"You told me not to laugh, and I'm picturing you bouncing in your seat trying not to pee, and…" His words were lost in his laughter.

And so went the next fifteen minutes as Dean figured out where she was and directed her to his house. By the time she got there she was ready to burst. She flew out of her car, tearing a path around gorgeous, overflowing gardens, and headed for Dean's front door. He came around the side yard, shirtless, carrying an enormous rock that covered his entire torso. His jaw was clenched tight. Veins bulged in his thick neck, broad chest, and massive arms as he bent his knees and set the rock at the edge of a garden.

Her breath whooshed from her lungs.

Holy mother of hotness.

She'd almost forgotten how large and powerful, how *commanding*, he was in person, and how from their very first glance, he'd made her stomach flip and tumble. His hair was the same honey-wheat color as hers, cropped so short he looked military. And *wow*, he'd kept the beard he'd grown over the winter after all. He'd told her he usually went clean-shaven over the summers, but she'd pleaded with him to keep it. She'd told him the girls would love it, and she knew she was right. He looked even tougher than usual, and coupled with his perpetually serious expression, he appeared as if he were going to snap at any moment.

The big faker.

Beneath that big, bad facade was the most patient man she'd ever met. That trait had taken her by surprise, and now she found herself swallowing hard to silence the lascivious woman inside her who was preparing for a coming-home party.

No way. Not happening. She'd dated friends before, and it never ended well. She'd long ago put Dean into the off-limits section of her brain, whether her body remembered that rule or not.

He rose to his full height of six-plus feet, spotting her. An amused look rose in his gunmetal-blue eyes, and she realized she was staring at him, with her thighs pressed together. *Aw, heck!* What could she do but laugh, which quickly sent an urgent sensation rippling through her bladder.

Dean jogged up to the front porch and threw the door open. "Go on, doll. Down the hall to the left."

"You're my hero." She planted a quick kiss on his cheek. She'd asked him why he called her that the first weekend they'd met, and his response had been, *No reason.*

He smacked her butt as she ran through the door.

"I swear I'll pee on your floor!"

"Not the response I usually get," he called after her. "But if that's what you're into…"

She couldn't stop grinning. It was so good to see him, so good to be back near Desiree and the other friends she'd made last winter. With her bladder finally empty, she washed her hands and took a moment to check herself out in the mirror. Yup, she looked like she'd spent all day in a car. Her hair was tied in a knot and secured with a pencil she'd found in the console. Several strands had sprung free, giving her a disheveled look. She pulled out the pencil, and her hair tumbled down her back. She cupped a hand over her mouth and breathed into it.

Ugh. Coffee breath.

She opened the vanity drawer and dug around looking for toothpaste. *Floss, Band-Aids, deodorant, nail clippers, beard oil, beard balm.* She picked up the beard oil and opened the top to sniff it. *Mm. Cedar.* She read the label. Organic. *Nice.* Scented with peppermint, eucalyptus, and lavender essential oils. Looked like her second-bestie treated himself well. She put the cap back on and set the beard oil in the drawer, then rifled through another drawer and found toothpaste. She squeezed a bit on her finger and scrubbed her teeth clean.

"Hey, doll. You okay in there?" Dean called through the door.

She pulled it open, held up her finger to indicate *one second,* and gathered her hair over one shoulder as she turned the faucet on and dipped her mouth under it. She rinsed her mouth and washed her hands as he watched with a curious expression.

"That's so much better. I borrowed your toothpaste."

He arched a brow. "Got a date?"

"Ha! I wish." She threw herself into his arms, hugging him so tight she could feel his heart pounding against hers. "I'm so glad to finally be here!"

"Me too." He set her on her feet. "Sorry about the dirt. I'm sure I smell pretty ripe, too." He hiked a thumb over his shoulder. "I'm landscaping out back."

She brushed the dirt from the front of her dress and dragged her eyes down his incredibly hot bod, wondering why he didn't have some chick there with him. Desiree had told her that girls hit on Dean all the time. "You smell like your beard oil, which I *might* have snooped into."

His eyes narrowed. "Snooped?"

She waved a hand dismissively. "Of course! I needed tooth-paste. Anyway, I like the way it smells, and it's good to know you take care of yourself in ways other than just building these bad boys up." She ran her hands over his bulbous biceps and he gritted his teeth. She laughed and patted his cheek. "You look like you want to growl at me."

Having grown up with three older brothers, she got along better with guys than girls and had always had more guy friends than girlfriends. She'd learned at a young age that guys had a hard time holding anything back. If he wanted to growl, she'd let him growl.

"Something like that," he said under his breath.

She followed him into the living room. "Why is your stuff in there anyway and not in the master bathroom?"

"Only one bathroom in the house."

"Really? Why?"

"I don't know. Why would a single guy need more than one bathroom? More importantly, I thought you weren't coming up until next week. What happened?"

Ever since Desiree moved away and she and Dean had become friends, Emery had felt like her life was here now, too. "I felt like I was waiting for water to boil, and I was so excited to come and start my life here, and see you, Des, Vi, and Serena and everyone else, I said the heck with it!" Serena ran the administrative offices of the resort Dean co-owned with Rick and Rick's brother, Drake. "And here I am! But with the traffic, I can't get to Desiree's, and she said it could be backed up for hours. Something about changeover day?"

"With only one road on and off the Cape, it's one big traffic jam on changeover days. Saturdays are the worst, but Sundays can be a headache, too."

"Do you know a back road to her place?"

He turned, brows knitted. "I can take you over on the Jet Ski."

"Oh, fun!" Her excitement deflated as quickly as it had arrived. "But then I can't bring my stuff."

"Why don't you hang out here and help me in my yard? We'll throw something on the grill for dinner, and you can go over when the traffic clears."

"You must landscape *all* the time. Your yard looks like it belongs in a magazine."

"Thanks." He shrugged and said, "Gotta do what you love, right?"

She knew that in addition to being co-owner of the resort, Dean maintained a few clients with his own landscape business—the hospital where he used to work as a trauma nurse and the local assisted living facility, where he worked in the gardens with the residents. Emery liked to tease him about his elderly fan club. Dean was great at keeping his emotions close to his chest, which made him difficult to read sometimes, but whether they were texting or talking on the phone, his passion for his work always came through loud and clear.

"Very true." She loved what she did for a living, but lately she'd craved more than the yoga classes she'd been teaching at a gym since leaving the rehab center. She hoped one day to return to being a yoga back-care specialist and to turn her passion for yoga back care into something more meaningful. But those were plans for another time.

One major life event at a time.

To distract herself from her thoughts, she focused on Dean's cottage. She took in the hardwood floors and wood-paneled walls that ran the length of the open living room and kitchen, which were separated only by a table for two. A black cast-iron oven and cooktop and fridge complemented earth-toned granite countertops atop rustic wood cabinets. Long, rough-hewn wooden shelves held dishes and cups, giving the place the brawny feel of a bachelor pad.

"I saw glimpses of your place when we FaceTimed and Skyped, but"—*like seeing you in person again*—"experiencing it firsthand has a much stronger impact. This is incredible. So earthy and rugged. I love it." She ran her fingers over the simple oak table.

"Thanks. This is the original house built on the property. When I renovated, I wanted to preserve the rustic feel, so I used old, sun-bleached scaffold boards for the walls and floors. Check this out. It's my favorite feature." He went to the wall that faced the kitchen, unhooked something near the top and then near the bottom, and slid the entire wall *into* the living room wall, like he would a pocket door. "These are barn doors I repurposed from another property."

At least ten or fifteen feet of wall space disappeared before her eyes, opening the small kitchen to a magnificent trellis-covered patio, with potted plants overflowing with life on top of enormous rocks, like the one Dean had been carrying when she arrived. Comfortable-looking rockers and two oversized loungers had a gorgeous view of more impeccable gardens.

"Wow, Dean. I've never seen anything like this." She followed him outside, where low stone walls lined either side of the patio. A fireplace anchored one end, and she spied the telltale wooden stall of an outdoor shower just beyond. Her gaze swept along the gorgeous pavers, and she imagined how wonderful it would be to meditate there in the early mornings, when the rest of the world was asleep. She'd seen the hardscaping he'd done at the resort, but this was even more breathtaking.

They walked along a rocky path between two garden beds. She recognized some of the flowers and was happy to see roses and lavender, which she could use to steep tea. As they wound through the path surrounded by vibrant flowers, with the sun shining down on them, it felt like she'd stepped into his private paradise.

"Sort of coaxes you into thinking about a simpler lifestyle, doesn't it?" he asked.

"Definitely. If I lived here, I might never want to leave. But what landscaping are you doing? Everything already looks gorgeous."

His hand pressed against her back as he guided her around a wall of bushes. She'd forgotten how often he'd done that the weekend they'd met, and how nice it felt. Most guys just said they'd show her something and expected her to follow. Her burly buddy might look standoffish to some, but he was the most gentlemanly guy she knew.

"Thank you for letting me use your bathroom and hang out for a while." She put her arms around his waist and hugged him. His entire body felt like one giant muscle. His hand moved up her back, returning the embrace. It wasn't the rushed embrace of a man looking to get lucky—which she was all too familiar with. It was a gentle yet powerful loving embrace that spoke volumes about their close friendship, and it made her feel like she'd come home instead of having left it all behind.

"Anytime, doll," he said. "And if it'll earn me hugs, then use my bathroom as often as you'd like."

They walked around more garden beds, and nestled between a rock garden and a grassy area with lounge chairs and a small table, there was a patch of tilled earth with all sorts of weeds growing around the edges.

"This is my latest project." The edges of his lips tipped up. "Are you in? Or do you want to sit in traffic?"

"Heck, yes, I'm in. But I warn you, I have a black thumb. I can kill a plant just by looking at it."

He laughed. "I highly doubt that. I'll go grab another trowel and a couple of cold drinks. Be right back."

Helping weed his garden was the least she could do. After all, he was the one who'd convinced her to give this move a go. During one of the many nights when they were FaceTiming, she'd mentioned that she was thinking about coming up for the summer to see if she could get a seasonal yoga business off the ground, hoping it would not only be a nice change of pace for her, but that it would also bring added value to the inn for Desiree and Violet's customers. Dean had asked, *How can you succeed at anything, giving only half an effort?* She'd seen it as a *huge* step, moving away for the summer, not half an effort, but then he'd followed that question with one that had stopped her in her tracks. *Are you always afraid to commit, or are you worried you'll miss your family?* And she'd found herself retracing the last few years of her life and realizing that maybe, *just maybe*, he'd figured out what she never had. And the more she'd thought about it, the more convinced she'd become that she had been the adventurous one, but only within the safety of her small hometown. It was time to blaze a new adventure and blow that girl out of the water.

She heard a phone ring in the house, jarring her from her memories. Shrugging off those thoughts, she set to work ripping out the weeds.

DEAN PRESSED HIS cell phone to his ear, trying to hurry his older brother, Jett, off the phone. But Jett was busy apologizing about having to be in Argentina to close a major investment deal, which would cause him to miss the upcoming benefit dinner for the Pediatric Neurology Foundation their late grandfather had established. It was just another in a long line of Jett's excuses, even if this one sounded valid. Their father was going to be a keynote speaker at the event and, as usual, Dean had given in to his mother's plea and agreed to attend in support of *the family*, while Jett did his own thing. Dean wasn't looking forward to attending the stuffy event, but he would put on his best face, if only to keep from hurting his mother's feelings. After all, their oldest brother, Doug, wouldn't be at the event either. Doug had married right after medical school and was working overseas. Being a physician, he had a very different relationship with their father than Jett or Dean, but that didn't affect his relationships with them. Although Dean was close to each of his brothers, equal parts of him respected and resented Jett's choices.

"I swear I'll make it up to you," Jett promised. As a real-estate investor, Jett owned plenty of properties in and out of the country, including a waterfront he'd purchased several years ago in Wellfleet, though he had yet to build on it. He stayed at whichever of his properties was closest to his current business, which meant he never stayed in any one place for very long.

"Whatever, dude. I've got this." *Like always.*

Dean had been dealing with the aftermath of Jett's distancing himself from the family for years. Jett had never forgiven their father for briefly separating from their mother when he and his brothers were young. To this day, Dean had no idea what had led to their father's leaving or what had transpired to bring him back home beyond being told that his parents *had hit a rough patch.* But that brief three-month separation had destroyed Jett's trust in their father. When Jett had gone off to college, rarely coming back to visit, and their oldest brother, Doug, was getting ready for medical school, Dean had taken it upon himself to make sure their mother didn't feel abandoned. He'd buried his own dark feelings toward his father in order to help smooth things over in the wake of Jett's rebellion.

"What's happening with the chick from Virginia?" Jett asked. "She comes next week, right?"

Dean loved his brother, but after months of getting to know Emery, and endless nights spent fantasizing about what it would be like when they were together again, she was finally within reach. He'd much rather spend time with her than explain to Jett that if anything were to develop between him and Emery, who'd sworn off dating friends, it would take a lot of finesse. *Or a miracle.*

"Listen, dude. I've got tons of work to get done today and I have to run. Hit me up when you return to the States and you can pay me back for attending the dinner from hell."

After he ended the call, he poured two glasses of iced tea, wishing he had fresh lemons, since he knew Emery's favorite drink was ice water with fresh lemon slices. He carried the drinks out to the yard, grabbing an extra trowel from the shed on his way.

He didn't know how he'd gotten lucky enough to be Emery's emergency bathroom stop, but he was in no hurry to get rid of her. When she'd first told him she was moving to the Cape, he'd thought he was the luckiest guy on earth and hoped he had a chance at convincing her to give up that nonsense about not going out with friends. Or more specifically, not going out with *him*. But he knew he had to bide his time. The last thing he wanted was to scare her off. And to make matters worse, when she'd come to him and his partners about the idea of offering yoga to their customers, he'd been torn. While it would mean she would be around more often, she'd told him months ago about how much she had loved working as a yoga back-care specialist with the elderly before she'd gone out with—then broken up with—her idiot boss and she'd been forced to resign in order to escape his stalkerish ways, and in doing so, she'd lost the career she'd loved. *The bastard.* Dean knew she wouldn't find that type of fulfillment teaching yoga to vacationers at the inn or the resort. But his desire to see her again had selfishly won out, and he'd agreed to the arrangement even though everything inside him had wanted to push her to take the time to network and figure out how to get involved with what she really wanted, despite the fact that it might have meant delaying her arrival.

He was a strong man, but Emery had become his Achilles' heel, and his best intentions and desires had been pushed aside in order to have her nearby—but that didn't mean he'd look the other way forever about making sure she didn't forgo the career she really wanted.

As he came around the bushes, he shoved those thoughts away and said, "Hey, doll, I brought iced—" *Holy. Smokes.*

Emery lay on her back on a lounge chair in a skimpy yellow bikini top and barely there brown bottoms with cutouts over her hips. Her body was sleek and toned, and so sexy he had to stifle a groan. Her long, golden-brown hair was spread out around her just like in his midnight fantasies, save for that itsy-bitsy bikini. A thin leather necklace rested against her tanned skin, two small silver charms lying between her breasts. He'd give anything to take their place.

She opened one gorgeous hazel eye, shading it with her hand. "Hey there." Her gaze flicked to the drinks. "Oh! Iced tea?" She jumped up from the chair, flaunting her gorgeous figure as she grabbed a drink from his hand and took a sip. "Mm. Needs sugar."

"Sugar," he mumbled, trying to untangle his lust-addled thoughts. The trowel dropped to the ground.

"No worries. I've got it." She bent over to pick up the trowel, and her butt cheeks peeked out from beneath her bikini bottom.

He turned away and bit his knuckle, hoping the spear of pain might keep his libido from rising any further.

When he turned around, she was taking off her bracelets. "I got your weeding done. It wasn't so hard after all," she said as she set several bracelets on the garden table and fiddled with a thick silver one.

He was vaguely aware of her speaking—*weeding?*—but that itsy-bitsy bikini revealed too much for him to concentrate, and he pretended to focus on her unscrewing something on her bracelet so she wouldn't catch him lusting after her. She tipped the bracelet over and poured white powder into her palm from some secret container within the shiny silver bangle.

His stomach sank. "Em, what is that? You're not into drugs,

are you?"

A mischievous smile played on her lips. "You have known me for five months. Don't you think you'd know if I were a druggy?"

She was right. He would. Emery wasn't the type of woman who held back her thoughts. Most of the time she had no filter whatsoever. He'd asked her about her candid comments once, and she'd said *growing up with three brothers did that to a girl.* She'd explained that she'd learned to speak her mind so she wouldn't get walked all over. Dean didn't have a sister, but he took Emery at her word. After all, she didn't seem to know how to do anything but tell the truth.

They'd shared hundreds of texts and late-night phone calls, during which she'd told him about everything from her work woes to her dating life, filling him in on more details than he could handle in some cases. He was surprised by how much he *wanted* to know everything about her—including the details of botched dates that made him want to kill the guys. Even if through gritted teeth, he loved talking with her. He liked knowing that her favorite shows were offbeat, and sometimes scary, adventures, and her favorite movies were sappy love stories, despite her not believing in true love. And he found her likes and dislikes in people interesting. She didn't shy away from aggressiveness the way some girls did. She seemed to thrive on it, which he'd learned had set her up for heartache too many times for his liking. He knew how lonely she'd been after Desiree had moved away, and in the hours they'd spent talking about it she'd unknowingly revealed the sensitive woman behind that tough-girl persona. Yes, Emery Andrews might be a complicated firecracker, but she'd been an open book from the moment they'd met. That was just one of the things he loved about her. He'd had his fill of women who played games.

Unfortunately, they'd become *such* good friends, and with her recent swearing off of dating friends, he had a feeling that's all he could ever be to her.

She licked her finger, then dipped it in the white powder and held it up to his mouth with a playful glimmer in her eyes. "Open."

Like a trained pup, he opened his mouth, wanting *her* to jump in. She put her finger in his mouth and rubbed it over his tongue. He grabbed her wrist and sucked her finger clean, puckering at the saccharine taste.

She pulled her finger away, laughing.

"What the heck was that?"

"Splenda!" She tapped the powder into her glass and set the bangle on the table beside her other bracelets. "I hate Equal and that's about all anyone ever has. I used to carry sugar, but I needed too much of it. So…Splenda it is. Do you want some?"

"Depends what you're offering," he said under his breath.

"Splenda, silly." She took a long drink, and his entire body came alive as she licked her plump lips. "Mm. That hit the spot."

I'd like to hit your spot.

He needed to get a freaking grip. It had been much easier to control himself when Emery was hundreds of miles away. He set his drink on the table and cleared his throat, as if that might help to scatter his dirty thoughts.

"Aren't you happy that I weeded?" she asked cheerfully. "Now you can just sit back and relax with me."

He followed her gaze to the garden, remembering something she'd said about weeding earlier, when he'd been too busy checking her out to process it. His stomach knotted at the sight of the plants he'd spent all morning planting lying in a pile on the dirt.

"Well?" She blinked up at him with a proud, enthusiastic expression. "Great, right?"

A disbelieving laugh fell from his lips, and he turned away. He pushed a hand through his hair, stroked his beard, and ground his back teeth together in an effort to quell his frustration. When he faced her again he hoped his expression was casual enough to mask his irritation.

"Oh no. Did I do it wrong?" Her eyes shifted to the plants she'd dug up.

She sounded devastated, and it took his frustration down from *Holy cow, my plants* to wanting to take her in his arms and make her smile again. Before he could think of the best way to handle the situation, she bent over in front of him, reaching for the plants—and exposing her gorgeous butt again.

"Should I have put them in a bucket or something?"

He grabbed her arm and hauled her upright. "No buckets. Didn't you have clothes on before? I think you need to put something on."

She looked up at the sky. "Why? It's gorgeous out. And you don't have a shirt on."

He muttered under his breath. "Never mind." The confused look in her eyes turned his insides to mush. "Okay, doll, time to teach you the difference between three-toothed cinquefoil and weeds."

"Three-toothed what?" She put her drink down and set her hands on her hips. "Oh no. I killed your weeds and you wanted them, didn't you? I'm so sorry!" She threw her arms around his waist, crushing her softness against him. "I told you I have a black thumb. I'm so sorry. I'll make it up to you."

Heat radiated from every point where their bodies connected, lighting him up like a bottle rocket. He reluctantly peeled her arms away and guzzled his drink. When that didn't cool him down, he dug into the glass for ice and rubbed it over his chest.

Her eyes opened wider. "You're so mad you're sweating? I really do suck. I'm sorry."

He shook his head and knelt beside the pile of plants, trying not to think about her *sucking*, or that slinky little bathing suit, and patted the ground beside him. "It was an honest mistake. I'm not mad. Come here, doll."

She squatted, resting her forearms on her thighs, which pushed her breasts together and made them nearly pop out of her top.

"Don't look at my boobs." She adjusted her bikini top, which did nothing to help. "The *girls* always want to come out and play."

"Geez, Em. Put a shirt on." *Before I take them up on their offer.*

"*You* put a shirt on."

"I'm not the one with overzealous tatas."

She smiled. "Did you just call my boobs 'tatas'?"

"Would you rather I said 'jugs'?"

"No. I hate that word."

"Boobs? Breasts? Knockers? Melons? Cupcakes?"

Laughter burst from her lungs.

He loved her loud, boisterous laugh and tried to prolong hearing it. "Hooters? Fun bags? Love apples?"

She fell to the side, holding her stomach. "Stop! Stop! I'm gonna pee!"

Laughing right along with her, he sat on the dirt. Dean had

spent years as a trauma nurse, and it had changed his outlook on life. He'd always been pretty serious, but trying to save people on death's doorstep changed a person. He couldn't remember the last time he'd lost himself in laughter.

Oh wait. Yes, he could. It was Valentine's Day, when he and Emery had FaceTimed. She'd been filling in for a friend, delivering singing telegrams, dressed up like a cupid in a skimpy red leotard complete with wings and foam arrows. She'd insisted on acting out every single telegram she'd delivered, and the recipients' reactions to them. What had started as a holy-cow-you-danced-around-in-*that* conversation had turned into rip-roaring hilarity.

"You should do that more often," she said, wiping happy tears from her eyes.

He reached over and wiped a tear that had slid all the way to the edge of her jaw. "Do what?"

"Smile."

Their eyes connected and his world halted, the temperature spiked, and the very air seemed to hum. But just as quickly as hope filled him, she pushed up to her knees, breaking the spell.

"Okay, *boob man*. Tell me about three-toothed squirrels."

He knelt beside her, wondering if he'd imagined the heat.

"Cinquefoil." He grabbed a plant, focusing on it instead of his overactive desires. "See the woody stem and evergreen leaves? They'll grow little white flowers."

"Sorry, Dean, but they still look like weeds to me."

"Okay, I'll give you that, because they're small. They're for groundcover, and really beautiful when they flower." He picked up the hand shovel and gave it to her. "Dig a hole."

"A hole? How big?"

"Big enough to replant this."

She thrust the shovel into the dirt deep enough to bury a small animal. He reached around her, stilling her hands.

"The earth is already tilled," he explained. His gaze caught on the glimmering gold bracelet on her wrist. The one he'd sent her for her birthday with the tiny delphinium flower charm. He slid his gaze to her other bracelets on the table. "Why didn't you take that bracelet off?"

"I don't know," she said absently. "I never take it off."

He wanted to read far more into that than she probably meant. Knowing Emery, the extra safety clasp he'd had put on the bracelet was just too much of a pain to fiddle with.

"You only need to cover what's left of the roots. Like this." He guided her efforts, his bare chest pressed against her warm, soft back. She smelled like sunshine and lavender, feminine and *pretty*, just like she had the weekend they'd first met. That weekend had passed in a whirlwind of celebrating Desiree and Rick's engagement. Dean had grown up with Rick and his siblings, Drake and Mira. The weekend of the party, they had all hung out together in a group. And although he and Emery had spent nearly every minute by each other's side, flirting like there was no tomorrow, he'd refrained from trying to take it any further because she was only there for a weekend and he wasn't looking for a quick, meaningless lay. But then they'd kept in touch, and the desire to be closer to her had grown. And now all he wanted to do was soak all of her in.

She dipped her chin, and her hair brushed against his shoulder. He imagined it sweeping across his chest, spread out over his pillow, brushing over his thighs...

Torture. Pure torture.

He put a few inches of space between them, hoping to temper his desires...*again.*

"Good job." He handed her the plant, giving him something else to focus on. "Now put this in and push the dirt around it."

"Put it in the hole," she said as she did it, "and pack it in good." She smiled up at him. "How'd I do?"

He was still hung up on putting it in the hole and packing it in good. He cleared his throat and said, "Great. See? You don't have a black thumb, just a confused one. Now we have to do the rest of them."

They worked side by side replanting the garden and teasing each other as they'd done for months long-distance. This was so much better. Their friendship was easy and natural, and as much as he wanted more, he knew if he pushed for it, he could ruin everything. If he could keep himself in check, at least he had a chance for something more developing naturally.

That was a big *if.*

When they finished planting he brought out the hose and watered the plants.

"What now?" she asked, surveying their work.

"Now we pray they don't go into shock."

"Oh no, really? I feel horrible, but they actually look prettier now. Not so much like weeds." With a hand on her slim hip, she said, "They obviously needed my touch."

He was pretty sure *he'd* look better if she had her hands all over him, too. He sprayed her with the hose and she shrieked, taking off right through the garden they'd just planted. He dropped the hose and thrust his hands out, catching her around the waist and lifting her straight up before she could trample the plants, her legs still moving. He tossed her over his shoulder and carried her toward the house.

"Hey! I'm sorry! Dean! Where are you taking me?"

"Keeping the chaos away from my gardens." If she were *his*, he'd carry her straight into the bedroom and keep her busy so she couldn't cause any more trouble. But she wasn't, and she'd told him enough horror stories over the last few months about dating friends to know better than to even try. He stopped at the patio and set her on her feet.

She crossed her arms and narrowed her beautiful eyes. "Are you calling me *chaos?*"

He was sure she meant to look mean, but she looked so cute, and he couldn't help but smile. "You said it, *whirlwind*, not me."

Tango, one of his two kittens, wound around her feet. She scooped him up, holding him against her chest and nuzzling his head. "I am *not* chaos *or* a whirlwind. Am I, little guy?" She glanced at Dean, rubbing her cheek against the area of the cat's head where his ear should have been. "I can't believe I can finally hold Tango. I wanted to *so* badly when I saw you feeding him and Cash on Skype."

In early spring, when he was out for a morning run, Dean had found the two kittens down by a marsh. They were nothing but skin and bones, shivering, with barely enough energy to lift their heads. Both had been severely injured. Tango, a calico, was missing one ear, and the wound had become infected. Cash, who was all gray, had an open wound on his tail. He'd taken them directly to the vet, and they'd clung to him like a lifeline. He'd bottle-fed them and cared for their wounds. They'd recovered well and had become mischievous little guys, and they'd been sleeping on his bed ever since.

She rubbed noses with the kitty and set him down. "Where's Cash?"

He shrugged. "Probably out prowling around somewhere."

"Speaking of prowling around, why aren't you out chasing hot chicks on your day off? You do landscaping all week long. Don't you want some *prowling* time?"

"Do I seem like the prowling type to you?" He had women hitting on him all day long at the resort, the assisted living facility, the hospital, and at the beach. Once upon a time, he'd enjoyed that availability to the fullest, but ever since getting to know Emery, there had been only one woman on his mind.

And at the moment, she was bending over to pet Tango, giving him an eyeful of her *playful girls* and driving him out of his ever-loving mind.

Chapter Two

"YOU MIGHT BE even better at grilling than Desiree is at making breakfast." Emery reached over and stole a pineapple chunk from Dean's plate. He'd grilled shrimp and steak kabobs with chunks of pineapple and peppers for dinner, and they were eating at the table on the patio. After the garden debacle, she'd been relegated to the patio, the house, or basically anywhere that wasn't green. "You know, that says something, considering Desiree's breakfast skills are driven by her sex life."

The running joke at Summer House Inn, where Dean, Rick, and the rest of their friends gathered for breakfast most mornings, was that the quality of Desiree's breakfasts was determined by how hot her love life with Rick had been the night before. Emery had to admit, she was a little jealous that Desiree had a five-star love life while hers was practically nonexistent. She'd had plenty of experience over the years, but watching her best friend fall madly in love had opened her eyes to what she'd never known she was missing. Not that she was capable of having such a loving, stable relationship. Her parents had divorced when she was young, and although she still had a close-knit family and had grown up splitting time between both parents' houses, neither she nor her brothers seemed capable of maintaining anything worthy of being called a *relationship*—much less finding everlasting love.

She pushed those thoughts away and snagged another pine-apple chunk from Dean's plate, having nearly licked her own clean. "By *Desiree* standards, you must be getting some pretty hot sex, too. That's not surprising. I mean look at you." She waved her hand at him. "You've got it all going on, with that killer smile, eyes that say, 'I'll take you and cherish you at once,' and a body that turn women's minds to mush from twenty feet away."

He raised his brows in quick succession. "Give you any ideas?"

"Like you need me on your list of lovers?" She laughed and took a sip of his iced tea, as hers was already gone. Dean had spoken often about hanging out with friends and his work over the past few months, but he'd only alluded to going on a few first dates. She was curious about his personal life. "As I said, you must be keeping busy."

He scoffed. "Hardly."

"Seriously? You cook this well *just because?*" Cash wound around her feet, purring. She'd loved him up while Dean was grilling, and he'd been following her around ever since. "I'm not buying it."

"I do everything well *just because.*"

Enjoying his cockiness, she said, "Careful saying that around women, big guy. They'll want you to *perform.*" Her phone vibrated with a text and she began licking her fingers while simultaneously looking around for her napkin. She spotted it on the ground and bent to retrieve it. "Can you check that text for me?"

"I'm a little busy," he said, eyeing her cleavage.

She glared at him and wiped her hands, but they stuck to the napkin. "Ugh. Still sticky. Maybe you could put your checking-out skills to better use and read my text for me."

"You really want me to *read* your text?"

It was cute to see such a large, confident man worrying about what he might see on her phone. "It's probably my brothers checking up on me. Come on, it's not like it's going to be a dirty text from a hot guy or anything." Dean had met her entire family over Easter, when her older brother Austin had walked in on the two of them FaceTiming at their mother's house. Austin had made a big deal of bringing the whole family in to meet Dean in a failed attempt to embarrass her. She didn't get embarrassed over friendships. He'd deemed Dean *Viking* that night because of his beard and the stern impression he'd left on Austin. Before she'd taken off for the Cape, Austin had told her not to call him in a month and say she was shacking up with Dean, or he'd come out and teach the poor bastard a lesson. Yes, being out from under her brothers' thumbs was a very good thing, though with her luck, there was no chance of making out with—much less shacking up with—anyone anytime soon.

She went into the house and washed her hands in the kitchen sink. "Not all of us have great love lives," she called out to Dean.

"I know your dating history, remember? I'm not checking your text."

She came outside and grabbed her phone. "I love that whole disappearing-wall thing you have going on." She read the text from Desiree. *Where are you? Did you find a new BFF?* "Des wants to know if I have a new BFF." She read her response aloud as she typed it. "*I'm with my number two BFF. You might know him. Big, bearded badboy with mad cooking skills.*"

She smiled at Dean and said, "We should get everyone together and go to that bar in Truro we went to at Christmastime. Do you think the traffic is gone yet? Can you give me directions to Desiree's?"

"Undercover? Sounds good, and yeah, the traffic is probably gone. I'll write down directions."

Her phone vibrated with Desiree's response, and she read it to Dean. "Tell the bearded cooker he'll never take my number one spot. Come over so I can see you!"

"Tell her the competition is on," Dean teased.

She smiled, imagining Dean trying to beat out Desiree as her very best bestie. How could he top more than twenty years of friendship? She sent a quick response to Desiree. *Okay. Be there soon. We're going to Undercover tonight. Can you and Rick come and bring Vi, Serena, and Drake?* She was glad she already had a small group of friends here. Back home, if she'd asked friends to meet her at a bar, at least thirty people she'd known her whole life would show up. And, she realized, not one of those people knew her as well as Desiree and Dean did.

"I'd better get going if I want to shower before we go out." She began clearing the table, wondering if people who lived at the beach just threw on a tank top over their bathing suits and headed out for the night? She waved at her bathing suit and asked, "I can't go like this. Can I?"

"Not with your *playful girls* on display, you can't."

She smirked. "Maybe I should. Who knows? Maybe I'll find a hot date that way."

He scowled and carried his dishes inside. He scribbled down directions to Desiree's, mumbling something about getting herself into trouble, and Emery went to get her belongings from the table by the garden. She slipped her dress over her head, admiring their planting job. Three of her footprints were evident through the middle of the garden. Remembering how quickly and easily Dean had intercepted her holy-garden terror, she got down on her hands and knees and filled the holes in with dirt. She grabbed her keys, bangle, and one of her other bracelets, searching high and low for the third bracelet. She finally gave up and headed back to the house.

"I lost one of my bracelets," she said as she joined Dean on the patio. "It's silver and says, 'Blame it on my gypsy soul,' I think. It might say, 'I solemnly swear I'm up to no good,' and it might actually be gold not silver. I can't remember which one I wore, but if you find it, can you hang on to it for me?"

"Are you sure you had it on when you got here?"

"Mm-hm. Pretty sure, anyway. It's not that big a deal if you can't find it. I have a ton of them."

He handed her the directions and walked her out front.

"Don't you want help cleaning up?"

"After seeing how you helped with the garden?" He cracked a smile, and he must have seen the guilt she felt written all over her face, because he touched her back and said, "I'm kidding, doll. The garden actually looks better now."

"You're the greatest for lying to me." She set her things on the passenger seat of her Jetta. "Thanks for letting me hang here for the day."

"Anytime, doll."

She gave him a kiss on the cheek. "Mm. You smell good after a hard day of lounging around with me." She climbed into the car and started it up. "See you at Undercover."

"Looking forward to it."

As she drove away, she felt like she'd been visiting Dean for a week, not just a handful of hours. Things were like that between them. When they talked on the phone hours would pass feeling like minutes. She was glad it was no different in person.

The roads were clear, and it took her less than ten minutes to get to the inn. This weekend traffic flow would take some getting used to. In Oak Falls heavy traffic meant it took seven minutes instead of five to get to work, and that was a rarity.

She parked beside Violet's motorcycle, taking in the gorgeous gardens, which she knew Dean had helped with in the spring, the cute cottages lining the right side of the property, and the magnificent Victorian overlooking Cape Cod Bay. Desiree and Rick lived in the main house, and they rented out the other rooms, as well as two of the four cottages. They used one of the cottages as Devi's Discoveries, the art gallery (with a lingerie and adult-*pleasure* shop in the back, which they called an *adult-exploration* shop) their flighty, vagabond mother, Lizza Vancroft, had left for them to run when she'd taken off for some sort of overseas meditation mission.

Emery climbed from the car feeling a thousand times calmer than she had when she'd left Virginia. Spending the day with Dean had centered her and eased her anxieties. Looking forward to her new adventure, she drew in a deep breath and grabbed a few of her bags from the trunk.

Desiree burst out of Violet's cottage. Her wavy blond hair was secured at the base of her neck, and her floral sundress swung around her thighs as she ran toward Emery. Emery squealed, dropped her bags, and plowed into her open arms, hugging, laughing, and talking at once as Violet sauntered out of the cottage and joined them.

"I can't believe you're here!" Desiree said.

Emery's cheeks hurt from grinning so hard. "Me either!"

"We're going to have so much fun!" Desiree stepped back, holding Emery's hands. "I've missed you *so* much."

"Me too. We need to have a slumber party and stay up all night catching up."

"A slumber party?" Violet asked. She was the antithesis of Desiree, with long raven hair and colorful tattoos snaking down her shoulder and arm from beneath a black tank top. Her gray miniskirt revealed more tattoos on the side of her thigh. "Are you going to do each other's hair and nails, too?"

Emery launched into Violet's arms, squeezing her tight.

Violet wasn't a hugger, but beneath the harsh exterior and verbal slaughter she'd dole out to anyone she pleased, she was a good, kind, and creative person who, Emery and Desiree believed, just needed love to soften her up. They were determined to break Violet of what they called her Wall of Warning.

"If you don't hug me back, I'll keep hugging you," Emery threatened. "And it's 'we' as in you, too, Vi."

Violet sighed, her arms briefly circling Emery. "I thought we were going out tonight, getting our groove on…"

"We are! I can't wait." Emery went back for her bags. "Do you mind if I stay with you, Vi? Just until Wednesday, when the room in the big house is free?"

"Nope. Desiree already dropped that bomb on me. I just hope you brought your earplugs, because I plan to work off some stress tonight." It was no secret that when it came to guys, Violet was of the opinion that *less* was definitely not *more.*

Emery followed them into Violet's cottage. "Do you have a steady boyfriend?"

Violet scoffed. "Heck, no. You two better get moving," she said as she headed for the kitchen. "That bar is packed on the weekends."

"I promise to be fast, Vi," Desiree said.

Emery followed her into the guest bedroom and dropped her bags. "Is Rick coming tonight?"

"Yes," Desiree said. "Drake and Serena, too, but Mira and Matt are taking Hagen to the children's theater, so you'll have to meet them another time. And since they're trying to get pregnant, I think they have better things to do at night anyway." Mira was Rick and Drake's younger sister. She and her husband, Matt, and their little boy, Hagen, lived in a cottage on the Bayside Resort property.

"I'll have to remember to show Mira some fertility-boosting yoga poses."

"She'd probably love that." Desiree hugged Emery again. "I still can't believe you're actually here for good and you're going to be working at the inn. Thank you!"

"Are you kidding? More like thank *you* for letting me crash your life." Emery had missed her so much, she had to hug her again.

"Okay, Sappy Sues," Violet called into the bedroom. "Move your pretty little butts or you'll never get into Undercover."

UNDERCOVER WAS ONE of the few happening night spots on the outer Cape, and as expected, it was jam-packed. Dean sat at a table with Rick and Desiree, while—like most of the guys in the bar—watching Emery and Violet dance like they were lovers: arms over their heads, breasts thrusting, hips gyrating, and sexy smirks challenging every man who tried to cut in. Emery looked like she might set the dance floor on fire in a skintight dress that showed every sinful curve. She'd done something with her makeup that made her eyes look *too* smoky and seductive. Dean couldn't take his eyes off her.

"Look at them," Desiree said a little breathlessly. "Violet with her cutoffs and fringed belly shirt and Emery in that tight yellow dress. They look like they were put on this earth with the sole purpose to drive men crazy. I would give my left arm to be able to dance like that."

Rick gave her an over-my-dead-body look. "If you danced like that I'd have to lock you up."

Which is exactly what I'd like to do to little Miss Shake Her Booty over there.

Desiree leaned closer to Rick and said, "Careful." Then, quieter, "I might like that."

Dean slid his gaze back to Emery and ground his teeth together as another guy approached her. He was tall, built, and about to get his butt kicked if he brushed against her again.

"Wow, Dean," Serena said as she arrived at the table with a pitcher of beer and Drake on her heels. Drake's six-plus feet dwarfed her petite frame. She tucked her dark hair behind her ear and said, "You look like you're about ready to kill someone."

Dean's fingers curled around his glass, mentally driving daggers into the jerk who was now deep in conversation with Emery.

"Why don't you go out there and stake your claim instead of drooling from here?" Serena suggested.

Dean was glad Desiree was too busy with Rick to have heard the comment. The last thing he needed was to have the girls pushing him or Emery, when he knew it might only cause Emery to run like the wind.

Drake grabbed the back of her dress and pulled her away

from Dean. "Causing trouble again?"

"Nope. Come on." Serena grabbed Drake's hand and tried to pull him toward the dance floor. As one of Mira's best friends, Serena had grown up with Drake and Rick, too. When they'd bought the resort, she'd been between interior design jobs and had agreed to temporarily help them get the resort under control and manage the office. That was three years ago.

Drake plunked himself down in a chair and poured a glass of beer. "Thanks, but I think I'll hang with the guys."

"You stinker." Serena turned pleading eyes to Desiree. "Dance with me?"

Rick gave Desiree a quick kiss and swatted her butt as she pushed to her feet. "Go, have fun."

"She's right," Drake said to Dean, eyes tracking Serena, who had stopped to talk to a guy by the edge of the dance floor. "You should dance with Emery. You know you're into her."

"Look who's talking." Dean chugged his beer. He wasn't sure if Drake was bluffing or if he was as transparent as his friends made him seem, but he'd never admitted his feelings for Emery to either of them. And if he was that transparent, then Emery must be the only one wearing blinders.

Drake scoffed. "Not even close. Besides, I don't dip the pen in the company ink."

"Neither do I," Dean said, silently reminding Drake that next week Emery was on their payroll. "I just don't want her getting hurt by some jerk."

He watched the girls dance to a few more songs, every minute more painful than the last, as Emery amped up her dirty dancing, catching the eyes of the few men who hadn't already been leering at her. Maybe he should fire her before she started working for them and make a move after all.

Shoot. The whole friendship thing would still be a problem.

Drake and Rick began planning the group's next tubing adventure. They'd enjoyed just about every water sport available on and off the Cape since they were kids. The three of them were always planning one adventure or another, but Dean could no more concentrate on their conversation than take his eyes off Emery.

"Dean?" Drake said sometime later. "Can you make it? Tubing a week from Thursday?"

He was only half listening. "Yeah, count me in. Are the girls coming?" If the girls were going to be there, chances were, Emery would be there, too.

"Yes. That's why we're going in the afternoon. Des has to be at the inn in the morning."

"Perfect." Dean's phone vibrated, and he took it out of his pocket, saw his father's name on the screen, and sent it to voicemail. He wasn't in the mood to deal with his overbearing father's bull about getting serious and going to medical school. Not today. *Not ever.* It was bad enough that he'd have to spend the night of the benefit dinner pretending to have a pleasant relationship with his father.

Dean gazed out at the dance floor, struggling to push those harsh feelings aside. By the time the girls made their way back to the table, hanging on to each other and giggling, he'd come out from under his father's shadow.

Emery sat down beside him and took a drink of his beer. He struggled to resist the urge to drape an arm around her and send the message to the rest of the jerks in the bar that she was taken.

But she wasn't taken.

And if he made a move, she'd probably give him a hard time for putting a damper on their friendship.

ADDISON COLE

In other words, he was trapped.

"Emery has a date tomorrow night," Violet announced while pouring herself a drink.

Dean felt Rick's and Drake's eyes on him, but he was too busy grinding his back teeth to react. "A *date*?"

Emery pointed across the dance floor to the guy he'd mentally slaughtered. "I'm going out with *him*. He's pretty hot, right?"

Dean wanted to wipe the floor with the guy's arrogant grin. "You just met the guy."

"So what?" Emery said. "He's a pretty good dancer, and it's not like I have anything better to do at the moment."

"Don't you mean any*one* better to do?" Violet waggled her brows. Then her eyes narrowed and she pointed at Emery. "I had to move out of the big house because Desiree and Rick kept that headboard banging at all hours of the night. If you're staying with me, just keep that kind of noise to a minimum."

"I'm not a skank, Vi." Emery reached for Dean's beer again. "Besides, you're the one who told me to bring earplugs."

"I was kidding," she said unconvincingly.

"Sounds like mixed messages to me," Serena said.

Emery took another sip of Dean's beer. He filled a glass and set it in front of her.

She wrinkled her nose, looking adorable. "I hate beer."

"You could have fooled me."

She put her hands around his glass and flashed the sexiest smile he'd ever seen. "It tastes better because it's *yours*. It's like eating a salad you make yourself and taking care to use all the same ingredients that they use at your favorite restaurant. No matter how you cut the lettuce and veggies, it's never as good as the salad you get at the restaurant, because someone *else* made

38

the other one."

Why did her ridiculous rationalizations make him smile? "I didn't make the beer," he pointed out. Not that he minded sharing with her. The first time he'd met her she'd sucked down his entire drink and that weekend she'd eaten half of nearly everything he had on his plate.

Emery rolled her beautiful eyes. "Same idea."

"Dean, what's going on over there? Are you trying to steal my best friend?" Desiree asked. "She used to drink *my* drinks."

Stealing doesn't come close to what I'd like to do to her. "Hardly."

"First you keep her at your place all day," Desiree said. "Now she's sharing your drinks. I think you're definitely trying to move into the number one BFF spot."

"I told you I couldn't get to the inn because of the traffic," Emery reminded her.

"Dean *lives* on Bayside Resort property," Desiree pointed out. "It's about a five-minute walk from his place to my front door. Why were you able to get there—" Her eyes widened. "Oh my gosh. Are you two…?"

"What? No." Emery sat up straighter, putting distance between her and Dean. "Wait. You live *on* the resort grounds? I didn't see the resort."

Dean scrubbed a hand down his face to try to hide his smile.

Rick belted out a laugh. "If you had followed the path through the tall bushes at the back of his yard, you would have come out near the far end of our property, near Matt and Mira's cottage."

Emery swatted Dean's arm. "What the heck, Dean? You said you'd have to take me on the Jet Ski!"

"Uh-oh," Drake said with a laugh.

"What?" Dean tried to play it off casually, as if it were no big deal. "I had no idea where the keys to the golf cart were, and it's a long walk with all your stuff. I was only thinking of you."

"Thinking of me, my *butt*," Emery said.

"Darn right he was thinking about your butt," Violet said.

"C'mon, Vi." Dean met Emery's angry gaze. "Is there something wrong with wanting to spend time with my friend? You said Des was busy anyway."

"She *was*, but you could have been honest with me." Hurt replaced the anger in Emery's eyes. "Besides, why did you give me directions all the way back to Route 6 if you're on the same property?"

Drake and Rick cracked up again, but the hurt in Emery's eyes cut him to his core.

Before he could answer, Desiree said, "You gave her the *long* way? Em, all you had to do was go out his driveway and turn left. It's literally a three-minute drive."

Dean shrugged. "I thought it might be best if she learned how to get there from the main road."

"You get more girls with truth than lies, Dean," Serena added.

"It wasn't a lie, and I wasn't trying to *get* Emery." He put an arm around Emery and pulled her closer. When she resisted, he tugged harder, unwilling to let this come between them. "I'm really sorry for wasting your time, doll, but is it a crime to want to spend time with the woman who texts me at two in the morning?"

"She texts you at two in the morning?" Serena slid Desiree a curious look.

"I can't very well text Desiree anymore, can I?" Emery answered. "Rick would have my head on a platter." She leaned back, giving Dean an eyeful of her *girls*, as she said, "Besides, Dean doesn't mind. He texts me all the time, too."

Mind? He waited with bated breath for those texts.

"Sounds like the cold winter nights were warmed with sexting frickery to me." Violet pushed to her feet and headed for the bar. "Speaking of *frickery*, I see an old friend. Catch y'all later."

"Frickery?" Amusement rose in Drake's eyes.

"Not my choice of words," Violet said as she eyed Desiree, "but my sister doesn't like the term fu—"

"Don't!" Desiree snapped.

Violet laughed. "Can we get back to the sexting between Emery and Dean? That's much more interesting than my toning down my language."

"We were not sexting!" Emery grabbed Dean's beer and took another drink.

"In any case"—Serena waved toward the dance floor—"I think Dean owes you a dance."

The last thing he needed was to dirty dance with Emery. He'd be aroused in seconds and Drake and Rick would have a blast teasing him about it. "I don't want to dance," he said sharply.

"Tough toenails. You owe me." Emery hauled him out of his seat and toward the dance floor.

Who was he kidding? He'd let her lead him around by the nose if she wanted to.

The song "Hands to Myself" began playing, and Emery fell into a hip-swaying, shoulders-rolling dance, singing about wanting him all to herself. Her voice—and those words—were as intoxicating as tequila. Her arms moved like graceful snakes over her head as she turned in a circle, her butt brushing against his hips. Man, the girl could make a dead man come alive. She glanced over her shoulder, her long hair curtaining one eye. A sultry smile curved her lips as she sang about not being able to keep her hands to herself and wanting his *all*.

I'll give you my all, all right—and then some.

She turned, her hips brushing against his, and he hauled her against him, matching her every move with a bump and grind of his own. He wedged his thigh between hers and guided her arms around his neck, bringing her soft, pliable body against him.

"Thought you couldn't dance," she said as he settled his hands on her hips, never missing a beat.

"I said I didn't *want* to dance. There's a difference." Now that he was deliciously wrapped up in her, he wasn't about to let go. "Hold tight, baby doll."

He dipped her over his arm and she followed his lead, arching and swaying, her hips pressed tightly against his. When she rose upright again, she held his gaze. Her hands played over his pecs and then wound around his neck, driving him out of his mind one touch at a time. She dragged her fingernails along the back of his neck, and he imagined dozens of dirty ways he could get those sexy nails to dig deeper.

"You're quite a dancer, big guy."

Her voice jarred him from his fantasies, but it was like swimming to the surface of a volcano. Every touch, every glance, brought more wicked desires. His hands slid down her hips, up her back, and into her hair. He loved her silky hair. Their eyes connected, holding for a long, sizzling moment. He was vaguely aware of the song ending, the beat changing, but he continued dancing, unwilling to break their spell. She licked her lips, and he was sure she was right there with him. She arched back again, holding on to his arms, her hair fanning out behind her as she swayed in an arc. He struggled to keep himself in check, but as she rose, her chest grazed his and his restraint snapped. He couldn't keep from lowering his mouth toward hers, to finally claim the kiss he'd dreamed about for so long. Her eyes closed, her shoulders rocked, and just as his lips hovered over hers, she dipped back again, headbutting him in the chin.

"Son of a—" He swallowed a string of curses.

"Oh my gosh! I'm so sorry! I was so lost in dancing, I didn't see your face there." She reached for his cheeks, stroking his beard. "Wow, that's so soft. That beard stuff really works, huh?"

He groaned. How could their bodies be so close, the heat be so intense, and their thoughts be that far apart? "I didn't know I needed a chin guard."

"How many times have I told you that I can be oblivious to things? I'm buying you a football helmet to wear around me. I'm so sorry. I just got carried away." She fluttered her sexy lashes and said, "Take it as a compliment. It means we connected."

Not exactly the connection I was hoping for.

Chapter Three

THE NEXT MORNING Emery woke with the sun, lying in Violet's guest bedroom planning the first day of her new life. She couldn't wait to check out her studios at the inn and at the resort. She planned to hold most of her yoga classes outdoors, but Desiree and Violet had renovated the den as a studio for when it rained. The guys at Bayside Resort had created a wonderful community center last summer, where she could hold classes in bad weather, and they were allowing her to use one of the offices there, too. She was excited to put up some of her decorations and make each of those spaces her own.

She climbed out of bed and stretched, thinking about last night. She'd had so much fun seeing everyone again, and spending time with Desiree. She couldn't believe she already had a date lined up with...*Oh gosh. What was his name?* She winced and then remembered it was Dave something or other. They were meeting at the Beachcomber, an oceanside restaurant and bar. Dean had looked annoyed about her date, but he would be happy once he realized she'd heeded the advice he'd given her over the winter. Or rather, the *mandate* he'd given her when he'd read her the riot act about leaving a bar with some guy she'd just met to go have pizza. *Safety 101, Emery! You don't give up control to a guy you don't know. You're in his car. You're under his control. No more of that nonsense. Got it?*

She smiled to herself with the memory. As if her older brothers hadn't taught her enough self-defense for her to be able to protect herself if things got out of hand. *Sheesh!* Though she had to admit, she liked Dean's protective nature. It was adorable. Especially when he'd sent her a mad-faced selfie afterward.

She scrolled to one of those pictures on her phone. Austin was right; he did look like a Viking. His thick arms were crossed over his massive chest. Tattoos covered his left shoulder, pecs, and biceps. His beard was trimmed into a neat V, making him appear even more serious. His piercing blue eyes stared straight ahead, both intimidating and a turn-on. Heat tiptoed up her chest, and she blew out a breath. *Don't even go there. You stink at relationships.*

She wasn't stupid enough to ruin their friendship or to put her job at risk. *Been there, done that.*

Thinking about their dance, and the way his big, strong body had moved with the fluidity of a man half his size, she absently rubbed her head where she'd bonked his chin.

I am such a klutz.

She zipped off a text to him, *Sorry for the headbutt*, added a smiley emoticon, and then typed, *You never told me you were secretly a dirty dancer.* It wasn't until after she sent it that she realized it was only six thirty in the morning. He was probably out running with Drake and Rick, like most mornings.

She set her phone on the dresser and padded out to the kitchen to get some ice water with lemon, her go-to morning drink. She opened the fridge and was surprised to find a pitcher of ice water with sliced lemons floating in it. Warmed by the thought that Violet had remembered, she took it as a sign that today was going to be a great day.

As she poured herself a glass of water, Violet's bedroom door opened and a very tall, very *naked* man sauntered out. He had a mop of dark hair on his head, a sprinkling on his chest, and *holy mother of hotness*, he was perfectly manscaped below the waist.

"Mornin'." His lips curved up in a crooked grin that reminded her of Dermot Mulroney.

"Morning," she mumbled, trying futilely not to stare at his impressive manhood.

He grabbed a carton of milk from the fridge and set it on the counter as if he did it every morning. For all Emery knew, he did.

"Watering the counter?" he asked.

She followed his gaze to the pitcher she'd forgotten she was holding, and the water spilling all over the counter. "Oh, shoot." She grabbed a dishcloth and scrambled to clean up the mess.

He chuckled, poured himself a glass of milk, and walked casually back into Violet's bedroom.

If finding the water with lemon had been the sign of a great day, what the heck kind of sign was that?

Reeling from the encounter, she decided to skip her morning meditation and yoga in case the nude guy decided he needed more milk. After a nice long shower, she dried her hair and threw on a pair of cutoffs and a peach tank top, all the while hoping Desiree had enjoyed amazing sex last night so she'd make one of her delicious, fancy breakfasts. She assumed Violet had had a fun night, although they hadn't made any noise that she could remember. Could Violet have had bad sex?

Maybe it really isn't the length of the sword, but how expertly they wield it. She laughed to herself, imagining if that had been the case, Violet would have kicked his butt out of the house long before morning.

She headed over to the inn to question Desiree about naked *six-pack Jack.* Cosmos, the dog Desiree and Violet had inherited along with the house, greeted Emery at the kitchen door, yapping and trying to crawl up her legs. He was some sort of terrier mix, with pointy ears, mostly gray, wiry fur, and big brown eyes. She scooped up the scruffy pup and he licked her chin. "Hey there, matchmaker."

Desiree's mother had lived in the house for a few months before tricking Desiree and Violet to come out and stay there last summer. Unbeknownst to them, as part of a grand matchmaking scheme to bring Rick and Desiree together, Lizza had trained Cosmos to climb the fence and swim in the pool at Bayside Resort. It had worked so well, and Desiree was so happy, Emery almost wished Cosmos would work some magic for her.

That would take a miracle.

Not a single person in her family seemed to know how to have a lasting relationship. They were a boisterous, opinionated bunch, and because of that, she knew they were not *easy* partners. Her brothers were constantly flirting and rarely held their tongues. She had the not-holding-her-tongue thing down pat, and as for flirting? Well, she was pretty good in that department, too. The trouble was, several men she'd gone out with had accused her of flirting with other guys even when she wasn't.

She stepped inside and set Cosmos on the kitchen floor. The sounds of spatulas on pans and laughter filled her ears.

Desiree stood at the stove flipping pancakes. Dean, Rick, and Drake sat at the table, shirtless, their bronze physiques on display as they scarfed down breakfast. They were all athletic, but *whoa*. Rick and Drake looked like boys next to Dean's Adonis-like body. The way they were shoveling food into their mouths, she wondered if they'd run the entire length of the Cape. She might not find love, like Desiree had, but she knew she'd find plenty of other types of happiness here at the Cape.

"Hey, Em," Desiree said.

The guys looked up, and Rick and Drake mumbled "good morning" around their food.

Dean smiled, lifting his chin in greeting as she plucked a piece of pancake from his plate and popped it in her mouth.

"Hey, doll. Sleep well?" Dean asked.

"Mm-hm." She reached around him and grabbed his coffee, helping herself to a sip. Dean intercepted the mug before she could set it back down and took a gulp. "But the naked guy in the kitchen kind of threw me for a loop."

Dean spit coffee all over the table. "What?"

"Watch it!" Drake flew from his chair, causing Cosmos to bark and setting Emery and Desiree laughing.

"C'mon, Dean." Rick brushed coffee from his chest. "What the...?"

Dean grumbled something that sounded like "sorry," his angry eyes locked on Emery. "What naked man?"

Desiree tossed Rick a towel and said, "There was a naked guy in Violet's kitchen?"

Emery shrugged. "Yup. Tall guy, well endowed. Des, any idea who Violet's banging these days?"

"No." She handed Emery a plate of pancakes. "I know she has an old friend who lives in the area, but she refuses to tell me anything about him."

"Well, they didn't make a sound, so either I slept like a log or their tryst should go down in the *Guinness Book of World Records* for the quietest ever. Do you have a tent I can borrow for the next few days?" Emery asked.

"You're staying at my place," Dean said adamantly. He carried his plate to the sink and began scrubbing it clean.

"I can't intrude on you," Emery said. "I'll mess up your mojo or something."

He turned off the water and faced her, arms crossed, jaw tight. "My mojo is already messed up, and I'm pretty sure 'or something' follows you everywhere you go. You can, and you *will*, stay with me. It's not safe for you to be around strange naked guys."

"Think it's safe for her to be around you?" Rick asked.

Dean glared at him.

"Dean would never hurt me." Emery sat down at the table and speared a pancake from the platter Desiree set before her. "You sure you don't mind, big guy? It's actually perfect, considering I can *walk* there," she teased. "But I have to warn you, I'm not the neatest person, and I stink at cooking, but I'll—"

"Keep her out of your kitchen," Desiree warned. "I've seen her cook. Not only will your kitchen never recover, but neither will your stomach."

"*Truth,*" Emery said, and ate another forkful of pancake.

"I don't need you to cook or clean. Just stay out of my gardens and we'll be fine." Dean glared out the window over the sink at Violet's cottage, looking like he was strategizing World War III.

"Okay, thanks. I'll get my stuff after breakfast," she said.

"*I'll* get your stuff and take it to my place while you eat," Dean said. "I'm working in the hospital gardens today. I'll make you a key while I'm out and text you when I get back."

Before she could say a word, he stormed out the door.

"That's a man on a mission," Desiree said as she sat down beside Rick.

"I thought I left my overprotective older brothers back in Oak Falls." She looked at Drake and Rick and said, "What is it about me that makes guys want to build a fortress and lock me away? I'm tough. I can handle myself. I don't take grief from anyone, and there's no guy on earth who's going to get anything I don't want to give. You'd think after knowing me for all this time Dean would know that."

The two men shared a serious glance she couldn't read.

"He just doesn't want you to get hurt," Drake said.

"Well, we had a blast yesterday. So, whatever his reasons, I'm glad he'll put up with me for a few days. And I'm sure Vi will appreciate her privacy." She stabbed a piece of pancake with her fork and pointed it at Rick. "These are good, but do you think you can up your game a bit? I'd really love some of Desiree's cranberry bliss crepes."

"Oh, man," Rick said.

Everyone laughed, and Emery said, "Maybe the naked stranger can give you some tips."

WHILE DESIREE MADE breakfast for the customers staying at the inn, which she always offered their first morning but didn't provide on a daily basis, Emery pulled out her phone to text Dean. She found a reply to the message she'd sent him earlier about being a secret dirty dancer, and read it on her way through the house to see her new studio.

You never told me you were a naked man magnet.

She smiled as she typed a reply. *I'm a woman of many talents. Thanks for letting me stay at your place. Going to check out my new studios. See you tonight, Patrick Swayze.*

Her phone vibrated a minute later with his response. *Forgot to tell you. I have one rule. No overnight guests.*

She gasped. Did he really think she'd do that? She zipped off a smart-alec reply. *Wait, let me rethink this...*

She pictured his overprotective scowl and decided he was being too nice to torture, and sent another text. *I'm KIDDING!*

A few seconds later a picture of his scowling face appeared on her screen, and she smiled. She really loved their banter. Why couldn't the guys she went out with be that easy and fun? Another text bubble popped up with the message, *Serena has a key to my place in the office. Use that if you need to get in before I get home.*

Feeling good about staying with him, she replied—*10-4, big guy*—and slipped her phone into the pocket of her cutoffs as she headed into her new studio.

The open, airy space was exactly as she'd envisioned. Worn hardwood floors led to two sets of oversized French doors that opened directly to a patio. She threw open the doors, inhaling the salty sea air, and stepped outside. The inn sat up high on a dune, giving her a gorgeous view of the sandy beach and Cape Cod Bay. In the distance, two sailboats made their way out to sea. Sounds of a young family down on the beach, gentle waves lapping at the shore, and a new life embraced her. She still couldn't believe she'd packed up her belongings and moved away. This was her new home—not for a vacation, not for the summer, but for the foreseeable future. Tears stung her eyes, but they weren't tears of sadness. They were tears of joy, tears of hope—and okay, maybe a few were for moving so far away from her family, but wasn't that to be expected?

She'd surprised herself when she'd started thinking about moving away from the only home she'd ever known. But with her best friend embarking on a wonderful new life, the voids in her life had magnified. Not only did she miss Desiree, but her friendships with Violet and Serena had quickly morphed into a sisterhood as strong as any she'd had back home. But it was Dean who had helped her make the final decision to try to make a *real* go of it in Wellfleet, permanently rather than just for the summer, as she'd originally planned. He pushed her to see things differently and said things that made her introspective. Even now she found herself wondering what it was about the guy at the bar that made her accept his invitation to go out with him. She'd never picked apart things like that before getting to know Dean.

"What do you think?"

Emery started at the sound of Desiree's voice, taking a moment to push her thoughts away before facing her friend. Cosmos darted over, and she knelt to love him up.

"It's gorgeous. I can't tell you how much it means to me that you're letting me try to get this business off the ground here with you guys."

Cosmos trotted into the grass tethered by his long leash.

"Are you kidding? I'm thrilled!" Desiree joined her in the sun. "I feel like my sister has come home."

"*Home.* Do you know how weird and wonderful that sounds?"

"I know. The very word has taken on new meaning for me.

Rick feels like home to me."

"And *you* worried that *I* found a new BFF in Dean?" Emery was only teasing, but she couldn't deny the sting of jealousy slipping down her back knowing she—or part of her relationship with Desiree—had been replaced by Rick. But she knew in her heart that she and Desiree were as close as biological sisters, and nothing could ever take that away. There was room in Desiree's heart for both of them, and Violet, and probably half the town.

"You know what I mean," Desiree said. "I never thought I'd leave Oak Falls, and then I met Rick and got to know Violet, and you were so supportive of me starting over here. Now this has become home, because it's where my future came together, and I'm hoping it will be the same for you."

"I hope so. I can't wait to bring my things in here and get started with my classes. Are you sure you want to do a percentage of monthly income instead of my paying rent? I'm happy to do either, but if I have an off month, you might be better off taking a set amount."

"Like I'd ever take rent money if you had an off month?" Desiree threaded her arm into Emery's, and they walked out to the grass, leaving the doors wide open.

Emery loved that Wellfleet was the type of community where she didn't have to worry about break-ins and theft. She'd never had to worry about those things in Oak Falls, and it would be a harder transition if she suddenly needed to.

"I should go see Vi and apologize for Dean barging in this morning."

"I'll walk with you," Desiree offered.

The sun smiled down on them as they walked toward Violet's cottage with Cosmos in tow. Emery spotted the sign for

Devi's Discoveries, and her thoughts turned to Desiree's mother. Besides being an artist, Lizza Vancroft had been an absentee mother. When Desiree was five years old, Lizza had divorced Desiree's father and moved overseas with Violet, returning only for brief, uncomfortable visits. Emery had been there to pick up the pieces of Desiree's broken heart after each one. Lizza had been visiting the weekend Desiree had gotten engaged, and it seemed as though she was making strides at keeping in better touch ever since. Emery hoped she still was.

"What do you hear from Lizza lately?"

"She sends postcards, and sometimes she'll call, but she's still *Lizza*. The conversations are mostly one-sided, with her sharing the details of her travels and me listening. But you know what? I'll take it. At least she's making an effort, and now I have a relationship with Vi." She looked lovingly at Violet's cottage, as if she could see through the walls to the sister she'd been separated from for too many years to count. "And we both know Lizza will never be the kind of mother yours is."

Marla Andrews was loud, opinionated, and strong in every sense of the word, but she was also loving, generous, and *present* in Emery's life. She made herself available to her children at all hours of the day and night, regardless of what she had going on. Unfortunately, Emery's father was also headstrong and opinionated, which probably explains why they'd raised four children who were not afraid to speak their minds, and why her parents fought like cats and dogs. But still, they were an affectionate family, with loads of hugs and friendly teasing between parents and children. But growing up in two homes with her big, loud family had its downfalls. They weren't the easiest people to have relationships with. They overshared *everything*, from opinions and food to belongings and secrets, and that wasn't about to change.

The door to Violet's cottage opened and she stepped outside wearing her black bikini and biker boots.

"Hey," Violet said as she clomped her way over to her motorcycle. "Your bodyguard was here to pick up your stuff."

"Yeah, sorry about that," Emery said. "I really appreciate you letting me stay here, but—"

"But seeing a stranger naked wigged you out? I get it." Violet flipped her keys into her palm and straddled her bike. "Sorry about that. He's an old friend, and he gave me a ride home last night." The bike roared to life, and she ran her hand down the sleek curves.

"You're not going out on that thing in just a bikini, are you?" Desiree touched the handlebar. "That's not safe. What if you have an accident?"

Violet revved the engine with an arrogant expression. She loved to pull Desiree's strings about as much as Emery liked to tease Dean. "Baby sister, are you *ever* going to stop mothering me?"

Desiree crossed her arms, hurt rising in her eyes.

"She's right, Vi," Emery said, and not just because Desiree was right. She'd always had Desiree's back, and she always would. "Shouldn't you wear leather or something?"

Violet cut the engine and dismounted the bike. "Relax, *mama bears*. My friends dropped it off this morning. I was just making sure she started up okay." She ran an assessing eye over Emery's face and said, "If you have an aversion to seeing naked men in the morning, are you sure it's a good idea to stay with Dean? I've seen him in his swim trunks, and he's definitely packing some major heat."

Tell me something I don't know. The man filled out his running shorts like a porn star. "We're friends. It's not like he's going to walk around naked," Emery said. "Besides, I'm not a prude. I just didn't expect to see your guy's junk, and Dean offered for me to stay there. It wasn't anything personal against you."

"He's not *my guy*," Violet said. "But the way Dean blew in here and barked at him, he acted like you two were an item. How did I miss that?"

"You didn't. We're not. We just became really close friends over the past few months and he's protective of me," Emery explained.

"If you call wanting to make love to you six ways to Sunday *protective*," Violet mumbled.

"He does *not*," Emery said. "Besides, he knows I don't date my guy friends anymore, and he also knows that I have a date tonight."

"Do you think that's a good idea? The date?" Desiree asked. "The way Dean looks at you, it does seem like he's into you."

Emery rolled her eyes, annoyed with this whole conversation. "Can you please stop saying that?"

"You share his food!" Desiree pointed out.

"So what? I share your food, too, and half the guys I grew up with. It's no different. That's who I am. I share food. I tease guys about being too cocky or too hot, or whatever. You know me, Des. I have always had far more guy friends than girlfriends. This is no different from me and all my guy friends back home, except he knows more about me, because…" *I didn't have you to talk to.* She wasn't about to make Desiree feel guilty for her happiness, and the truth was, she had a feeling that even if Desiree had moved back home, she and Dean would have continued to become just as close as they had.

"That is true," Desiree agreed. "But does Dean know that?"

"Of course he does," Emery insisted. There was no denying the blazing heat that had burned between them when they'd first met, but their friendship overrode the instant lust they'd experienced, and she'd grown to love a lot more about him than his looks. "Dean and I are *friends*. We've been talking nearly every night since I was here at Christmas. What did you think I was doing for all these months while you and Rick were building a life together?"

"I can see that," Desiree agreed. "You are most comfortable with guys."

"Like I said, *six ways to Sunday*," Violet said.

"Believe it or not, Vi, I'm friends with tons of guys that I do not sleep with. Regardless of your whole bang-your-friend policy, I've sworn off sleeping with friends. Dean and I might have started out with sexy innuendos and flirting, but it's not like that anymore. Dean's like you, Des. Careful and stable. He brings me back down to earth when I go off on a tangent, and he makes me laugh. And if you have any lingering questions, I told him about all of my dates over the winter, and *everything* that you and I would usually talk about until all hours of the morning. For goodness sakes, I tell him I love him half the time when we end our phone calls, the same way I do to you, Des. He's a *friend*. If there's one thing I can do, it's read guys. Y'all must be seeing what you want to see, not what's really there."

"My money is still on him wanting to bang you," Violet said with a shrug. "But what do I know?"

"Maybe you're right, Em," Desiree relented.

Emery sighed with relief. "*Now* can we get back to what really matters?"

"Whoa." Violet held her hands up. "Sex matters."

"Okay, yeah, it does. Not that I'm having any luck in that department," Emery said with a sigh. "But more importantly, Vi, I'm really sorry for bailing after you were nice enough to let me stay with you. No hard feelings about me staying with Dean until I move into the inn?"

"I don't do hard feelings," Violet said. Emery embraced her, and Violet added, "Do we really have to do this *all* the time?"

"Yes," Emery and Desiree said in unison.

Chapter Four

AFTER SPENDING THE day tending to the hospital serenity gardens, Dean went to the resort and landscaped around the new patio he was creating on the far side of the property. He dragged his forearm over his brow as he finally headed down to the office later that afternoon. Emery had texted earlier and said that she'd picked up the key from Serena, and no matter how hard he'd worked since, he hadn't been able to stop thinking about her. His mind had gone straight to the places he told it not to, imagining her in the guest bed, in the shower, and eventually his mind made the jump, putting her gorgeous body and effervescent smile in *his* bed.

Had he made a mistake by offering her a place to stay? She was like his grandmother's cherry pie cooling on the window-sill—something he'd never been able to resist.

"Hey," Rick said as he climbed the steps to the office and pulled open the door. "How's the landscaping coming along?"

"Great. I should have it done in a few weeks. The plantings are mostly done, but I'm still figuring out the final designs for the hardscaping."

"I don't know what bug got up your butt about needing another patio, but I'm sure it's going to be awesome."

The same bug that has been burrowing under my skin since the holidays. Over the winter, Emery had told Dean about a meditation garden in Oak Falls where she liked to do yoga at sunrise. She'd spoken of it like it was a part of her. When she'd made the decision not to come to the Cape for just the summer, but to move there for good, she'd said she'd miss that garden as much as she'd miss her family. Dean had gone online and found pictures of the area she'd spoken of, and by spring, with Emery as his inspiration, his new project had taken shape.

He followed Rick inside and found Brody Brewer, their new surf instructor, talking with Serena. Brody was a good, honest guy with boundless energy and a casualness that people gravitated toward.

Brody turned to greet them, flashing a killer smile that probably opened more bedroom doors than he could handle and ensured a full docket of women wanting to learn to surf on a daily basis. "Dudes, you should have seen the waves on the ocean this morning. I was just telling Serena that one of these days I've got to get her out on a board."

Dean and Rick exchanged an amused glance. Like them, there wasn't a water sport Serena couldn't do. That was one of the great things about living where the land was bordered by the ocean on one side and the bay on the other. The possibilities were endless.

"Serena didn't tell you? She's been surfing since she was a kid," Rick said.

"Seriously?" Brody's eyes widened.

"Rick and Drake's dad taught us all how to surf," Serena said.

"Why didn't you say something?" Brody asked.

"Because it was fun to see you so excited."

Brody laughed. "I tend to get that way about surfing. Oh, and I met the new yoga instructor, Emery?" He whistled. "She is a sassy one." He rolled his shoulders back, and a satisfied grin spread across his face. "I'm taking her out tomorrow."

Dean's hand fisted by his side. "Out?"

"On the water, after my morning class," Brody said casually. "She said she's never surfed." He shrugged. "I figured, what better way to get to know my new co-worker." His gaze flicked to the clock on the wall, then back to them. "I gotta jet. I met some girls on the beach today and they invited me to a bonfire over on Cahoon Hollow. Want to come along?"

"No, thanks," Rick said. "I'm taking Des out to dinner."

"Dean?" Brody asked.

Dean shook his head, chewing nails over the idea of Brody hanging out with Emery in her barely there bikini.

The second Brody left, laughter fell from Serena's lips. She came around the desk and unfurled Dean's fingers. "Don't even try to pretend you don't have a thing for Emery! First you give her a key and now you want to kill Brody?"

"Never said I wanted to kill him." *Maim, maybe, but not kill.*

Serena grabbed her keys from the desk drawer. "You know she has a date tonight, right?"

"Mm-hm." He'd been trying to forget about it all day.

"You sure you're not setting yourself up for trouble inviting Emery to stay with you?" Rick asked.

"I'm not sure of anything, but I'm not about to let her stay in a house with naked guys roaming around."

"*Guy,*" Serena corrected. "*Singular.* And from what she told me, he wasn't a bad sight to wake up to. He just surprised her."

Dean trapped a growl in his throat. "TMI, Serena."

She laughed softly.

He was glad *she* found this humorous, because it was eating him up inside.

Rick lowered his voice and said, "You could fire her before she starts working here."

"There's no reason to fire her. We're just *friends*." Firing Emery was sounding better by the second, but he knew how she felt about dating friends. *If this keeps up, I'm liable to say or do something I can't take back, and there will be no friendship to worry about.* He pointed at Serena and said, "And don't go spouting off to the girls about this thing you think is going on. That's all I need, for you and the girls to make Emery feel weird around me."

Unable to remember why he'd come into the office in the first place, he stormed out the door and headed across the grounds toward his place. Every step amped up his frustration as thoughts of Brody putting his hands on Emery in that tiny bikini of hers peppered his mind. By the time he reached his cottage, he was sure steam was coming out his ears.

The kitchen doors were wide open, and Emery's bright orange Jetta was parked out front. He went inside and tossed his keys in the bowl on the kitchen counter—where he usually kept his golf cart keys. The darn things had been missing for two days, and he'd searched high and low for them. He usually used the cart to carry supplies around the property, but he didn't have time to worry about that now. Besides, with Emery around, he'd likely have an overload of built-up frustration to walk off.

The cottage was too quiet for his sweet, infuriating *chaos* to be there. He stalked to her open bedroom door. *Man, I'm already thinking about it as her room.*

The room looked like it had been hit by a tornado. Suitcases lay open on the bed. Emery's clothes were strewn over the sides, across the bed, and a few stray pieces lay on the floor, like someone had raided her luggage. Tango and Cash were curled up in the center of the mess. Tango opened one eye, but he must have found him boring, because he went right back to sleep.

Dean stepped into the room, inhaling Emery's unique scent, which wound through him, softening his frustration and tightening his gut at once. He reached out and touched a slinky black dress hanging over the closet door. Soft. Silky. *And you're not wearing it for me.* He took a step and nearly tripped over several pairs of heels lying in a heap beneath the window. The dresser was already littered with her things—hairbrush, comb, perfume bottles—and boy did he like seeing her things in his house.

The devil on his shoulder sneered. *She's out on a date, you idiot.*

The idea of another guy picking her up at his house sent fire through his veins. That probably made him a jerk, but he didn't care. Would she have left for her date without closing up the house? *It's Emery. Of course she would.* He should be more annoyed by her leaving the house wide open, but there was no room for that with the image of Emery and another guy front and center in his mind.

He tore off his T-shirt and headed for the bathroom to take a cold shower, hoping it would ease his mounting frustration. As he neared the bathroom, he heard water splashing, and an undeniable feminine scent filled his senses. He stopped cold, envisioning Emery lying naked in the tub, and he became aware of steam seeping through the slightly ajar door. One step backward might bring her into view.

"Dean? Is that you?"

Her voice jerked him from his reverie. "Uh-huh."

"Oh, thank goodness. I got in the tub and forgot my razor. Would you mind grabbing it from the pink bag on my bed?"

"Seriously?" He closed his eyes, unable to shake the vision of her lying in his tub naked. He was a nice guy, but there was no way he could go in that bathroom without giving away his true feelings, and risking their friendship.

"*Please?* I have to meet Dave at six, and my legs feel like sandpaper."

"Then don't let him touch your legs," he growled before he could stop himself. He clenched his teeth together and said, "You know it's five thirty-five, right?"

"What? No!"

The panic in her voice startled him. He heard splashing and then the sound of the tub draining. The bathroom door swung open and Emery bolted out holding a towel to her chest—the back was wide open, giving him a clear view of her heart-shaped butt as she ran toward her bedroom, yelling, "I'm going to be late!"

He should look away, but a guy could only be *so* good.

She flew into her bedroom, talking as she pushed the door *almost* closed behind her. "I was reading in the tub and must have lost track of time. Sorry for getting the floor wet."

His gaze dropped to the floor long enough to see a trail of water, then moved right back to that tempting sliver of space between the doorframe and the door. He'd gone from *semi-nice guy* to *lust-filled roommate* in the space of a breath, secretly hoping she happened to fill that sliver with her naked body.

A few seconds later her door opened, and she walked out

wearing a skimpy black spaghetti-strap dress, holding the front against her chest with one hand as she ran her fingers through her wet hair with the other. She turned around and said, "Can you zip me, please?" Her sky-high wedged heels brought her closer to the perfect kissing height.

Her zipper was open all the way to the base of her spine, revealing her braless back and the seductive T of a thong. All his blood rushed south, leaving him a little dizzy—and very turned on. It was all he could do to stare at the tanned expanse of toned skin before him.

She glanced over her shoulder. "What's wrong?"

"Wrong?"

"You're not zipping." She gathered her hair over her shoulder, and he noticed she was wearing a wrist full of bracelets— including the one he'd given her *and* the one that contained Splenda.

Ready for anything.

Great. Anything conjured too many infuriating images.

She stood up straighter, holding her hair away from the zipper. "Better?"

No way. It would be better if the dress was on the floor and your legs were wrapped around my waist.

"Dean…?"

He zipped up her dress. "You sure you want to wear that? I mean, with your unshaven legs, you might want to go with jeans." *Or a sweat suit. How about a snowsuit? Yeah, that'd be even better.*

She looked down at her outfit and lifted her long leg. "You think he'll notice?"

She blinked up at him with so much trust in her eyes he couldn't lie. "No, doll. You look like a million bucks."

"Thank you!" She hugged him.

His arms circled her, holding her lush curves tight against him as she kissed his cheek. His entire body ignited like a frigging teenager.

"I need to dry my hair." She walked into the bathroom. "You'll be happy to know I'm meeting him there."

"Where?" *Shoot.* He sounded angry. He softened his tone and said, "I mean, just in case you have trouble. I should know where you're going."

"Beachcomber." She flipped her head over and dried her hair.

Just perfect. Dancing, good food, and lots of alcohol. "Call me if you have any trouble."

"I'll be *fine.*" She flipped her hair to the other side, and continued drying it.

Dean couldn't take his eyes off the nape of her neck. He wanted to press his lips to the exposed skin, to tangle his fingers in her hair and bury his tongue in her mouth until she was moaning for more.

She turned off the hair dryer, shook her head, and her hair tumbled over her shoulders, startling him back to reality.

Flashing a radiant smile, she said, "What do you think?"

His thoughts were still struggling to clean themselves up. He wanted to tell her she was going out with the wrong guy. To say the heck with friendships and working relationships, take her into his arms and kiss her like she deserved to be kissed— slow and sensual, until her entire body trembled with need, and then hard and possessive so she felt everything he had to give— but all that came out was "*Gorgeous.*"

"Well, then. It sounds like it won't matter that I'm going to be a little late." She fluttered her lashes flirtatiously. "I'll scope out hot chicks for you while I'm out."

"I can get my own women, thank you very much."

"Then why aren't you going out tonight?"

"Who says I'm not going out?"

She set her hands on her hips and her expression turned serious—or annoyed—he couldn't be sure.

"Dean Masters, are you holding out on me? I tell you about all my dates."

He chuckled. *Annoyed* it was.

"So...? Who is she?" She crossed her arms and thrust out her hip.

"Who?"

"Your date. Geez!"

"Who says I have a date? Drake's coming over for a cook-out."

"But you just said—"

"Don't assume."

"What*ever*. You can tell me if you have a date, you know."

"And I have many times," he reminded her as she headed toward the door. "Don't you need your keys? A purse? Your phone, just in case...?" And here he thought she was prepared for anything.

She bent at the waist and fiddled with her heel, opening some sort of secret compartment in the wedge. She curled her fingers around something and did the same to the back of her other heel.

She popped upright holding her keys in one hand and her phone in the other. "Never underestimate a resourceful woman, big guy."

He wondered what else she was hiding. His fingers itched to go on a treasure hunt and explore every inch of her until he discovered all her most coveted *secret spots.*

EMERY GAZED INTO the crowd as Dave rambled on about being a stockbroker, which she had decided more than two hours ago was the most boring job on earth. Or maybe she was just out with the most boring *man* on the planet. Since he'd asked her what she did for a living, only half listening to her answer, every conversation had revolved around him and his stellar ability to select solid investments. Investments she didn't give a hoot about. Then there was the issue of his wandering eyes. Throughout dinner, and while they'd been dancing, he'd ogled nearly every woman in the place. Luckily, the Beach-comber was built on a bluff overlooking the ocean, and there was enough of a chilly breeze sweeping up the dune to douse the hot air coming from his blowhole, and the glorious view gave her something to disappear into.

Her mind wandered back to Dean and their time together yesterday afternoon. They'd had such a good time, well, other than her pulling his flowers, but replanting them was fun. And last night when they'd danced together, his eyes had never once strayed. It had all been so easy. So friendly. She'd much rather hang out with him than with this guy. But didn't that confirm what she'd known for a while now? She was much better at friendships than she was at dating. Either she chose the wrong guys, or she messed up somewhere along the way by simply being herself. She'd heard it all—she was too flirtatious, too outgoing, too *unfiltered.* She might be overly friendly, and maybe some people saw that as flirtatious, but that was their problem, not hers. In a world where political affairs created anxiety so palpable they practically deserved their own state to live in, how could a person be *too* outgoing or friendly? And too *unfiltered?* That one really pissed her off. So what if she was overly confident and said what was on her mind?

She turned her attention back to Dave, who didn't seem to notice her zoning out and was now spouting off about his personal investments and setting himself up to retire in twenty years. What was he? Twenty-eight or -nine? She couldn't imagine wanting to stop working that young. She wanted to do *more* with her life, not less.

She took a moment to really study him. He was a handsome guy, with classic good looks and a nice body. She was sure some women would be all caught up in the idea of retiring young and doing whatever guys like him enjoyed doing, but he hadn't paid a lick of attention to her, and she was *this close* to ending the date. Not that she needed a lot of attention, but was it too much to want two-sided conversation and a few laughs?

Dave's eyes finally landed on her, and she forced a smile. Maybe *she* was the boring one. Yoga wasn't exciting to people who didn't practice it, but there was more to her than what she did for a living. Maybe he was sitting there trying to think of a reason to leave, too.

She nixed that ridiculous thought instantly and, in the same breath, decided she was done with this date.

He leaned closer, his blue eyes darkening as he put his hand on her thigh and said, "What do you say we get out of here and head back to my place?"

Laughter fell from her lips before she could stop it. "Are you serious?"

He cocked a smile that told her just how serious he was. *Unbelieveable.*

She pushed his hand from her leg, suddenly *needing* to know what had led him to believe he could get her to go back to his place—*into his bed?*—after the horrendous date they'd just shared. She opened her mouth to ask, and something Dean had said to her over the winter stopped her. She'd made a smart-alec remark to something he'd said when she'd complained about the guy she had gone out with, and he'd said, *Doll, when the right guy comes around, you won't need to spend your energy on all those snarky comebacks.*

She'd like to believe her dating history was riddled with the wrong guys and assume Dean was right. But she knew better. *She* was the problem, because she was the only person making the decisions about who she went out with. In any case, Dave wasn't worth the energy. She politely declined his offer, ignored his put-off expression, and left with her head held high.

The drive to Dean's went quickly. Everything was so close here it reminded her of home—especially now that she was closer to her two best friends. As she parked next to Dean's truck, relief swept through her, and the stress that had been her constant companion all evening fell away.

Chapter Five

DEAN'S COTTAGE WAS dark save for the light thrown from the television. Emery stepped inside quietly, and Dean looked up from where he was sprawled on the couch wearing a pair of gym shorts and a tight tank top, his feet propped up on the coffee table. Did the man own anything that wasn't tight across all those muscles?

"Hey, doll." He pushed to his feet.

"Hi." She tossed her keys on the counter, and that tingling feeling she got when a good-looking guy approached shot through her. She bent down to take off her heels—and to regain control of her overactive hormones. Clearly her body was confused, getting turned on by Dean when she'd sworn off messing around with friends. *Going months without a man's touch will do that to a girl.*

"I figured you'd be back much later." He put a hand on her hip to steady her as she wrestled with her second heel.

He smelled woodsy and rugged, so much nicer than the acrid citrus cologne Dave had worn.

"Me too," she admitted. "Dave turned out to be a dud." She took her phone from the hidden compartment in her heel and set it on the counter and then set her heels on the floor.

Without them she was a good head and a half shorter than Dean, and stared directly at his chest. She tipped her face up and caught him grinning. "Why do you look so pleased?"

"Just glad you're home. Now I have someone to watch movies with."

Home. There was that word again. She had felt comfortable there from the moment she'd walked in yesterday afternoon. Maybe Desiree was right—home was more about the people they were with than the place they happened to be.

She walked into her bedroom and rifled through her clothes until she found a pair of sweats, pulling them on beneath her dress as she called out to him, "Would you believe after doing nothing but talking about himself all night, he had the gall to ask me to go back to his place?" She grabbed a tank top from her bag and laid it out before her, then gathered her hair over her shoulder and said, "Can you please unzip me?"

"What did you expect him to do?" Dean asked as he came over and unzipped her dress. "You picked him up in a bar."

With her back to Dean, she whipped her dress over her head. For a sliver of a second before she pulled her tank top over her head, she felt the heat of his stare.

"Whoa, girl."

"What? My back was to you," she said, as if she'd felt nothing, and then circled back to his question. "I don't know what I was expecting. Maybe that he would talk to me about anything other than himself. Take an interest in me? Not that I'm needy, but honestly, a girl needs a *little* something." She twined her hair into a messy bun and rifled one-handed through her toiletries bag, searching for her hair clip.

Dean reached around her, grabbed a clip and handed it to her.

"Thanks. Would you ever treat a girl that way?" she asked as she secured her hair and headed out of the bedroom.

"No, but I don't pick up girls in bars, either."

"Really? Then where do you meet women?"

He shrugged. "At my friends' Christmas parties."

"Good one." She pulled open the fridge and spied a plate of ribs. "Oh, yum! I guess you had a good cookout?" She grabbed a rib from the plate and caught Dean looking at her chest. "Dean! Eyes up here."

"What do you expect when you flaunt those eye magnets?" He chuckled.

She sighed. "At least you're honest, and not a jerk." She offered him a rib, and when he shook his head, she bit into the tender meat. Sweet deliciousness burst over her tongue. "Mm. This is amazing."

"Thanks."

She took another bite. "Sure you don't want some?"

The corners of his lips curved up in a wicked smile, and he stepped closer. The small kitchen suddenly seemed even tighter as heat climbed up her torso. *Uh-oh.* She needed to cure herself of the disease she was suffering from—*lackanookie*—before she jumped her roommate. Maybe she should visit the girls' pleasure shop and take care of things herself.

"That's not really what I'm hungry for." He reached up and wiped something from the edge of her mouth with his thumb.

Shivers raced through her with the intimate touch, knocking her a little off-kilter. She was *definitely* visiting the girls' shop—and she was *never* talking to Violet again, because she had obviously planted ideas in her head about Dean.

Before she could misconstrue anything else, she said, "I know just what you need."

She pulled open the freezer, and exactly as she'd thought, it was stocked with nearly every flavor of Dean's favorite ice cream, Halo Top. He ate it by the pint, and she teased him relentlessly about it because he gave her such a hard time for eating Ben and Jerry's. But sometimes a girl had to indulge in Karamel Sutra. *That core. Mercy!* She reached inside and grabbed a pint of Halo Top Chocolate Almond Crunch, and beneath it, she found a pint of Karamel Sutra.

"What is this?" She plucked it from the freezer and held it up. "You're secretly indulging in Ben and Jerry's?"

"Hardly. You were supposed to arrive next week, remember?"

"Yeah. And?"

"And that was for you. I figured you'd want to binge-watch something at some point, and I wanted to be prepared. I even bought the first season of that show you keep begging me to watch. *Outsiders.*"

Her heart skipped a beat. She and Desiree used to do things like that for each other, but her guy friends would be more likely to toss her a beer when she showed up than prepare for her visit. Her older brother Alec had told her about the series, and she'd been dying to watch it. But Alec had a fledgling entertainment magazine he was trying to get off the ground, and he traveled often. He always seemed to have time to watch over Emery in a big-brotherly way, but rewatching a television series with her wasn't how he wanted to spend the little free time he had.

"I think you just inched up a notch closer to the number one BFF spot. But…" She opened the fridge again and scanned the contents—*fresh veggies, Greek yogurt, farm-raised chicken thighs…* "Let's see if you make the cut…"

He reached around her and pulled a can of whipped cream from the back of the top shelf. "Is this what you're looking for?"

He set it on the counter and reached into a cabinet above her. His chest brushed against her back, and for a fleeing moment she allowed herself to enjoy the feel of his hard frame pressed against her. *Friends, friends, friends,* she reminded herself, struggling to ignore how good he felt. Could a person go through withdrawals from human touch? When the *friends* reminder didn't take away the tingling in her lower belly, she pulled out the big guns—*boss, boss, boss!*

He took a step back, and cooler air rushed over her skin. Her breath left her lungs with a long, relieved exhalation.

There. That's better.

Worse. But safer.

He set containers of chocolate and rainbow sprinkles beside the can of whipped cream, flashing a knowing grin. "What do you call nights like this again? Who-needs-*men*-when-I-have-*Ben* nights?"

And just like that her head cleared and she needed no more reminders. This man had become one of her closest friends. He knew her—*all of her*—the good, the bad, and the annoying, and he still spent hours on the phone with her, had helped her figure things out so she could come to the Cape, *and* he had offered her a place to stay without hesitation. Only an idiot would take a chance at messing that up.

"I can't believe you remembered that." She opened the ice cream as he took two bowls down from a shelf.

He scooped the ice cream into the bowls. "Kind of hard to forget when it seemed to be your mantra for a while there."

She opened the can of whipped cream and sprayed some in her mouth, thinking about what he'd said. "Not all of us are lucky in love. Open up."

She aimed the can and filled his open mouth with creamy goodness, earning a dark look that made her mouth water. She turned her attention to spraying whipped cream onto their ice cream to avoid getting swept up in the wrong direction again.

He added chocolate and rainbow sprinkles to hers, leaving his without. After putting away the ice cream and condiments, he handed her a bowl and spoon and said, "Ready to binge-watch *Outsiders*?"

"You mean am I ready to bury my bad date?"

The muscles in the side of his jaw pulsed. "Thought we already did that."

She followed him to the living room and curled up on the couch as he set up the DVD. "Girls don't just bounce back from bad dates. Do guys?"

"How should I know?" he said as he sat down beside her.

"You had a string of first dates that you said were boring or the women were too into themselves."

He filled his spoon with ice cream and grinned. "I guess we do, because you and I talked after each of those dates, and I don't remember having anything to bounce back from."

She stuck her spoon in his bowl and tasted his ice cream. "That's not bad. Here, try mine." She filled her spoon with Karamel Sutra and fed it to him. "See? You didn't keel over from Ben and Jerry's. Anyway, getting over bad dates takes time. Think of life as the stem of a rose. You know how it has all those prickly things on it?"

"*Thorns*," he said.

"Yes. They're like bad dates, and in between them, you have this lovely, smooth stem, the *good* dates." She ate a spoonful of ice cream.

"And…?"

"I don't know. It seemed like a good analogy at the time. Thorns draw blood. Bad dates draw bad feelings. It takes time to get over the sting of it. I'll meditate it out of my system in the morning."

He picked up the remote and said, "What you need is to skip the thorns and go straight to the calyx."

"The what?"

"You know those green things at the bottom of the rose petals? Those are called sepals, and collectively, they're called the calyx. It protects the flower in bud and supports the petals when it blooms." He ate a bite of ice cream and turned on the first episode of *Outsiders*.

"Dating should be so easy."

"You don't need to date every guy in Wellfleet the first week you're here," he said under his breath.

She reached over and pushed the pause button on the remote, glaring at him. "What does that mean?"

"I heard you have a date with Brody tomorrow. What happened to not dating the guys you work with?" The bite in his tone didn't go unnoticed.

"We don't have a *date*. He asked if I wanted to learn to surf."

"Trust me, doll, in his mind, it's a *date*."

"It is *not*." She pushed the play button, and they ate their ice cream in silence. She was annoyed with the possibility that Brody had misconstrued her acceptance of his offer to teach her to surf. Brody was hot, funny, and nice, but even during their short conversation she could see that he was the kind of guy who floated from one thing to the next—surf instructor this summer, traveling with a band last winter. She loved to have fun, but at her core she was a small-town girl who liked stability. Plus, she didn't want to go out with anyone she worked with.

Her appetite gone, she set her bowl on the table and sat back to watch the show, mulling over what Dean had said. "Do you really think he believes it's a *date?*"

"Guys think differently than girls. In his mind it's a date, regardless of what you want to call it."

She tucked her feet beside her on the cushion, stifling a yawn as the last twenty-four hours caught up with her. "Well, I'll just have to make it clear tomorrow that it's not a date."

Dean placed his empty bowl beside hers and put an arm around her shoulder, pulling her against his side. "Let me know if you have any trouble."

"Thanks. But I've got this. Telling guys what I think has never been my problem."

"I like that about you."

"Because you're not *dating* me," she said honestly.

"That wouldn't make a difference, doll. I *like* who you are, and that doesn't change because two people become a couple."

She shifted so she could see his face, and it was as serious as ever. The longer she looked at him, the softer his expression became. And when she smiled, a slow smile lifted his lips, smoothing the remaining serious edges.

"That's a good thing, roomie," she said, "because I like who you are, too."

They fell into comfortable silence as they watched the show. Dean's fingers moved in an intoxicating pattern up and down her arm, lulling her worries away. It turned out all his ridiculously large muscles weren't hard as stone. His chest was firm, but cushiony enough to use as a pillow, and his arm was heavy around her, practically crushing her against his side, but it felt good to be embraced by the man who had literally brought a smile to her face every day for months on end.

By the middle of the second episode, Tango and Cash were curled up beside her, purring as they slept, and she was struggling to keep her eyes open, but too engrossed in the show to want to stop watching. After watching shows together from hundreds of miles apart while video chatting, she was enjoying finally spending time—and cuddling up—with Dean in person, like best friends should. For weeks she'd wondered if their friendship would change once she moved here and they were no longer restricted to long-distance phone calls. If after being reunited with Desiree, she and Dean would drift further apart. Even after only a day she knew their friendship had already changed. It was more real than ever.

As she lay against him, safe and comfortable, she realized that it hadn't been Desiree she'd thought of first thing this morning, even though she hadn't lived in the same area as her for ages. It was Dean. In fact, it hadn't been Desiree for a very long time.

THERE WAS PROBABLY some sort of sin wrapped up in allowing himself to soak in every second of this closeness with Emery, but it was worth it. Dean was acutely aware of her every breath, of the way her body relaxed into his and of her hand resting on his thigh. How many nights had he longed to hold her? Watching her on a screen didn't come close to being able to feel her in his arms and brush his cheek over the top of her head, enjoying the feel of her silky hair against his skin, the scent of her shampoo.

This was so good.

A fantasy.

Literally.

She was a friend resting in his arms. She wasn't his in the way he wanted her to be.

Not yet, anyway.

He ran his fingers along her arm from her bracelets to her elbow. Her skin was just as soft as he'd imagined, and he told himself this would have to be enough until he could figure out how to convince Emery that what had happened with the so-called friends she'd dated in the past would not happen between them. Their friendship *would* turn into something more—into *everything* more. How could it not? He had no idea how she could be oblivious to the thrum of heat between them. He'd dated Diana Longhorn, his father's business partner's daughter, for about six months, and he'd never felt for her what he felt for Emery a month after knowing her long-distance. Emery was everything the women he'd dated weren't. She was spontaneous, unfiltered, and so full of life, she was like the brightest of lights on the darkest of nights, outshining everyone and everything around her. He'd never met anyone so enthralling—or so infuriating—and it didn't matter how long it took, he wasn't about to give up on showing her how great they could be together.

"We got so sidetracked with Brody," Emery said, pulling him from his thoughts. "I forgot to tell you that I saw my office at the resort. It's perfect, and I love the color."

Of course you do. It's buttercup, your favorite. He wondered if she even remembered telling him that. He was mesmerized by her sleepy, breathy voice and her slightly Southern drawl as she told him about how, on Desiree's recommendation, she'd designed flyers for her yoga practice while she was at the inn earlier and planned to put them out at local stores later in the week.

"I wish I knew where to go, but Des said just to hit every store along the main drag. That's what they did for their shop. She already has tons of signups for next week when I start teaching, so I don't even know how much promoting I need to do. But it can't hurt, right?"

"I'll drive you around and show you the most likely places where you'll get clients, if you'd like."

"Don't you have to work?"

"Let me worry about that." There were perks to being his own boss, and one of them was taking as much time as he wanted with Emery.

She relaxed against his lap again, and they watched the rest of the episode in silence. When it came to an end, he noticed that Emery's eyes were nearly closed. Moving slowly, so as not to jostle her, he used the remote to turn off the television.

She started. "Hey!"

Tango lifted his head. Cash opened one eye, watching them as if they bored him.

"You're half asleep, doll. We can watch tomorrow."

"I am *not*." She sat up, blinking excessively, as if that would make her appear less exhausted. Tango and Cash repositioned themselves, watching Emery. Tango patted her leg with his paw. Emery stroked his head and said, "We can't stop now. The very definition of binge-watching is to watch so many episodes your eyes cross."

He chuckled. How many times had she nearly fallen asleep while they were Skyping and watching movies, only to get upset when he suggested they end the call so she could go to bed? She was a funny one, this sweet, feisty woman he adored.

"Okay," he agreed. "One more episode, but you need to lie down before you fall over." He set a pillow on his lap and patted it.

"*Two* more episodes," she said rebelliously, and lay down on her side with her head on the pillow. He covered her with a throw blanket from the back of the couch, and she wiggled closer, sighing as the kitties curled up beside her. "Why can't dates be just like *this*? It's perfect."

They can be was on the tip of his tongue. But Emery had just moved into his guest room, she was coming off a bad date, *and* she was half asleep. Now was not the time for him to bare his soul. Instead, he ran his hand along her back, trying to think of an innocuous response that would comfort her. He was pretty sure telling her she was dating jerks was the wrong thing to say. He tried to concentrate on the show, but his brain wasn't on board with the plan. He couldn't silence the debate going on in his head between telling her how he felt and risking it all, or letting it ride for...what? *Another day? A week? A month?* The thought killed him.

She made a dreamy sound and wrapped her arms around his legs, hugging them tight. Hope climbed up his chest. Maybe she already knew how he felt. He leaned forward so he could see her face—and she was *fast asleep*. For some reason that warmed him to his core.

He stroked her hair, glad she'd finally allowed herself to rest. He let her sleep, listening to the even cadence of her breathing and reveling in how nice it felt to be together, even if only as friends. *For now.*

Afraid to wake her, he left the television on, and after the episode ended, he lifted her into his arms. She wound her arms around his neck in her sleep. He carried her through the dark house to her bedroom with Tango and Cash by his side. Moonlight streamed in through the window, illuminating her luggage and the piles of clothes still littering her bed.

"Only you, doll," he whispered with a smile, and carried her to his bedroom.

He pulled the covers back and laid her in his bed. She made another sleepy noise as he pulled his blankets up around her. Cash jumped onto the bed and curled up behind her, and Tango followed.

Dean wanted to be next in line, but he knew better. Instead, he brushed a kiss over Emery's forehead and whispered, "Night, doll. Sleep well."

"Love you, Dean" came out breathy and slow, the way it often did when they ended their phone calls, but hearing it in person hit him square in the center of his chest.

He stilled, his heart hammering as he searched her face. But her eyelids didn't flutter, and her lips didn't curve up in a smile. She'd said it in her sleep.

He scrubbed a hand down his face, telling himself to get a grip, and quietly collected running clothes for the morning. He'd need a long run after what was sure to be a sleepless night knowing she was just a few feet away *in his bed*. This wasn't quite how he'd pictured it in his fantasies. He closed the curtains and took one last, adoring look at Emery before heading out to the couch for the night.

Chapter Six

EMERY AWOKE TO the feel of gentle vibrations against her belly and found Tango curled up beside her, purring like his little life depended on it. She blinked away the haze of sleep, the scent of *Dean* surrounding her like an embrace. She turned her nose into the pillow and inhaled.

Mm. Dean.

Her eyes flew open wider. *Holy cow! Dean!*

She bolted upright, and Tango darted out of the room. Emery pulled the soft brown blanket up to her chest, scanning the bedroom as her mind traveled back to last night, when she must have fallen asleep on his lap. She was still dressed and obviously hadn't been drunk last night, so they definitely hadn't hooked up. But why was she in his bed?

Her gaze crawled over the rustic wooden headboard, to the timbers that trimmed the doorframe and cathedral ceiling. A cat's toy sat in the center of a black leather chair in the corner of the room. The far wall was home to a single heavy wooden dresser, and the windows were draped in caramel-colored curtains and flanked by heavy granite planters with lush greenery spilling over the sides. Simple lines, no clutter, masculine. *Perfectly Dean.*

She pushed from the bed, burying her toes in the dark throw rug sneaking out from beneath the bed. A few steps later her feet met hardwood, and she went in search of him, stopping cold at the sight of his big body sprawled out on the too-small couch. He lay on his back wearing only the gym shorts he'd worn last night. The material was bunched up at the top of his thighs, making *everything* look even more impressive.

Wow. Violet wasn't kidding…

She forced her eyes away from the land of temptation to the sleeping kitty cradled in his arm. Dean's other arm hung off the edge of the couch, the back of his fingers grazing the floor. She glanced across the cottage to her messy bed. Her heart squeezed. *Instead of waking me up or moving my things, you gave me your bed.* He was a gentleman to the bone.

Her eyes slid back to his gym shorts, and her stomach dipped.

Great. He was just about the kindest man on earth, he'd opened his home to her and given her his bed, and here she was, ogling all his off-limits hotness while he slept.

Disgusted with herself, she hurried into the bathroom, where she brushed her teeth and hair and washed her face. Then she tiptoed past Dean and changed into her sports bra and yoga pants. Maybe she could meditate her mind back into submission. She went to get her car keys so she could grab her yoga mat from the car, but they weren't on the counter where she was sure she'd left them. She searched the kitchen, quietly tiptoed around the living room, and circled back to her bedroom, but her keys were nowhere in sight.

She finally gave up and headed out to the backyard. The path of plush lawn around the patio would do just fine.

The brisk morning air teased over her skin as she moved

through her morning yoga routine. It was chillier there than it was in Virginia at six in the morning, but she welcomed the cooler air, the hint of sea in the breeze. Emery always began her routine with the most basic positions. The sun salutation was the perfect eye-opener, before moving on to more advanced, core-strengthening moves.

She raised her hands upward, palms facing overhead, focusing on inhaling as she bent backward, stretching her core, then bent forward, bringing her hands to her feet and her face to her shins. Eyes closed, she exhaled. The image of Dean lying on the couch appeared behind her closed lids, making her insides quiver. She opened her eyes, annoyed with herself, and pushed that image aside as she transitioned seamlessly and sank into a lunge position, inhaling deeply. But Dean's terse voice swam into her mind. *You don't need to date every guy in Wellfleet the first week you're here.*

Tension climbed up her limbs, making her moves rigid and difficult. Dean and his *skip the thorns and go straight to the calyx.* Did he really think dating was that easy? And if so, why was he still single?

The thought brought a thread of guilt. She knew it wasn't that easy for him. He'd told her that he'd rarely strayed from dating the kind of women his overbearing tool of a father approved of. It was such a stupid way to live his life, hoping to use the most personal aspect of his life to appease an unworthy man. She'd told Dean enough times that she hoped one day he'd throw caution to the wind and go out and find the most exciting and daring woman he could, just to break free from his father's stranglehold.

She moved through a few more positions, trying to calm the thoughts ping-ponging in her head, but it was the ache in her chest that had tension clinging to her like a second skin. Dean went out of his way to help everyone, checking on Desiree when Rick had to travel back to DC for meetings and playing peacemaker in his family for his older brother, Jett, who had turned his back on their father, and in turn, it seemed, his family. *Giving me your bed.* The mountain of a man had a heart of gold, and while she wanted him to break free from the stifling confines his father had drilled into his head, the idea of him doing so with a desperate stranger made her queasy.

She was definitely losing it.

She stretched her arms up and bent forward, closing her eyes and exhaling as she grabbed her elbows with opposite hands, maintaining the Uttanasana pose, an intense forward-bending position. At this rate she was *never* going to clear her head. She tried to focus on her spine lengthening, the stretch in the back of her legs, the air flowing through her lungs. And when a sense of calm descended upon her, she exhaled a long breath. *Finally.*

"Now, that's a good morning welcome if I ever saw one."

Her eyes sprang open, and her stomach pitched at the sight of Dean standing behind her, staring at her butt. "So you're a butt man, too?" She straightened her spine, set a hand on her hip, and glared at him, hoping to scare away the misguided heat missiles darting through her.

"I don't discriminate. I like every aspect of a beautiful woman's body." He stepped closer, clearly ignoring the scowl on her face. "Is this the way you greet every morning? If so, I'm going to have to get up a little earlier."

He was messing with her. Well, she'd mess with him right back. Her gaze slid down his bare chest, stopping just shy of his shorts. Awareness zinged through her body like lightning. She was dancing on a slippery slope, but she couldn't keep herself from engaging in the flirtation.

"Maybe you should come out and learn how to *thread the needle* with me." She pretended to gaze out over the gardens as she stretched her arms over her head, hoping he didn't sense the way he'd affected her.

"*Mm.* Now, that sounds worth an early alarm."

Her mind took the ball and ran with it, wondering what it would be like to feel his bare body against hers. His gaze rolled over her face, and sparks ignited beneath her skin.

"What's going on, doll? Thinking about how much you want me to *thread your needle?*"

"No," she lied. "You just…you got in my head last night and it's making me mad."

"Did I?" He stepped closer. His eyes darkened, boring into her and leaving no room for misinterpretation. "In what way did I get in your head?"

Her pulse went crazy, and not the kind of crazy it should be going toward a friend. It was going I-want-to-touch-you-kiss-you-and-devour-you crazy. *Holy hotness. Violet was right.* How had she missed this blazing inferno between them?

She wasn't about to admit that, so she fell back on the other thing that was bugging her. "You said those things about Brody, and now I'm going to be uncomfortable when I see him today."

His long legs ate up the last bit of space between them, bringing them so close his body heat seeped into her pores.

"Dean?" fell from her lips, full of confusion and inescapable desire.

"Emery," he said in the richest, most seductive voice she'd ever heard.

He touched her hip. She opened her mouth to say something snarky, to sever their connection, but her sass was trapped beneath simmering lust. "What…? What are you doing?"

"What I should have done the minute you showed up on my doorstep." His gaze moved slowly over her face, as if he were seeing her in a new light. "Being completely honest with you about how I feel."

Her entire being was on fire, but she couldn't do this, no matter how much she might want to. "Dean. We're *friends*."

"We are." His gaze did not waver from hers.

"You don't want to do this. I'm not even your *type*." She knew his father would never approve of a small-town, uneducated yoga teacher for his precious son, which meant they could never have anything real and lasting even if she was willing to risk everything.

"You're wrong, doll. I've wanted to do this since the first night we met, and every phone call, every text, every freaking thought of you since, has only made me want you more."

Panic swelled inside her, warring with the manic butterflies that had taken flight. She'd done such a good job of not letting herself see him as anything more than a friend for so long, she couldn't relent now. It would only lead to the beginning of the end of their friendship, and their friendship was too important to risk.

His fingers tightened around her hip, hot and enticing. She held her breath, fighting against what felt like an unrelenting force between them.

"What's wrong, Emery? You don't like my *killer smile*? My *eyes that say I'll take you and cherish you at once*? Or is it my *hot body* that you're opposed to?"

A half laugh, half oh-shoot-me-now sound fell from her lips as he threw her own words back at her. "That's a stupid question. How could any woman in her right mind not find you attractive?"

To prove—*to herself?*—he hadn't opened some sort of floodgate, she pressed her hands to his chest, but heat seared up her arms, and she pulled them away as if she'd been burned. His lips curled up in a satisfied smile.

"We can't do this, Dean. *I* can't. I'll mess us up."

"I won't let you," he said, steady and confident.

"You can't stop it." Fear exploded inside her at the thought of losing his friendship—and at revealing the truth she'd never shared with anyone. But with Dean, she suddenly couldn't hold back. She didn't want to. He needed to know why this was a bad idea.

"It's who I am, Dean. I don't know how to be whatever it is that you want."

"Emery." He cupped her jaw, and *mercy*, she leaned in to his reassuring touch. "I want you. Emery Andrews. The girl who downs ice cream when she's had a bad date, watches creepy movies from behind splayed fingers, and refuses to admit she's too tired to stay awake. You don't have to be anything other than yourself."

Oh, how she wished that were true! She forced herself to step out of his reach, her heart thundering so hard she was sure he could see it, and she did what she knew she had to in order to redirect the heat between them, even if it felt wrong. "Was this your plan all along? To get me here so you could make your move?"

Anger crawled up his features, but it was the deeper emotions keeping that anger at bay that had her dumbstruck. "Do you think I planted the naked guy in Violet's cottage? C'mon, Emery. I saw you were uncomfortable and I gave you a solution." His gaze softened. "You blew into my life last Christmas, and you've been there with me nearly every night since. Of *course* I wanted to protect you from that situation."

"What else do you want from me?" she snapped reflexively. "Because a one-night stand will ruin us—"

"That's the *last* thing I want." He closed the distance between them. "You know me better than that. You know I don't sleep around. I'm a one-woman guy—"

"Right. That's *you*. But did you forget who you're talking to? I don't even know what that looks like. My parents split up, remember? I've never dated anyone for longer than a week." Her chest constricted with her confession, even though he already knew this about her. Saying it face-to-face drove the ugly truth of it home. "My brothers and I are broken or something."

"You're not broken, Emery. You just haven't been with the right guy. You haven't been with *me*. I'll show you how."

Her heart stumbled, and it took a moment before she could find her voice again.

"You can't show me. I ruin everything that even *begins* to look like a relationship."

"You're wrong." His face was serious, his blue eyes determined and authoritative, as if he were silently challenging her to give him all she had, so he could prove her wrong.

"I wish I was," she admitted. "But if there's one thing I finally figured out about myself, it's *this*. I've told you about all the guy friends I've dated—"

"They were the *wrong* guys. They weren't *me*," he said adamantly.

She opened her mouth, but no words came.

"Think about it, Em. We've been in a relationship for

months."

"It's different" fell from her lips. "Over the phone is one thing, but in person? As a couple? And let's not forget that I'm going to be working *for* you. There is no doubt in my mind, Dean. I'll mess this up big-time. I only know how to be *me*, and apparently I'm too—" Her mind reeled back through the last twenty-four hours, and the truth sank in. She *was* flirtatious and unfiltered. Tears burned her eyes and she turned away. Unwilling to be one of those weak girls who fell apart in the face of hard times, she straightened her spine, keeping those stupid tears at bay as she turned to face him again.

"I'm not willing to risk our friendship." But she wanted to because, *oh*, she loved everything about him. He was confident and funny, honest and rational. And they got along so well. To experience all of that in an intimate way for one night would be more than she ever had, but if they shared even one kiss, everything would change—and not only because she wouldn't want to stop.

She met his gaze, and the hurt and desire she saw there nearly did her in. She felt gutted.

Everything had already changed.

"Why did you have to tell me how you felt?" she spat. "How can we ever go back to being just friends? Now I'm going to question everything I do around you—and everything you do for me."

"How could I not tell you, when the woman I've been falling for every day for months is finally within reach? Do you really want me to pretend I feel nothing? To watch you go out with guys who aren't worthy of you? I tried, Emery, because I know how you feel about going out with friends or with your boss, but I can't do it. I'm not going to be one of the guys who lies to you."

"But…" she said weakly. "I love our friendship, and I don't want to lose it."

His arm circled her waist, and he drew her against his hard frame. "Neither do I."

For a brief moment, she allowed herself to enjoy the feel of him embracing her, the way he calmed the mounting panic that had threatened to consume her. She wanted to stay right there in the circle of his arms and forget that anything had the power to break them—least of all *her*. But she knew better.

"I've been down this road before," she finally managed, "and it never ends well. Within a few dates, all those things you like about me will become the very things that'll drive you away."

"You're wrong, doll."

"Oh, *right*," she said as an incredulous laugh fell from her lips. "Like you're going to be okay with me flirting with other guys?"

His brows knitted. "You wouldn't do that if you were with me."

She pushed from his arms and paced, feeling like her insides were being ripped to shreds as she prepared to lay her true self out in the most vulnerable way she ever had. She inhaled deeply and gazed directly into his hopeful eyes. "Not on purpose, I wouldn't," she admitted. "But don't you see? I don't realize I'm doing it half the time. It's who I am. Look at how you reacted when I changed into my shirt in front of you last night. I trust you as a friend, so for you to see my bare back was no big deal to me. Nothing about that was meant to feel sexual or flirtatious, but you probably thought it was."

"You may not have meant it to entice me, but you can't tell

me that you felt nothing when you had your top off in front of me," he challenged, closing the distance between them again, sparks igniting all around them. "That you feel nothing now."

She froze. "What I feel isn't the point. The point is, when I took my dress off, I wasn't thinking about reeling you in or turning you on. I wasn't thinking past the conversation we were having. I don't know if that's because I'm so used to being around guys from growing up in a house full of them or what, but it is what it is. And it's the only *me* I know how to be."

His eyes narrowed and he quickly schooled his expression, but not before she saw his frustration.

"See?" She crossed her arms, needing the barrier between them. "You know it's true. I could do that around other guy friends without even thinking about it, and you would want to rip their heads off for seeing me—and rip mine off for doing it. And I wouldn't blame you."

Her confession drained her. If ever she thought there was a man she could love, it was Dean. But being loved for her true self? Forever? That was a pipe dream at best.

DEAN CLENCHED HIS teeth together so hard he was sure he'd crack a molar. There was no way he was okay with being just friends with the woman who had captured his heart one phone call at a time for months on end. But he swallowed those words and reached for her.

"Come here, doll." Holding her close, he tried to get a handle on his emotions.

She rested her cheek on his chest, and he guided her arms around his waist.

"You're one of my best friends. I can't explore my feelings for you because I can't imagine my life without you in it," she said, holding him tighter. "I'm too broken to be fixed, and that's okay as long as I don't lose *this*."

Dean's heart ached. She was the same woman who'd cursed a blue streak when she'd told him what happened with her ex-boss at the yoga back-care practice and had sworn she'd never work for someone else again. The woman who'd cried when she'd first seen him bottle-feed the wounded kittens and when her favorite character died on *Game of Thrones*, swearing she'd never watch another episode—until he said he'd watch it with her via Skype so she wouldn't be alone. She could be strong and stubborn, but he knew about her softer side. The side that needed to be held and nurtured, loved and supported in *all* her endeavors. The part of her that needed to be pushed and challenged so she didn't sell herself short.

He'd seen, and adored, the side of her that needed protecting...*from herself*. A pang of hurt speared through him with the harsh thought, but it was true. She didn't believe she knew how to have a relationship, but even without being in the same state, they'd shared their highest highs and lowest lows. And he was the best man—the *only* man—to prove that to her.

But if there was one thing he was sure of about his sassy, stubborn doll, she was too *scared* to give in, despite that he was one hundred percent certain they belonged together. She was in Wellfleet starting a new life because he'd pushed her buttons enough to make her open her eyes and finally take charge of her happiness, and he intended to do it again and again until she realized friendship was good—but true love could, and would, be even better.

He cradled her face in his hands and gazed into her beautiful eyes. There was no denying the emotions he saw there—or the fear simmering on the surface. He had a feeling that winning Emery's heart was going to be like scaling a dune barefoot in the scalding heat, but he knew it would be worth every painful second.

"The last thing I want is to lose our friendship," he assured her. "I know you've been hurt by guys in the past, but I'm not them. I'll never hurt you." She opened her mouth to speak, and he placed his finger over her lips, wishing he could silence her with a kiss. But that was part of the problem. Emery was used to burning hot and hectic with the guys she dated, and although that was a hard pill for him to swallow, he wasn't surprised that she had completely shut him down. Because if she didn't, if she allowed herself to explore what was so obviously there, she'd wake up tomorrow expecting their friendship to disintegrate.

He was determined to show her they were different— *better*—in every way.

"Being friends is not enough for me," he said honestly, and felt her body go rigid against him. He continued cradling her face and holding her gaze, unwilling to let her escape before she heard him out. "I understand why you're afraid to give us a chance, and I respect your fears, but I'm not going to sit back while you hurt yourself over and over again, picking up guys who are looking for only one thing, when you're worth so much more. Everything you want, Emery, everything you need, is standing right in front of you."

Her eyes took on that dreamy look women got when they saw babies and puppies, and it made his insides turn to mush.

A second later the look washed away, and she said, "Dean, I'm not going to suddenly change my mind."

"I'm not asking you to." He was confident that once she

experienced the difference between spending time with a man who desired, respected, and cared about her, rather than one who simply wanted to get laid, he wouldn't have to *ask* her to do anything.

He lowered his hands to her hips, his fingers pressing into her softness. "All I want is to show you how you deserve to be treated. Let me take you on three"—he paused before the word *dates* could escape—"example outings." *Example outings? What is that?*

A soft laugh fell from her lips. "Seriously? Do you think you're pulling the wool over my eyes by calling them that?"

"I'll call them whatever will make you give us a shot, so you can realize we belong together."

"What if I say no?" she asked with pleading eyes—eyes that told him she didn't want him to accept no for an answer.

"Then we'll both be missing out on what I'm sure will be the best thing in our lives."

"How can I even stay here with all this laid out between us?"

His gut clenched. "Because we're still the same people we were last night when you fell asleep on my lap. Only now I've said what you probably already knew but were afraid to acknowledge."

"Well, take it back," she said playfully. "I *need* that guy from last night. The one that doesn't expect intimacy."

"Em, don't you see? It's you I want, not just your body. Spend time with me and I promise, when we finally come together, it won't be about *sex*." He leaned in closer, and she breathed harder. "It'll be about us."

Dean held his breath as silence stretched between them. When Emery took a step back, the fear in her eyes fell away, replaced with strength and conviction. He prepared himself for her to storm away.

"How do you think Brody will take it when I cancel?"

He blinked several times, unable to believe his ears. "I don't care how Brody feels. Are you saying what I think you're saying?"

With a cheeky smile and a sway of her hips, she headed for the house. "I'm saying you better get your run over with fast, because if I'm going on *example outings* with anyone, it's not going to be Brody."

He had no idea what had flipped her switch, but his sassy girl was back, and he felt like he'd been given the gift of a lifetime. But he also knew Emery, knew what she liked, and a challenge was on the top of that list.

"Hey, doll face," he called after her.

She looked over her shoulder, and man, *those eyes, that smile...*

"Real men have work to do. Get your pretty little butt cleaned up. You're coming with me. I'll take you surfing when I'm good and ready."

Her eyes widened. "Wow, big guy. That's some alpha*disiac* stuff you have goin' on."

"Darn right. Be ready in an hour."

Chapter Seven

THERE WERE THREE things wrong with Dean's *example outings*, the first of which was...*example. Yeah right.* The second was that now his truck smelled like Emery, from the sweetness of her shampoo to the desire that practically seeped from her pores every time she stole a glance at him. She probably thought she hid it well, but she was seriously impaired in that department. She couldn't hide squat, which created the third issue. There was no way he was going to be able to keep his hands, or his mouth, to himself if she kept looking at him like she was deciding if she should kiss him or pretend she didn't want to, especially while she was wearing hot little cutoffs and a lacy yellow top over a blue and white tie-dyed bikini. Her top had enough decorative holes to be used as a fishing net.

He parked in front of Lower Cape Assisted Living, or as everyone called it, LOCAL, and cut the engine.

"I think I just figured out why you're still single," Emery said with a fair amount of snark. "I gave up learning to surf so I could help you landscape? You could have at least clued me in so I could change out of my bathing suit."

"You gave up *going out with Brody* because you wanted to spend the day with me," he reminded her. "And I like your bathing suit." He stepped from the truck. He felt her watching him as he walked around to the passenger side and opened her door.

"*This* is your example outing? How you think guys should treat me? Take me to work with them?" She lifted her brows inquisitively.

He reached into the truck and, in one swift move, turned her by her hips, bringing them face-to-face. "Wipe that smirk off your face, doll. I'll teach you to surf, but first I have work to do, and you need to network."

"Network?" She gazed up at the building, and understanding dawned in her beautiful eyes. "You think I should put flyers out here? I didn't even bring them with me."

He reached behind the seat and waved a stack of the flyers he'd found, along with a stack of yoga magazines, two of his gardening magazines, and a tube of cherry lip balm, littering *his* bed.

When he'd returned from his run, Emery had been meditating in the garden. She'd looked so serene he could hardly believe she was the same whirlwind of a woman who moved from one thought to the next without skipping a breath. And when he'd gone inside, he'd found evidence of her inner chaos everywhere. A pile of hair ties, two kinds of hair product, and a wide-toothed comb lay on the bathroom sink. A flowered notebook on the kitchen counter with a fuzzy pink pen and two crumpled papers. Not one, but *three* pairs of flip-flops in the living room, and his personal favorite, the charm necklace she'd worn the other day, lying on the living room couch. It was like she was marking her territory.

"Where did you find those?" she asked, reaching for the flyers.

"On my *bed*." He slid his hands along her hips, bringing their mouths a whisper apart and earning a sharp and sexy inhalation. "What were you doing on my bed, Emery?"

"Um…" A surprisingly shy smile lifted her lips. "I haven't put my clothes away yet, and I wanted to look at the flyers."

"And my gardening magazines?"

"I wanted to see what makes you tick."

He felt himself grinning again. "And the magazines of skimpy yoga outfits?" Oh yeah, he'd flipped through them, imagining taking each article of clothing *off* Emery.

"I wanted to see the summer styles."

"On my *bed*?" He brushed his lips over her cheek and said, "And the lip balm on my pillow?"

She inhaled a ragged breath, and he drew back just far enough to look into her lust-filled eyes. "Were you thinking of me when you were lying on my bed, Emery? How about when you put that balm on your lips?"

"Dean, I…" She closed her mouth and swallowed hard.

"Did you leave it there just to torture me? To make me fantasize about how incredible your lips would taste with it on?"

"I…" Her eyes narrowed, and all that heat turned to challenge. "I told you I don't think about what I do. I just do it."

She pushed past him, landing on her feet, but the way her cheeks flushed and her breathing quickened, he knew he'd struck a nerve. And he knew her claim about not thinking about what she did wasn't exactly true—otherwise she would have thrown caution to the wind when he'd told her how he felt. That told him more than a verbal confession ever could.

"Are we going to go inside, or what?" She stalked toward the entrance.

He chuckled, catching up to her. "Denial looks cute on

you."

"Don't make this weird," she said without looking at him.

"Don't make this harder than it has to be." He leaned down as they approached the front door and lowered his voice. "And get that hungry look off your face. The residents here will call you on it in a hot second."

She laughed. "Were you always this cocky, or did I just not notice before?"

"Trust me, doll. You noticed *everything* about me." He pulled open the door and swatted her butt. "And one day you'll stop standing in your own way and admit it."

STANDING IN MY own way. Give me a break. Emery stewed over Dean's accusation as he spoke to the cute twentysomething receptionist who was literally twirling her shoulder-length curly dark hair around her finger and flirting unabashedly. Dean leaned his bulky forearms on the counter, looking hot as sin in his shorts and tight T-shirt, all *Mr. Casual Sweet-Talker.*

An unfamiliar feeling clawed at Emery, making her stomach squirrely. Dean rose to his full height and winked at Emery as the receptionist picked up the phone and spoke into it.

Winking at me while you're flirting with her? I don't think so!

Her words from earlier came rushing back. *I don't realize I'm doing it half the time. It's who I am.* The truth hit her like a bullet. Was this the way guys felt when she was just being who she was and they thought she was flirting? This was an awful feeling.

While she tried to crawl out from under the uncomfortable truth, a petite blonde with a cute pixie haircut came through a door behind the reception desk.

"Dean, didn't I just see you three days ago?" The blonde's eyes met Dean's and she tilted her head, looking at him with a playful smile, the way women who had intimate knowledge of a man did.

It was a look Emery knew well. It said, *Hey there, big boy. What kind of trouble are you getting into now, and can I come?*

"Did you miss me already?" Pixie Cut asked.

Three days ago? Emery suddenly recognized the emotion coursing through her for what it was. *Jealousy.*

She wasn't proud of the ugly emotion. In fact, she was shocked by it, but not too stunned to flash her best he's-all-mine smile as she stepped beside Dean and purposely brushed her arm against his. She knew it was wrong to claim him when she'd just given him a diatribe about how she couldn't go out with him on a real date, but she was powerless against the viscous monster gnawing at her gut.

"I always miss you, Chloe," Dean said.

You always miss her? Then what on earth are you doing claiming to want me? Emery felt like she was swimming in a sea of quicksand. But quicksand would probably be easier to handle than the jealousy that was winding around her insides, stringing her muscles so tight she thought they might burst.

Dean put a hand on Emery's lower back, dragging her to the surface again.

"But that's not why I'm here," he said. "Chloe Mallery, this is Emery Andrews, the yoga instructor I told you about."

What? She shot a curious look at Dean, whose sexy smile was now aimed at her, sending her insides into a whole different type of flurry.

Chloe's eyes widened. "You're the back-care Wonder Woman Dean raves about?" She opened her arms and pulled Emery into an unexpected hug. "I am so glad to meet you. Dean said you worked wonders at Oak Falls Back Care and Rehab."

Emery was at a loss for words. He'd networked for her? Did he also tell Chloe why she had left the practice? She finally managed, "He did?"

"Yes! He sings your praises like he's your marketing rep," she answered. "Didn't he tell you? And of course my sister, Serena, told me all about how nice you were."

Serena's sister? The puzzle pieces were falling into place, and Emery felt like a fool, being jealous of someone Dean had grown up with. *Being jealous at all.* She didn't like that feeling, and since she'd never been jealous before, she wasn't sure she liked what it meant about how she felt about Dean.

Denial looks cute on you.

Like jealousy, denial wasn't an emotion in which she was well versed. She glanced at Dean, who winked again. When did he start winking? Had he always done that? She tried to push past the truth in his observation and said, "He didn't tell me."

"Well, after I heard you were coming here, I *had* to Google you," Chloe exclaimed. "I read the archived articles you wrote for the back-care center you worked for. I was astonished by the article about the sixty-five-year-old man who was bedridden after suffering a back injury at work. You were able to help him get back on his feet so quickly."

"Mr. Wiles. The doctors had pumped him up on pain meds and basically left him to believe he'd suffer for the rest of his life. Patients don't realize the negative impact becoming sedentary can have on them." She remembered Mr. Wiles well. He was a curmudgeonly man who lived in the next town over. When they first started working together, he'd hated every session and had told her he was only doing it because his daughter, who had worked at the hospital and had referred patients to the back-care center, had insisted. With time and gentle care, he'd come to trust Emery, and with that trust had come a desire, and drive, to heal.

"I read that. But with your help, he was walking again within two months and nearly pain free four months later. That is *very* impressive." Chloe pointed to the flyers in Emery's hand. "Are those for your new business?"

"Thank you, and yes, well, sort of. They're for my yoga classes, and they have my website address, which has my experience on it." Emery handed her a flyer and then remembered how casually she was dressed. "I didn't realize we were coming here to meet you today. I would have dressed more appropriately."

Chloe waved a hand dismissively. "No worries. No one dresses up on the Cape in the summer. You look great."

As Chloe scanned the flyer, Emery turned to thank Dean, but he was busy talking with the receptionist again. Just as he glanced her way, a tall brunette pushed a wheelchair into the lobby, and the elderly woman sitting in it said, "Dean, what a surprise. Are you here to take me out to tend to the flowers?"

Dean knelt beside the wheelchair and took the elderly woman's hand in his. "How are you, Agnes?"

Her thin lips curved in a smile that reached her eyes. "I woke up this morning and saw a bright light. Thought I'd died and gone to heaven. Then I realized I had forgotten to close my curtains. I've been blessed with another day. That's a good day in my book."

"And in mine." Dean rose to his feet, still holding the woman's frail hand, and greeted the brunette behind the wheelchair.

"Jenny, would you mind if I took Agnes out for a walk?"

He really did have a heart of gold.

"Not at all. But you know," Jenny said with a mischievous grin, "once the ladies get wind of this, they're *all* going to want to come out and work in the garden with you today."

Dean held a finger in front of his lips. "Shh. This is mine and Agnes's private date."

He turned to Emery with a question in his eyes, as if he was asking if she wanted to come, or if she was okay with him disappearing for their walk. Her insides had gone all warm and fuzzy. She'd known he was generous to a fault. And now he'd not only gone out of his way to help her, but he was willing to put everything else aside to take this lovely woman out to see the gardens. She tried to close the emotional floodgates she'd so eagerly denied existed, but they were near to bursting.

Before she could say a word, Chloe said, "This is perfect. Now I can pick Emery's brain and show her around."

"Yes, perfect," Emery said with her eyes on Dean and her heart in a quandary.

Chloe gave Emery a thorough tour of the facility, which was warm and homey and reminded Emery of the assisted living facility in Oak Falls where many of her clients had lived. During the tour, Chloe asking about the work Emery had done at the back-care specialty practice, and the more Emery talked about working with the patients, the stronger the pull became to get back into it.

They stepped outside and into a beautiful courtyard. The warmth of the sun shone down on them as they walked by several elderly men and women seated around a table playing cards. Chloe stopped to say a brief hello, and it was clear by the enthusiastic greetings how much the residents liked her. But

Emery noticed more than their smiles. She noticed the way the woman on her right was favoring her right shoulder and the way the man on her left continually shifted in his chair, as if his hips were bothering him.

As they walked away, Chloe said, "You've got to watch Nelson, the one with the gray shirt. If you buy into the gossip, he's some kind of cardshark." She smiled and said, "And apparently has quite the social life, too. Anyway, now you've moved here for good, but you're not starting a back-care specialty practice? Dean made it sound like that was what you loved most. I was really hoping you might want to get involved with our residents."

"I would love to help the people here. There are so many ways to make a difference in their lives. But I'm going to be working at my friend Desiree Cleary's—"

"I love Des! She and Violet are members of BNI, the business networking group I belong to. We shared a table at a local networking fair in the spring."

"Really? Des and I grew up together, and she invited me to come stay at the inn and offer yoga to her customers. I'll be working at Dean's resort, too, so I really can't start a full-blown back-care specialist practice, which would be my dream. I wouldn't feel good about leaving either of them hanging after they've given me such a great opportunity and enabled me to move here and start over." She noticed an elderly woman sitting in a wheelchair, hunched over a table. Her face was pinched, as if she was in pain, as she sorted flowers. Several flowers fell off the edge of the table and she mumbled something indiscernible.

"But I love working with the elderly, and I'd like to take on a few clients maybe once a week or so." Emery walked over and picked up the flowers. She handed them to the woman and said,

"Hi. These are beautiful."

The woman's pinched expression morphed into a pained smile. "Thank you, dear. This darn wheelchair has me hamstrung."

"Good morning, Rose. I see you've been busy." Chloe turned to Emery and said, "Rose is very particular about the arrangements in the dining room. She likes to rearrange them and make them just right for everyone to enjoy."

Rose shook her head, mumbling about the arrangements. She picked up a daisy and pointed it at Chloe. "What I wouldn't give to get back to my beloved gardens. When I'm on my feet again, I'm going to drive myself over to that florist and give him a lesson or two. He should be ashamed, sending these over the way he does."

"It can be hard to have reduced mobility if you're used to an active lifestyle." Emery touched her shoulder, unsurprised by the spastic muscles she felt. "Are you in much pain?"

"Ha!" Rose stuck the flower in a vase and said, "That's like asking if I breathe air."

"Rose refuses to take the stronger pain medications the doctors have prescribed," Chloe explained.

"They dull the pain and make my brain fuzzy," Rose said sharply. "The pain is my reminder to get my butt in gear and find a way out of this darn chair."

"I understand, and I'm sorry for what you are going through. Have you found anything that has given you relief?" Emery asked. "Exercises? Stretches?"

"Exercises? That would be like a dream come true. Every time I move I'm in pain." Rose set another daisy in a vase and began picking through the flowers on the table. "I can only stand getting out of this ride to death's door for short periods of time. I've had scoliosis forever, but it was a darn herniated disc that finally did me in. I've tried everything. Chiropractors, physical therapy, acupuncture..."

Emery looked at Chloe, whose empathetic expression mirrored her own feelings—*almost*. Hope sprouted inside Emery, the type of hope that brought her hands to Rose's shoulders again and then lovingly down over the hump on her back. She felt Rose tense up and said, "I'm sorry. I can be overly touchy."

Rose studied her for a moment. "Most people shy away from that ugly deformity."

"I don't find it ugly. Did you know that some spine curvatures can be fixed with the right care and therapies? If it's not a rigid deformity, meaning a deformity of your spine, which would require surgery, there might be ways to help reduce the curvature." She didn't want to give Rose false hope, but she couldn't resist asking, "If someone thought they could help, would you be willing to try?"

"Sweetheart, I'd sell my soul to the devil if it offered me a chance to get out of this chair and into my beloved gardens again."

They talked for a few more minutes, and as Emery and Chloe headed back toward the lobby, Emery said, "I would love to try and help her. Do you know if there were other mitigating factors that led to her being wheelchair-bound?"

"No. I'd have to ask her doctor. As Rose mentioned, she's seen the best doctors and physical therapists, but they've gotten nowhere," Chloe said. "The herniated disc she's speaking of happened when she slipped going up a flight of stairs shortly before she moved in here. She's been wheelchair-bound ever since. It's been several months. She's gone through a lot. At first she was flat-out angry, and then she fell into a depression. I know she seemed uppity, but I'm so happy she finally is getting her personality back. I would have to speak to her doctor to get his approval for you to work with her."

"Thank you. I would appreciate that. And I'm happy to speak with her doctor if you'd like me to. I can't make any promises, and a lot of her success will depend on how much she's willing to endure, because it will probably hurt at first. We're going to stretch muscles that probably haven't been stretched in years. But, Chloe, this is what I did for so long back home. I've seen patients with hunchback-like posture resulting from scoliosis, osteoporosis, disc issues…We had tremendous success with the programs I put together. I think I can help, and I assure you, I won't give her false hope, but I will share her determination to help her feel better. I'll make it clear that the goal is to give her more mobility with less pain but that there are no guarantees."

Chloe put a hand on her hip and smiled. "Dean was right. You are passionate about the work you do. Let me make some phone calls."

"Thank you." She was still a little shocked at how Dean had built her up. He was just full of surprises.

"If you don't mind me asking, are you and Dean *together?*" Chloe asked in a hushed tone. "You don't have to tell me, but I've known him all my life, and I've never seen him light up when he talks about a friend the way he does with you."

Emery spotted Dean pushing Agnes's wheelchair toward the lobby. Agnes had a bouquet of fresh-cut flowers in her hands and a smile on her lips. "We're…" She paused, searching for the right words to describe their relationship. "He's one of my best friends," she said honestly, because she was pretty sure, *Today we're friends, but if he keeps up these heart-melting outings, I'm not sure what we'll be tomorrow,* wasn't an appropriate answer.

Chapter Eight

"I CAN'T BELIEVE you told Chloe so much about me. Thank you. That was really beyond nice of you," Emery said excitedly as Dean drove out of the parking lot.

He glanced at her, meeting her curious gaze. "No problem, doll. It was nothing."

"No, it wasn't *nothing*. It was really thoughtful. I was going to put off working anywhere but at the inn and your resort until I was settled in. Desiree has classes scheduled three mornings a week, and Serena said she was booking the other two mornings for me at the resort. We left open the afternoons until we see how the mornings pan out. I think I can squeeze in an additional client or two one or two afternoons a week. Chloe is going to see if she can get authorization for me to start working with one of the residents. And there were other residents who I could tell would benefit from working with me. Just talking about working with people who really need my help got my blood pumping."

Her voice escalated, and he stole a glance at her, thrilled that she wasn't upset with him for pushing her in that direction.

She reached across the seat and touched his arm. "I really mean it, Dean. Thank you for everything."

Her hand slid from his arm, and it took all of his willpower not to grab her hand and hold on tight. Emery was generally a happy person, but right now she was radiant.

"We're not done yet." He nodded toward the stack of flyers on the seat between them. "Let's go distribute those and see what else you can line up."

"No way. You said you had to work, and you've done enough for me today." She flashed an effervescent smile. "What's next on *your* agenda?"

"You," he said, biting back an even more sexually charged response.

Her cheeks flushed, and a soft laugh slipped from her lips. "I meant next on your workday agenda."

"Darn," he said teasingly, and headed for Cape Stone, to choose the hardscape materials for the new patio at the resort.

Emery sang along to the radio on the way. Every once in a while she'd look at Dean while she sang sexy lyrics, and he found himself confused by her seductive and playful smiles. He wanted to believe each one was meant just for him, but knowing Emery, the emotions of the song were simply playing out in her expressions.

He was sure that one day they'd be meant solely for him.

One day couldn't come soon enough.

Half an hour later they walked into the Cape Stone showroom, a hardscaper's heaven. As Emery took in the displays of stone fountains, pillars, fireplaces, and other design samples, Blaine Wicked approached. Blaine's whole family worked in the building industry on the Cape. He and his brother Justin owned Cape Stone, while his father and two other brothers specialized in renovations. Blaine was a dead ringer for actor James Marsden, from his dark, always-tousled hair to his shockingly blue eyes and playful nature. His gaze raked appreciatively down the length of Emery's body.

Dean moved his hand possessively to Emery's lower back before his competition reached them. Blaine's gaze shifted to Dean, and a quick raise of his chin told Dean his *she's-taken* message was received loud and clear.

"How's it going, Dean?" Blaine asked, passing a friendly smile to Emery and keeping his eyes respectfully on hers.

"Blaine," Dean said. "This is Emery Andrews. I want to get her opinion on a few things. Mind if we use one of the worktables?"

"Hi." Emery smiled, and he swore the room lit up like the sun had come out.

He wanted to bottle up that smile and keep it all to himself, but he wasn't that much of a possessive jerk. Or at least he had never been before. Now, he wasn't so sure.

"Nice to meet you," Blaine said. "Is this guy getting all your *dirty work* done?"

Dean glared at Blaine.

"Not yet," Emery said. Then her eyes narrowed, and she said, "But he definitely has strong hands and the right *tools* for the job," with enough sass to wipe the grin off Blaine's face. She wrapped her hot little hand around Dean's biceps and said, "Chiseled from head to toe, and every hard inch in between."

Blaine chuckled and slid a defeated look to Dean. "Use whatever you need, buddy, and grab me if I can help."

As Blaine walked away, Emery leaned in, like she was preparing to share a secret.

Dean slid his hand around her waist, pulling her closer. "Darn, girl. What do you say we forget work and go get stuck between a rock and a hard place?"

She laughed, glancing at Blaine. "We should set him up with Violet. He's got a *wild* look in his eyes."

She thought he was kidding? His fingers tightened around her, bringing her attention back to him. The air sizzled, and her amused expression quickly faded, replaced briefly with surprise and then undeniable hunger.

"Dean," she said softly. "Put away your *hammer*, big guy." She pressed her hands to his chest, forcing space between them. "We have work to do."

He pulled her against him again, holding her gaze. "What do you see in my eyes, doll?"

As she searched his face, her eyes darkened. "A hurricane," she said softly. "As dangerous as it is mesmerizing."

She pushed away again and closed her eyes for the briefest of seconds. When they opened, his hurricane was met with a storm—heat and wariness battling for dominance.

He stepped closer again, their chests touching. Lust thrummed like a heartbeat between them as he brushed his beard over her cheek and spoke in a low voice, "You want the hurricane, but you need the safety of knowing it won't demolish your shelter. Let me show you we can have both." He drew back just far enough to gaze into her eyes, recognizing the uneasy look of reluctant acceptance beneath a host of conflicted emotions.

"Breathe, doll." He felt himself smiling, and with a hand on her back, he guided her toward a worktable by the windows.

"I *am* breathing," she snapped, walking slowly beside him. "Geez, Dean. Give a girl a minute to recuperate after blowing her away."

"That was a *whisper*," he said confidently. "When I *blow you away*, you'll need *hours* to recuperate."

Her cheeks flushed, but that spark he loved rose in her eyes, and she said, "That almost makes me want to throw caution to the wind and accept the challenge."

"Almost?"

She stopped beside the worktable and stared at him. The longer she looked, the softer her expression became.

"Yeah. *Almost.*" She turned abruptly away and motioned toward the showroom displays. He noticed her hand was trembling ever so slightly. "This is like a texture wonderland. How do you decide what to use? It's all so pretty."

Nice redirect.

He wanted to push her over the hump between friendship and something more, but her abrupt subject change told him to hold back. Struggling to douse the inferno inside him, he set the landscape plans on the table and said, "Most of the time the right materials speak to me as I design the project, and I know immediately which will be a perfect match." *Like I did with you.* "But this is a really special project, and it's got me a bit perplexed. I'd like your opinion."

"You really *do* want my opinion? I thought you were just saying that to Blaine."

"Yes, Emery. I truly want your opinion." *And so much more.*

AS DEAN ROLLED out the landscaping plans, Emery tried to calm her racing heart. She'd seen the way Blaine had looked at her, and normally, a good-looking guy like that would capture her attention. But she hadn't felt a single belly tingle or had any lingering lustful thoughts. She'd felt nothing. *Nothing!* Her body had been too consumed with the rush of sensations caused by Dean's nearness. And every word he said, every heated glance, every *breath* since had proven she'd been dead wrong earlier, when she'd thought she could lock her emotional floodgates closed. Even now, as he leaned over the table, holding down the edges of the plans to keep them from curling up—not looking at her, not speaking to her—her stomach fluttered and her pulse skyrocketed.

How could she possibly process all of the emotions crawling up from the depths of her soul, where she must have been unknowingly hoarding them away?

"Here, let me show you," Dean said, drawing her from her thoughts.

She told herself she was just getting carried away because of his earlier confession and his brazen comments. She could totally regain control. *No problem. Just switch back into friend mode.*

She tried to look over his shoulder, but he was too big. She went up on her toes, but he was still too bulky for her to get a clear view of the plans. She ducked under his arm and stood within the confines of his body. See? She could handle this.

His chest grazed her back, and she fought the urge to lean into him. He reached around her with his right hand, still holding the edge of the plans with his left, and pointed to the drawing, bringing his chest tighter against her back. Her temperature spiked, obliterating her ability to concentrate on what he was saying. Every time he moved, his body pressed closer, making her hyperaware of every blessed inch of him, from his abs moving with every inhalation, to his hips, and lower… She clenched her teeth, trying desperately to catch his words so she could hold on tight and climb free from the lust dragging her under, but his breath smelled minty, and her mind spiraled down a dark path. What would his mouth taste like? How would he kiss? Rough and demanding? Or would his kisses be tender and giving?

"*Doll?*"

She started, her body burning and flustered. She'd never been so affected by a man. *Ever.* The truth of their situation hit hard. She inhaled a calming breath, but there was no calming her racing heart. Weren't there steps for dealing with denial like there were for grief and addiction? She felt like she'd been cut off cold turkey from her safe haven. The gates leading to Denial Palace had slammed closed and locked up tight—leaving her to face her attraction to Dean head-on.

Turning to face him, she was immediately drawn into his piercing blue eyes. Fear and lust coalesced, as she mentally batted away the darts of friendship and career that bombarded her. He was so confident about them. Could he be right? Did she want him to be? *Oh, yes! Yes, I want you to be.*

She inhaled deeply, hoping she wasn't about to ruin their friendship and everything she'd pinned her future on, and said, "Let's do this."

Chapter Nine

DEAN WASN'T SURE how to take Emery's sudden all-in attitude. He wasn't sure if she was talking about deciding on materials for the landscape plans or moving forward with the two of them. Because of that, he played it cool, which was next to impossible. Over the course of the next hour, Emery went from barely breathing, emanating body heat like the Sahara and clearly struggling to focus on Dean's explanations of Ashlar patterns, cobblestones, and flagstone, to being drawn in to the beauty of the plans. She'd become so swept up in ideas for the garden and patio, she was mesmerizing.

Her eyes sparkled with possibilities as she described her ideas for the project. "Can't you see it?" She waved her finger over the designs as she spoke. "A free-form flagstone patio here, instead of making those edges sharp. Sharp isn't warm. Sharp says, 'Don't come over here,' while rounded edges say, 'I'm easy, come over and relax.' Oh! Can you use recycled flagstones? The ones that are all different sizes and colors?"

He loved the way she thought. "Definitely. I use recycled materials whenever I can."

"A man after my own heart." She paused, her gaze finding his. Then quickly, nervously, she pointed to the plans again.

"And what's over here?"

"A view of the water."

"That makes it even more beautiful. And this?" She put her finger on the center of the patio where he'd marked the tree he was going to build the patio around.

"A gorgeous oak tree."

"I love that," she said dreamily. "Such a wonderful patio should be surrounded by flowers. What are those tall orange flowers I love so much?"

She scrunched her nose, looking so adorable he couldn't resist slipping his arm around her waist and tugging her closer. "Tiger lilies. They're all over the Cape."

"Yes! I adore them. What were those yellow flowers you just showed me a picture of?" Her hand dove into his back pocket and retrieved his phone. She navigated to the browser.

Maybe he should be bothered by her breaching his privacy like that, but how could he be bothered by Emery *being* Emery?

"Yellow flag blossoms," they said in unison.

"Yes! And Queen Anne's lace, and"—she studied his phone, flipping through the pictures he'd shown her—"purple lace cap. This will be so pretty. The perfect meditation spot. Can you see it? All billowy with color and life with the sounds of the bay beckoning your inner calm?"

He felt himself falling for her a little more with each excited word she uttered. He didn't have the heart to tell her that he'd already planted most of the gardens. Luckily, they were quite similar to what she'd described. "I can see it perfectly."

She slid his phone into his back pocket, leaving her fingers tucked there as she gazed up at him a little nervously. "Me too," fell breathlessly from her lips.

The showroom and the people in it fell away as his arms

circled her. One hand came to rest at the top of her spine, the other on her lower back, pressing her closer. Her heart beat rapidly against his, and her breathing shallowed. Her fingers dug into him through the thick denim of his pocket. *Finally*, she was right there with him.

"Emery—"

"Did you get it all worked out?" Blaine's voice broke through their connection but didn't sever it completely.

Emery's gaze never left Dean's. He expected her to pull away at any second, but her fingers pressed harder. Oh, how he wished they were someplace private.

"We did," he finally said to Blaine, unwilling to look away from Emery.

In the next moment, her gaze dropped to his mouth, hovering long enough for him to weave a quick and dirty fantasy about what he'd like to do with said mouth. Dean cleared his throat to try to erase the image he'd conjured of Emery propped up on the edge of the worktable, moaning his name as he devoured her sweetness, but the image had burned into his mind. She was looking at him like she could read his mind— *and liked it.* Getting turned on in front of Blaine was not on his agenda.

Emery bit her lower lip, her eyes dancing with devilish mischief. She stepped sideways, her fingers slipping from his pocket, leaving him to bear the brunt of his fantasy in front of his buddy. He scrubbed a hand down his face and quickly glanced down, relieved to find his shirt was long enough to hide his arousal.

"Yeah," Dean uttered, trying not to sound as sexually frustrated as he was. He gathered and rolled the plans, holding them in one hand as he took Emery's arm in the other. "We're good. I'll email you the order."

She giggled as he hurried her toward the door.

Outside, he said, "You think that's funny?"

He turned her in his arms, backing her up against the side of the truck, and boxed her in with his body.

"Seeing your bad self out of control?" she asked with another sweet, infuriating laugh. "Heck, yes, it's funny."

He grabbed her wrists and pinned them beside her head. The plans sailed to the pavement. He sank down and arched forward, pressing against her, and her eyes took on that hazy, sensual look he was earning so often today. Her skin flushed, and her lips parted. For all her sass, and self-pronounced strength and resilience, she looked anything but *in control*.

He dipped his head, touching his lips to her neck, and dragged his tongue along her heated flesh until he reached her earlobe, which he took between his teeth, biting just hard enough for her to inhale sharply. She struggled against his grip, but her head tilted away, exposing more of her neck for him to devour. But he had something else in mind. A little lesson.

Using his fingers, he stretched her hand flat against the truck, and he lowered his mouth to the tender skin of her palm, lavishing it with a long, hot, openmouthed kiss. She sighed wantonly, her back bowing off the truck, and she rubbed her body against him like a cat in heat. He grazed his teeth along her wrist and followed the sleek lines of her smooth skin all the way up her arm to her shoulder.

Needy, sinful sounds escaped her, and when he brushed his lips over her cheek, his name sailed from her lungs like a plea— "*Dean*—" Her fingers stretched to touch him. "Please," she begged.

"Oh yeah, doll," he practically growled into her ear, before sliding his tongue along the shell, earning another lustful sound. He lifted her hands higher, grasping them both within one of his, and ran his fingers lightly down her side, making her shiver. "That's it, sweetness."

He flattened his hand over her hip and slipped it around her, bringing her even tighter against him. "Don't even try to tell me you don't want me. You don't want *this*." He accentuated his words with a pulse of his body against hers. "Friends or not, *I'm* the man you crave."

She was breathing fast, her eyes narrowing. His hand slid to her butt and she held her breath, her eyes pleading for more.

"I'd bet my life, if I were to touch you, I'd find you ready for me."

Her cheeks flamed.

"Tell me I'm wrong, doll." He kissed the corner of her mouth. "You can see my arousal. I can *sense* yours."

Her mouth clamped shut.

Still holding her wrists in one hand, he cupped her jaw with the other and brushed his thumb over her lips. Her tongue slid across her lower lip, and it took all of his control not to seal his mouth over hers. He laced his fingers with hers, moving both hands beside her head, and nibbled on her neck again, until she was panting, eyes closed, skin flushed. She was the sexiest woman he'd ever seen, and she'd had him wanting her since the very day they'd met, but as badly as he wanted her, he reminded himself this was a lesson in control.

He touched his forehead to hers, soaking in the rising and falling of her chest with every needful breath. He released her hands and bent to retrieve the plans. As his face neared the juncture of her thighs, he looked up at her, and the air rushed from her lungs. Plans in hand, he pressed the unlock button on his key fob and headed for the driver's side, leaving her trembling, panting, and, he knew, *beyond* needy, as he ground out, "Not so funny now, is it, doll?"

BY MIDAFTERNOON, EMERY had accepted that the idea of not getting hot and bothered every time Dean looked at her was hopeless, much less when he put his hand on her lower back as they ordered lunch at Mac's Seafood by the Wellfleet Pier. Her body had become a ticking time bomb. She had no idea how she made it through lunch. She needed relief, but there was no relief in sight. Every glance, every joke, every brush of Dean's hot skin against hers stoked the needy woman inside her.

After lunch, as they drove around town leaving flyers for her yoga classes at local businesses, her traitorous body remembered the weight of him pressed against her, the feel of his breath on her cheek, his tongue on her neck, hand, *wrist*, and the hungry look in his eyes as he shredded her walls, one touch, one word, one *look* at a time. Who knew Dean was such a master seducer?

Holy cow. She had definitely met her match.

By late afternoon, when they stopped at Dean's place so he could put on his swim trunks and pick up two of his surfboards, she *finally* felt a modicum of control.

"We'll get a wet suit for you at my buddy Jonny's shop," he said as he came out of the house carrying his wet suit and headed for a shed in the backyard.

"A wet suit? No thanks. Too confining."

"Em, you'll freeze without one."

"I'll be fine. I've swam in an ocean before."

"Yeah, in the *South*." He opened the shed, but before he

stepped inside, he closed the gap between them, staring down at her with a serious expression. "Why do you fight everything I say?"

"I don—" She realized she was doing exactly that and swallowed her words. "Knee-jerk reaction. I hate being told what to do."

His brows knitted. "You take the long way around everything you do. Just this once, trust me enough to do as I ask, okay?"

She huffed out a breath. "I hate being confined."

"By the wet suit, or by me?"

After a beat of silence, she said, "The wet suit."

He cocked his head, as if he didn't quite believe her. Planting her hands on her hips, she opened her mouth to refute his thoughts, but she knew Dean would never buy it. They may not have been face-to-face all these months, but she'd been honest with him about everything. She'd even shared her dream of one day becoming a yoga back-care specialist, primarily for the elderly, on a full-time basis.

She closed her mouth, warmed by the realization of how seriously he'd taken her dream. *Seriously enough to have built me up to the one person who has the connections to open doors.*

"Not you, specifically," she explained. "But...I'll try a wet suit if you really think I should."

He stepped closer. He was good at this space-invader thing he did. Her heart skipped as he tipped her chin up with one finger and said, "And a real date? Think you can trust me enough for that?"

Her lungs constricted. "Our friendship...?"

"Is already on the line, regardless of what happens next."

"You're going to be my boss."

"You're fired," he said with an impish grin.

She laughed. "I can't let down Drake and Rick like that. I said I'd offer yoga to your customers."

"We'll send them to your classes at the inn."

"Dean, I can't just back out on commitments because you want me to. What would that make me?"

"Smart," he said, tugging her closer again, softening her to his plight. "You'd have one less reason to pull away. One less excuse to keep your distance. One less reason to fight your own happiness."

She inhaled deeply, trying to weed through right and wrong. *Am I clinging to the best excuse I've got to keep my heart intact?* She didn't know why she was suddenly worried about her *heart*.

My heart?

Her hand drifted absently to her chest, her heart kicking against her palm. She'd never given that particular organ much thought beyond remaining healthy. It was their friendship and her career she'd worried about. She swallowed hard, suddenly aware of Dean watching her intently. Her heart beat faster.

"What do you say, Em?"

She wanted to accept the challenge. *Or was it an offer? Suggestion?* No, she realized, this wasn't any of those things. This was a *gift*. He was offering her an olive branch, giving her a way to set aside one of her worries and give them a chance. No one had ever given her the gift of happiness.

Except sometimes they did. Her father had done it when he'd paid for her back-care specialist courses, and hadn't Desiree given her a gift when she'd offered a space at the inn for Emery and her business?

Okay, sometimes people who really care about me, really know me and love me, despite my faults, have done that for me.

Dean cocked a brow, and she opened her mouth to accept, but "Can I think about it?" came out before she could stop it. The hope in Dean's eyes faded. *Oh my gosh. I really do stand in my own way.*

"Sure," he said, looking at her for a long moment before breaking their connection and heading into the shed to retrieve the surfboards.

She watched his muscles flex as he carried the boards out of the shed. "I'm sorry."

"Don't be. It's actually good that you're giving this some thought. I think it means something."

There it was again, a glaring difference between what she usually did and what she did with Dean. "Maybe," she said noncommittally.

As he loaded the boards into the truck, he didn't push, didn't make her feel guilty. He smiled and patted her butt, joking around like they always did, until she was breathing normally again.

"Hey," she asked as he locked up the shed. "Why is your board so big?"

He chuckled. "You noticed?"

The dark look in his eyes revved her up again. "Your *surfboard*, big guy."

"Like I said…"

How would she ever make it through the next few hours? Everything he said brought her right back to the dark desires she'd been trying to outrun. "You're impossible."

"Trust me, doll. I'm *very* possible." He backed her up against the truck again, leering like a hungry wolf. "With you, I'm a sure thing. Although *that* longboard is meant for you, as a beginner. It's easier to balance on a longboard." He pressed his hips against her again and said, "But this *longboard's* got your name on it."

Drawing all her wits about her, which at the moment weren't much, she knew she had to try to ignore that comment and cling to the one that would keep her from jumping into bed with Dean. "I know how to balance. I don't need a special board. Maybe I should ride the shortboard."

"Not happening, doll," he said as he pulled the keys from his pocket. "You want to get up on the board, not fall off it."

She wanted to get up on something all right, but it wasn't the surfboard.

Not helping.

"So, you're riding the shortboard because you think you have better balance than me?"

"I'm riding the shortboard because I know how to surf." He opened the passenger door of the truck, laughing under his breath. "Riding the shortboard," he mumbled as he helped her in. "That's not the thing I'm hoping to ride, *short*cake." He smacked her butt and strutted around the truck, climbing into the driver's seat.

"Get over here where you belong." He hauled her beside him, and she didn't even try to complain as he hooked her seat belt.

She didn't want to.

He draped one arm around her, holding her against him, and drove out to the main road.

"I didn't even accept a real date yet," she pointed out.

"You take the long way around things. I know this about you. But maybe you don't know me as well as you think you do. I tend to find the most efficient route."

"So that's what this is? *Efficiency?* I'm living in your house. Kill two birds with one stone?"

He shook his head. "That smart-alec bull might work on other guys to goad them into a senseless debate and throw them off-track, but not me. You're living in my house because it was a better place for you. You're living there because you *want* to be living there."

She opened her mouth to rebut him again, but before she could get a word out he said, "You could have stayed at Violet's, but you made a big show out of the whole naked-dude thing. I think you wanted me to offer my place."

"Right," she said sarcastically. "Delusional much?"

"Did you fight it?"

"No, but—"

"I rest my case. Like I said, *denial* looks cute on you." Dean parked the truck in front of Surf Magnet, which she assumed was his friend Jonny's surf shop. He cut the engine and said, "But I have a feeling *clarity* will look *smoking hot.*"

He stepped from the truck and came around to help her out. She knew a thing or two about clarity. She found it as she greeted each morning with yoga and meditation. Wasn't she always preaching the benefits of centering oneself to her clients? Praising mindfulness, the coming together of mind, body, and soul? But where Dean was concerned, clarity was shrouded in worry.

She stewed on those thoughts as she was measured and fitted for a wet suit, which she assumed they'd rent, but Dean insisted on buying. *You're a Cape girl now. You'll need it.*

By the time they reached Newcomb Hollow Beach, the sun had dipped low in the sky and the waves looked enticing. Emery was excited and nervous about learning to surf, and she was glad that Dean was going to teach her instead of Brody. She was equally aware and excited by her newly discovered—*accepted?*—feelings toward Dean.

Brisk ocean air swept up the dune, bringing a world of freeing sensations with it. Emery had forgotten how different it felt to be at the ocean than the bay. The bay was calming, while the ocean seemed to rejuvenate her entire being. She reveled in the way the salty air made her skin feel tacky as they kicked off their flip-flops and stepped into the warm sand. She carried the towels and wet suits down the steep walkway toward the beach. Dean had a surfboard under each arm. She walked behind him, trying not to stare at his perfect butt beneath his swim trunks, but what else was there to look at? A beach full of swimmers? No one compared to him. Not in looks, or as much as he'd hate hearing it, not in sweetness, either. His heart was as tender as his muscles were strong.

There went *her* heart again, quickening, making it hard to breathe. That organ she'd never paid much attention to wasn't fading back into the background anytime soon.

Dean set the boards on the shore and took the wet suits and towels from her, setting them down, too. He pulled his shirt over his head and tossed it to the sand, exposing another of his most dangerous weapons—his powerful physique. She was dying to know the meaning behind the ink covering his shoulder, biceps, and pecs, but each time she'd brought it up over the last few months he'd changed the subject. Now that her true emotions had not just surfaced, but crashed into her like rolling waves against the shore, she was more curious than ever.

Dean stretched his arms over his head, then out to the sides, twisting and stretching. His muscles pulsed as he flaunted every angle of his deliciousness. Suddenly Emery was very hungry.

Ravenous.

He laced his long, thick fingers together and extended his arms forward with another deep stretch. Her spine tingled with the memory of how those adept fingers felt on her skin as they trailed down her ribs and beneath the hem of her shorts.

Dean stepped closer, his blue eyes boring into her. She must have been dipped in ice for all these months to have kept her distance, because his eyes, his very presence…She could catch fire from the heat of this man.

"You ready to get wet, doll?" he asked with a haughty look.

Oh boy…

Chapter Ten

DEAN HAD THOUGHT covering up that skimpy bikini he'd been fantasizing about stripping off Emery all day would make it easier to concentrate on teaching her to surf. But it turned out that helping Emery into a wet suit was even more of a lesson in self-control than the bikini had been. She wiggled her hips, shimmied her shoulders, arched and stretched, all of which caused her luscious curves to appear even more pronounced and tempting. When she was finally zipped in tight, her gorgeous body encased in black neoprene, she looked *absolutely* scorching hot.

Emery was back to being her sassy self, complaining about being shown how to wax her board and about having to practice the various stages of surfing—paddling, popping up to her feet, proper stance—on the sand before getting in the water. She was a spitfire of rebellion, and she tried his patience at every turn. While that should be a great mood killer, coming from Emery, it was also strangely a huge turn-on. He prayed he could control himself long enough to get into the water, because there was no hiding being aroused in a wet suit.

He left his board on the shore, wanting to be *right there* if she needed him. "Remember, you want to cut through the waves head-on, not at a glancing angle, or you'll lose your momentum."

Emery dropped her board in thigh-high water. One hand on the board, the other shading her eyes, she scanned the water. "What if I see a shark?"

"Don't try to pet it."

"I'm serious."

"So am I." He looked her dead in the eyes, recognizing the fear lingering there. "It's an ocean, and there are sharks. We have a high seal population. But the chance of you encountering one is slim."

"Not helpful. The chances that I'd end up living in your house and getting all hot and bothered because of *you* were less than *slim* when I arrived."

He chuckled. "Duly noted. If you see a shark, keep it in sight as you head for shore."

"And when it chomps my leg off?" she asked.

"Hope it doesn't like the way you taste and get out of there."

Her jaw gaped.

"Emery," he said in his most reassuring tone, "I will be nearby. If there's a shark, my priority will be to get you out of the water, even if that means taking a hit myself."

She sighed nervously. "That doesn't make me feel better."

"Want to skip surfing?"

She shook her head.

"Want to paddle out and see how you feel? Find your sweet spot on the board?" As he said the words *sweet spot* his body heated up again. He walked into deeper water, submerging his lower half, and said, "If you're too frightened, you're not going to get up on the board. You'll just get frustrated."

She gazed out at the sea. "I'm not too scared." In the next breath, she was on her board, plowing through the waves head-on, just as he'd advised.

Dean swam after her, impressed with her resilience. When she began drifting sideways, he grabbed her butt, redirecting her.

She glowered.

He laughed and patted her butt. "Move a little lower on the board, so the nose is slightly above the water."

"Got it, Mr. Handsy." She shifted lower and paddled with long, deep strokes, with Dean swimming beside her. "This feels good. I think I found my sweet spot."

He felt himself grinning. "I'd like to find your sweet spot. I can guarantee you'll feel good."

"There you go, bragging again," she said with a sexy smile. "I think I've got this."

He motioned toward the oncoming waves. "You know what to do, doll. Pick your spot, paddle like crazy, and keep looking forward."

He swam away, watching her like a hawk as she sat up on the board, used her hands and feet to turn toward the shore, and looked over her shoulder with the confidence of a lifelong surfer. She was stunning with the late-afternoon sun glistening over her damp skin.

As the wave swelled she paddled forward. Every muscle in Dean's body tensed as the momentum of the wave built and she tried to stand on shaky legs. The board tipped, sending her flying backward, into the crashing wave. His heart lurched as he quickly swam toward her. She broke the surface as his arm circled her.

Swiping at her eyes and gasping, she yelled, "Stupid wave!"

and reached for her board.

"You're okay?"

"Yes, I'm okay! I'm mad. I slipped right off the stupid board."

"It takes time. You did great. It's really hard to find your footing when the world's moving out from under you. You looked amazing out there."

She faced the waves again and climbed onto her board. "I looked awful, but not for long."

She paddled away, and after four more failed attempts, each one bringing more frustration than the last, he held her trembling body, both of them bouncing with the force of the water.

"You gave it a good shot. Let's call it a day and try again—"

"No way. If you can do this, so can I. I have balance. I'm the *queen* of balance. Watch." She pushed away from him and paddled past the waves to calmer waters.

He swam after her, stunned when she unhooked the leash from her ankle and *stood* on the board, fluidly arching backward into a backbend. How the...? He swam closer, careful not to create waves, and when she kicked her feet up into a perfect handstand and then lowered them perpendicular to the board in an even more precise handstand split, he saw her not as the temptress he lusted after, but for the experienced, intense, determined yogi she was.

A wide smile graced her beautiful face as her legs moved fluidly toward the board, and swiftly beneath her, until she was doing splits along the length of the board.

"See?" she said, a little out of breath. "*Balance* isn't my is-sue."

She straddled the board and reached for his hand. He

climbed on, mimicking her position, her knees tucked against his inner thighs. She pressed her hands to her thighs, her brows knitted in concentration.

"It takes a different type of balance when the board is cruising along a wave. It takes time, but you'll get it," he reassured her.

"Will you help me learn?"

He moved closer, her request touching him deeply. Emery wasn't the type of woman who asked for help. Earning another level of her trust meant the world to him. "I'd love to."

EMERY LAY ON the surfboard with Dean perched above. His strength radiated in the small gap between their bodies, making her feel safe and excited at once as the swell of a wave propelled them forward. Her heart thundered as adrenaline and something even more thrilling, sexier, and unexpected coursed through her veins. He'd gone over what she was supposed to do so many times it ran through her mind like a mantra.

I'll stand, then you push up. Concentrate on your stance, knees bent, arms loose and extended, torso forward. Look straight ahead and know I've got you.

Suddenly Dean's hands disappeared, and the board tilted with his weight as he rose to his feet. It happened so fast, Emery didn't have time to think. She gripped the edges of the board, pushing her chest up as her feet moved beneath her. Dean clutched her hips, strong and stable, helping her pop to her feet. One of his arms circled her waist, holding her back against his chest as they rode the wave.

As they surfed along the shores of the Cape, the sounds of

the rushing waves, distant voices in the wind, and the pounding of blood in her ears gave Emery a sense of freedom, euphoria, and at the same time, disbelief. The overwhelming sensations should bowl her over, or at least give her pause, but instead they gave her a sense of clarity.

Dean held her until the very end of their ride, when he lowered her to a sitting position and hopped off the board.

She was delirious with happiness and adrenaline, and her words tumbled out too fast. "That was amazing. Incredible. *Life changing.* Like the first time I did yoga. It felt like taking the clearest, deepest, soul-reaching breath, only the breath was inside *and* outside my body."

She swung her legs over the side, and Dean moved between them, his strong arms circling her hips. Her thighs pressed against his chest. The depth of emotions swimming in his blue eyes sent pulses of something warm and electric straight to her heart. She didn't think, didn't contemplate what it all meant or why her heart felt like it was trying to climb out of her body to reach him. She let it guide her and lowered her lips to Dean's. Her head spun with the first touch of his warm, soft lips. In an instant, he took control. His hands flattened on her back, his arms squeezed her hips, tugging her closer, and his mouth—*his gloriously hot, heavenly eager mouth*—consumed her. The kiss turned rough and unstoppable. Amid sensual sighs and rough kisses, he hauled her forward, while simultaneously lifting himself higher on the board, as if he couldn't get enough of her and might not ever have another chance. Her body slid against him hard. She clung to him with her arms and legs, never breaking their connection.

His arm wrapped around her waist, pinning her to his hard frame. His other hand moved along her back, into her hair, tangling and tugging demandingly, angling her face so he could intensify the kiss. His beard scratched her skin, giving her bursts of slight pain with insurmountable pleasure. She knew her face would be abraded, and she didn't care. She kissed him harder, digging her fingers into his wet suit. A purely masculine sound erupted within him. It was the hottest thing she'd ever heard. Fireworks ignited inside her, sparking and exploding in rapid succession, shattering her ability to think of anything but *Dean*. He squeezed her tighter, and she could barely breathe.

She didn't *want* to breathe.

Never in her life had a kiss made her feel so alive, so intimately bound to a man. She wanted *more*. More electric kisses. More of his chest heaving against her, *because* of her. More of *him*.

Heaven help her, because she wanted *all* of him.

When he eased his efforts, kissing her softer and somehow more deeply, too, her body vibrated like a live wire. Their bodies swayed with the force of the waves. They weren't in danger of the waves breaking on them, but she wouldn't care if the tide took them out to sea. She clung to his shoulders, her legs wrapped tightly around his waist, feeling his strength, his corded muscles, his *resistance*.

Oh, mama. If this was Dean holding back, what would it be like when he gave her his all? When he kissed her with reckless abandon? Oh, how she wanted to find out!

He explored every inch of her mouth, slow and steady, like she was a fine dessert and he didn't want to miss a single taste. Even while she was lost in his decadence, her overactive mind wondered *why* he was holding back. She tried to pull away, but he tightened his grip on her hair, taking her in a rougher, more controlling kiss, and her curiosity fell away.

Oh yeah, big guy. That's what I want.

She surrendered herself to his demands, meeting every stroke of his tongue with one of her own, grinding against him. A guttural groan escaped him as he tore his mouth away, leaving her panting and bereft.

"Emery," he ground out.

His fingers clenched tighter in her hair, stinging her scalp, and their surroundings slowly came into focus. The surfboard bobbed by the shore. The beach was nearly empty, the sun barely visible over the horizon. How long had they been making out?

"Sorry" came tumbling out, though the reasons for the apology escaped her. She wasn't sorry. Not one bit.

"What the heck, Emery? *Sorry?*"

"I'm not," she said quickly. "I'm not sorry. I didn't know what to say."

His hand pushed into her hair again and he recaptured her mouth, taking her in another wet-suit-melting kiss. This time, he didn't hold back, kissing her forcefully, holding her with the strength of ten men, his entire being demanding more, until she was a writhing, boneless mess, clinging to him for dear life, because if she tried to stand, tried to use her legs at all, she was sure she'd sink to the bottom of the ocean.

When they finally drew apart, it was a slow separation. Dean brushed tender kisses over her lips, whispering in between each sensual touch. "That was a *taste* of how much I want you." *Kiss, kiss.* "No regrets." *Kiss, kiss.* "Don't deny us." *Kiss, kiss.* "Tell me you want us, Emery. Let's stop playing games."

When his words weren't followed up with another kiss, she opened her eyes, and found him watching her intently, his gaze a demand. And she loved it.

"I'm not playing games." She wanted their friendship, and she was still supposed to work with him. But he was right. Their friendship was already in jeopardy, regardless of what they did next. She swallowed hard, trying to calm her frenzied swirling thoughts, and said, "I'm tendering my resignation from your company."

His hearty laughter smothered against her lips as he crashed his mouth to hers again, alighting her every nerve anew. "I already fired you."

"I didn't accept your dismissal. I *quit*."

He laughed again, gracing her with several more tantalizing kisses. "You're a rebellious, beautiful, funny pain in the neck."

She smiled into their kisses. "I gave you fair warning. I'll drive you crazy."

"You already are. In the very best way possible."

Chapter Eleven

AFTER THEIR IMPROMPTU make-out session and her *resignation*, Emery had pulled back a little, as if she wasn't sure how close she should allow herself to get to Dean. While Dean respected her need for space, their smoking-hot connection made him surer than ever that they belonged together. He wasn't about to back down.

They had dinner at PJ's Restaurant, and when Emery sat across the table from him, he moved beside her, earning a slightly uneasy look that was so opposite of what he was used to, it took all his resolve not to take a step back. Instead, he put his arm around her and said, "Stop fighting it, Emery. This is exactly where you're supposed to be."

She was stunned into silence, but he'd broken the ice, and they recovered quickly, falling into the comfortable, fun friendship they'd enjoyed for the last few months—with underlying promises of much more.

Emery insisted she didn't want fries with her lobster roll, and she ended up eating most of Dean's. His quirky girl was nothing like the women he was used to. She ate like she didn't care if she gained an ounce of weight and seemed to prefer to eat everything as if it were a finger food, licking the salt from her fingertips. She looked so hot, he'd been aroused most of the evening. She also cursed often, laughed too loud, and fought him on everything—and for whatever reason, each of those things made him fall harder for her.

When they arrived back at his place, she headed outside to shower *beneath the moonlight*. Being the gentleman he was, Dean had offered to join her, to help her wash her back, of course. But she'd gotten that uneasy expression of not knowing if she should cross that line...*yet*. He relented, showering alone inside the house, thinking about his naked beauty beneath the warm shower spray. Even turning the shower to Nordic temperatures didn't help.

Showered and dressed, he carried a blanket outside and tossed it on a lounger. Emery's melodic voice sailed into his ears. "What if...I might hurt you." *Hum, hum, hum.* "...or leave you..." *Hum, hum, hum.* "Find someone else...or don't need you..."

His chest constricted. Was it a coincidence, or was she giving him a message? He knew the song by Kane Brown, and the tune was right, but she had the lyrics wrong. He, Rick, and Drake had played in a band together when they were growing up. Drake now owned a chain of East Coast music stores, and they all still played from time to time. "What Ifs" had become one of his favorite songs over the winter. Now, as Emery sang about the sky falling and if the sun stopped burning, he finally understood why. The lyrics were Emery's deepest fears.

He stepped closer to the shower, cutting her off mid-lyric as he sang his own rendition of the song. "I hear you, doll. I feel your worry. But before you make up your mind, I gotta know..."

He heard her gasp, and he let the words fall free. "What if

we were made for each other? What if we were meant to be? What if the stars aligned and we had our *last* first kiss in the deep blue sea?"

The water turned off, and the towel slipped from the top of the stall. Dean held his breath, and just when he was sure he'd blown it, her melodic voice filled the cool night air.

"What if I mess us up? Break our hearts in two?" She was quiet again, and he heard the sound of her pulling on her shorts and hoodie. The wooden door opened, and she stood before him, a vision of beautiful vulnerability. Her hazel eyes were shadowed with trepidation, a few wayward strands of hair stuck to her cheek, dripping water onto her clothes.

She nibbled at her lower lip, her long lashes fluttering as she whisper-sang, "What if I don't know how to do this? What if I hurt you? What if—"

He reached behind her, taking the towel from where it hung on a hook, and used it to gently blot her hair dry as he sang, "You won't hurt me, because hurting me will hurt you, too." He tossed the towel onto the bench inside the stall and tucked her hair behind her ear. Gazing into her eyes, he gathered her close, swaying to the soft tune he heard in his head, and sang, "What if I show you how incredible you can be?"

"Dean," she whispered, touching her forehead to his chest.

He tipped up her chin and gazed into her eyes. "What will it take for you to believe that whatever happened with your previous guy friends will not happen with us?"

"I know that now," she said, surprising him. "Whatever this is between us is nothing like anything I've felt before. It's stronger. I can't, and I don't want to, deny it. But that doesn't mean I'm not worried that I'll mess it up."

"I have faith in my woman," he said earnestly.

"Your *woman?*"

"Don't fight me." He grabbed her, holding her bottom. Her eyes widened with surprise. "You know we belong together. I just watched you attack the waves until you figured out a way to conquer them. You asked for help, which I'm sure you struggled with as if your life depended on it, and the end result wasn't conventional, but I don't think there's a single thing about you that's conventional. And because I know you, *because* I have spoken to you nearly every single day since the day we met and I know how caring and strong a person you are, I am one hundred percent certain, without a shadow of a doubt, that if you *want* this to work, you won't allow yourself to mess it up."

"I told you I don't know when I do things that make guys angry."

Her response came too fast. It was too much of a knee-jerk reaction to be anything but an old standby. He knew she hadn't really heard and processed what he'd said, so he tried a different approach. "You know what, doll? While I believe that you might not be cognitively aware of the things you do, I'm not buying that you don't know *exactly* what you're doing on some level. Even if subconsciously."

Her eyes narrowed, and he felt her stiffen against him. "Did you just call me a liar?"

"No, *Miss Rebellion.* I called you *human.* We all hide from ourselves on some level. Maybe you knew those guys weren't right for you, or maybe you were scared of getting too close. I don't know, and frankly, it doesn't matter. What does matter is *this.* You might not have been aware of your actions before, but that doesn't mean you'll keep yourself in the dark in the future."

"Don't hold your breath," she said, her shoulders dropping a fraction of an inch.

He flattened his hand on her lower back, keeping their bodies flush, until the defeat in her eyes turned darker and her body began to melt against him. And then he remained quiet, letting their silent seduction take over. The desire that had been there all day, that had exploded to epic proportions in their kisses, thrummed between them. An inescapable force she'd refused to see for too long.

When her tongue swept across her lower lip, leaving it shiny and alluring, he brushed his lips over hers, lingering there in the silence, reveling in the quickening of her breathing, the press of her fingers into his chest. Oh yeah, she was too into him to mess this up. He was sure of it.

"You're worth holding my breath for," he said in a voice so raw with lust he didn't recognize it. "We'll just have to spend a lot of time together so you can expose me to all those supposed-ly horrible things you do. Only then will I know the truth. And make no mistake, beautiful girl. I am fully aware that if you want to mess this up, you will. I'm willing to take that risk."

"Promise if I screw up, we can still be friends?" she asked.

There was no thought involved with his answer. Honesty didn't take thought; it only took courage. Dean was the *king* of courage. He'd spent his life going against his father's wishes.

He threaded his hands into Emery's hair, greedily soaking in the desire in her eyes. He tangled her hair around his fingers, shifting her mouth beneath his, and said, "No. I won't promise you that, because if you mess this up, it'll be intentional."

DEAN'S MOUTH HOVERED above Emery's, his warm, minty breath teasing over her lips. She'd always thought she had her act together, except in the relationship department. She knew she was broken. Her whole family was broken. *The Andrews: Too Messed Up for Happily Ever Afters.* But if what Dean said was true, if she was sabotaging any chance she had at happiness, she was *really* messed up.

She swallowed hard, knowing she'd practically worn a neon sign telling him to run away. Only he refused to go—and she didn't want him to!

He stayed.

He pushed.

She loved his pushiness, and she craved his intensity. He'd catapulted her right out of denial and into the land of desire so powerful she was drowning in it. And she only wanted to satisfy it with *him*.

His lips grazed hers, sending shivers down her spine.

"Kiss me," she said breathlessly.

Then his hands were in her hair, his mouth on hers, pushing away all thought. The insanely sensual scratch of his beard made her core burn and ache. When he pressed his entire body to hers, hips, chest, thighs, she stumbled back against the side of the shower stall. She barely caught her breath before he was taking their kisses deeper, and only one thought flashed in her mind. *Please let him be right. Let me be capable of not messing this up.*

His kisses were rough yet sensual, demanding. *Always demanding.* She opened her mouth wider, accepting his magnificent assault. His hips ground against her in a dizzying rhythm as his hands caged her in—one around her waist, the other buried in her hair. She'd already come to crave his possessive hold as his hands moved up along her waist. His kisses unraveled her, but his fierce domination *annihilated* her.

She'd always wanted a man who knew how to *be* a man, who knew how to *take* without forcing, how to *give* without becoming too soft, and was sensitive enough to listen and care without losing his edge. Yes, she craved it all, even if she didn't think she could hold on to such a magnificent creature. But she didn't worry about that too much as she dreamed about the perfect potent male, because until Dean, she'd never come across a single one.

As their lips parted, a whimper escaped. *No!* She wasn't done yet. Maybe not ever if he kept up these mind-blowing kisses. How could she have denied this heat? The passion arcing between them? She grabbed his shirt and pulled his mouth back to hers. Electric currents *zing*ed along the surface of her skin, and her entire body exhaled, like she needed Dean to breathe. His hands were everywhere at once, on her shoulders, arms, hips, trailing up her sides. His heavy palms grazed her ribs, and she heard herself moaning, willing him to take more as he nipped a path along her jaw. Each stinging bite heightened her arousal.

He clutched her hips, holding her exactly where he wanted her. His mouth took up residence in the sensitive area beneath her earlobe, devastating her one openmouthed kiss at a time. The delicious friction between them, coupled with his insistent mouth on her neck, and the firm press of his hands on her hips set off an explosion inside her.

"Dean! Don't stop—"

The desperation in her voice mirrored the agonizing pleasures tearing through her. She dug her nails into his shoulders as her entire body pulsed erratically. He didn't relent. His mouth crashed over hers, muffling her pleas as he drove her out of her mind, intensifying *everything*, sending pleasure rippling from her scalp all the way to the tips of her toes.

When she came down from the clouds, she collapsed, spent and sated, against him. He lifted her into his arms, lavishing her with tender kisses as he carried her to the lounger. He sank down, tucking her safely along his side, and covered them with a blanket. Shocked by what he was capable of without so much as touching her in the places she always thought needed it most, Emery was lost in a sea of emotions.

She turned toward him and his leg moved over hers. His arm circled her waist, bringing her into the safety of *him*. He was wearing shorts, and his skin was warm despite the cool temperature. She snuggled closer, awakening her body again. Just as quickly as she reignited, she cringed inside. She'd been so swept up in him, she hadn't reciprocated. *Way to go, selfish.*

She pressed a kiss just above the collar of his T-shirt and began kissing her way south. A niggling of worry stepped in, and she froze. Putting her mouth on him ranked right up there with full-on sex. In fact, it was even more intimate. Once they moved past their clothing, there was no turning back. *Is there really any turning back now?* She didn't want to turn back, but what if things got awkward? Would they look at each other differently afterward? Would she ever be able to look at him again and not see him naked?

And then there was the other issue she was trying to push to the side. What if when she told Rick and Drake she preferred not to work for them directly—*because I want to be with Dean*—they got upset because she'd been the one who had approached them about the job in the first place? She could omit the part about Dean, but they'd figure it out. She was horrible at lying. Denial came much easier. But there was no denying her feelings anymore.

She glanced at the house and her stomach clenched.

Being outside, under the cover of night, gave her a sense of freedom and made her feel like everything was okay. She realized she'd felt freer, and like herself, more often today than ever before, and she knew it was because of her deep connection with Dean more than her surroundings. But once they went inside his house, they'd face a whole new landscape, with questions and boundaries that might no longer exist.

Dean tightened his hold. "You feel like you're deciding if you should bolt."

"I'm…" *Trying to decide what to do.* "Not bolting."

"Darn right you're not," he said firmly.

"Don't tell me what to do." *Darn it.* Why did her habits have to be so ingrained?

He shifted his leg off her and waved his hand. "No one's holding you hostage, doll. If Miss Rebellious wants to sabotage the best thing she's ever had, have at it."

Ouch. That stung, but the element of truth buzzed like a firefly. She tried to tease it away. "My, aren't we cocky?"

He arched a brow, amusement playing in his eyes. "After pleasuring you, I have a right to be."

She had to agree. "Okay, I'll give you that. You're quite *talented.*"

He put his leg over her again, and in one move, he was lying above her, his hips between her legs. "You haven't seen talented yet."

She knew he wasn't bluffing, and the hard press of his body made her want to find out. But as much as she wanted him, and wanted to reciprocate the incredible way he'd made her feel, it was more important to know that when they woke up tomorrow, nothing will have changed for the worse. Then they could make clearheaded decisions.

His mouth came coaxingly down over hers, and like a fish to water, her body instantly responded, arching and grinding.

He perched on his forearms, smiling down at her.

"I really like when you do that." She reached up and stroked his face.

"Kiss you?"

She shook her head. "Smile." That earned an even wider smile. "You're always hot, but you're *dangerously* hot when you smile."

"I'm only dangerous to those who mess with me." He kissed her neck. "Or anyone who dares mess with you."

"That made you even hotter."

"Good. Remember that when we go out on real dates, like in a few weeks, for example."

"*In a few weeks?*" Was this his way of telling her he was busy until then? She'd had such a good time today, she'd assumed they'd spend more time together. She was surprised by the disappointment swamping her.

"What's the matter, doll? I'm not hot enough for you to go on real dates with?"

The spark of tease in his eyes told her that he didn't believe that his being hot enough was even a consideration. With anyone else, that arrogance would be a turn-off, but with Dean, it was a major aphrodisiac, making it easier to push aside the disappointment of not knowing if they'd spend time together in the days between now and their date. "That depends. Will our date include one of those epic, outside-shower moments afterward?"

He trailed kisses down her neck. "Before, during, and after that Friday night, if I have my way."

Oh boy... How would she survive that? "The odds are tipping in your favor."

He winked.

"Where are we going on *that* Friday night?"

He tugged down her neckline and pressed a kiss to the center of her breastbone. "A benefit dinner for my grandfather's foundation. My father is the keynote speaker."

She knew his grandfather had been one of the nation's first pediatric neurosurgeons, and he'd started the Pediatric Neurology Foundation, with which his family was still very involved. But her gut fisted at the thought of attending a dinner with Dean's family. More specifically, his father, a well-known, and arrogant, physician who ran one of the most prestigious pediatric neurosurgery practices on the East Coast. Knowing how he was constantly riding Dean to sell his share in the resort and go to medical school made her more likely to slap his father than speak to him.

"What are you trying to do, pick a fight with your father? You know how I feel about the things he says to you, and I'm not good at holding my tongue. When he starts giving you a hard time about not going to medical school, I'm going to say something I shouldn't. It's not a good idea."

Dean moved lower, and the blanket fell to the ground. She didn't need it anyway. He kept her so revved up, she didn't have time to cool down. He pushed her hoodie above her ribs, exposing her belly to the air. His warm lips trailed across her stomach, bringing rise to goose bumps.

"You're my girl now, and I want you with me."

His *girl*? She'd never been one of those women who needed to be, or wanted to be, *claimed* by a man, but in the space of a day spent with Dean, it felt like the only thing she'd ever wanted. She reminded herself that it hadn't only been a day. They'd been building up to this for months, but she'd been buried too deep in denial to let herself enjoy it.

"Will Jett be there?" she asked cautiously.

He scoffed. "He's conveniently going to be out of the country dealing with investments."

"That's another man I won't hold my tongue around. I know he's your brother, but he's too weak to be in the same room as your dad. He should show up once in a while."

"Jett might argue that I'm the weak one. But can we *not* talk about my brother right now?"

"You? Weak? Ha!"

He circled her belly button with his tongue, sending scintillating pleasures feathering outward from her core and dragging her back to the delicious heat of the moment. She'd made a lot of bad decisions in her life, and though she knew Dean wasn't one of them, she wanted to be completely clearheaded when they took the next step. She needed to see for herself that in the light of day, when her head wasn't foggy with lust and her body wasn't acting like a ravenous beast, they'd still be on the same page.

Maybe just a few more belly kisses.

"I don't know about that dinner," she said breathlessly. The last thing she wanted to do was cause trouble between Dean and his father, but she also wanted to be there for Dean. She went with levity while she thought it over. "There are several weeks between now and then. What if I get a better offer?"

He lifted his face, meeting her gaze with a serious expression. "Has someone forgotten our three-example-outings deal?"

Her heart soared. He wasn't busy after all? Well, except with her. "No…"

"Tomorrow, six p.m., be ready for outing number two."

"Is that how I should expect guys to ask me out? Because that was pretty much a demand." And *oh*, how she loved his demands. But she wouldn't like any other man taking such liberties.

His lips curved up in a smile. "My apologies. Beautiful doll, will you go on an example outing with me tomorrow evening at six?"

"I will," she said sassily. "But a few more belly kisses might seal the deal."

"As you wish." He lowered his open mouth to her belly.

He kissed just above the waist of her shorts. Her fingers curled into fists as he continued his oral assault, snaking that talented tongue from one hip to the other. She was so desperate for more, she dug her heels into the lounger. Her body screamed *yes!* but the organ she'd ignored for so long—her heart—told her to wait. *Don't mess this up.*

She squeezed her eyes shut. And then she squeezed her thighs together. Dean lifted his head again, confusion riddling his handsome face. She had to say something, but her words refused to come.

"I know I'm your girl now," she managed, and saying it out loud magnified the meaning behind it, rejuvenating her resolve. "But you said this time together was an example of how I should expect guys to treat me. Is this what I should expect when I go out on first dates, to let them go further?" Even talking about other guys seemed wrong on too many levels, but it was the only reason she could come up with in her current frazzled state.

The muscles in his jaw twitched. "Absolutely not."

"Then maybe…" She sat up and wrapped her arms around

her trembling legs. "We should call it a night."

He nodded curtly, his face stoic, eyes still dark as night, clearly struggling as he pushed to his feet, picked up the blanket, and offered her his hand. He helped her to her feet, and they walked awkwardly, and silently, inside. She felt a fissure forming inside her, and at the same time, she knew she'd done the right thing. But she worried about what was going on in Dean's head.

"I should get the towel from the shower," she said to break the ice, and turned to go back outside.

He grabbed her around the waist, hauling her against him with that same stoic expression. But his eyes softened, filled with worry. So much worry it caused the fissure to tear wide open.

"I'm sorry," they both said at once.

"No. It's my fault," she said quickly. "I want to be with you, but I'm afraid of what the morning will bring. I'm not good at this, and I've ruined enough friendships. I can't ruin ours."

"I shouldn't have rushed you. I know better, but I'm so into you, Emery, I can barely control myself."

He pressed a hand to the back of her head, bringing her cheek against his chest, and held her so tight she was sure his handprint would be branded into her skull. It was a *good* hold, a solid hold. The hold of a man who was fighting against everything inside him.

Join the party.

"You can't ruin us," he said vehemently. "You're not capable of it, Emery. One day you'll understand that."

He drew back and gazed into her eyes. "It's late. Go get ready for bed. I'll grab the towel."

He pressed his lips to her forehead, and as she watched him disappear into the darkness, it took everything she had to force her legs to carry her into the bathroom instead of running after him. She closed the door and leaned her back against it. If she'd had any reservations before, now she knew for sure that whether she'd let him go further or not, everything had already changed.

Chapter Twelve

DEAN LINGERED OUTSIDE, giving Emery time to use the bathroom and get safely within the confines of her bedroom before he ventured inside. He could kick himself for rushing her when he knew perfectly well it was the wrong thing to do. He wanted to set them apart from all her other relationships—*dates*, he corrected himself. Emery didn't *do* relationships. She dated guys a few times, slept with some—the pit of his stomach pinched with that bullet—but she'd told him that she'd never had a lasting relationship. From what she'd said about her ex-boss, that had looked like it could lead to something more. She'd gone out with him a handful of times, but according to Emery, the guy had become stalkerish. He'd wanted to see her every night, and she'd needed space. Then things had become uncomfortable at work and she'd quit.

He paced the yard, his gut churning with the thought of her ex making her uncomfortable. *Wanting to see her every night.*

Dean stopped cold. *He'd wanted a relationship?*

Could that have been it? Had she overreacted? Self-sabotaged?

He began pacing again. And here he was mentally making plans together for every night of the week. She didn't need to mess this up, because he probably already had. That would explain her hesitation to going with him to the benefit dinner. Although his father could be a pompous tool, and Emery did have a pretty thin filter.

He had to fix this, and he knew there was only one way to do that. He'd have to give her space, no matter how much he wanted to barge into her bedroom and sweep her into his arms. That was a surefire way to lose the wild child, afraid-of-commitment Emery Andrews. Why hadn't he seen that before? She might have been in denial about her true feelings, but he'd clearly been blinded by his.

When enough time had passed that he was sure she was in her room, he headed inside. Her bedroom door was closed. Cash was curled up in front of it like a tiny sentry. *Don't worry, buddy. I know the boundaries.*

The bathroom smelled like her. A pink comb and brush sat on one side of the sink. A small white tube, glass jar, and pump bottle, all with MEANINGFUL BEAUTY labels, littered the other side. He picked up the glass jar and read the label. WRINKLE SMOOTHING CAPSULES. Was she kidding? She wasn't even thirty years old yet. *Girls worry too much.* She had gorgeous skin, and he was sure it wasn't because of some expensive face stuff.

He opened a drawer and began transferring his toiletries to another, clearing that one out for Emery. He put her things in the empty drawer and reached for his electric toothbrush, beside which was a child's electric toothbrush with a character on it. He chuckled. He'd forgotten about that. She used children's talking toothbrushes because she didn't like how big adult toothbrush heads were. She also said she got distracted when she brushed and could never remember if she'd brushed long enough. The talking toothbrush did the remembering for her.

She was quirky, all right, and that just endeared him toward her even more.

He brushed his teeth and washed his face, and when he went to his room, he found all the things Emery had left there earlier. He set the magazines and other paraphernalia on the bedside table, stripped, and climbed between the sheets. Plagued by the scent of her on his pillow, memories of the look on her face seconds before she'd kissed him in the water, the sensual sounds she'd made when they were making out assaulted him. He'd never forgive himself if he screwed up things between them.

He threw an arm over his eyes, ground out a curse, and tried to ignore the lust coursing through his body.

EMERY SLID BENEATH the sheets. Dean turned onto his side, reaching for her, bringing her soft, warm body against his. He was in that hazy gray space, not fully asleep, but not fully awake, and this was the best dream he'd ever had. He could feel her soft curves beneath a thin layer of silk. He pressed his hips forward, inhaling her sweetness. She nuzzled against him, making those addicting noises he loved so much. As his mouth came down over hers, it felt so real, all he could think was, Please don't let me wake up. Let me live in this dream forever.

"No, big guy. I just want you to hold me."

Her voice was so real, but she was saying all the wrong things. This was his dream, his fantasy. What the...? He covered her mouth with his again, but she squirmed out of reach, toward the edge of the bed. No! Don't go!

"Sorry, I shouldn't have come."

His eyes flew open, and he realized he hadn't been dreaming. One of the kittens scampered off the edge of the bed beside Emery, who was sitting with her back to him. The clock on the bedside table read 2:13 a.m. "Em? Sorry. I thought I was dreaming."

She glanced over her shoulder, her hair covering one eye. She looked nervous, and sinfully sexy in a silky spaghetti-strap top and matching shorts. "I shouldn't have—"

His arm circled her waist before she could finish what she was saying, and he pulled her beneath the sheet. A nervous smile crawled across her face.

"I wanted to be with you," she whispered. "But not to fool around. I mean, not yet. I need to be sure that if we—when we—if we…" Her gaze slid away, and she inhaled deeply. When she looked his way, it was with pleading eyes that made him want to shelter her from the world. "I need to know that if we spend the night together, we'll still wake up as friends and things won't get weird. But it was unfair of me to expect you to hold me and not want to do more."

"I want *you*, doll. I'll take what I can get." He locked her within the circle of his arms, bringing them nose to nose. "I want you here, and I can refrain from doing more." He had no idea if he could or not, but he'd sure as heck try. Even if it meant taking a quick ice bath first. Emery Andrews finally, *willingly*, in his bed? *Heaven.* Resisting her? *Torture.*

"Thank you." Her hand moved down his back to his butt, and her eyes widened. "You're naked!" She gasped. "And you're aroused!" She wiggled her lower half away from him, but he didn't release his hold on her. "Why do you sleep naked? How did I not know this about you?"

He laughed. "Because it's comfortable, and you never

asked."

"I can't sleep with you if you're naked! I won't sleep!"

"I'll remember that." He sat up on the edge of the bed.

She threw herself flat on her back, staring up at the ceiling. "What are you doing now?" she practically yelled. "Now you're *really* naked."

He chuckled as he walked leisurely across the room to his dresser to retrieve a pair of boxer briefs. "I assure you, I was really naked when you woke me up."

He glanced over and caught her staring. Her cheeks flamed and she shifted her eyes away. As he stepped into his briefs, he caught her looking again, and stopped with his briefs knee high. "Should I leave them off?"

She covered her face with her hand, but her radiant smile was like a beacon lighting up the room. "No!"

He began pulling them up.

"*Yes*," she said softly.

He hesitated.

Her fingers parted, and she peeked over at him, then said, "No! Definitely don't leave them off. *Ohmygosh*." She rolled to her side, turning her back to Dean.

With his briefs on, he crawled beneath the sheets behind her, gathered her into the haven of his body, and kissed her shoulder. "Embarrassed or afraid?" He was very well endowed. It was a blessing and a curse.

"Shocked and excited." She giggled and added softly, "And a little embarrassed. I'm not used to seeing you *naked*."

He nipped at her shoulder, earning a sexy gasp. "If I have my way, you'll not only get used to it, but you'll crave it, thinking about me and the pleasure I'll bring you day and night."

"Dean!" she whispered. "You're not helping!"

"And if you wiggle like that again, I can't be held responsible for my actions."

She turned in his arms and put her hand on his cheek, smiling right along with him. She did that a lot, caressed his face. He wasn't a needy guy, but the intimate touch made him feel special, and he hoped she never stopped.

"Think we can do this for real?" she asked. "Sleep together and still be okay in the morning? Still be close friends, and more, without it being awkward or different?"

"I think we can stay up all night, make love like bunnies, and fall asleep in the morning closer than we've *ever* been."

The air rushed from her lungs. Man, he loved that response. But he was still trying to climb out from under the biggest realization of all. "I thought I blew it tonight, and it killed me to think you might bolt."

"It's my job to blow it, not yours," she said with a raise of her brows.

She'd destroy him with her double entendres, and by the satisfied look in her eyes, he was sure she knew it. "Is your plan to torture me all night long?"

"No. That was just a bonus." She touched her lips to his, then rested her head on the pillow. "Maybe this wasn't a good idea. It's torture for both of us."

He pulled her closer again, their bodies touching from thigh to chest. "A good test, then." He lowered his cheek to the pillow and gazed into her sleepy eyes. "I'm glad you're here."

"Me too," she whispered.

"I'll try to behave."

She giggled. "Ditto."

He leaned in and kissed her, tender and slow, savoring every second as her hand moved from his cheek to his hip. *Behave*, he reminded himself.

As he drew back from the kiss, he was holding on to his control by a thread. He knew he could probably persuade her to let him make love to her, or at least pleasure her. But that wasn't how he wanted their first time to happen. He wanted her to crave him so badly she couldn't hold back. He wanted her to be out of her mind with desire. As he struggled to regain control, he realized he not only wanted to be the best lover of her lifetime, but he wanted to be her last.

"Sleep?" he asked reluctantly.

She nodded, snuggled in close, and closed her eyes. "Sleep."

Chapter Thirteen

EMERY DIDN'T KNOW how long she lay awake last night, but she'd been keenly aware of every inch of Dean's body, from his muscular legs, to the dusting of chest hair tickling her skin, all the way to his long lashes moving ever so slightly when he dreamed. He'd slept with one arm tightly around her. About an hour ago he'd rolled onto his back, and she'd snuck from the bed long enough to pee and brush her teeth. Tango and Cash had followed her into the bathroom and then cuddled up beside Dean when she'd returned to the bedroom. She'd been lying awake ever since, trying to draw her eyes away from the tented sheet bunched around his hips. But after dreaming about him all night long, and waking herself up with a moan, it was proving to be an impossible feat.

It seemed like hours before the predawn light crept across his tanned and toned abs. *Finally. That was the longest night of my life!* Emery's pulse quickened as she leaned up on one elbow, her gaze rolling over Dean's face. The face she'd thought she'd memorized, but as he'd slept, she'd cataloged a few things she'd missed. His brows were blonder than his hair, and the upper half of his mustache and beard were lighter, too. Even in his slumber he had the serious face of a warrior. *A Viking. My*

Viking? Her insides trembled with memories of the way he'd made her feel last night. Her body was on fire, her breathing erratic. She needed a Dean fix.

She continued visually devouring him. His flawless skin only slightly softened his sharp features. *But that smile*, she thought dreamily. His smile made her stomach tumble and flip, and the way he'd looked at her last night, and the way he'd spoken to her, like she was his entire world, had an even more powerful effect. Had it always been that way?

His eyes opened slowly, and she watched the fog of sleep clear, bringing rise to that heart-melting grin.

"*Finally*" fell from her lips like she'd been stranded on a desert island and he was her rescuer. "Are we good? Still friends?"

His brows knitted. "Of course, why?"

"Thank goodness!"

She *pounced*, straddling his body as she crashed her mouth to his in a fury of feverish kisses. "I've been waiting so long," she said as she stripped off her top and tossed it away, touching her chest to his. That first skin-to-skin contact sent magic dancing along her skin.

Dean swept her beneath him, his eyes ablaze with desire. "I like the way you greet the morning."

He trapped her hands beside her head with a glimmer of demand in his eyes, and he took her in a fierce kiss that sent tingles zipping through her. Their lips parted with a rush of heat, and he kissed her cheek, her forehead, the corner of her mouth, the sensitive spot beside her ear. They were only kisses, but each one felt more erotic than the last. And when he put his mouth beside her ear, his warm breath sinking into her pores, she hung on every second, waiting for him to speak, or kiss, or—

His tongue moved along the shell of her ear. "There will be no rushing today, sweetheart."

A whimper escaped before she could stop it.

"Those noises make me lose my mind. I'm going to make you whimper, moan, and *beg*."

"*Yes*," she pleaded.

He circled her ear again, this time with kisses. When he got to her lobe, he whispered dirty things in her ear.

She was surprised by how his words made her cheeks burn. She wasn't intimidated by dirty talk. She'd always known she'd love it, and as she'd lain awake, she realized she'd fantasized about dirty talk coming from *Dean's* voice for months, and she'd buried that acknowledgment right along with the rest of her feelings. But actually hearing him talk like he did in her dreams as the room became brighter by the second was a whole different ball game.

He bit into her earlobe, and she sucked in air between clenched teeth. "Do you want me, Emery?"

"More than anything." The truth felt so good, she felt like a great weight had lifted from within her, and her eyes fluttered closed.

"You're trembling for me."

"Yes," she said, closing her eyes against the embarrassment.

He dragged his beard along her neck and nipped at her chin. "Open your eyes for me. I want you here with me. Don't hide from us."

Her eyes opened, and the look in his eyes wasn't erotic—it was deep and emotional—and she realized he'd repeated *for me*. He was setting this moment apart from all others. Showing her—and himself?—that when they were together, they were different. And he was right. The guys she'd been with had never wanted, *demanded*, such defining lines.

"You're so beautiful," he murmured as he brushed his lips over hers. "I'm going to make you feel so good, you're never going to want to leave this bed."

Before she could respond, he kissed her. Her whole body arched and swayed.

"I've waited my whole life for someone like you," she said breathlessly.

He sank his teeth into her shoulder, and she bowed off the bed, but he held her down, glaring at her. He dipped his head and laved his tongue over the tender spot he'd caused, then whispered, "I'm beginning to understand how you get into trouble with guys."

"What did I say?" She tried to recall her words, but she'd said them too quickly.

"When I'm thinking about all the ways I want to pleasure you, the last thing I want to hear is that you've been waiting for *someone like me* your whole life."

She blinked several times, trying to figure out what was wrong with her statement. "So, I should lie?"

He chuckled. "How about just removing references to anyone else? We both know you've been waiting for *me* your whole life."

She laughed and grabbed his head with both hands, pulling his mouth closer to hers. "You are so cocky, and because you somehow got me to quit my job—"

"You were fired," he reminded her with a tender nip of her lower lip.

"Because you somehow got me to *quit* my job," she reiterated, "and I'm lying in your bed, you'll probably never believe I'll stick to my guns about anything ever again."

"Not true. You're as stubborn as I am cocky, and it makes you sinfully hot." He dragged his tongue along her lower lip, making her entire body shudder. "I'm about to get very intimate with all that heat, and I want to know you're thinking of me, not that I could be *any* guy who knows how to turn you on."

His sensitivity caught her off guard. As she lay there turning his words over in her mind, wondering how she'd feel if he'd said he'd been waiting for a woman *like her* all his life, she realized just how powerful words were. She wasn't ready to say she'd been waiting for him her whole life, but she was surprised to find the words riding pretty close to the surface. Worry over where they would be tomorrow, the next day, and for the foreseeable future lingered like a ghost waiting to kick her feet out from under her. But she refused to let that worry sabotage them.

She turned her face toward his arm and licked the length of his biceps. "Maybe you should convince me that you're the one I've been waiting for."

With a wicked grin, he buried both hands in her hair and took her in a savagely fierce kiss.

He devoured.

Consumed.

He *possessed* with everything he had. Just when she started to focus on one sensation, he'd move, shattering her thoughts.

EMERY'S EYELIDS FLUTTERED closed. Her cheeks were flushed, her beautiful swollen, pink lips were parted, and her body was covered in a sheen of sweat. She was beyond stunning as she reached for him, pulling him into another kiss.

"My turn," she said against his lips, and pushed him onto his back.

Her gaze trailed down his body. She inhaled a shaky breath, her hands playing over his chest and thigh.

"You're like the perf—" She paused, her hands stilling as she met his gaze. The brown and greens in her eyes were darker, and the gold around the edges glittered like stars. "You're *my* perfect playground."

She destroyed him. He reached up and pulled her down by the nape of her neck, kissing her deeply. He imagined his heart opening and wrapping itself around her, and he never wanted to let her go.

Banging on the front door startled them, and he glanced at the clock. *Aw, hell.*

She sat back and pulled the sheet up to cover her chest. "Were you expecting someone?"

He ground his teeth together. "Drake and Rick." The banging continued. "They're here to go running. I forgot we were going early today. Drake has to meet some guy at eight. Sorry, doll. I'll get rid of them." He sat up on the edge of the bed as they banged on the door again. "I'm sorry."

"It's okay." She moved next to him. "You should go running. I don't want to monopolize your time. Besides, I really need to meditate if I'm going to get anything done today besides thinking about you."

He put an arm around her neck and pulled her into another kiss. "I'd rather make love to you."

"I know, but it's kind of embarrassing to send them away for that, and I'll feel guilty."

Just his lousy luck. "I'll make it up to you tonight."

"I think that should be me making it up to you. She dropped her gaze to his very noticeable arousal. "Maybe *I* should answer the door."

He kissed her shoulder. "Not naked, you're not." He grabbed his T-shirt from the chair by the window and pulled it over her head. When she stood, it fell to the middle of her thighs. She looked adorably hot. He liked seeing her in his shirt almost as much as he liked seeing her in his bed.

"I'll tell them you'll be right out." She took a step away, and he grabbed her hand, guiding her back, until she stood between his legs.

He slipped both hands beneath the T-shirt and pulled her forward.

"Oh my," she said dreamily. "Or…maybe we should ignore them."

Another loud bang brought a curse from both of them, followed by laughter.

"Go take a fast icy shower. I'll tell them you'll be right there."

As she stepped away, he hauled her back again. "You are *not* going out there without underwear."

She looked down, as if she hadn't noticed. "Your shirt covers me."

He narrowed his eyes and she bit her lower lip.

"This is another one of those Emery-is-oblivious times, isn't it?"

She wrinkled her nose. "I told you." She peered over his shoulder at the tangle of sheets. "I have no idea where my pajama shorts are."

He pushed to his feet, stripped the blankets off the bed, and retrieved her silky bottoms. He held them open for her to step into and said, "I'm not a prude, but wearing underwear around other guys isn't negotiable."

"What if I'm not wearing underwear under my skirt when I'm out with you in public"—mischief sparked in her eyes—"if the sole purpose of said nakedness is for easy, *discreet* access?"

"I'm going to need an hour-long cold shower." He smacked her butt and she left the room giggling.

Underwear wasn't negotiable, but he had a feeling there was a host of Emeryisms he'd have to get used to. As he ducked into the bathroom and stepped beneath the cold water, he wondered how many times a day he'd be biting his tongue.

An hour later, as Dean, Drake, Rick, and Matt neared the end of their run, Dean was still fielding questions about Emery. "I don't remember you guys ever giving me the third degree like this about any other woman."

"No other woman has ever answered your door wearing your shirt before," Drake pointed out.

"Yeah, well, I was lucky she put that on," he said, biting back the reminder of how nonchalantly she'd almost answered the door buck naked beneath that shirt. "She doesn't always think things through."

Rick and Drake exchanged a glance he couldn't read.

"Spit it out," Dean said as the resort came into view.

"I was all for this the other night, but then she picked up that guy at the bar," Drake said carefully. "And now she's answering your door wearing your shirt. We don't want to see you get hurt."

He'd finally gotten that jerk out of his mind. That guy didn't matter. She was with him now. "I'm a big boy. I can handle myself."

"You just said she doesn't think things through, and although Des loves Emery like a sister," Rick said, "she's alluded to the fact that Emery is pretty uninhibited. Think about it. That's all we're saying. I can count the number of women you've had in your place on one hand, and they're all related to us in one way or another—sister, sister's best friend, mother..."

"You've had my wife in your place?" Matt asked with a teasing glare. "Something I should know about?"

Dean shook his head. "You were there, too. Halloween barbecue."

As they came to the resort grounds, they slowed to a walk. "Listen," Dean said. "I know Emery is a whirlwind, and I understand why you're concerned. She's nothing like the women I've gone out with, and there was that guy at the bar, but that's because she'd put me in some sort of friend zone. She was in complete denial about what was going on between us."

"In Emery's defense, friends to lovers is a hard bridge to cross," Matt said. "I've said it before and I'll say it again. I held back from being with Mira until I was sure I had the time and energy to devote to her. It took me a year to finally ask her out, and it only took me a few weeks to ask her to marry me. When you've met your soul mate, you *know*. In Dean's defense, I wish I hadn't wasted that year."

"Sometimes crossing bridges bites you in the butt," Drake ground out. "I'm glad it didn't for you and our sister, and I hope it doesn't for Dean and Emery."

Another strained look passed between Rick and Drake, and then Rick turned his attention back to Dean.

"After three days she's answering the door in your shirt? Come on, man," Rick said. "She might be good in bed, but just be careful. We care about you."

Dean's hands fisted by his sides as he closed the distance

between them, chest out, shoulders back. He was sure he was breathing fire. It took everything he had to not lay into Rick physically. "It hasn't been *three days*. I spent months getting to know her before we got intimate. *Months*, Rick. Talking every single night, video chatting. I can tell you what her puppy's name was when she was growing up, who her first kiss was with, and probably hundreds of things that would seem insignificant to you, but to me, they're everything, because they made her who she is. And I freaking love who she is. She's honest, smart, and she's got a love for life like no one else. She doesn't care about the nonsense most women care about." As he said the words, he recalled how he and Drake had been just as worried about Rick when he'd fallen for Desiree. "You fell in love with Desiree after knowing her for just a few *days*, remember?"

"Pretty much overnight," Drake pointed out.

"We've had *months*, Rick. And not months of rolling between the sheets. Months of *talking*, getting to know what makes each other tick. I was there for her when she had bad dates and decided to swear off dating guys who were friends. I know what she wants out of life." *And I know how she sabotages it.* "I was there for her when she was deciding whether she should leave Virginia, and I'll be there when she misses her family." He took a step back, pausing to rein in his emotions. "And she has been there for me. She's been a calming force every time my father has left me so angry I wanted to kill someone. Just like you guys have been."

Regret rose in Rick's eyes. "I'm sorry, man." He opened his arms and Dean reluctantly stepped into the embrace of the guy he'd known since they were both kids. "I should have known you've thought this through. And for the record, she looked very *satisfied* when she answered the door."

She hasn't even begun to be satisfied, thanks to you guys. "What do you say we go see how satisfied you made your fiancée last night? I'm starved."

"I've got to take off," Matt said.

"More baby making?" Drake teased. Matt and Mira had just begun trying to get pregnant.

Matt laughed. "Not this time. We're taking Hagen to the Woods Hole Science Aquarium. I'll catch up with you guys the next time I can make it out for a run."

"I've got to head out right after breakfast," Drake said. "I'm meeting a guy about that empty retail space in town. Thinking about opening my fifth store." When they'd bought the resort, Drake had put his plans for opening another music store on hold. It made sense, now that the resort was fully functional, with administrative processes in place, that he'd want to move forward.

"Good luck with it," Rick said.

"I've got a few places I'm checking out next week, too," Drake said. "I figured I'd start looking now, but I won't make any offers until the off-season. Better prices that way."

They headed up to the Summer House, and Dean caught sight of Emery talking animatedly with Desiree in the side yard as they set the table. She was smiling and waving her hands, wearing a pair of tight black yoga pants and a bright pink sports bra, which he couldn't wait to take off her. He wished she had a shirt on so the other guys wouldn't get to enjoy the view of her gorgeous body, but he wasn't a Neanderthal. At least she had pants on.

"I'm really sorry for coming across as a jerk," Rick said.

"It's all right. I get it. I know what it looks like, but, man, I've been hooked on her since the first time she opened that sassy mouth of hers the night you proposed." He understood why his friends worried, and the truth was, if Emery had appeared on his doorstep and they had never shared months of deep conversations, as well as light, ridiculous ones, he might worry too. But he knew his feisty girl, and once she stepped out of her own way, no one would question her feelings for him.

Chapter Fourteen

"I AM NOT humming!" Emery insisted, although not only was she buzzing like a hummingbird, but little spasms were quaking through her every time she thought of Dean. She was surprised she wasn't causing the ground to shake.

"You started humming after Oscar Martin popped your cherry," Desiree reminded her as she headed back inside for another tray of food, Emery and Cosmos at her heels. "And the only time you hum since is when you've had great sex. Why are you denying it?"

Desiree stopped walking, and Emery bumped into her with an *oomph!*

Desiree spun around, her jaw hanging open, her green eyes wide with horror. "Oh my gosh. We're growing apart, aren't we? You used to tell me about your sexy escapades. First we stop telling each other things, and then we'll stop hanging out, and it'll only get worse from there…"

"No, we are *not* growing apart." Hearing the guys in the yard, Emery took her by the arm and dragged her away from the door. Cosmos scampered back outside. "I share *everything* with you. I haven't had any escapades to speak of for months."

"But you're *humming*, and you swore there was nothing

between you and Dean. Oh no, please tell me you aren't staying at his place and sleeping with someone else."

"Yeah, that's it. I've turned into a flaming slut. You'd better lock up the men, or I'll jump all of them." They both laughed, and Emery admitted, "There wasn't anything between me and Dean before, or maybe there was and I didn't let myself see it. But we haven't done it!" she whispered emphatically. "At least not full-on *it*."

"Ha! I knew it!" Desiree set her hands on her hips and smiled. "The way he looked at you over Christmas is nothing compared to how he looks at you now that you're here. I knew you two would hook up."

"Then you're more intuitive than me, because I didn't," Emery confessed. She glanced toward the yard, where Dean's distinct voice rose among the others', and her stomach flipped. "Please don't be mad, but I quit working at the resort and told Dean I'd see their customers here. I know I shouldn't have said anything without asking you first, but I couldn't fool around with my *boss* after what happened with the nimrod in Virginia."

"That's fine, of course, but I'm not buying that you didn't know you and Dean would hook up."

"I swear it!" She stopped talking as Violet descended the steps, eyeing them curiously. "Hey, Vi. I love your skirt."

Violet looked down at the tie-dyed miniskirt covering the bottom of her black bikini. "Thanks. I made it." She made a dramatic show of sniffing the air and said, "*Ah*, Rick's a good man."

Desiree blushed as Violet made a beeline for the crepes Desiree had set out for everyone. Then Desiree narrowed her eyes and crossed her arms, staring at Emery expectantly.

"*Denial*," Emery said flatly. "That's my only defense."

"Denial? Really? So are you two a thing now?" A smile lifted her lips, and before Emery could respond, concern wiped it away. "Em, he's Rick's business partner. Please tell me this isn't a fling."

"I don't know what it is, but it doesn't feel like a fling," she whispered. "It feels right. Righter than anything ever has, other than doing *serious* yoga back-care. It feels as right as that, only better. And that scares me to death."

"Why?"

Emery gazed in the direction of the voices coming from outside. The voices of her new life, her new friends, and the deep, sexy voice of the man who was singlehandedly upending her plans. "Because I feel all these things I haven't felt before, and now that I'm not in denial, I know I didn't stop dating friends *just* because I always screwed up our friendships. I stopped dating *anyone* because I preferred to spend the evenings with Dean, even if long-distance."

"But, Em, those are good things. Wonderful things. Certainly not things to be scared of."

"That's not what scares me. What scares me is that I will probably mess this up, and I don't want to."

"Would you stop? You're not going to mess anything up." Desiree hugged her tight. "You gave me the courage to move forward with Rick, and I'm here for you, Em. Day or night. Whatever you need."

"Thanks. I'm sure I gave Dean whiplash yesterday the way I was scared one minute and jumping in with two feet the next. But you know what? He didn't freak out or run away. I think he really gets me."

"You're not that hard to get, Em. You're pretty amazing."

"Right back at ya, sister." On the way back outside, Emery

told her about Dean introducing her to Chloe. "I'm hoping she can get the approval for me to work with some of the residents there, but I promise it won't interfere with my work here."

When they stepped outside, Emery was sure all the guys looked up from the table, but she saw only Dean. He rose from his seat wearing nothing but running shorts and a predatory grin. As he ate up the distance between them, every determined step made her heart beat faster, her blood pump hotter. Oh man. She was so far past denial, she'd entered *he's mine* territory.

"Hey, doll." Dean planted a kiss on her cheek.

She was surprised by his open affection, but as she thought about the way he'd acted around Blaine and then around his friend Jonny as Jonny had measured her for a wet suit, she realized she shouldn't be surprised. Dean was a possessive man, and boy, did she like him just the way he was.

"Looks like Em doesn't have a problem with naked men in the morning after all." Violet lifted her glass in a toast. "To fantastic frickery for all."

Everyone laughed except Dean, who growled.

Emery turned his handsome face back toward her. She couldn't help but giggle at his serious expression. "You didn't really think you could kiss me without Violet announcing it to the world, did you?"

"This isn't *frickery*," he said angrily.

"That blush on her cheeks tells a different story," Violet chimed in.

"Does it matter what she calls it?" Emery asked Dean. "All that matters is what we think we are." As the words left her lips, she wondered where her confidence in their relationship came from.

He gathered her in his arms, but his expression did not

soften. Why was that such a turn-on?

"And what is it, doll? What are we to you?"

She drew in a deep breath, gathering her courage and choosing her words carefully. "The start of something that feels too right to be wrong."

He lowered his mouth to hers, causing everyone to whistle and cheer. Cosmos barked up a storm.

"Did I just see a smoking-hot kiss between you two?" Serena asked as she came through the gate.

"The frickery has begun," Violet explained.

"Enough, Vi." Dean led Emery to the chair beside his, and she immediately snatched a strawberry from his plate. He smiled and leaned in for another kiss.

"I guess Dean told you guys that I won't be working at the resort," Emery said as she plucked another piece of fruit from Dean's plate.

"What?" Rick glared at Dean. "No, he didn't tell us that."

"She can't work for me if we're going to be together," Dean explained.

"What about the classes I've booked?" Serena held a hand over her plate to stop Drake from putting a third crepe on it. "I can't eat three, but thanks."

"I'll see your clients here at Summer House, if that's okay with you guys. I'll still give the resort a commission from each person you refer. I feel really bad about letting you down, but I swear I'll teach just as many classes, and—"

"You didn't have to quit," Drake said with a hint of frustration as his gaze slid to Dean.

"I fired her," Dean mumbled.

"No, you didn't. I quit," she insisted.

"We could have worked around it," Drake said. "We're all

friends, after all."

The relief of not having the pressure of working for Dean hanging over Emery's head was indescribable, and she wasn't about to go back to worrying about that. But she owed them a better explanation. "Thanks, Drake, but I wouldn't have asked you guys to do that, and I couldn't have done it. I had a really bad experience back home when I made the mistake of going out with my boss. I couldn't take the chance of ruining everything if for some reason Dean and I don't work out."

Dean squeezed her shoulder. "We're going to work out."

"By that twinkle in her eyes, I'd say you already *worked out*," Violet teased.

"Vi," Dean warned.

Suddenly Emery worried that she'd put Dean in a difficult position by quitting. "Drake, if it's a problem, I can…" *Not see Dean?* That wasn't even an option anymore. "I can find someone else to teach at the resort if you want me to. I'm sure there are lots of yoga instructors here."

"No, it's fine," Drake said. "And don't worry about the commission. We don't need it. I just didn't want you to think you had to quit."

"It's fine, Emery. It's not like we went to any great expense to prepare for you to work there," Rick clarified. "We might have to repaint the office you were going to use, because Dean insisted on painting it buttercup yellow, but that's not a big deal."

Emery's heart filled up. Dean hadn't mentioned that he'd chosen the color. "You did that for me?"

"I would have built you an ashram," Dean said casually. "Painting a room your favorite color was hardly difficult."

"No, but it was the most thoughtful thing you could have

done." She mentally corrected herself. *The second most thoughtful thing. Talking to Chloe about me was even more thoughtful.*

"Does this mean I can use the office? You don't even have to paint it! I love buttercup yellow," Serena piped in. "I've been talking to Shift Home Interior about working with them part-time. Having an office here would allow me to see clients without having to drive all the way to Hyannis."

"You have a job," Drake reminded her.

"A *temporary* job," Serena said. "I told you guys I'd get the resort office up and running, but hopefully by next summer I can find a replacement and get my *real* career back on track."

As Serena and Drake discussed the office, Emery felt a weight lift from her shoulders. With the morning sun shining down on them and the bay kissing the shores in the distance, she thought about how much her life changed in just a few days. How much she was changing. Was she really doing this? Reorganizing her life around a man? Her brothers would have her head on a platter if they found out. Either that or they would keel over from disbelief.

Dean speared a piece of crepe from his plate and offered it to her. She glanced down at her empty plate and at his, which was overflowing with fruit and crepes.

"My girl thinks everything tastes better when it's mine," he said. "So I doubled up."

Oh yeah, she was rearranging her life, all right, but not just for any man. For one of her closest friends. A very patient, caring, sinfully hot, and talented man.

AFTER A LONG day of running around town and setting up

her yoga studio at Summer House, Emery raced home to shower for her and Dean's date. *Example outing*, she corrected with a smile. *Example, right!* The bugger had known exactly what he was doing when he'd offered that up. And when he'd sent her sexy texts throughout the day. She'd been revved up all afternoon from his playful texts, which had made her imagination work overtime, like, *Looking forward to getting dirty with you later.*

She hurried into her room, which still looked like a tornado had hit it. Tango and Cash were curled up in her open suitcase. She really needed to unpack. This morning she'd run around the house looking for her keys for twenty minutes before giving up and borrowing Desiree's car to pick up the plants and picture hangers for her yoga studio. While she was out, she'd handed out a few flyers—and got lost. *Twice.* She'd called Dean and he'd patiently directed her better than any fancy GPS system ever could. She'd probably find her keys buried somewhere beneath the clothes, but she didn't have time to look now. It was almost six, and she promised Dean she'd be ready on time.

She moved the kitties to the bed and dug through her suitcase, choosing her favorite pink miniskirt, a cute cotton number that went perfectly with the new flowy gray tank top with a colorful dream catcher embroidered into it. She'd bought it from her friend Morgyn Montgomery's boutique before leaving Oak Falls.

Her toiletries were scattered on top of her dresser, but for the life of her, she couldn't find her razor.

She showered, used Dean's razor so she wouldn't have furry legs, and then quickly dried her hair and got ready to go. She took one last look in the mirror. Her hair was perfect, fluffy and wavy but not overdone. She smoked up her eyes the way she had the night they'd gone to the bar. A few bangles around her wrist and a pair of pretty dangling earrings and cute strappy heels took her outfit from beachy to beautiful. She was excited to go out with Dean. No matter what they were calling it, in her mind, it was a *date*.

Hoping to make a grand entrance so she could see his appreciative expression, she straightened her spine, inhaled a calming breath to combat the butterflies swarming in her belly, and opened her bedroom door.

DEAN LIFTED HIS gaze slowly, drinking in every inch of Emery's long legs to the edge of her pink *ultramini* miniskirt, which covered the light brown birthmark he'd discovered on her inner thigh earlier that morning. *Mm.* He'd spent the day in a state of heightened desire, remembering those addicting sounds she'd made that morning.

He continued his visual feast, moving up her torso to the outline of her curves in a cute tank top that would look even cuter on his floor. His gaze trailed up her long, graceful neck. His mouth watered with the memory of how sweet and hot her skin tasted.

His gaze lingered on her mouth. He could stare at her lips all day long. He forced his gaze north and lost his breath at the emotions staring back at him. He needed her in his arms.

He stepped forward, one arm sweeping around her waist, the other holding the bouquet he'd made for her, of tiger lilies, purple lace cap, Queen Anne's lace, yellow flag bottoms, daisies, and other flowers he knew she'd love. "Hi, beautiful."

"Flowers?" she said softly. "You should give dating lessons. I've never been given flowers. They're gorgeous. Thank you."

He liked knowing he'd achieved another *first* with Emery. "Not nearly as gorgeous as you."

He'd missed her so much today he'd ached with it. He tried to go slow, but his body would have no part of *slow*. He kissed her ravenously, causing them to stumble. Her back met the wall, and she made a mewling sound.

He tore his mouth away. "Sorry. I got carried away. Are you okay?"

"Yes," she panted out. "That wasn't a cry of pain."

She grabbed his shirt and tugged him into another fierce kiss. He wanted to drop the flowers and strip her bare, so they could finish what they'd started that morning. But this wasn't what he'd planned for tonight. This was their second *example outing*, and he wanted her to know she was worth more than just sex, that together they could enjoy more than hot make-out sessions. He forced himself to pull away, groaning as their lips parted.

"That was *not* meant as an example," he said sharply.

She giggled. "I have a feeling I won't have to worry about any other guys kissing me for a while."

A while my eye. He tightened his grip on her. Yeah, he was fiercely possessive about her, and he wasn't about to let anything come between them.

Emery must have read his mind, because she said, "We can delete those last three words."

"Wow, you're amazing." He kissed her, quick and tender, so he didn't get sidetracked again. He released her only to pick up the tall green gardening boots he'd bought for her earlier in the day.

"Flowers and *rain boots*? Is my man into something kinky?"

"Doll, you just keep calling me your man, and rest assured, I'm into *you*. We'll be as kinky as you want to be." He dropped to one knee and began removing her sandals. He couldn't resist sliding his hands up her outer thighs and kissing the soft expanse of tanned skin just beneath the hem of her skirt.

Her breath left her lungs in one fast breath. An invitation? When her eyes fluttered closed, he knew it was, but one taste of her would unravel him, and he had plans for them tonight. He forced himself to finish taking off her sandals.

Later, he'd take more than a taste.

She gazed down at him as he withdrew a pair of pink ankle socks from his pocket. "Socks," she whispered. "You thought of everything."

When it came to Emery, thinking of the little things wasn't difficult. It came naturally. He wanted her to be comfortable. But he wasn't going to miss an opportunity to mark his territory. He held up the socks for her to read the message written across the toes: TAKEN.

"Only you, big guy…" She smiled as he put the socks and boots on her feet. "How did you know my size?"

He pointed to her flip-flops, which he'd collected from around the living room and lined up by the patio doors.

"My, aren't you a clever boy," she said as he rose to his feet. She wrapped her arms around his neck and kissed him softly. "These boots are super cute. Do you know something about the weather that I don't?"

"No, and no more questions."

"If you're not going to tell me where we're going, at least tell me if I should change my clothes."

He was thrilled by how openly affectionate and accepting of

their budding relationship she'd become. When he'd kissed her at breakfast in front of their friends, he'd expected her to recoil. Not only hadn't she recoiled, but she'd said they felt *too right to be wrong*. He felt like he'd won the lottery. He was determined to prove to her that their long-distance friendship was the foundation of their future.

Dean took her hand and led her to the kitchen. He filled a vase with water and said, "You're this landscaper's fantasy come true. You're not changing a thing."

He put her bouquet in the vase and held her hand, guiding her as they walked out the back door. "If that outfit gets dirty or ruined, I'll buy you a new one." Her skirt barely covered her butt, and she looked so delectable, he said, "I'll buy you a closetful of them."

They wound through the gardens and around the tall bushes buffering his house from the rest of the resort property. He loved his privacy, and when he'd bought into the resort with Rick and Drake, he'd considered remaining in the cottage he owned in Eastham. But the minute he'd seen the cottage he now lived in, he'd fallen in love with it. Cordoning it off from the rest of the property in a way that looked natural made all the difference. He had no commute to work, except on the days he worked at the gardens at the hospital or LOCAL, where he enjoyed teaching residents how to care for the gardens.

They followed the narrow path lined with wildflowers and low-lying shrubs he'd planted in the spring. The solar lights in the ground hadn't turned on yet, but they would soon, as the evening swallowed the last of the daylight.

A breeze swept over the dunes, and Dean pulled Emery closer. "Cold?"

"No. This is wonderful compared to home, where the humidity sucks the life out of you."

"Careful talking about *sucking*, doll. I'm trying not to think about how sexy you look in that skimpy outfit."

She pretended to write in the air. "Buy more skimpy outfits. *Check.*"

Chapter Fifteen

AS THEY NEARED the end of the path, he said, "Close your eyes, doll."

"Hm. A long romantic walk, a mysterious request to close my eyes." She closed her eyes and leaned into him. "You've got me wondering what's up your sleeve. Not that I think you can fit much beyond those muscles of yours. But the rain boots have me curious. What exactly do you have in mind, Mr. Masters?"

"Our second example outing."

She squeezed his arm. "You really think you can cover *all* the bases of how I deserve to be treated in *three* example outings? When I move into the Summer House on Wednesday, will I be well schooled in all things relationship related? That seems awfully fast."

He bristled with the reminder that she hadn't moved into his place for good. He hated the idea of her moving out, but with any luck, by the time tomorrow afternoon came, she wouldn't want to go anywhere other than directly into his bed.

"I assure you, by the end of our third date—"

"Outing," she corrected him with a teasing giggle.

"Right. By the end of tomorrow, I will have ruined you for any other man."

When they reached the end of the path, the gardens Dean had planted over the spring, the area he'd cleared and prepared for the patio, and the view of the bay came into focus, along with pallets of flagstone, various tools, and other landscape paraphernalia. He'd left an unfinished border between the gardens and the area where the patio would be installed, to be filled in and planted afterward. In the center of what would become the patio stood a massive northern red oak, beneath which there was a table set for two. As if by magic, the solar lights in the tree sparked to life, twinkling above the table, where a chilled bottle of wine and dinner he'd picked up at Van Rensselaer's, one of the best restaurants on the Cape, awaited. Their meal was hidden within fancy serving dishes he'd borrowed from his buddy who owned the restaurant.

"Okay, Em. Open your eyes."

She gasped with awe as she took it all in. "Dean."

Still holding on to his arm, she gazed up at the sparkling lights, at the pretty serving dishes on the table, and the view of the bay. "You did all of this for me?"

"Yes, but don't get too excited yet, because look around us."

She glanced around and her brows knitted, as if she'd only just noticed the pallets of flagstone and the accouterments needed for creating a patio. "Um…?"

"We're going to lay the flagstone together."

Her beautiful eyes widened. "This is where you're making the patio? Really? I get to help?"

Her excitement made him laugh. "Yes. If you don't mind."

She threw her arms around his neck, sending him stumbling backward as he caught her around the waist.

"This is the best example outing *ever*!" she said with a mile-wide smile. She trapped her lower lip with her teeth, and her eyes darkened as she tightened her hold around his neck. "I have a confession to make."

"Should I be worried?"

"When you said you were looking forward to getting dirty with me, my mind went elsewhere."

"Don't worry, doll. We are getting down and dirty tonight. *Very dirty.*"

She put her mouth beside his ear and whispered, "I'm not wearing any panties."

Holy...

His hand slid down her back, and just as his fingers grazed the curve at the base of her spine, she grabbed his wrist, stopping him.

"*Uh, uh, uh*, Mr. Masters. Unless you think it's appropriate for a guy to grab my bare butt on the second date?" She wiggled out of his arms and made a show of smoothing her tiny skirt over her thighs.

"Obviously *you* think it's okay, since you came on this date naked under that skirt." He ground out a curse.

She wrinkled her nose. "Sorry?"

He tugged her against him again. "You are a little temptress." He put his hand on her rear, leaving the skirt between them, and squeezed. "I ought to back you up against that tree and till *your* garden." He had no idea how he'd get through another minute, much less the evening, with this new information taunting him.

She feigned a gasp. "Mr. Masters, that is totally inappropriate. I'm not that type of girl."

"Just what type of girl are you?" It was a loaded question, one he knew the answer to. Emery was a street-savvy, smart, sexy woman who owned her sexuality, and he loved that about her.

She slithered out of his arms again and took his hand. "The kind that is going to enjoy being wined and dined by her man so she can fulfill all his fantasies after she puts these pretty new boots to use."

OVER THE PAST few days, Dean had been more thoughtful and made Emery laugh more than any guy she'd ever gone out with. But tonight? This romantic dinner of shrimp cocktail, lobster cakes, and salad? These adorable boots and oh so very *Dean* socks? And most exciting, the thought that he wanted her to help him with the patio? The idea of creating something beautiful and lasting together was more than she could have hoped for. Even if they didn't get *dirty* later, the night was already the best date she'd ever been on.

They laughed about using one plate, which they did, and fed each other like those sickeningly romantic couples she'd seen in movies. Only none of it felt sickening or over the top. They were falling into their relationship just as naturally as they'd fallen into their friendship.

After they finished eating, Dean leaned in, kissing her slowly and sensually. He put his hand on her thigh, inching it up to the edge of her skirt. He'd made advances throughout dinner, and Emery was having trouble remembering why she should fend them off. But for the first time in her life, she wanted *more* time with a man. She wanted all of tonight—the romantic dinner, working side by side, and much later, after they'd squeezed every bit they could out of the evening, she wanted the *rest* of him.

"I'm so glad you're not hundreds of miles away anymore."

"Me too. I still can't believe we're *together*." She removed his hand from her leg and said with a prim and proper air she had no business conveying, "Mr. Masters, please keep your hands to yourself." She wasn't just denying him; she was denying herself the pleasures she knew he would bring. And she was surprised to find her arousal heightening with each refusal.

"My hands have a mind all their own, but I'll try to distract them. How are you making out here without your family?" He lowered his mouth to her neck, placing several tender kisses along her shoulder.

She tried to concentrate on his question and not the heat rising between them. "I think we *made out* pretty well this morning. I'm not sure why you would want my family involved."

He drew back and smirked. "You are one dirty-minded girl."

"No, I'm *your* dirty-minded girl," she said, feeling a little high from the wine—and from the sexy banter. "Words matter, Mr. Masters. When enjoying a romantic dinner, a girl likes to feel as though she's the *only* woman on her man's mind, not that she could be any female on the planet."

"There's no one else on the planet I'd rather be with than you." He tucked her hair behind her ear and said, "Now, tell me, Emery. How are you holding up hundreds of miles away from your family?"

She was momentarily caught off guard by his question. With all the heat swirling around them, he was wondering if she was homesick? She wasn't used to anyone other than her family caring enough about her to think about that type of thing. "I'm good. I haven't had time to miss them yet."

He studied her face for a minute, as if he were weighing her answer. "One of your concerns before moving here was missing your family. I just wanted to be sure you were okay."

He pushed to his feet and brought her up with him. "Are you ready to get down and dirty?" He waggled his brows.

"Okay, Casanova. Show me how to lay this flagstone."

"I'll show you how to lay something, but it's not going to be flagstone." He tugged her against him and kissed her deeply. Smiling against her lips, he said, "I told you we could be friends and more."

"Let's get this patio done so we can get to the *more* part."

Chuckling, Dean stepped back and turned away to adjust himself. "I'm ready for the *more* part now."

"No way. You promised I could help you with the patio, and I think my example outing should include a man who keeps his promises." She came up behind him and hugged him, running her hands up his chest, then down his abs, and lower.

When he spun around, she dashed away. He caught her by the waist and she giggled and wiggled as he carried her to the garden. He turned her in his arms and took her in a deliciously hot kiss.

He clutched her bottom, and she inhaled a sharp breath.

"You're a tease," he said against her lips, with a smile that made her want to tease him even more.

"I'm *your* tease. Mind your words, Mr. Masters." She didn't know what had gotten into her, exclaiming so openly that she was *his* as she pressed herself against him, but she was going with it. For once, she felt like she could be her real, true self without holding back, and it felt *amazing*. "What's wrong, big guy? Can't handle the heat? Am I too much for you?"

"Never," he said through gritted teeth.

She loved seeing him barely able to restrain himself. She wanted him so crazy with desire, by the time they went to his cottage he *couldn't* control himself. The thought of experiencing all of the raw passion she saw simmering in his eyes, felt in his every touch, made every advance more difficult to deny than the last.

"Can't keep your mind on the task before you? I think there's a name for that. *Chaos? Whirlwind?*" she said playfully, as she sauntered toward the flagstone.

"Two can play at this game." He reached behind his back and pulled his shirt over his head. "Come on, sweet thing. Let's lay some flagstone."

Emery could deal with a lot of things, but a shirtless Dean Masters lifting and carrying large pieces of flagstone and practically oozing pheromones was a force not to be ignored. He moved with fluid determination, hefting and maneuvering, their bodies brushing against each other as he showed her how to place the pretty slabs and choose the angles, explaining details she was sure held some importance, but processing Dean's words while he flaunted his body was a futile effort.

He carried the larger pieces of flagstone, but Emery insisted on carrying the smaller pieces. They were both covered in a layer of dust and dirt. Her outfit was filthy, but she didn't care. Working with Dean was exciting and inspiring. Not only was he extremely generous with his kisses and sexy touches, but he was a veritable Picasso of flagstone, taking her vision of a sunbeam and helping to create it within the confines of the patio. They chose their pieces carefully, picking longer, slimmer slabs for the rays and a bulky piece for the heart of the sun. Conversation was fun, steamy, and gloriously comfortable. Emery told him how excited she was at the prospect of working at the assisted living facility, and Dean asked her again about going to the benefit dinner. This time she gave him a firm acceptance. She wanted to be there for him. If she could only learn to keep her mouth shut, she might not be so nervous about meeting his father.

"Wait until my brothers catch wind of me going to a highfalutin benefit dinner. They won't believe it."

Dean looked up from where he was setting a piece of flagstone. Moonlight flickered in his eyes. His body glistened from his hard work, despite the cool breeze whisking over the dunes. She'd never seen anyone more rugged or masculine, but that wasn't what had her stomach doing that flip-floppy thing again. It was the way he was looking at her, like she'd always been part of his life and always would be. If she removed the underlying heat and sensuality, the strength of their friendship remained.

"We'll take a picture of us all dolled up and send it to them."

"*Us,*" she mused. "You are a possessive man."

"I never was until you, doll." He finished setting the flagstone and pushed to his feet. "I think Ethan, Alec, and Austin should see who's taking care of their baby sister."

"Do you, now?" Normally, a comment like that would upset her. The thought of any man saying he was *taking care of* her was too similar to her brothers' watchful eyes. But nothing about her relationship with Dean fit her norm, and she liked the way it sounded when he said it. She felt protected in a different way. A *better* way. Maybe the wine had gotten to her more than she thought.

Or maybe Dean was right and they were meant to be together.

"How fancy *is* this dinner?" she asked.

"It's country-club fancy, but not little-black-dress-slit-up-to-there fancy. I don't want to upset any of the wives because their husbands are ogling my girl all night."

She bent to pick up the water bottle, and he whistled. "Baby, you bend over like that again, and I can't be held responsible for my actions."

She liked the sound of that, dirt and all. Taking in the gorgeous mosaic of colorful stones they'd laid, she said, "This has been the best night of my life."

"Mine too, doll," he said thoughtfully. "But it's only the beginning. We make a great team."

"Yeah," she said a little breathlessly. "How much are we doing tonight?"

His eyes swept over the ground, coming to rest on her boots, then crawled up her body, lingering around her thighs and sending her stomach into another wild flurry. He licked his lips, stepping closer, his gaze traveling up to her chest. She could do little more than watch him moving like a lion on the prowl, eyes narrow and solely focused on her as he took the water bottle from her hand and set it on the ground.

His gaze never left hers as his arms circled her waist and she melted against him.

"I think it's time we focus on something else for a while. I think it's time"—he kissed her shoulder—"that we focus on you." He groped her bottom, firm and insistent. "And this pantiless perfection."

His hand was rough and warm as he drew her body flush against his and took her in a deep kiss that tasted of wine and the unique manly essence of *Dean*. Rivers of desire slithered through her veins. When he tangled his other hand in her hair, angling her mouth in that possessive way she'd already come to expect, sparks *zing*ed from her head to her toes, and something inside her snapped. Suddenly she couldn't wait another second to have more of him, to be emotionally and physically closer. Using his shoulders for leverage, she went up on her toes, trying to climb him like the big, stable man he was. Her thigh moved up his, and she gave a little jump. He smiled against her lips, easily lifting her into his arms. She exhaled in relief as her legs wound around his waist.

Her hands roved over his warm flesh, over the hard ridges of his muscles and into his short hair. He was breathing as hard as she was. His strong touch brought another sense of relief, and she moaned into the kiss, rocking against his abs, needing so much more.

His fingers tightened, and he began walking—*fast*—toward the path.

"Where are we going?" she said between kisses. "No one can see us here!"

He kicked up his speed to a run. "I'm not making love to you in public—and I'm too dirty to touch you the way I want to."

Oh, she loved the sound of that! "What about the dishes and the patio stuff?"

"I'll deal with it tomorrow."

He bolted toward his house, their teeth knocking as they kissed. Then they were in his yard, and he carried her into the outdoor shower.

"I need all of you," he said as he turned on the shower and warm water rained down on them, fully dressed, devouring each other as they washed the dirt away.

He stripped off her shirt, kissing her all over. Sharp pleasure radiated through her.

She went up on her toes, and he tore his mouth away long enough to tug her skirt down over her boots. His mouth crashed against hers as she wrestled with the button on his shorts and made quick work of pushing them down. They got stuck on his boots, and he hopped and cursed as he tugged his boots and pants off. He tried to pull off her boots, but they were stuck, filled with water, and every tug brought more laughter. He finally gave up, standing naked before her. Adonis, personified. Only better, because he was hers. Her heart tumbled at the deeper emotions he'd unearthed. She felt out of breath and like she could breathe forever at the same time.

His gaze swept down her body as his arms circled her again. "Good heavens, Emery. You are perfect."

She wound her arms around his neck and said, "We both know I'm nowhere near perfect, but I'm *yours*." The words came so easily, so honestly, she had no doubts.

He stilled for only a few seconds before lifting her into his arms, but in that brief moment, she knew everything had changed.

"You are mine, and I am yours," he said. "I haven't even been intimate with a woman since I met you."

Her heart took another unexpected hit, and the truth tumbled out. "I haven't been with anyone either. Dean, I realized that I didn't just want to stop dating friends. I stopped dating because I wanted to spend the evenings with you, even if long-distance." She could practically see the gears in his mind churning, and she knew she'd thrown him for a loop with her confession.

"And your old boss? He wanted more than you could give?"

She nodded. "I guess I wasn't ready to admit it, but I only wanted you." As she lowered her mouth to his, she whispered,

"Now make love to me like you mean it before I go out of my mind."

"You," he said sweetly, "are *my* perfect."

Chapter Sixteen

THE LINE BETWEEN real life and fantasy blurred in the wee hours of Wednesday morning, when, after Dean and Emery's frantic and fantastic shower lovefest, they'd landed in his bed, where he'd loved her properly. *And then not so properly*, he thought with a grin. Emery was a sweet tigress between the sheets. She liked control as much as he did, which led to the hottest sex of Dean's life. He lay beside her now, only a couple hours after they'd fallen asleep, with his heart full, overwhelmed by the desperate need to make love to her again, slowly and sensually. Hot sex was amazing, but he wanted her to feel his love for her more deeply, to understand that what they had went deeper than anything he'd experienced before—and deeper than anything she had, either.

She lay on her stomach, the sheets strewn across one leg. He scooted lower, trailing his fingers lightly along the back of her legs, and followed them with kisses. His heart ached as reality slowly filtered in. Today was Wednesday. Emery was moving out. He'd waited so long to be with her, and he didn't know how he would survive waking up without her in his arms.

Struggling to push past that ache, he pressed his lips to the soft skin behind her knee, vowing not to let reality ruin the last few hours they had together under one roof. He kissed his way up the back of her thigh. She made a sweet sound and turned over onto her back.

"Good morning, beautiful." He sealed his mouth over hers.

She went up on her elbows. "Wow," came out breathy and sexy. "Your mouth is the best alarm clock ever."

He gave her all he had, loving her with his whole heart.

Afterwards, he embraced her sated body, and lowered his mouth to hers. She kissed him eagerly, igniting even more heat. Gone was his ability to slow down and love her carefully. Would he ever be able to? She was the soil to his seed, the sun to his bud. She was the other half he'd never known he was looking for.

He drew back quickly, catching her glassy eyes. A spear of pain ravaged his heart.

"I'm sorry, doll. Are you okay?"

She nodded and closed her eyes for a second, and when they fluttered open, so full of emotions, the ache in his heart dissipated. "You're *my* perfect, too."

AFTER THEIR BREATHING calmed and they came back down from the clouds, Dean stepped from the bed, bringing a groggy, sated Emery up beside him. She groaned, going boneless against him. He'd made love to her with the love of a thousand Cupids and the grace of a prisoner just freed from jail. It wasn't slow or careful, but it was wonderfully, perfectly *them*.

"A quick shower, and then we'll watch the sunrise. Example outing number three." That got her attention.

She peered around him, squinting in the direction of the

nightstand. "Is that…?" She leaned forward and peered into the half-open drawer. "My necklace?"

He reached into the drawer and withdrew her leather necklace with the two little charms. "I found it on the couch right after you moved in."

"And you kept it," she said with a playful smile.

"I should have asked, but yes. It makes me feel closer to you."

"Hm. I wonder if that's what serial killers say when they keep a lock of their victim's hair."

He clenched his jaw even though she said it teasingly. "You make me sound creepy. Here." He set the necklace in her hand, and she closed her fingers around it.

"Do you know what the charms mean?"

He shook his head.

"You know I'm a Gemini, which means I'm an air sign. My father used to tell me that I was like the wind, hard to catch and easy to get swept up in, but too adventurous to settle down." She turned the charms over and pointed to the one with three squiggles on it. "Air sign. When I graduated from high school and didn't want to go away to college, I tried attending community college. But I could not sit through the classes. My mind wandered, and I was bored to death. I was basically horrible at school. Well, that type of school, anyway. My mom suggested I try taking an exercise class to combat my boredom. I must have signed up for twenty different exercise classes over the next year, each one less fun than the next. I stayed *away* from yoga because I was…"

"A whirlwind?" he offered.

She laughed softly. "Exactly. Anyway, one day Desiree, who'd tried her best to never talk about her mother back then, told me that her mother meditated religiously. You know her mother never stays in one place very long. I figured, what could it hurt? And I took a yoga class. I swear to you, that first class changed my life. For the first time ever, my mind calmed enough for me to sit still. The next time Lizza blew into town for a visit with Desiree, I was there when she arrived. I told her about how yoga had affected me. By then yoga had become my saving grace. You know I never feel complete unless I make it to the mat, and she understood that. I'll never forget, she put one hand on my arm and said, 'You're a water sign. You need that.' Of course, I'm not a water sign, so I told her she was wrong. But she insisted, and said she could see water all around me. That's when I remembered that my mother had delivered me in an underwater birth. It was all the rage back then. And Lizza said, 'See? You're a unique person. You're an air and a water sign.'"

She pointed to the other charm, which looked like waves. "The next time I went into town, I bought these charms."

"What does the water sign signify?" he asked curiously.

"Water signs are intuitive and emotional. They're overly sensitive, and a little mysterious."

"For all Lizza's faults, I have to agree with her there, doll. When I look into your eyes, I could drown in their depths."

She curled against his side. "You're softening that Viking image of yours with all this romance." Smiling up at him she said, "I like that you wanted to keep a part of me with you. I want you to have it." She set the necklace in the drawer and took his hand, leading him out of the bedroom. "You can thank me during our *quick* shower."

The shower was anything but quick, but how could he have even tried to fool himself about being fast with his sexy tigress's hands all over him. He buried his hands in her hair, holding tight.

"Tighter," she demanded. "Geez, big guy. Don't you know me by now?"

Perfectly matched didn't begin to describe how good they were together. More like two of the same being.

After thoroughly loving each other, he said, "You gotta stop me if I get too caught up in you and push too hard."

"I promise."

Dean gathered her in a towel, stealing more steamy kisses.

"If you keep that up, we'll miss the sunrise!"

Her giggles and threats filled the air—and his heart. "We have thousands of sunrises in our future."

"Maybe," she said teasingly.

"C'mon, woman." He smacked her butt and she scurried out of the bathroom toward her room. It felt weird to return to his bedroom alone, where Emery's scent hung in the air. As he dressed, his mind skipped ahead, and his stomach clenched tight. How could he let her move out?

Twenty minutes later they were sitting on a blanket on the dunes in their sweatshirts and shorts, overlooking the water. Ribbons of red, orange, and lavender crept across the sky. Emery rested her head on his shoulder, fitting to him like a piece of a puzzle. He'd brought a thermos of ice water with lemon slices for them to share. This, he decided, was the perfect way to greet the day.

"This is my favorite time of day to do yoga, before the world wakes up, when it's just me and the gift of a new day."

"I like the way you said that. A *gift*."

"Oh, I might blow through life like I think it's all here for my taking, but trust me, I know each day is a gift. It's a chance to renew ourselves in so many ways."

"How's that?"

"The way I see it, if we mess up one day, the next day is a chance to make it better or move past it. It's a gift of another chance. A new beginning." She gazed up at him and said, "That's what I love so much about doing yoga first thing in the morning. It centers me in a way nothing else ever has. It's like my mind, body, and soul all have this one chance to come together without any clutter."

"You, without any chaos?" He leaned down and kissed her. "I'm not sure I'd want to even imagine that."

She laughed softly. "You sort of center me, too."

Her confession warmed him all over. "Is that so? How?"

"I'm not sure, but you push me to see things differently. I know this will seem weird, because you have already made me act so differently than I normally do. But I feel more like myself than I ever have." She looked out over the water as the sun crept higher. "Ever since our first kiss, which I know wasn't months ago or anything, but ever since that kiss, I haven't wanted to hold back."

He brushed her hair over her shoulder so he could see her face more clearly, and when she turned, her cheeks were flushed.

"I tried to fight it," she admitted, "because I didn't want to risk our friendship. But I feel completely uninhibited when we're close. I never realized until now that I *wasn't* uninhibited with anyone else."

"It's because you feel safe with me," he said. "We've shared a lot over the months we were apart. Some things I would have rather not heard about, and I'm sure there were times you didn't want to hear about things I shared. But I never judged you, and you never judged me. That creates a sense of safety."

"I didn't see it that way. I saw our talks as two friends sharing their daily lives. When you told me about the dates you went on, I wanted you to be happy, but now I know that the reason I ate nearly a half gallon of ice cream on those nights was because I was jealous."

"No way." He pulled her closer. "I can't even imagine you being jealous."

"No? I could have clawed Chloe's eyes out in the first thirty seconds of seeing her. The way she looked at you was proprietary and intimate."

That surprised him. "We've known each other forever, but we've never gone out. She's a friend, unlike all those horseback-riding, lasso-swinging cowboys you call *friends* back home."

She buried her face in his chest. "And yet you still want me."

He lifted her chin and gazed into her eyes. "More than you can imagine. I like who you are. I told you, there's nothing you can do that will scare me away, and I'm not going to let you sabotage our relationship when you get scared."

She scowled. "You think you know me so well?"

"Hardly. You're not the type of woman a man can ever be done getting to know. You're power and passion, too wild to be tamed and too smart to let anyone dull your shine. You're like the ocean, shaping the landscape around you as you go through life. I know better than to stand in your way. You'd find a way to blow right through me."

She went up on her knees and moved between his legs, looking hauntingly beautiful against the rising sun.

"You really see me like that? Powerful? Wanting others to change to fit my needs?"

The sadness in her eyes told him that she'd misunderstood

the beauty he meant to convey. "I do see you as powerful and beautiful, but not asking others to change to fit your needs. You own who you are, and you do what it takes to get where you want to be. There's nothing wrong with that."

He kissed her softly, but the uncertainty in her eyes remained. "Emery, you don't ask for anything. You're beautiful and passionate. You're bright lights and steamy nights. You're the little girl who would move heaven and earth to make her best friend feel safe and happy after her mother broke her heart and the strong woman who won't settle for anything less than she deserves."

Her eyes glossed over again, as they had in the bedroom.

"You don't ask others to change. But you don't take any crap. When you're not treated right, you walk away. I'll never ask you to change, either. But as you know, I have asked that you open your eyes with regard to our relationship, to make sure you don't *accidentally* blow us both out of the water."

She wrapped her arms around his neck and rested her head on his shoulder. "You see me clearer than anyone ever has in my entire life."

He held her close, wishing the sun would take hours to rise so they could remain right there together, keeping the rest of the world at bay. He couldn't hold back from asking for what he really wanted. "I wish you'd consider staying, and not move to the inn."

She was quiet for a long moment.

"It's too soon," he said, more heartbroken than he'd like to admit and wishing he'd kept his mouth shut. "Sorry I mentioned it."

She moved back and gazed into his eyes with a serious expression. "It would be easy to say okay, but I'm still worried I'll somehow drive you away, and I don't want what we have to end."

"You won't drive me away."

"Then let me prove that to myself. Moving out will be hard, especially since you're so addicting. I can't even begin to imagine what it will be like to wake up in a separate house, much less a separate room. But I have to know this is real, and if it is, then a short walk won't make a difference."

He wanted to push her, but even if he didn't need proof that their relationship could withstand a little distance—*for Pete's sake, they'd been hundreds of miles apart for months*—he acquiesced to ease her mind. "Okay, doll."

She rested her head on his shoulder again, remaining quiet for so long this time, he hoped she was reconsidering.

"You're really good at these example outings," she finally said. "I don't want them to end. Because once they stop, it means we've decided to date, and when people date, they find flaws in each other. Everything will change. And when you couple that with me moving out…"

She lifted her head again, and the worry in her eyes brought his hands to her cheeks, holding her so she couldn't look away, couldn't avoid seeing the honesty in his eyes. "No, sweet girl. We've had months of getting to know each other's flaws. When they come out, we'll embrace them, and the ones we can't, we'll talk about until we find a way to accept them. Not everything good ends with disappointment. We're moving from example outings to a real, claim-me-as-your-guy relationship, and I'll do everything within my power to make sure you never regret that decision."

Chapter Seventeen

EMERY SPENT WEDNESDAY evening hanging out with Desiree in Provincetown. She needed a little girl time, and it was a good distraction to keep from running back over to Dean's house and crawling into his bed. She hadn't even spent one night alone yet, and already she missed him. When she'd visited over Christmas, the inn had felt homey, and it had been easy to see herself there. Now, at a little after midnight, as she closed her bedroom door, leaving the expansive emptiness on the other side of it, everything felt different. Over Christmas, the big Victorian had been bustling with their friends. She'd been by Dean's side even then, sharing his drinks and dinners, laughing and joking.

Flirting.

She sat on the edge of the bed, staring at her still-packed suitcases and thinking about how they'd gone from shamelessly flirting to falling for each other. She ran her finger over the bracelet he'd given her, missing everything about him. His laugh, that serious expression that would suddenly flash so hot her heart would stutter. She even missed the way he touched her when he walked by, and the scratch of his beard on her cheek when they kissed. Oh, she missed that. But she'd made the right decision to follow up with her plans and move into the inn. For once in her life, she was thinking things through.

And it sucked.

She fidgeted with the edge of her sundress, wondering if Dean was asleep yet. Were Tango and Cash curled up in her spot beside him? Or was Dean lying awake wondering what *she* was doing? They'd texted before she'd gone out with Desiree, and he'd told her he missed her already and to have fun.

She did have fun.

They even made plans to start looking at wedding dresses in the fall, even though Desiree and Rick hadn't picked a date yet.

But now she was done. She'd caught up with her bestie.

Now she was ready for *Dean*.

She pushed from the bed, stepping around the open suitcases and clothes that were hanging over the sides, and went into the bathroom. She washed her face and brushed her teeth. When she set her toothbrush down on the counter, even that felt lonely without Dean's right next to it. Geez, she was really losing it. Since when did she even *think* this way? She pulled off her dress and tossed it in the hamper. She changed into a cami and sleeping shorts and sat on the edge of her bed again, this time holding her phone. Her finger hovered over Dean's name on her recent call list.

Would he think she was clingy if she called? He'd asked her to stay. Surely he would be happy?

Or sleeping…

Ugh. But she missed him. How could she go to sleep without hearing his voice after having talked with him nearly every night for months on end, and being together every day since she'd come to the Cape?

She couldn't be expected to go *cold turkey*.

That would be torture, and Dean would not want her tortured. Of that she was sure.

But maybe he wouldn't want her *at all* if she were clingy…

She glanced at the bathroom, and an idea came to light. With her heart dancing to a nervous beat, she called him.

He answered on the first ring. "Hey, doll. Everything okay?"

The sound of his voice sent relief *whoosh*ing through her. She flopped onto her back and said, "Yeah, great." Okay, she *lied*.

"Did you have fun with Des?"

"Mm-hm. We walked all over P-town, talked, you know. Caught up."

"Good. And how's your room?"

Lonely without you. She kept that to herself and said, "It's fine, except…I was, um, just wondering if you could come check out my sink? It's…not working right."

"Your sink? Sure, when?"

"Now?" She closed her eyes, hoping that didn't make her sound needy.

"Of course." He made a noise like he was pushing to his feet, and she wondered if he was on the couch or in his bed.

"I don't want to inconvenience you."

"You are never an inconvenience." His keys jingled. "I'm on my way, doll. Don't you worry."

THANK THE FREAKING powers that be. Dean had been lying on his bed looking at what he knew would be a long, sleepless night spent thinking about Emery. He climbed into his truck and sped over to the inn. It was faster than walking, and he needed her in his arms *now*.

The inn was dark, save for the lights in Emery's second-floor bedroom. With his toolbox in hand, he took the porch steps two at a time, reminding himself she'd asked him to look at her sink, not sweep her into his arms. The last thing he needed was to scare her off by wanting too much too fast.

He forced himself to slow down, and when he lifted his hand to knock, the door opened before he had a chance to. Emery peered up at him, looking beautiful and sexy in a spaghetti-strap top and silky pajama bottoms.

"Hi," she said softly.

"Hi." He fought the urge to drop the toolbox and haul her into his arms. Why was he so nervous? He felt like everything was riding on how he handled things right this second. She'd called him for help, not to be carried back home. He didn't know when that mental transition had happened, but he already considered his house her *home*—regardless of how few days they'd spent together there. He had the feeling it had started before she'd even moved to the Cape, when coming home at night had meant hearing her voice on the phone or over video chat.

He leaned down and kissed her. She tasted of toothpaste and blessed relief. How could a few hours apart feel like a lifetime?

"Thanks for coming over. My, um, sink is in my room, upstairs." She glanced at the stairs.

"Okay, let's take a look."

He followed her up the stairs. The sway of her hips in those little silky bottoms filled him with hope. *Down, boy.*

She pushed open her bedroom door, and his gaze swept over a handful of fancy pillows scattered across the four-poster bed, her open suitcases lying on the floor, a pile of clothes on a chair. The room smelled pretty, like roses, but markedly *not* like Emery. The bed was too frilly, the furniture too fancy. Everything felt wrong. She belonged with him.

"Can you close the door?" she asked. "I don't want to wake anyone."

As he closed the door, he told himself once again not to read too much into it or allow his desires to take over.

"The bathroom's in here." She pointed to a door at the far end of the room.

She stepped just inside the bathroom door, and though it was a large bathroom, the space between the antique vanity and where she stood was barely enough for his large frame. He put a hand on her hip as he set the toolbox down, bringing his mouth to chest height. He wanted to slip that slinky top off and make her go wild.

Their eyes connected, and he couldn't resist cradling her face in his hands and gazing into her eyes. He wanted to say so many things. *I miss you. Come home with me. You look beautiful. You belong with me.* But he'd already asked her to stay, and he had to respect her need for this time apart if only to prove to her what they had was real.

He pressed his lips to her forehead instead, breathing in her unique and alluring scent. "I'll always be here when you need me." Drawing upon his feelings for her, he stepped back. "Let's get your sink fixed."

He turned on the faucets and felt the water. They were appropriately hot and cold.

"It seems to be running fine." He looked under the sink to see if there was a leak, but it was bone dry. When his gaze caught Emery's in the mirror, she was biting her lower lip, but her smile shone through. And the blush on her cheeks kicked his brain into gear. How could he have been so thickheaded?

"I think I know what's wrong with your sink," he said, turning to face her.

"You do?" She blinked up at him, her entrancing hazel eyes all surprise and curiosity, as if she really thought he'd figured something out.

He lifted her onto the sink and wedged himself between her legs, holding her tight against him. Lust brimmed in her eyes, telling him he'd guessed right. "It obviously hasn't been properly broken in yet."

As he lowered his mouth to hers, she touched his cheek, and he realized she was stroking his beard, as if she'd missed every inch of him just as much as he'd missed her.

"I missed you, too, doll." His fingers threaded into her hair, and he kissed her again, deeper, his pent-up desires spilling out.

She gasped with pleasure, arching into him and pushing up at his shirt at the same time. "I think my mattress might need to be inspected, too."

He chuckled and crashed his mouth to hers. He lifted her into his arms, and carried her into the bedroom. "Baby, I swear I like you for more than sex." He laid her on the bed and came down over her. "I know you need to make sure we've thought this through, and I'm not pushing, but you need to know. I want you with me. *Always.*"

"I want to—"

He silenced her with a long, sensual kiss, and when she made one of those little murmurs he loved so much, he kissed her longer. When their lips finally parted, her eyelids were heavy, eyes dark and alluring.

"Don't say a word, doll," he whispered, refusing to push

her. "I feel how much you care for me in your kisses. I see it in your eyes. When the time is right, we'll both know."

"Stay with me tonight?" she asked breathlessly.

"It would take an army to drag me from your bed."

Chapter Eighteen

EMERY TURNED HER yoga bag upside down in her bedroom at the inn Friday morning and dumped the contents onto her bed amid the piles of clothes and belongings. It had been two days since she'd moved out of Dean's cottage, and she was still living out of her suitcases. Between planning her classes, helping Dean with the patio yesterday, and staying up for hours at night talking to him on the phone, like they used to...*only sexier*, unpacking hadn't been on the top of her priority list. *I actually have my priorities straight*, she thought proudly.

She sorted through her yoga props for the hundredth time, searching for one of her yoga straps. Chloe had called Wednesday afternoon and told her she was approved to work with Rose, and Rose's daughter, Patty Gable, was managing her finances and was going to take care of the bills. She'd already exchanged emails with Patty, who seemed lovely and was excited to see if Emery could help her mother. She'd also spoken to Rose, who was so eager to get started, they'd set up her first session for today. Emery was just as excited to begin, and thrilled that Rose had the support of her daughter.

"Still no keys?"

She looked up and found Dean leaning against, *and filling*, her doorframe, looking sexy in his shorts and tight T-shirt, his hair still wet from their shower. She'd gotten up early to meditate and had seen Dean leaving for his run with Rick and Drake. When he'd come home, she'd been waiting for him at his place. They'd made love like they'd been apart for weeks. It was a cycle she very much enjoyed, but she'd had to hurry back to the inn to get ready to see Rose, and as Desiree had so lovingly pointed out, she'd been humming all morning.

"The keys are a lost cause. Are you still okay lending me your truck to go see my first client at LOCAL?" She put her hands on her hips and visually scanned her open suitcases. "I'm looking for one of my yoga straps."

"Yoga straps? Sounds kinky. Did you check those little compartments in your shoes for your keys?"

It figured he'd ignore her question about his truck and focus on the sexy stuff instead. Man, she loved that about him.

His gaze slid down her body. "Any other secret compartments I should check?"

"Not in my yoga pants."

Dean reached into his pocket and placed a set of keys in her hand.

"You found my keys? What about my bracelet? And your golf cart keys?"

"No, sorry. I'm afraid my house has turned into the Bermuda Triangle. I called Austin yesterday when you told me you'd lost your keys. He went to the dealership to get you a new set and overnighted them. They just arrived."

She exhaled with relief. "You did that? He did that?"

"We've got your back, doll." He tugged her closer. "Now, tell me about these straps. Maybe we should try them out." He waggled his brows.

"No naughtiness with my yoga props! Besides, silk is always better, don't you think?" She went up on her toes and gave him a quick kiss. "I'm going to be late if I don't get out of here." She stuffed her props back in the bag. "We'll have to grab my yoga mat and blankets from my studio."

He glanced at her open suitcases. "You should unpack. Maybe then you'd find your things. You said you were missing your razor, too?"

"Yeah. I'm going to get one today. I've been borrowing yours." She flashed a cheesy smile and slung her bag over her shoulder. "I'm also going to stop by the girls' shop."

His arm circled her waist and he drew her closer. "I'm not keeping you satisfied?"

"Oh, yes, you are, Mr. Masters. I want to check out the paintings for my yoga studio. Classes start tomorrow." She went up on her toes and kissed him, feeling like they'd been together forever. "If you're lucky, maybe I'll stop into the *adult-exploration* shop and bring us home a little something special."

"Now you're talking." He nuzzled her neck and said, "Are you still going shopping with Des and the girls later?"

"Yes. That's the plan."

"Remember, no hot dresses. I don't want my father's colleagues gawking at you." He leaned in for another delicious kiss. "I'll miss working with you on the patio. I'm getting used to having you with me."

"I'm going to miss you, too," she admitted. She was enjoying creating the patio with him. Dean might be an aggressive and demanding lover, which she adored, and a bit picky about his gardens, which she respected, but when it came to the patio, he was uncharacteristically easygoing. Yesterday she'd brought over several potted basil plants to ward off bad mojo and set them along the edge of the gardens that surrounded the patio—because she knew better than to try to *plant* them—and he seemed not only happy she'd brought them, but curious about her knowledge of herbs. It turned out that they had even more in common than she'd imagined. And when she was struck with inspiration while meditating this morning and she asked if they could change some of the remaining flagstone design to incorporate a few earth signs, he was totally open to it. Even though he was doing the bulk of the work, she felt like she was an integral part of the creative process, making it even more special.

She pulled her bag over her shoulder and asked, "What are you working on today?"

"I have a few surprises up my sleeve. Good luck with your first client." He smacked her butt.

She glared at him as he followed her out the door, but inside she was thrilled that she could finally be herself with a man. Not only did he not find fault in her moving from one thing to the next without slowing down, or changing direction midstream, but he supported her endeavors. *Encouraged them, even when I was ready to put them off.* He seemed to genuinely adore everything about her, which made her worry less about messing things up.

She called Austin on the way to LOCAL. Of all her brothers, she was closest to Austin, in age and in relationship. They were different in many ways, including how they handled things. Like their oldest brother, Ethan, Austin was careful and thoughtful, thinking through ramifications before acting, while Emery and Alec, who was almost two years older than Austin, were impulsive and could have hair triggers if provoked. But she couldn't remember a time she and Austin weren't close.

"Hey, sis. How's beach life besides keyless?"

She heard the smile in his voice and felt a pang of home-sickness. "Beach life is *interesting*. Different from home, of course."

"I'd say. You have that big Viking to do your bidding."

She winced. Had Dean told him about them? She had been so relieved to have a set of keys she'd forgotten to ask. "Yeah, Dean's great," she said, fishing to see how much he'd told Austin.

Austin was silent for so long, she looked at the phone to see if she had service. "Aus?"

"I'm waiting for you to tell me about you and Viking."

Shoot. Okay, she could do this. All of her brothers were protective, and when things had gone down at the rehab center, Ethan had wanted to sue her boss and Alec had wanted to kick the life out of him. But Austin had talked some sense into them, and he'd taken it upon himself to go down to the office, unbeknownst to Emery, and he'd had a long discussion with her ex-boss. He wouldn't tell her what had transpired, but whatever it was had stopped his excessive texts and phone calls immedi-ately. Like Dean, her brothers weren't afraid of anything, and they were loyal to the bone.

"I guess he mentioned that we're dating?" *Dating?* She never used that word when referencing a guy with any of her brothers before. *Going out with*, sure. *Hooking up with*, yup. *Dating?* Nope. In their family, the word was rarely spoken. They were the broken ones, after all. Or so she used to think.

"Dating?" Austin cleared his throat. "No."

Uh-oh. She was equally surprised and touched that her pos-sessive boyfriend hadn't staked claim and had left it up to her to reveal their relationship to her family. Although she could think of a hundred better ways than what she'd just done. Emery drew in a deep, calming breath that did not calm her nerves one iota, and explained, as best she could, how she hadn't realized what was developing between them until recently. She didn't tell him she had stayed with Dean when she'd first arrived. Why add fuel to the fire?

"You expect me to believe that for all this time you had no clue? Come on, pistol. You're no dummy."

Her heart squeezed at the endearment he'd called her since she was thirteen and their father had taken them to the shooting range. They'd grown up on a rural farm, and her father had insisted they all know how to defend their property. She'd been a better shot than all three of her brothers even though she hated firearms.

"I know, it's weird," she admitted. "But I swear, I blocked out my feelings or something. Austin, I know I've kept some things from you in the past, but I've never been happier."

"You mean like keeping *everything* from me since you met Viking?"

She thought about that. Yeah, she had shared more with Austin before she and Dean began talking every night. "See? I hadn't even put that together in my head until just now."

"C'mon, pistol. I could see it in your eyes at Easter. It took me a while to figure out that was why you broke up with your old boss, which, by the way, you could have told me and saved me a big showdown with the guy. The poor guy only wanted you to go out with him more and to commit to only seeing him. Even though that was never going to happen, I could have approached him in a less threatening way."

She winced. "Sorry?"

"Geez, P. How could you *not* know?"

"What? There was nothing *to* know at that point." At least she hadn't realized it at the time.

Austin was silent, which meant he was deciding how to react.

"Aus?" When he said nothing, Emery knew he was being extra careful. "He's more like you than me, if that helps. He's thoughtful and protective. He's not going to hurt me. I know that's what you're worried about, but he's different from anyone I've ever known. I can feel how much he cares for me. I'm happy we're dating."

"You used the *D* word."

"Yeah. Scary, right? It just came out. But like I said, this feels like nothing ever has. It feels real, and I *want* it to be real."

He was quiet for a long moment. And then he said, "What if something goes wrong? You've got no one there."

"I have Desiree," she said. "And I'm perfectly capable of handling myself. I know you like to think of me as your angelic sister who doesn't go out with guys."

He laughed. "Hardly. But the *D* word? That takes guts, P."

"I know, but with Dean it doesn't feel like it does."

"So weird. I hate you being that far away. And we haven't met Viking in person. Maybe I need to take a weekend trip to the Cape."

She pulled into the facility parking lot, smiling. "Austin…"

"I'm just pulling your leg. *Sort of.* He seems like a good guy, and if he's not, *then* I'll break his legs."

They joked about who would break whose legs, and he filled her in on her brothers' latest shenanigans, which included a midnight rodeo with the usual rowdy crowd. She had a pang of longing for the life she'd left behind and the friends who did crazy things at all hours. But even as the thought hit her, she knew that somehow she'd grown up in the days since she'd left. Maybe it was traveling so far on her own and knowing she had no family here to fall back on, or perhaps it was the idea that now her nights were spent in the arms of a man who wasn't interested in being wild and crazy, but being stable and loving. No man had ever made her *want* to climb into his bed and just be held. Until Dean.

She tried to push those thoughts to the side, but they refused to be contained as she told Austin about the fancy dinner they were going to in a few weeks and promised to text him pictures—and to tell Dean to behave himself. She'd crossed her fingers on that last part.

As she headed inside with her yoga bag and mats for her first appointment with Rose, the empty spot she'd felt at being so far away from her brothers seemed a little fuller. And having admitted to Austin that she was *dating* Dean was proof that she was indeed stepping into a new phase in her life.

EMERY HAD LEARNED from Chloe that the assisted living facility had several wings, designated by the level of care the residents needed. The wings ranged from Helper's Hand, which meant someone was always a call away, to Live-in Assistance, for those who had hired full-time, live-in care providers, to the Nursing Care and Hospice wings. Rose lived in the Helper's Hand area. Emery squared her shoulders and knocked on the door, her friendliest smile in place. When a tall, broad, and intimidatingly stern, gray-haired man answered the door wearing an expensive, perfectly tailored suit and a pinched expression, she was thrown a little off her game. His cold blue eyes swept over her tank top and yoga pants with a look of irritation.

"Yes?" he snapped.

"Hi...I'm Emery Andrews. I have an appointment with Rose."

"Oh, yes! Come in, sweetheart," Rose called out from behind the stoic door blocker. Her wheelchair appeared beside him and she pushed at his hip. "Step aside, will you? Let the girl in. Where are your manners?"

The man let out an annoyed *harrumph* as he motioned for Emery to enter the cozy apartment, which felt stifling beneath the weight of the man's negative energy. "What kind of cockamamie scheme are you up to now, Mother?"

Rose grumbled as she wheeled herself into the living room. She waved a dismissive hand in his direction. "Don't mind him. My son is brilliant, but he failed in the bedside-manner department."

Emery's stomach clenched at the man's disapproving glare. The way his hair was slicked back, exposing a sharp widow's peak, made him look even more daunting. She forced a smile and turned her attention to Rose. "Would you like to reschedule our yoga session for after your visit?" For the life of her, Emery couldn't imagine wanting to spend a second with this poor excuse of a man.

"Yoga? Good grief, Mother. How much are you paying this woman? What kind of nonsense—"

"I'll have you know," Emery interrupted, not about to let some guy with a stick up his butt disrespect her. "Many types of injuries that physicians have written off as untreatable have been healed through yoga, without medication or expensive medical treatments. A person's emotional state, and the ability to free themselves from the medicated confines that too much of society has embraced, has led to many incredible healings." She was shaking, but she stood pin straight, refusing to back down on her principles.

The man scoffed. "People like you are the reason so many patients end up with more trouble—"

Rose held up a hand, silencing him. In that moment, Emery saw the power struggle between mother and son. Rose pointed to the door, her gray-blue eyes locked on her son. "I believe it's time for you to go."

His gaze never left Rose's. "I'll send Chloe a list of approved live-in caregivers for you to interview."

"Save your energy. I'll have no part of live-in care." She motioned toward the door again. "Now please go. I'm sure you have more pressing things to attend to than my exercises."

Without another glance Emery's way, the man left, taking his cancerous aura with him. The loud sigh that rushed from her lungs brought a laugh from Rose.

"I'm sorry. That was rude of me," Emery said, setting her bag and supplies down beside the couch.

"He's my son, and I love him, but that man makes me crave scotch too early in the morning." She shook her head, her snow-white waves moving with the motion. "He wasn't always that way, but when he took over the business, he became…well," she said thoughtfully. "He became someone other than the person I raised." She waved her hand again and said, "Let's get this show on the road. I'm good and ready to make some progress."

"You've just answered my first question about how hard you're willing to work." Relieved to have moved on to a different subject, Emery walked behind Rose's chair and began kneading her shoulders. "How about we loosen up some of these muscles while you tell me about your lifestyle and how it's changed over the years."

"You want to talk? Shouldn't we be doing some downward dog or something?"

Emery laughed. "You've done some research."

"I'm good at that online research. But you have to be careful with your search words. Why, my friends and I searched Dick's—you know, the sporting goods store? Mag wanted to order a yoga mat when she heard you were coming. The results were quite eye-opening."

She glanced up at Emery, who had stopped kneading her shoulders to try to keep a snort from following her laughter. "Maybe you should leave the research to me."

"And miss out on all those hotties?"

Oh my! Rose was a live wire. Circling back to her question, Emery said, "We will get to yoga, but right now I'd like to get to know more about you. And these muscles could use a little extra attention."

Rose smiled. "I like the sound of that." Her muscles tightened again and she added, "If my son has his way, I'll never have to do anything myself again."

"Sometimes family members feel a sense of inadequacy when they can't help, or even a sense of despair."

"Perhaps," Rose said thoughtfully. She was quiet for a moment, as if she were mulling over what Emery had said. "Let's see. How has my lifestyle changed? Well, I was always active. I ran around after my three children, volunteered, gardened, danced. Oh, how I loved to dance. But you don't want to know about that."

"I would love to hear about that, and any other activities you've enjoyed and would like to get back to." She began massaging Rose's arm, gently working her way down to her fingers, checking the range of motion in her shoulder, elbow, and wrist, while Rose painted a picture of a happy family life, including dancing, family vacations, and picnics with her children. Emery wondered how such a close-knit family could have resulted in the man she'd seen treating his mother so harshly.

"There was a time when my husband loved to dance. And, of course, as we got older, real life took over, and we did those things without my husband because he had to work." Rose paused, twisting her wedding band with a pained expression.

Emery turned her attention to Rose's other arm, soaking in every word she shared, and also, the way she reacted to certain touches and shifted in her wheelchair, indicating painful positions. This getting-to-know-you period was the most telling with new clients. As they talked, she noticed Rose moving her fingers a little more easily. Those signs gave Emery hope for what she could achieve. Yoga had turned into a trend, and people were capitalizing on it every way they could—goat yoga, cat yoga. Heaven only knew what would be next. While she enjoyed teaching classes, regardless of the reasons people attended, it was these one-on-one sessions that allowed for deeper relationships, which in turn allowed her to help her clients on a different level, filling her with joy.

"You must have enjoyed those things with him after he retired," Emery said.

Rose's pained expression returned, and a cynical laugh fell from her lips. "I thought I would, too, but it seems the early years were our best. By the time our children had lives of their own, my husband and I were virtual strangers. It was a shame, but there was not a lot of love left in my husband by the time we lost him unexpectedly to a heart attack. After he passed, as much as I missed him, it was a relief, to be honest. It has taken me years to admit that, but he was not a happy man. That was more than a decade ago, when we should have been looking at our golden years together after all his hard work. Anyway, I continued gardening and seeing friends, but his death took a toll on our family, and other parts of my life became more difficult. My daughter went through a bout of depression for a while, and my youngest son didn't deal with his grief at all. He just swept it under the carpet and moved on. And my eldest, the son you met. The *angry* one," she said with a small smile that could only be forged by the mother of someone so bitter. "He buried himself in work at the expense of his own family. When you watch your children suffer, it takes a toll on you. Little aches and pains became more noticeable at that point."

"That's not surprising. Emotional heartache can lead to all sorts of health issues. We'll work on ways to alleviate stress so you're not so knotted up from it."

"Oh, there's a bit more," Rose explained. "Several years after I lost my husband, something I never imagined happened." She twirled her ring again, and a genuine smile lifted her lips. "I fell in love for a second time. This time, with a good man, my Leon," she said warmly. "He was good to me, kind, and affectionate. Always made me his first priority. I thought the universe had given him to me as a gift, that's how wonderful he was. The kind of wonderful I couldn't turn away from."

"That's lucky, to find love twice in your lifetime." Emery was still hoping to get lucky enough to find it once and hold on to it. Her blossoming feelings for Dean made her wonder if they were heading in that direction. Her stomach fluttered with the thought. She pushed those warm feelings aside and focused on

Rose.

"They were two very different types of love," Rose said, and her expression saddened. "The first might have started as love, and lust, to be honest. But a few years into our marriage, it had become duty that kept us together. In those days, you didn't divorce. You stuck things out, even if you were miserable. My love for Leon, however, was the truest type of love, because it was fully reciprocated. We were married for two years and three months. One morning I woke up, and…" Tears welled in her eyes. She inhaled deeply, blinking repeatedly until her tears dried. "He was gone."

"Oh, Rose." Without thinking, she leaned in and embraced her. "I'm sorry."

"Thank you. Do you have a man in your life?"

Emery hesitated. She knew Dean was friends with many of the residents, and she didn't want to make that awkward for him, so she was careful with her answer. "I do, and he's a good man."

"That's good, Emery. With age comes wisdom, and if I have any to share, it would be not to give your heart to a man simply because he makes your body feel alive. The physical part is easy. Love is hard. You should give your heart to the man who treats you like a treasure, who cherishes you and wants you beside him always. Someone who helps you become a smarter, *better* person. He might keep you up all night beneath the sheets, because let's face it, lust is good, and it's part of love. But it's not everything."

There was a knock at the door, and a gray-haired woman peeked her head in the door. "Is the coast clear?" she whispered loudly.

Rose smiled and waved her in. "Yes. He's gone."

Emery was still processing all the things Rose had said. It saddened her to know Rose had endured an unhappy marriage, but she was glad she'd found true love in the end, even if only for two years.

Rose glanced at her as two women hurried into the room whispering like teenagers. "If there's one thing my son is good at, it's clearing a room."

"You can say that again," the younger of the two women said as she plunked a knitting bag down on the coffee table. She was tall and wiry, with short, layered brown and gray hair and bright brown eyes. "I'm Magdeline. You can call me Mag."

"Or Magpie," the other woman added. "I'm Arlin. You can call me *beautiful*, or *sweets*. I personally like sweets, but anything other than *ma'am* or *grandma* works for me." She had a happy, round face with rosy cheeks, and her orange-tinged hair was peppered with breakthrough white. Her brows were painted on, but her smile was real as the day was long. "Have you started the bendy class yet?"

"I hear yoga is great for sex," Magdeline said as she sank down to the couch.

"That's something else about my lifestyle that has changed," Rose said. "There was a time when I could bend pretty well, and my husbands, *oh*, they both liked that."

"Mm-hm," Magdeline agreed with an emphatic nod. "Men do like us to be flexible."

"You would know," Arlin chimed in. "We used to call her Mad-Shag Magdeline."

Emery stifled a laugh, feeling like she'd stumbled across the Dirty Grandma Club.

Arlin patted her hair with an air of primness and said, "I, on the other hand, made my men work for it."

"You made them raise the cow from birth, milk it, *and* pasteurize it," Rose said. "And then, maybe, if they jumped through all the other hoops on your list, they could get to second base."

The women chatted throughout their session as she continued working with Rose. Emery not only learned about how Rose's activity level had changed over the years and how a fall had led to her current pain, but she also realized how determined Rose was to get back on her feet. Rose's range of motion was fairly good, and Emery was sure with the right care and the support of her friends and daughter, Rose was on a good path toward achieving the mobility she desired. While Emery usually started new clients with once-a-week sessions so they didn't find their therapies or the payment for them a nuisance, she was pleased when Rose insisted they work together three times each week. They scheduled sessions for Mondays, Wednesdays, and Fridays.

After their session, Emery headed to the inn to check out the paintings at Devi's Discoveries before going shopping with Desiree. *And maybe I'll pick up a little something at the adult-exploration shop, too.* The idea sent her stomach into a wild swirl. She'd never used anything like that with a man before.

Surprisingly, the idea of exploring with Dean didn't make her cringe with embarrassment. Instead, her girly parts twitched with anticipation, even if she wasn't quite sure she would actually go through with it.

As she turned down the street toward the inn, she thought about her upcoming shopping trip with Desiree. She was excited about getting all dolled up for Dean, though she was nervous about meeting his parents. From everything Dean had told her, his mother was wonderful, but his father had gone from being a typical hardworking parent who spent time with his kids in the evenings and weekends to being a total jerk. She was not good at holding her tongue, and it had gotten her into trouble enough times that if she were capable of changing it, she would have by now.

She parked by the cottages and found Desiree looking care-free and happy, wearing a cute flowered sundress, her blond hair tied back in a low ponytail. Her paintbrush moved over the canvas on an easel in front of Devi's Discoveries. Desiree had been a preschool teacher in Virginia, and when she'd moved to the Cape and taken over Lizza's art gallery, her mother's paintings had inspired her to start painting again. According to Desiree, the income from the inn, the shop, and the sales of their paintings, along with the batik wall hangings and pottery Violet made, earned more than enough to pay the bills. But Desiree also taught art to children during the schoolyear. She had their pictures hanging up throughout the inn.

Desiree turned as she approached, her smile quickly fading. She put her brush down and ran over to Emery. "What is it? What's wrong?"

Emery walked into Desiree's open arms and said, "Tell me I'm not crazy for feeling like I'm falling, like *really* falling, for Dean."

"You're definitely *not* crazy. Am I allowed to be super happy that my bestie is *finally* admitting to her real feelings for our amazing neighbor?"

"Yes!"

"Good, because he's an amazing guy, and he clearly adores you."

Emery held her tighter. "Now tell me I'm not going to mess up our relationship by telling his father what I really think of him."

"Um…"

"Oh, that's helpful," she said sarcastically, and headed into the shop.

Desiree followed her in. "Emery, what's going on? Are you worried about going to the dinner?"

"No, the idea of meeting someone who tells my boyfriend he's wasting his life instead of seeing him for the incredible man he is has me *giddy*." She focused on the paintings to distract herself from the way her nerves were knotting up. She was surprised by how many paintings Desiree had completed over the winter. The walls were chock-full of gorgeous, colorful paintings of sunsets and children playing in the sand, Cosmos lying in the snow, and beautiful gardens.

"Gosh, Des, you've been busy this winter. These paintings are incredible. I'm so glad you started painting again."

"Thanks. For the first time in forever, I'm not all blocked up because of Lizza. I think working things out and coming here, getting to know Vi, falling in love with Rick"—she sighed dreamily—"all helped. And now that you're here, my life is perfect."

"I think it was pretty perfect before I got here, too. But I really do need some advice about how to handle things with Dean's dad."

"I saw the planters covered in plastic wrap on the window-sills. Violet said they weren't hers. Did you consult Morgyn about this little problem of yours? Did she tell you to grow some filter-enhancing herbs?"

Emery gave her a deadpan look. Morgyn was the same friend whom Emery had bought the dream catcher tank top from. She reminded Emery of Desiree's mother, in that she was a total throwback to the seventies, but she was only in her early twenties and wasn't at all flighty or nomadic. She was grounded and stable. *Like Dean.* Morgyn ran an eclectic clothing store, where she patched and accessorized—or as she called it, *enhanced*—gently used clothing, turning them into spectacular and unique items. She was also a talented jewelry maker and herbalist.

"No, although that's a great idea. I'm growing something for Dean." After reading several of his botany magazines, Emery had gone online to find something she could grow for him that he wouldn't think to grow himself. Something spiritual and meaningful. "I'm trying to grow a lemon tree, which symbolizes longevity, friendship, and…" She paused, wondering if Desiree would think she was out of her mind.

"And?"

"Don't laugh, but lemons represent purification and longevity. And I'm really trying to make this relationship work and be more conscious of the things I do. Because, you know, I'm not always the best at that. So, while I learn how to be more mindful, it's sort of a purification of myself." She sighed and said, "I really want this to last, Des, and you know me. It might take a little help from the universe."

"Oh, Em." Desiree's tone softened, and she pulled her into another hug. "You really do care about him."

"More than I ever thought I was capable of caring for a person, other than you and my family, of course."

"It's a wonderful feeling, isn't it?" Desiree's eyes lit up. "And the fact that you're being so introspective tells me that this is real. You're the if-you-don't-like-who-I-am-then-kiss-off girl."

Emery laughed. "I'm still that girl." She studied a beautiful painting of the sun rising over the bay, thinking about the sunrise she and Dean had watched the other morning.

"Only better," Desiree said. "And as far as his father goes, I think I know a little something about having a less-than-perfect parent."

"Life is so weird," Emery said. "I had two loving, very present parents while you and Dean each had two loving parents for a while, and then Lizza turned gypsy and Dean's dad turned into a jerk. And here I am, the one who has a hard time committing and finding love, while you two seem to know just how to handle things. I don't think I'll ever understand how we turn out to be the people we are, or how a parent can turn their back on their family."

"I gave up on understanding Lizza a long time ago," Desiree said.

"The thing is," Emery said as she carried the picture to the counter. "I need some lessons in biting my tongue. Oh, and I want to buy this for my studio."

"Okay, first, you're not paying me a penny. Take it. It's yours." Desiree motioned toward the painting as Violet came through the door to the pleasure shop. "And second, I'm not even going to touch that lesson-on-biting-your-tongue thing. But I can give you some advice about how to keep quiet."

"I can give you a ball gag," Violet said.

Emery laughed. "That might be necessary."

"And fun." Violet snort-laughed.

Desiree shook her head at her sister. "Getting back to *helpful* advice…When someone says something I really want to respond to in a negative way, I count to ten before saying anything. Or at least I try to. It doesn't always work."

"Yeah, I don't think that'll work for me," Emery said. "I'm not big on self-control."

"Obviously, given that you were riding the bearded man's *viper* within hours of moving in with him," Violet teased.

"I was not!" Emery put her hands on her hips. "I'll have you know, I showed tremendous restraint."

"Ah. So you *are* into bondage," Violet said with a smirk. She was all sleek lines and colorful tattoos in a gray tank top and cutoffs, both of which were speckled with dried pottery clay.

"No!" Emery insisted. "I mean, maybe silk ties or something, but that's not what I meant." Remembering how she'd woken up in Dean's bed and practically attacked him, she added, "I waited until I couldn't wait anymore."

"That must have been a painful ten minutes." Violet glanced at the painting. "That's a good choice. Very *you*. And if you're really trying to not say something in front of someone, then you're hanging out with the wrong people. If you can't be yourself, why be anything at all?"

"Because it's Dean's dad, and he's a total jerk, but I want to support Dean by attending a benefit dinner with him where his father is speaking." Emery pointed at the door to the pleasure shop. "And…I kind of want to check things out in there before we go shopping."

"You do?" Desiree's eyes widened. "*Already?*"

"Don't judge!"

"Ha! Oh yeah, baby. Let's go." Violet grabbed Emery's arm and hauled her toward the back room. "Now, let's talk ball gags…"

Chapter Nineteen

OVER THE NEXT week, Emery didn't just fall into her new teaching schedule; she *charged*, planning her classes to the nth degree and taking extra time to get to know each student. Her client list was growing daily, with referrals from the inn, the resort, and from the flyers they'd distributed. She'd picked up several new clients at LOCAL, and she was more passionate than ever about her yoga back-care work. Dean was glad he'd pushed her toward not waiting to expand her business in the direction she enjoyed most. She and Dean had fallen deeper into their relationship, spending most evenings together, and she continued to leave pieces of herself all over his cottage. Forgotten panties tangled in the sheets, body wash in the bathroom, earrings on the coffee table. She still spent some nights at the inn, so she and Desiree could have some girl time. But on the following mornings, they'd seek each other out. Sunday morning she'd been waiting for him *in* his shower when he'd returned from his run. *That* was the best surprise he'd ever experienced. Until Monday, when having kept the key to his cottage at his insistence, she'd crawled into his bed at two o'clock in the morning because she *couldn't stand being apart a second longer*.

That was the beauty of being with Emery. Not only did she wear her emotions on her sleeve, but she *owned* them. Whether they were in bed, or eating one of Desiree's fancy breakfasts with their friends, where she scarfed down more of his food than her own and kissed him between each bite. Or when she relayed a story about one of her new clients at LOCAL who had been all knotted up because of losing a grandchild. Chloe had suggested Emery try to help center the woman's mind and teach her to relax, which Emery said she'd done well. But when Emery showed up yesterday afternoon in the gardens near the pool where he'd been working, her eyes puffy and red from crying, it was all he could do to hold and console her. She was strong, opinionated, and rarely slowed down enough to take a breath, but his girlfriend was the most sensitive person he knew.

He gazed at her now, sunbathing with Desiree, Violet, and Serena on the enormous yellow raft that was tethered to the boat. It was late Thursday afternoon, and they were in the middle of the bay, anchored after a few hours of tubing. She was smiling, eyes shut, her hand intertwined with Desiree's. Dean wondered if she felt like she'd come *home* by moving here as much as he did. She'd told him yesterday that she'd missed doing little things with Desiree, like eating ice cream out of the carton, creating new inside jokes, and catching up, which they'd been enjoying since she'd moved into the inn. Was it ridiculous that even though he was happy for her to have that time with her friend, he'd felt a pang of jealousy, wanting to be the one doing those things with her?

"Remember the days when we used to actually *go* tubing and waterskiing from sunup until sundown?" Rick said as he sat down beside Dean. His dark hair was damp and brushed away from his deeply tanned face, making his strong features look even more pronounced.

He looked so much like his father, Dean's chest constricted. Before Rick's father had drowned at sea in a freak storm, he'd been like a second father to Dean. But those were also the days when his own father had spent time with friends outside of the medical field, like the Savages. When his father had been accepting and less judgmental, easier to deal with. He missed those days so much.

"I remember those days," Dean finally answered, his gaze finding Emery once again. The girls had decided they were *done* tubing and had been lying on the raft for the past forty minutes, giggling and talking. "But I wouldn't go back to them for the world."

"Yeah, me neither." Rick clinked water bottles with Dean and drained half of his in one swig.

Drake pulled his shirt over his head and tossed it on the deck. "I don't know about you wimps, but I'm done waiting for the princesses to feel like having some fun. I think it's time for a shark attack."

Dean and Rick exchanged an *oh-yeah* glance, set their drinks down, and pushed to their feet. The three men were a formidable force, but they slipped into the cold water as stealthily as ninjas.

Swimming underwater, so as not to cause ripples, they lined up beneath the raft. Drake gave a quick nod, and they burst through the surface in perfect sync, lifting the raft on end and sending the girls shrieking and sprawling into the cold water as the guys hollered, "Shark attack!"

Dean dove for Emery as she went under. He caught her around her waist and propelled them both to the surface. She clung to his shoulders, droplets of water hanging on her spiky lashes, her slippery body sliding against him in all the best places.

"I can't believe you did that!" Her words tumbled out on the tail end of laughter.

He pressed his lips to hers, smiling into their kiss. "You've got to watch out for sharks in deep water."

He squeezed her bottom, earning an expected swat on his shoulder. He kissed her again, harder, and they sank beneath the surface. He propelled them up again, holding her tight and stealing kisses while Rick and Desiree bobbed in the water a few feet away and Violet hollered threats at Drake as she and Serena dunked him.

Best. Summer. Ever.

They swam and hung out in the boat until it was nearly dark. Sun drenched and happy, they docked and made their way down to Newcomb Hollow Beach for their bonfire. Open fires weren't allowed on the bay beaches, and it was nice to be on the ocean side for a change. They cooked hot dogs and burgers, and Rick did his best to embarrass Dean by sharing stories about his youth with Emery. But each story only made her hazel eyes grow warmer and the inches between them on the blanket lessen.

After dinner Dean and Emery had taken a walk, and now Desiree and Serena roasted marshmallows while Dean played the guitar and Drake told him and Rick about another property he was going to check out for the music store. Dean was only half listening as he strummed the guitar, thinking of Emery and how often she'd been humming lately. He hadn't realized she was so musical.

Emery turned, the moonlight catching in her eyes as she headed up the beach toward him, arms crossed over her shirt, which hung low enough to cover her bathing suit. He imagined her naked beneath that shirt, as she moved gracefully up the beach, gazing at the sand and smiling as she spoke to Violet. It was easy to imagine Emery in all facets of his life, dressed, naked, in a wet suit. But now, with the stars sparkling above, he imagined her in the winter months, bundled up in a parka and cap, still wanting to stroll in the moonlight on the snowy, windy beach, and in the spring, when flowers had just begun to bloom and she could finally leave the jacket behind and don jeans and a hoodie, he imagined her cute toes digging into the sand.

"Everything feels different tonight," Drake said as he reached for the guitar.

Dean hadn't realized he'd stopped strumming until Drake took the guitar from his hands. Drake was right. Everything felt different. Dean wasn't just enjoying the evening with friends and a girlfriend. Emery had already become so much more than just a girlfriend. For the first time in his life, he didn't feel like something was missing. If he never had anything more than he did at that moment, he could be happy forever. As long as he had Emery by his side and good friends to enjoy, life was better than good. Life was beautiful.

Emery smiled as she lowered herself to the blanket beside him, and he leaned in for a kiss. Her nose was cold, but her lips were warm and soft. She smelled like sunscreen and happiness. As he gazed into her smiling eyes, he realized she'd become his world.

"Do you know what the koshas are?" Emery asked.

Violet sank down beside Serena on a blanket and said, "Here's a hint. They're not Polish hot dogs."

Dean shook his head. "I can't say that I do. Why?"

Emery shrugged. "Violet and I were just talking about them, and I wondered if you had ever heard of the concept."

"They're the five layers of being," Violet explained. She waved at Dean, Drake, and Rick. "You guys run like your life depends on it, and that's great for keeping your physical body in shape."

Emery put her hand on Dean's thigh. "I do like Dean's shape."

"Not half as much as I adore yours." He pulled her into a kiss.

"That's great," Violet said. "Anyway, you run, but what do you do for your subtle body? Your casual body?"

Dean nipped at Emery's neck. "Trust me, *all* of her bodies get great workouts."

"That's right," Emery said softly. "But…"

Dean arched a brow. "Seriously? You're going to dis my skills in front of everyone?"

"No!" She laughed. "Not *those* skills! You've got great skills in that department."

"TMI, Emery," Rick said.

"Most bearded guys are skilled," Serena said.

Drake glared at her. "How would you know?"

She lifted one shoulder and pushed a marshmallow onto her stick. "I dated a bearded guy one summer in college. He was pretty amazing."

Drake's knuckles turned white around the neck of the guitar. Dean took it from him before he broke it and began strumming another tune.

"We weren't talking about sex," Emery explained. "We were actually talking about meditation and how sometimes we can meditate so deeply it's hard to come out of it, while other times our minds are too chaotic to even begin to find mindfulness. And I said that my go-to image for relaxation is the koshas. If you can visualize a circle with five layers, that's pretty much what it looks like. The outer circle is your physical body, and as the layers get closer to the center, each one is made of increasingly finer grades of energy, until you get to the innermost circle and you find what some people refer to as your *true self*."

Dean had seen the image she'd described before, but he couldn't place where. As Emery explained the meaning of each layer, he tried to remember where he'd seen it.

"I think we should try to reach your innermost layer tonight," Rick said to Desiree.

"Shh," Desiree warned.

"That would be experienced as happiness and delight. *Sheer bliss.*" Emery popped up to her feet and grabbed her backpack. "Des, can you and Serena hold up towels so I can change out of my wet bathing suit?"

"Sure." Desiree and Serena pushed to their feet and held up the towels to shield her from the others.

Dean stole a glance at Drake and Rick, who were pointedly looking away. This was Emery in action. He bit his tongue and blew her a kiss when she looked over, reminding himself that in Emery's mind, these were her most trusted friends. *At least she asked for towels.*

"Actually," Emery said, moving out from between the towels. "I'll go change in the ladies' room."

A knot Dean hadn't realized had formed unfurled in his gut. "I'll walk you up."

He set down the guitar and reached for Emery's backpack. His other arm circled her waist as they headed for the path that led up toward the parking lot and the bathrooms.

When they were out of earshot from the others he said, "You didn't have to do that because of me."

"I didn't," she said, and put her head on his shoulder. "I did it for us."

Dean didn't know much about layers, or what needed to happen internally or externally to a person for each layer to pass for having been fully experienced and nurtured. But he was pretty sure the all-consuming happiness burrowing down and taking root in his soul counted as having found his *sheer bliss*.

Chapter Twenty

"LOOKS LIKE OUR *flexibend* class has spectators today," Magdeline whispered, pointing to a small group of elderly men peering in through the glass doors. She ran her hand along her polyester-pant-covered hip and pushed out her chest. "We are the *hot* ladies of LOCAL, after all. Everyone is talking about how much younger we look now that we're doing flexibend."

Emery chuckled. She was working with Rose today, or at least Rose was her main focus, as this was one of their one-on-one sessions. Magdeline and Arlin accompanied Rose to each of their thrice weekly sessions, gently reminding Rose to sit up straight, breathe deeper, relax her shoulders, and other loving nags, like sisters might. They cheered Rose on with every ounce of progress she made. And Rose *was* making progress. Not only was she carrying herself differently, sitting up straighter, holding her head up higher, and moving more comfortably, but her eyes were brighter, and most importantly, she was breathing more easily.

"Okay, sexy ladies. How about we concentrate on aligning our spines and do some deep breathing to show those handsome men what you're really made of?" Emery pointed to three sets of blankets she'd folded and set on the floor. One for each of the three incredible women who had already stolen a piece of her heart.

In addition to the support they showed Rose, Magdeline and Arlin had also weaseled their way into taking part in Rose's sessions, showing up to Emery's second session with Rose armed with their own mats and a handful of yoga props. *Did you know Amazon sells everything?* Arlin had said during Emery and Rose's first session. *They delivered our goodies right to our door!*

Emery helped Rose kneel on the blanket, and Arlin placed a bolster, a long, thick and dense cushion used to help support certain positions, under Rose's bottom so her hips were higher than her knees. Arlin and Magdeline had not only taken a very active role in their friend's therapy, but they had raved so much about Emery's *efficient and sweet but take-charge ways* that Chloe had been bombarded from families of the residents with inquiries about Emery's help. Emery had agreed to teach two weekly afternoon yoga classes at LOCAL. Between hanging out with Dean, squeezing in girl time with Desiree, Vi, and Serena, and the classes at the inn, Emery hadn't even had time to miss her family very much. When her oldest brother, Ethan, had called her earlier that morning, he'd made a comment about how happy she sounded. Of course, being the protective older brother he was, he'd asked if he should worry about that, which made her giggle.

"That's it, Rosie," Magdeline said as she and Arlin got into the same position. "Emmie, have you decided where to take your man?"

Emery smiled at the term of endearment they'd adopted toward her. Her mother would cringe if she ever heard it. For as long as she could remember, her mother had made a point of correcting people when they called her anything but Emery. *I didn't name you, Emmie. I gave you a strong name so you would always be respected.* She often wondered what her mother would think of Dean's calling her *doll*. But she let these women call her Emmie, because it made her feel like she had even more family here than Dean, Des, Vi, and the others. She felt like she had three grandmothers watching out for her in a way that only women of a certain age could, and that felt really good.

"I'm still thinking about it," she answered. "How about if we work on our breathing, and talk about it later?" They asked her about her personal life often, but she'd been careful about keeping Dean's name and profession out of their conversations. She could just see these three gals trying to get all the dirt on him.

"She's afraid we'll give her *old-lady* ideas," Arlin said with a sigh.

"That's not true!" Emery had been trying to plan a special date for Dean, but having been in town for only a few weeks and being so busy during that time, she was coming up empty. He was always doing little things for her, like stopping by after her yoga classes when he could just to see how she was doing, bringing her flowers, and keeping fresh lemons on hand for her water. They took long walks on the beach, and he was always sending sweet, sexy texts. He'd even purchased a subscription to *Yoga* magazine. She'd teased him about wanting to see women in their yoga clothes, since every time he saw her in hers, he got a hungry look in his eyes and they usually ended up making out. But he'd said he wanted to learn everything he could about the things she enjoyed. It was then that she knew she was truly the luckiest woman alive. She knew he didn't need a big, elaborate special date, but she wanted to take him someplace meaningful, and she just hadn't found or heard about the right spot yet.

"We *are* old ladies," Rose pointed out.

"But we've still got it," Magdeline said.

Listening to them made it easy to see what she and Desiree would be like when they were older. They'd had so much fun when they'd gone dress shopping for the benefit dinner next Friday. She could see them in forty years having just as much fun. While there were plenty of sundresses, finding a dress fancy enough for the event had been like finding a needle in a haystack. They'd finally found an elegant blush-colored strapless dress with a sash that ran from the hemline of one side to the center of the bodice. The underskirt ended midthigh, and a transparent top layer, split down the middle, hung to just above her knees in the front and dusted her calves in the back. It was fancier than anything she'd ever owned, but it was also comfortably stretchy and it fit like a glove. She couldn't wait to see Dean's face when he saw her wearing it.

"Heck, Magpie," Arlin said, bringing Emery's mind back to the moment. "We *defined* it, but we're not exactly twentysomething anymore. Maybe we should ask our grandchildren for date ideas for Emmie."

"No, really. I want to hear *your* ideas," Emery assured them. "I just want to make sure Rose's therapy doesn't get pushed aside."

"Oh, no," Arlin said. "We'd never do that. You're absolutely right. You tell us what to do, and we'll talk later."

"Thank you. Okay, ladies, inhale through your nose. Remember to inhale deeply. Feel the air moving through you. Visualize it filling your lungs." Emery inhaled deeply, watching the women's lips curve up in a smile as they followed her instructions. She blew out her breath and said, "Exhale through your mouth, and let me hear it." A collective *ha* sound filled the air. "That's it. Very nice. Now let's do it again, but let's take it deeper. Allow yourself to feel your lungs expanding. Become one with your breath, and let everything else go."

Over the next hour, as they worked through Rose's therapy, the women peppered Emery with ideas for what they were now calling her *big date*. Getting Arlin and Magdeline to focus on one thing was like trying to corral mosquitoes.

"How about the drive-in theater?" Arlin asked after the session, as Emery packed up her supplies.

"The drive-in was all the rage when it first opened," Magdeline said excitedly. "We went there, and of course we took our children there."

"Yes, and our children took their dates there." Rose waggled her brows. "They didn't think we were onto what really went on at drive-ins. Coming home with their hair all tousled and their clothes rumpled." She laughed and shook her head. "As if they'd invented fooling around in cars and could put one over on us. Ha!"

"Just remember, Emmie, dear," Arlin said. "If you go, park in the row closest to the movie screen and all the way down on the far right."

"But won't that make it hard to see the movie?" Emery asked.

All three women grinned.

"That's the idea," Rose said.

Magdeline picked up her mat and flashed a wicked smile. "And if you park on the end, no one is going to be looking your way."

"O…*kay*. Let's not go there right now." Emery laughed and dug around in her bag, withdrawing a box of tea. "I appreciate your suggestions, and I'll think about the drive-in. In the meantime, I bought this for you, Rose." She handed her the box. "It's tea made with a special blend of anti-inflammatory herbs that helps with achy joints. My friend Morgyn Montgomery makes it. She owns a little shop back home in Virginia. If you like it, I can get you more, and a few other flavors to try."

"Thank you, Emery." Rose, who was now seated in her wheelchair, set the box in her lap and took hold of Emery's hand. "Darling, I know you want your big date to be special, but you must know that what you plan is not nearly as important as the fact that you are spending time together. Whether you're out at a five-star restaurant, the drive-in theater, or just walking along the shore together isn't what matters. *Time* in and of itself is a precious commodity."

Magdeline and Arlin nodded in agreement.

"We know just how unexpectedly the future can be whisked away," Rose said thoughtfully. "You'll find the perfect date. Just follow your heart. It will never lead you astray."

LATER THAT EVENING, Emery stood in the kitchen at the inn, wrapping yellow ribbons around the pots with the lemon tree sprouts in them. Her phone vibrated with a text. Dean's name flashed on the screen, and the familiar *zing* of excitement she'd come to expect skittered through her. They had plans to watch a few more episodes of *Outsiders*, even though when she'd spoken to her brother Alec earlier, after giving her the third degree about Dean—*Thank you, Austin*—he'd told her that the show had been canceled and there would be no future episodes.

She opened and read the message. *I should be done working in about half an hour. Grilled salmon sound good for dinner?*

She loved that he didn't mind cooking, since she was horrible at it. She briefly pondered taking a cooking class and had visions of setting the classroom on fire. Nixing that idea, she sent Dean a quick response. *Naked boyfriend sounds better.*

Cosmos bolted in the doggy door and tried to climb her legs. She scooped him into her arms without realizing his tiny body was covered in sand, promptly holding him at arm's length. "What did you get into?"

"We were down at the beach," Violet said as she came through the door.

Emery set Cosmos on the floor. "Hey, Vi."

"Today is lemon tree delivery day?"

"Lemon tree seedlings is more like it. I hope they don't die. I'm taking them over in a few minutes." She picked up the box she'd brought to carry them and set each of the planters inside, while Violet dug around in the refrigerator. "I've been wanting to ask you. Who *was* that naked man?"

"Just a friend." She bit into a peach and closed the refrigerator door. "We didn't sleep together, if that's what you're wondering."

"Right," Emery said sarcastically.

"You guys are all hung up on what it means to be naked with someone. But it's not like that for me. I've been naked with lots of guys I haven't slept with." She took another bite, and as she headed out of the kitchen she added, "And lots of guys I have."

Emery had thought she was enlightened, but *wow*. Violet took enlightenment to a whole new level.

Her phone vibrated with another message from Dean. She opened it and stared at the shirtless selfie he'd sent, and thoughts of Violet flitted away like the wind.

Ten minutes later she was carrying the box of seedlings down the path toward the new patio where Dean was working. The bay breeze carried the scents of flowers and carefree summer nights. It had been a long time since Emery had been carefree, but every morning when she meditated and every evening when she was in Dean's arms, she felt something close. Over the course of just a few weeks, Dean had helped her stop worrying that being herself might somehow scare him away. He'd helped her feel safe and whole. *Centered* in a way she never had been. Caring about Dean and his feelings had made her slow down enough to think before she acted…most of the time, anyway.

Her pulse quickened as she approached the end of the path and saw Dean standing shirtless with his back to her. One hand rested on his waist, and the other lifted as he took a drink from a water bottle. As she watched him, his words came back to her. *We've been in a relationship for months.* He was right. Those changes hadn't occurred because of the past few weeks. They were the culmination of months of friendship. And she wasn't just *falling* for him; she was *falling in love* with him.

He turned, his eyes catching hers. His lips curved up in that bearded smile she adored. As he closed the distance between them, all power and determined fluidity, her heart stumbled. That beautiful, thoughtful man was all hers.

"There's my favorite girl." He leaned in, bringing his rugged scent with him, and kissed her so deeply her knees weakened.

Forget falling. I've already fallen.

"You didn't have to come all the way out here," he said as he peeked into the box with a curious expression. "But you are the best thing I've seen all day."

"I couldn't wait to see you." *I love you* was on the tip of her tongue, but she held it back, a little unsteady on her feet because of the enormity of her realization.

He peered into the box again. "What's this?"

"Lemon tree seedlings. For you." She held out the box and he took it with one hand. "You can't grow them outdoors here on the Cape, but you probably know that already," she said nervously, closing her mouth before she rambled any more.

He slipped an arm around her waist and kissed her again. "I know a few things about trees. Is this your way of telling me that you're here to stay? That you never want me to run out of lemons for your ice water? Because, doll, I'll grow so many lemon trees we'll have to get a bigger house."

Yes, please.

Her emotions soared, making her too nervous to answer. She glanced over his shoulder, where the setting sun cast a golden hue over the patio, and she blinked several times, sure she was imagining things.

Dean followed her gaze. "I was hoping to reveal this to you with some grand gesture."

"Did you...?" She walked on shaky legs toward the patio. Awestruck at the trouble he must have gone to, she took in the meticulous and breathtaking design of the koshas. What must be a hundred or more artfully placed flagstones created the most beautiful vision of the five layers of being she'd ever seen. It had to be ten feet in diameter, at the far end of the patio, where she'd thought the firepit should go. She'd been wrong. This was perfect.

"Dean, this is absolutely gorgeous."

He set the box down, took her hand, and walked closer to the patio. "It's your design."

"My...No." She shook her head. "I didn't make up the

koshas."

"I know you didn't, but last week when we went tubing, you described them, and I knew I'd seen the image before, but I couldn't put my finger on where." He withdrew his wallet from his back pocket and took out what looked like a folded envelope. "I went through the things you'd sent to me while you were in Virginia, and there it was."

He unfolded it and handed it to her. On the back of the envelope she'd sent him for Valentine's Day was a doodle of the koshas. Even then he must have been touching the deepest parts of her. She had truly been in denial. How could she have missed all the signs?

"And you kept the envelope for all this time?" Her heart swelled. She'd kept everything he'd ever sent, too. The cards he'd sent were tucked into the front of her unpacked suitcase, along with the box the bracelet had come in.

"I've kept everything you've ever given me." He took her hand and led her over to a toolbox on the other side of the patio.

He lifted the top and handed her a magazine. It was the one she'd sent him in early spring featuring the actors and actresses from *Game of Thrones*. She studied the faces of the actors, shaking her head with confusion.

"You were my muse for this garden, doll."

He flipped through the pages, and when he stopped, tears welled in her eyes. There, on an advertisement for an upcoming Netflix movie, were her doodles of the meditation garden she'd always dreamed of.

She swallowed against the rising lump in her throat. "I didn't realize I'd doodled it on that."

"This is *your* meditation garden, made even more special

because you had a hand in creating it. I wanted you to have all the things you've ever dreamed of. I'm sorry I didn't have it done before you moved here, but I really wanted you to be a part of it."

A tear slid down her cheek. "You—" Her voice was choked out by emotions. "You did all this for me?"

"For *us*, doll. You can meditate or do yoga. Whatever you want."

She reached for him to combat her shaky legs. "But how is that for us?" she asked with a laugh. "And what do Rick and Drake think about you using resort property for this?"

"It's for us because I care about you and I want you to have all your dreams come true. Seeing this smile?" He touched his lips to hers. "Knowing that every time you enjoy this patio you'll think of us? That's my happiness. And honestly, Rick and Drake don't know the reasons behind it. I wasn't even sure I was going to tell you."

She threw her arms around his neck, tears of joy sliding down her cheeks. "I'm so happy right now. I don't ever want anything to change."

"Nothing ever will. We're too good together for anything to come between us."

She pulled back and raised her brows. "You do know who you're going out with, right?"

Amusement filled his eyes like she'd said the most ridiculous thing on earth, and as he lifted her into his arms, she filled with hope that her incredible boyfriend was right once again.

Chapter Twenty-One

STANDING ON THE front porch of the inn the following Friday evening, Dean was as nervous as a jackrabbit in a field of wolves. He took several deep breaths, telling himself to calm down. He wasn't thrilled that their first fancy dinner date would be spent with his father, but he was the only one of his brothers who would attend. Tonight was about supporting their family, fulfilling a duty. He planned to do that as quickly and as painlessly as possible, and then get out.

Usually he entered the inn without knocking, but he didn't want to miss out on picking up Emery in proper date fashion. He knocked on the door and heard the sounds of female voices, the *clickity-click* of high heels on hardwood, and his sweet Emery's laughter. The door opened, and he was rendered speechless at the beauty before him in a light pink strapless dress. Emery's eyes were made up dark and alluring, her lips were painted with a sheer gloss, and her shiny hair spilled over her shoulders in gentle waves. His gaze drifted down her bare shoulders and over her gorgeous curves. He could practically feel the flare of her hips against his palms. And her long, tanned legs…

"Eyes up here, big guy."

Desiree and Violet laughed.

He'd been so enamored, he hadn't noticed them standing a few feet away by the sweeping staircase.

"I'm sorry, doll. You literally took my breath away."

"Thank you." Her gaze drifted down his body, and he felt a rush of heat. "*You* look utterly delicious, too."

"Thank you." He stepped forward, his hand circling her waist as her perfume sent his heart into another spiral.

She picked up his tie and ran her fingers down the length of it. "I can think of a few things we can do with this silk puppy after dinner."

"If I can hold out that long."

"Okay, that's my exit." Violet brushed past them. "You guys look gorgeous. Have fun. And if Daddy Warbucks gets out of line, just give me a call. I'm happy to show up and embarrass the heck out of him."

"Violet!" Desiree gave her a nudge toward the door. "They don't need to hear that. We're going to think positive. Nothing bad will happen."

"Hey, just offering to set the guy straight." Violet waved and disappeared out the door.

Desiree turned to them with a tender smile. "Sorry, you guys. You both look amazing. Want me to take a picture?"

Dean glanced down at his tan trousers, navy sport coat, and light blue shirt. The sight of his dark-chocolate-colored tie jolted his brain into gear. "Yes, in a moment. Something is missing from your outfit."

Emery looked down at her dress. "Missing? It's not fancy enough?"

Rick came down the stairs and whistled at them.

Dean shot him an I'm-nervous-enough glance. "You look

perfect," he said to Emery, then lowered his voice and added, "Although I did ask for something that wasn't hot."

Her cheeks flushed. "Should I change? I don't want to look inappropriate."

"You not only look appropriate, but you look like a goddess. You could wear my sweatpants and you'd still make men drool." He leaned in for a kiss. "And you taste like cherries."

"Lip gloss." She wrinkled her nose adorably. "I didn't want to get lipstick all over you."

"So thoughtful." He kissed her again, earning another whistle from Rick. He withdrew a long black velvet box from his pocket and opened the top. "For our first fancy date."

Emery and Desiree both gasped. Desiree peered around Emery at the dainty, three-tiered choker he'd had made for her.

"You don't strike me as a diamond or pearls girl," he said, "but if I've messed up—"

Emery pressed her lips to his, blinking repeatedly. "It's perfect. You're perfect. I'm not a diamond and pearls girl, but for you to know that…"

Rick put his arm around Desiree as she watched with a dreamy look in her eyes.

Dean took the choker from the case, and Emery lifted her hair, turning for him to put it on her.

"I know lots of things about you, but I have a feeling that just when I think I've discovered all your secrets, you'll have a hundred more things for me to unveil." He kissed the back of Emery's neck.

He secured the hook on the thin brown leather choker first and then the clasp on the attached silver chains that connected in the front with a silver heart in the center of her neck, and just below, where the thinnest chain met a silver hoop, a beautiful quartz dangled.

Emery turned to face him, lightly touching the choker. "How does it look?" she asked.

The brown leather and delicate silver chains against her slender neck looked even sexier on her than he'd imagined they would. "*You* look spectacular, and the necklace makes you look even more beautiful." He leaned closer and whispered, "And erotic."

"Mm. I like that." She framed his face between her soft, warm hands and gazed longingly into his eyes. "Thank you." She pressed her lips to his. "I love it. Did you know the charm was quartz when you bought it?"

"What do you think?"

"I think if you did, then you're an even more incredible boyfriend than I thought."

"Quartz helps relieve stress and anxiety," he said proudly. "I knew you were nervous about meeting my family. And I know how spiritual you are, even if you don't talk about it. You once told me that yoga was a lifestyle, not a job. I want to be part of your life, which means I need to learn about your lifestyle. So, yes. I did know."

"Mr. Masters, you do know how to impress a girl."

"I only want to impress *you*." He glanced over her outfit again, noticing that she was wearing the thick bangle where she'd hidden Splenda—*always prepared*—and strappy heels. "No hidden compartment for a phone in those. Do you want me to carry yours, or are there other secret compartments I should check out?"

She shook her head with a mischievous grin. "There's *nothing* hidden in the secret places I want you to inspect, and I'm not taking my phone. I don't want any outside distractions tonight. Just you, me, and a room full of highfalutin people who, thanks to you, I'll be a little less nervous around."

He withdrew his phone from his pocket and took a selfie of the two of them. Right before taking another picture, he turned and kissed her cheek, earning her melodic laughter, which led to several more pictures of them kissing. Rick and Desiree snagged Dean's phone to take more *appropriate* pictures of them, and then Emery insisted that Dean take a selfie of the four of them huddled together. They were all grinning like fools, and he knew it would forever be one of his favorite pictures.

Forty minutes later they were still kissing and laughing as they entered one of the two Victorian-style mansions at the Ocean Edge Resort. Emery clung to Dean's arm as they crossed the marble floor, following throngs of women in gorgeous dresses and men in designer suits toward the main ballroom.

"I've never been anywhere this luxurious," she said in an excited, though hushed, tone. "I don't even think we *have* mansions like this back home."

"And you're the most gorgeous woman here." Dean felt like his skin was stretched too tight beneath his clothes. He didn't enjoy these snooty dinners, but as they passed a sign directing attendees to the ballroom, his father's name was noted as the speaker, and a sense of pride washed through him. He was proud of his father's accomplishments, even if he didn't agree with the way his father pushed him, or his elitist attitude.

Emery stopped outside the ballroom, breathing deeply. "How will I know your parents?" She realized she hadn't seen any family photographs in his house.

"My father will be the one everyone's kissing up to, and my mother..." He followed the distinct sound of high heels clicking on marble at a fast pace and saw his mother hurrying toward them. While Dean shared his mother's honey-wheat hair, hers had turned mostly silver in the past few years, and it was Jett who'd ended up with her vibrant personality. Dean took after his father's more reserved nature. "Is right here."

"Baby!" His mother threw her arms around his neck. She looked beautiful in a dark blue dress, a string of pearls around her neck, and a smile as welcoming as the sun.

Emery mouthed, *Baby?* with an amused smile.

Dean couldn't suppress his smile. There was something about being doted on by his mother that always made him want to go back in time, to the years before his father had taken over his grandfather's medical practice and become a tool. Not for the first time, or the hundredth, he wondered why she put up with him. Granted, they never seemed to fight when he was around, and he'd seen her give his father looks that had, on occasion, kept his sharp comments at bay. Their whole relationship confused him, but he'd decided a long time ago, it wasn't his place to worry about their life choices. So he did what he could to make sure Jett's feelings didn't make her life any worse.

"Oh, sweetheart, don't you look dashing," his mother said, straightening his tie. "And you matched your tie to your gorgeous date's beautiful necklace. Doesn't *that* tell us something special?" She turned her attention to Emery, whose eyes sparkled like she'd already decided she liked his mother. "If you haven't guessed, I'm Dean's sugar mama."

His mother laughed a little loud and throaty, the laugh he'd heard all his life. And it made him laugh, too.

"Mom, *please.*" Dean shook his head. "Emery, this is my *mother*, Sherry. Mom, this is Emery Andrews."

"Emery…?" His mother hugged her. "It's such a pleasure to

meet you. But your name is familiar." Her eyes widened and she glanced at Dean. "Emery, from *Virginia*? The one you were chatting with over Easter?"

"Yes," Emery said. "Sorry we stole Dean away to meet my brothers on FaceTime. They can be pretty demanding."

"Oh, honey, are you kidding? I've never seen him smile so much." She touched Dean's cheek. "Until tonight. Sweetheart, why don't you go say hello to your father." She put her arm around Emery and said, "Come on, beautiful. Let's get to know each other."

Dean knew his mother was making an effort to shield Emery from his father, which meant his father must be in prime form tonight. He opened his mouth to say he'd rather go with them, but his mother said, "I promise I'll bring her back," and guided Emery away.

Emery glanced over her shoulder, smiling so brightly he knew she'd be just fine without him.

Dean followed them into the ballroom, which was decked out in shades of gold and accented with black and white. There were enough designer suits and diamonds in the place to open a store. He lifted a flute of champagne from a passing tray and watched Emery and his mother sipping the same. His mother held Emery's arm like they were old friends, and knowing the two of them, they probably already felt like they were.

He took a long pull of his drink and scanned the crowd for his father. The familiar sinking feeling in the pit of his stomach hit at the same second his gaze landed on the man his mother had so wisely guided Emery away from.

He glanced across the room, where Emery and his mother were now talking with his ex, Diana. He gritted his teeth. He hadn't thought about her being here. He should have warned

Emery. Could tonight get any more awkward? Diana looked…well…like *Diana*. Prim and proper in a blue and white striped dress. Her dark hair was twisted on the top of her head in a complicated knot that had probably cost a fortune and taken several hours to get just right. She was a beautiful woman, and she'd make a different man a good wife, planning every minute of their lives to perfection, tossing out *yes, honey*s, laughing, and building up her man's ego at every opportunity. She'd been groomed to be a doctor's wife, which was probably why she and Dean were not well suited for each other.

As he watched Diana, he wondered how he'd ever let their relationship go on for so long. They were compatible friends at best. Dean had gone out with her at the request of his father, and she was eager to please, always available, and she had filled a gap in his life. Going out with her was easier than hanging out in bars trying to meet women, or hooking up with random tourists.

Emery said something that made the three of them laugh, and she touched Diana's arm. Diana covered her mouth, her laughing eyes turned in his direction. Dean shifted his gaze to his father again, feeling as though he were caught between a lion and a spider web. His father looked regal in his dark pinstripe suit with a matching pocket square and tie. Dean didn't have to look to know the buttons on his father's shirt were mother-of-pearl, and his cuff links were twenty-four-karat gold with sapphires or yellow diamonds surrounded by enough high-quality diamonds to feed a family of four for a month.

Dean guzzled his drink and set the empty glass on a table. He brushed a hand down one of the three non-designer dress shirts he owned, trying to talk himself into walking over and saying hello. His father was speaking with his business partners,

Carl Longhorn—Diana's father—Prescott LaRue, and Tim Macalbee.

Four of the sharpest minds in medicine. His father's voice trampled through his mind, and his gut twisted. He turned away, reminding himself they only needed to make an appearance. He searched the room for another glass of champagne and spotted Emery and his mother heading his way. Thankfully, without Diana. They were both smiling, and Emery wasn't good at faking a thing. Maybe she hadn't made the connection between him and Diana yet.

Emery looked graceful and somehow also fierce as their eyes connected.

He reached for her. "Everything okay, doll?"

His father's cologne infiltrated his senses seconds before he felt his heavy hand clamp down on his shoulder and noticed the familiar straightening of his mother's spine, the narrowing of her eyes, and the silent *Behave yourself, Douglas* she cast toward his father before being swept away by a group of women.

Emery's gaze moved from him to his father, and her body stiffened. Dean looked at his father, whose eyes were filled with malevolence. He instinctively tightened his grip on Emery.

EMERY COULDN'T BREATHE as she stared into the cold eyes of Rose's son and tried to make sense of his hand on Dean's shoulder.

"Son," the man said, shifting his eyes deliberately away from Emery and pinning them on Dean with an accusatory slant.

Shivers crawled up Emery's spine. *Son?* Her mind scrambled back to her visit with Rose, and the pieces began falling into place like dirt filling a hole. *And my eldest, the son you met. The angry one. He buried himself in work at the expense of his own family.*

She gripped Dean's side, remembering the weeks after they'd met, when he'd told her about how, years earlier, when he'd been drowning emotionally as a trauma nurse, his grandmother had convinced him to leave the medical field and follow his heart.

She tried to find some semblance of balance in her mind, tried to imagine Rose going against her own son's wishes. The thing was, she *could* imagine that, but the realization sparked an unexpected softening inside her toward the man who was looking at her like he wanted to say something hateful.

"Dad," Dean said stoically, shifting his body as if he were doing his best to form a barrier between his father and Emery. "This is my girlfriend, Emery Andrews."

His father's lips tipped up in a terse smile. "The *yoga* girl?"

Dean bristled. His eyes narrowed, and his chest expanded. Emery was still processing that Mr. Stick Up His Butt was Dean's father. She bit back the verbal lashing she wanted to hurl at him, and when Dean opened his mouth to say something, Emery squeezed his hand and gave a barely discernible shake of her head. She knew Dean would stand up for her, but she didn't want to be the cause of a scene.

"Yoga *back-care specialist*. Yes," she said proudly, and extended her hand in greeting.

His father looked down at her hand so long she didn't think he was going to shake it.

Dean's glare told of his disapproval, and in the next second, his father lifted his drink in a feigned toast and his lips curved up in a wry smile as he shook her hand.

"It's a pleasure to meet you, Emery."

There wasn't enough alcohol on the planet to ease this situation. Luckily, an announcement came over the loudspeaker for the guests to find their tables, and Dean swept her away from the Big Bad Wolf.

"I'm sorry. I shouldn't have brought you anywhere near him," he said as he guided her toward their table.

"I'm fine," she said, although she was not *fine*. Hearing about his father was one thing, but experiencing him in person? She was barely holding her tongue, despite the initial softening she'd felt. The muscles in Dean's jaw jumped repeatedly as he visually tracked his father up to the podium.

Dean had enough worries tonight. He didn't need to be put in a position to stick up for her, or feel as though he was to blame for the way his father had treated her. She reached up and cupped his jaw, drawing his gaze back to hers. "I'm here for you, not for your father."

"I still shouldn't have exposed you to him."

They took their seats, and Emery caught sight of his mother heading toward their table. "I didn't realize Rose was your grandmother," she said quietly. "She was my first client at LOCAL. Is she here?"

"My grandmother?" A smile lifted his lips. "She and my father don't get along. She hasn't attended these dinners for quite some time. But my aunt Patty is with her tonight. She took her out for a nice dinner."

The tightening in her chest eased. She was glad Rose hadn't witnessed what had just happened. "I love Rose, and her friends Magdeline and Arlin. I met your father the first time I went to see her, but of course I had no idea he was your father." She explained what had transpired between them.

"I'm going to murder him," Dean said between gritted teeth.

"No, you're not. Rose said he wasn't always like this, that he buried his emotions in work after your grandfather died. I kind of feel bad for him. Not enough to think the way he treated me, or the things he says to you, are okay but enough to make me hold my tongue. Besides, he's your father, Dean, and you don't need to add my big mouth to the list of trouble between you two."

His father tapped the microphone, and a hush fell over the room. Tension rolled off Dean like the winter wind, cold and insistent, as his mother slid into the seat beside Emery and whispered, "Did my husband behave himself?"

"He was fine," Emery lied, wondering why such a lovely woman would put up with a man like him. There was no sense in upsetting her. The evening would be over soon enough.

Dean's father's authoritative voice brought all eyes forward, as he thanked everyone for attending and talked proudly about his father, Douglas Masters Sr., and his father's reasons for establishing the Pediatric Neurology Foundation. He went on to detail the strides that have taken place in the field and how proud he was to carry on in his father's footsteps by having taken over his pediatric neurosurgery practice. He spoke eloquently, injecting humor amid the technical details of the collaborative center that was the heart of the foundation. As Emery listened to him describe how the foundation served pediatric patients through advocacy, education, research, and support initiatives, she understood just how important the foundation was, and in turn, how vital his father's medical prowess had been for the industry.

It became clear that both the pride *and* irritation in Dean's eyes were well earned, and the more his father spoke, the more she realized just how much pressure he was probably under. It didn't make his actions or his attitude forgivable, but it gave her a little better understanding of the man behind them.

Emery reached over and squeezed Dean's hand.

He draped an arm around her shoulder and scooted his chair closer. "I'm glad you're here," he whispered, making the ordeal with his father worth every uncomfortable second.

After his father's speech and a round of applause that shook the ballroom, his father made his way toward their table, stopping at least a dozen times to shake the hands of appreciative people along the way. Emery watched him with interest. He was unassumingly charming, kissing the cheeks of women and patting the backs of men, as if they were all his closest friends. A stab of hurt slid through her. If he had greeted her with that smile, things would be very different right now.

When he arrived at the table and took his seat, the easygoing air he'd carried only seconds earlier disappeared with a weary exhalation.

It had to be exhausting carrying the weight of the world on his shoulders. Didn't he realize he had a family who could help him find some relief and happiness amid the pressure? Something as easy to share as a smile like he gave the others would go a long way for Dean and probably Jett and Doug, too. If only she could convince him to allow her to show him how to relax. But it would be a cold day in Hades before that man reached out to a *yoga girl*.

His piercing blue eyes moved slowly around the table, lingering on Dean for so long, Emery found herself holding her breath.

Some sort of silent, stressful message passed between father and son before his father said, "Thank you both for attending tonight. It's nice to see family here."

Dean nodded curtly, his fingers curling around Emery's shoulder.

Thankfully, dinner was served quickly, and they ate while carrying on strained conversation about nothing of importance. The only saving grace were the stories Dean's mother shared of when he was young and how much he enjoyed the beach, the water, and helping his grandmother in the gardens. Emery had wanted to tell her about her sessions with Rose, but she feared it might elicit another nasty comment from his father.

"Dean was always very precocious," Sherry explained. "While Jett couldn't be bothered with slowing down enough to read a book and Doug was too busy reading everything he could get his hands on to want anyone else to read to him, Dean's favorite bedtime stories were ones his father told about his patients. I remember Douglas coming home exhausted and Dean, as a young boy, pleading for *one more story*. He would tell Dean one story after another, until they both fell asleep right there in Dean's twin bed." She squeezed her husband's arm, smiling warmly.

"I can't imagine it," Emery said before she could catch herself. "I mean, Dean wanting to hear so many stories."

Dean and his father exchanged another glance she couldn't read, but oh, how she could feel this one. It was markedly different from the tension that had been hovering around them like buzzards. This was warm, and it brought a smile to both of them, but those smiles disappeared just as quickly as they'd come, taking a piece of Emery's heart with them.

"When the boys were teenagers, they'd drive me crazy, playing catch out back in the dark." Sherry smiled at Dean's father and said, "Remember when the boys would toss you a baseball mitt the minute you came in the door and bug you until you finally put down your work and threw the ball with them? Dean must have been twelve? Thirteen?"

His father wiped his mouth and set the linen napkin on the table. "That was a long time ago, when, like most young boys, Dean still saw me through starry eyes."

Emery made a split-second decision to try her hardest to rise above the hurt she'd felt from his earlier dismissal and make the best of it. All she needed was common ground, and having worked in a physician's office, she felt she had that.

"I enjoyed your speech," she said to his father, hoping she didn't sound as nervous as she felt. "You mentioned several neurological disorders that I've had some experience dealing with. When I worked for the yoga back-care practice in Virginia, I worked with patients who suffered from many different types of ailments. With specialized yoga plans and meditation techniques, we saw physiological and psychological improvements in patients who suffered from several neurological diseases, like epilepsy, stroke, multiple sclerosis, even Alzheimer's. I realize you're personally not a fan of yoga, but does your practice work hand in hand with any yoga professionals as complementary therapy to your patients' medical treatments?"

His gaze flicked between her and Dean. "That would be like putting a Band-Aid on a gaping wound. It might soothe the patient's anxiety temporarily, but there is *no* replacement for modern medicine."

"Obviously I'm not implying that you forgo medical treatment for your patients," she said more forcefully than she meant to, but *what the heck*? Did he really believe medicine was the *only* answer to everything?

Dean pushed to his feet and took Emery's hand. "If you'll excuse us, I'd like to dance with my date." He lifted Emery to her feet and quickly guided her away from the table.

"Dean!" she whispered. "I was trying to make some progress with him."

His arms circled her waist, and the moment his hard chest pressed against her, the tension in her body eased.

"You mean well, doll, but you won't win. He's a man of science. He relates to statistics, facts, and documented research."

"There have been studies—"

Dean pressed his lips to hers, kissing her slowly and tenderly, and just when she tried to pull away for a breath, he deepened the kiss. She came away a little dizzy, and warm all over.

"He's arrogant, sweetheart. You think you're having a rational conversation, but in his mind he knows more than anyone in the entire room. You're not going to get through to him, and you'll only get frustrated by trying."

She sighed. "I just wanted to find some common ground. I hate that I'm causing more trouble between you two. And even though I hate that he just dismisses everything I stand for, which is wrong on so many levels, I wasn't going to be confrontational. I just feel like, as a doctor, he should want to try everything possible for his patients. I was hoping if we could connect on some level things would be easier."

"I adore you even more for trying, but I don't want him to ruin this evening. Not when you look so beautiful and smell so sexy."

His hand slid to the base of her spine, the other threaded into her hair. The familiar possessive and sensual hold was enough to melt some of her resolve. She rested her cheek on his chest and said, "Okay, but I still can't believe Rose is his mother. She's so nice. He should put her on a pedestal. It's like he's so busy keeping up this facade of who he wants people to see that he's lost sight of the people who matter most."

DEAN'S CHEST FELT full to near bursting. He didn't think it was possible to fall deeper in love with Emery than he already had, but the combination of her determination to connect with his jerk of a father and her desire to see him cherish the people who should matter most solidified what he'd already known. While he and Emery might be as different as day and night on some levels, the very foundations of their beliefs were perfectly aligned. Family and love came before all else.

He rubbed his beard along her cheek, enjoying the feel of her shuddering against him. He was glad he hadn't shaved it off this summer. He still remembered the night they were FaceTiming and she'd begged him to keep it, the way her eyes had turned sultry. It boggled his mind that a person could be so deep in denial about emotions so strong they had practically reached through the phone and gobbled him up.

"I'll never become him, Em," he assured her. "I'll never put anything ahead of you, and I'll never treat people poorly. I need you to know that."

"I know. You care too much. Besides, you're the most loyal man I know."

"Thank you, but that's not why." He held her closer, swaying to the music as he spoke into her ear, wanting her to hear every word. "It's because I'm falling for you, Emery, and I could never hurt the person I value most."

She gazed up at him, looking deeply into his eyes, as if the answers to the questions in hers lingered there.

He smiled and touched his lips to hers. "From the very first day I saw you wrapped up in that big red ribbon, positive energy radiating off of you brighter than the sun, and you opened that beautiful mouth of yours and sassed me all night long, I was a goner."

"Dean," she said with watery, surprised eyes.

"I don't want you to get freaked out and run away. I just need you to know that I'm all in, Emery. I want you in my life."

"I'm all in, too," she said joyfully, rendering him momentarily speechless. "I am, Dean. I know I'm not experienced at relationships, and I'll probably still mess things up a bunch of times, but not in the really bad ways, like cheating or anything. Just in doing-dumb-things-without-thinking ways."

Remembering the night of the bonfire and the way she'd decided to change her clothes in the bathroom instead of on the beach, he said, "We all do things without thinking sometimes, but I have faith in us. If either of us stumbles, we'll be there to help each other find our footing."

She pressed her body to his with the biggest grin he'd ever seen and said, "You have to at least pretend to dance, or everyone's going to look at us."

He hadn't realized he'd stopped. "I want to remember you just like this for the rest of my life," he said without moving. "Right here, in this dress, telling me you're falling for me."

As couples danced around them and the darkness peered in through the windows, he didn't want to waste another second in this stuffy ballroom. All he wanted was to be alone with the woman he adored. "What do you say we get out of here? Go for a walk on the beach where it's not so stuffy?"

"That sounds wonderful. Right after you dance with your mom." She pointed to his mother, who was sitting at the table watching them with an appreciative smile. His father stood across the room talking with two of his partners. "She deserves to have a happy night, too."

She gave him a chaste kiss and said, "I'm going to the ladies' room. Don't find a new girlfriend while I'm gone."

He tugged her against him again, feeling happier than he could ever remember being. "No one could ever replace you. Do you know where it is? You have to go out of the ballroom and down the hall. Want me to walk you there?"

"No. I want you to dance with your mom. I know where it is. I saw it on our way in."

"Okay. Don't take too long." Despite her fancy dress and the formalness of the event, he gave her butt a pat, and she walked away smiling.

Dean approached his mother and extended his hand. "May I have this dance?"

"Thank you." His mother placed her delicate hand in his.

She moved gracefully in his arms. "I forgot how well you danced."

"I used to go dancing quite often with your father," she said, smiling.

"Before Grandpa died."

"Yes, but I still remember it like it was yesterday." She was quiet for a moment before saying, "I like Emery. She's got spunk."

"That she does."

"You look at her like you can't breathe without her," she said with the intuitive tone he remembered from his youth.

"Do I?" He knew he did, but this wasn't a conversation he'd been prepared for, even if he liked knowing she'd noticed.

"She's good for you. I can tell." She glanced at his serious-faced father, who was still deep in conversation with the two other men. "But she'll try your father's patience, and we all know he'll try hers." Bringing her attention back to Dean, her expression turned serious. "Don't let that dissuade you. Follow your heart, baby. It'll never lead you astray."

He couldn't imagine letting his father dissuade him from anything, other than further confirming that he did not belong in the medical field.

After their dance, two of his mother's closest friends, Elsa Longhorn and Aimee LaRue, the wives of his father's business partners, appeared by her side.

"Dean, it's so wonderful to see you," Elsa said.

He hugged her briefly. Elsa had always been good to him, and unlike his father, she understood that he and Diana were simply not meant to be together.

"It's nice to see you, too." Having practically grown up with these women, Dean also embraced Aimee. "You ladies look beautiful tonight."

"You are a charmer," Elsa said. "And Diana tells me your date is as lovely in person as she looks."

Dean looked in the direction of the ladies' room, missing Emery already. "She is. Thank you. How is Diana?"

"She's doing well," Elsa said thoughtfully. "She had to leave early. Harvey, her new boyfriend, is an up-and-coming obstetrician, and you know how that goes. When the babies are ready to enter the world, they'll wait for nothing."

The women spirited away his mother, who left him with a kiss, a pat on the cheek, and a promise to call him in the coming days. Dean gazed out the windows into the darkness. He was glad his mother had close friends, and he wondered if she was happy.

He caught sight of his father's reflection in the glass as he stepped up beside him. The muscles in Dean's neck pulled tight as he turned to face the man who had once left their family, and had returned a loving, attentive father. He wondered where that man had gone. As he studied his father's face, noticing crevices etched across his forehead, the loosened jowls that came with age, and his ever-sharp blue eyes, Dean wished he knew what had changed when he'd gone away to college and they'd lost his grandfather. How many stars had to have misaligned for his father to have turned into a bitter, angry man—the very reflection of Dean's grandfather, whom his father more often than not had abhorred.

"I think tonight's event has gone well, don't you?" His father sipped his drink and slid one hand into his trouser pocket, his steady gaze holding Dean's.

Dean nodded, struggling to quell the familiar battle waging inside of him. He wanted to walk away and never look back as badly as he wanted to tell his father exactly what he really thought of him. But respect and loyalty went a long way, and normally Dean was careful not to do or say anything that could cause a rift big enough to hurt his mother. Jett had taken care of that all on his own. But tonight Dean had been chewing on the way his father had mistreated Emery, and he wasn't about to let that go.

"I do think the event has gone rather well. But in the future, please treat Emery with the same level of respect you expect from others."

His father's glass stopped halfway to his mouth. He lowered

it slowly, his brows lifting slightly. "You sure you want to do this now?"

Dean drew his shoulders back. "It seems appropriate, given that you practically laughed at her career. She's a brilliant, kind woman, and more importantly, she's *my* girlfriend."

A long, drawn-out sigh left his father's lips. He glanced out the window, the extended silence clawing at Dean's nerves. His fingers curled and flexed as his father slowly brought his attention back to him.

"You're a *Masters*, son," he said evenly. "For generations, the Masters men have not only been doctors, but we've been leaders in our fields. Don't you think it's about time to put this resort business on the back burner and get serious about your career? You've had a solid break after tinkering with trauma nursing. It's time to get in the trenches and make a difference in this world."

"If making a difference, in your mind, also means treating people the way you do, then I want no part of it." He stepped closer, his tone deathly calm. "And for the record, my years spent as a trauma nurse were not only every bit as intense and important as your career, but they proved to me that while you can shut off your emotions, I cannot. The people I watched die were someone's relatives. They mattered to them, and the moment they were on my table, they mattered to me."

His father gave a half-cocked smile. "I forgot that you were too weak to handle trauma nursing. But there are other types of medicine—"

"Stop," Dean interrupted. "I'm thirty-two years old, not a child you can direct as you see fit or demean at your will. There are many types of weaknesses, and the ability to connect with humans is *not* one of them. You used to know how to do that.

The resort, working with men I respect and love like brothers, and nurturing life through nature makes me happy *and* proud. It's a shame you don't appreciate the value in those things, but I'm not going to waste any more of my breath trying to convince you otherwise."

His father seemed to mull that over with a lingering sip of his drink. "Fair enough. Then let's talk about your personal life. Diana is still unmarried."

"Seriously, Dad? Are you really going to try to pawn that poor woman off on me again?"

"She's good for you, son. She'll never try your patience or speak against you." His father looked out the window again and said, "This woman, Emery, is clearly intelligent, but she's a distraction, a—"

Dean grabbed his father's arm, turning him forcefully so he had no choice but to look him in the eyes. With his heart slamming inside his chest and his teeth clenched tight, he seethed, "It's one thing to push me toward a profession I don't want, but don't you ever—*ever*—talk about the woman I love that way." He dropped his father's arm. "I'm done with this. Whatever *this* is between us." He stalked away, and his eyes connected with Emery's. His heart lurched as she turned and bolted toward the exit.

Chapter Twenty-Two

EMERY'S HEART THUNDERED against her ribs so hard it hurt. She pressed her hand to the center of her chest and burst out of the ballroom door, struggling to drag air into her lungs. She didn't know exactly what type of argument she'd come upon when she'd seen Dean clutching his father's arm, but hearing Dean profess his love for her in one breath and threaten his father in the next had knocked the wind out of her.

She broke into a jog when she hit the lobby.

"Emery, wait!" Dean caught her by the waist, but she twisted away and continued running toward the exit. "Em, please, slow down."

"I can't!" She was shaking all over as she stormed out of the resort. The crisp night air stung her cheeks as she ran down the steps.

Tears blurred her vision, slowing her down enough for Dean to tug her against him so hard she smacked into his chest, and her tears broke free. He was shaking too, his chest expanding against hers with each harsh inhalation.

"Please, Emery. Stop!" He held her at arm's length, an immovable force trapping her in place. "I'm done with him. You'll never have to deal with him again. He's an arrogant, infuriating jackass."

"And he's your *father*," she cried. "You've spent years trying to keep peace within your family because of Jett, and now—" She gasped, trying to regain control of her emotions. "You *love* me? Oh, Dean! You *love* me!" Her heart soared, and just as quickly, it tore right down the middle. "And you threatened your father because of me? I don't want to be the thing that tears you away from your family! You shouldn't love me!" Sobs racked her body and she twisted away from him before he could see she didn't mean it, but his grip was too tight and he yanked her back.

She pushed at his chest, her mind whirring like a hurricane. *Don't let me go*, she tried to say, but all that came out was "Don't—" before another sob stole her voice.

"Don't *what* Emery?" he seethed. "Don't *feel* what I already feel?"

She turned her face away, slamming her eyes closed to try to stop the flow of tears, but the river continued, her heart crumbling to pieces. He jerked her toward him again, his free hand pressing to her back so firmly she could hardly breathe.

"That's not going to happen," he said through gritted teeth. "Do you hear me? You are *not* the cause of any of this. Don't you see that? It's *him*, Emery."

"Because he wants to see you with someone like Diana?" She swiped at her tears, inhaling sharply. "I met her! She's lovely"—*sob, sob*—"and nice"—*gasp*—"and totally wrong for you!" She couldn't stop the words from coming out. "I'm sorry, but of course she bored you to oblivion. She's...*vanilla*."

A soft laugh fell from Dean's lips.

"Don't laugh at me!" *Why am I yelling?* "She's not right for you, but I liked her, and she's coming to my yoga class tomorrow morning!"

He framed her face with his rough hands and gazed into her teary eyes. "You're incredible, do you know that?"

She shook her head, struggling to regain control, then nodded. "I am pretty incredible."

He laughed, drawing a half laugh, half cry from her.

"My father was in there spouting bull about being with a woman who won't get under my skin, and you meet my ex, and instead of getting jealous, like any other woman would, you make friends with her? I *want* you under my skin, Emery. I want you to speak your mind, even when it's not what someone else wants to hear. I want *you* at *any* cost."

Her mind spun, and she was still too upset and confused to speak rationally. "I know that!" she snapped. "I want you, too, and I want you to want me! But your father *hates* me."

Fresh tears spilled from her eyes, the sting of the truth too much to bear. She turned away, but he pulled her close again and kissed the top of her head. He smelled familiar and safe, and her fingers curled naturally into the fabric of his sport coat. She didn't try to push away, because the truth was, the only person she wanted to run to was Dean.

"I'm *not* letting you go," he said adamantly. "I *love* you, and I'm not going to let you sabotage our happiness."

How could something feel so good and hurt so bad at the same time? "I *want* you to love me," she managed. "But I can't be the thing that drives you and your father farther apart. How could I ever live with myself if I made things harder for you? It'll break my heart every time I think about it."

"The only thing that would make things hard for me would be if you push me away. Don't do it, doll," he warned. "Don't ruin what we have."

"I'm trying to save your family so you don't end up resenting me. That's what you do when you care about someone, isn't it? You step back and make yourself miserable so they can be happy?"

He put space between them, still holding her with a death grip, his confused eyes boring into her. "No, Emery. It's not. When you love someone, you never let them go. You do everything within your power to help them be the best person they can, to achieve their dreams, *and* to get through nights like tonight. But you don't run away. You don't become a martyr. Love isn't easy, Emery, but we *will* be worth it."

"I told you I didn't know how to do this! I don't even know what's right or wrong anymore." She threw her arms up, tears flooding her eyes. "I'm pretty sure this stupid pain in my chest is my heart exploding because by being *myself*..." She closed her eyes as the truth stabbed her again. She was trembling all over, and vaguely aware of other couples watching them as they came and went from the resort. She tried to lower her voice and said, "By being myself, I've caused even more trouble between you and your dad."

He grabbed her wrist, stepping closer, and said, "Stop right there. This has been coming for a long time."

"This *what*? This *fight*?" She crossed her arms. "I knew I'd mess us up!"

He shook his head and gathered her in his arms again. "No," he said gently. "Putting an end to my father's wrath."

He brushed his lips over hers, the slow, intimate touch taking her by surprise.

"And you and I coming together was also long overdue," he said firmly. "I love you, and I want you back in my house. In *our* house. *Our* bed, Em. You know you love me, and you know you want this—*us*—just as much as I do."

She buried her face in his shirt, unsure of what she should do or say. She loved him so much she was ready to walk away just to keep from hurting him more. But walking away would hurt them both.

He lifted her chin as he'd done so many times before and gazed lovingly into her eyes. "You deserve me, and I deserve you. Don't let my father make you think otherwise."

"I *know* we deserve each other. I'm pretty great, and you're *beyond* amazing. But that doesn't mean I'm okay with coming between you and your father."

"You didn't. He did this. Not you."

He kissed her softly, and though she tried to pull away, he held her tighter, kissed her deeper, soothing and exciting her at once. His grip loosened, and his fingers tangled in her hair. And in that moment, Dean's warm comfort eased the tension in her chest, and she gave herself over to their kiss. He sighed against her lips, a long, deep breath that filled her lungs, as if he needed to feel her love as much as she needed to feel his.

Their lips parted slowly, and he pressed a series of tender kisses over her mouth, cheeks, and forehead. When his lips brushed over hers again, he whispered, "I love you, Emery, and I'm not going to let you go."

His father had somehow used her to get to him, and that gutted her, but if she'd ever been certain of anything in her entire life, it was that she didn't want to lose Dean. She pressed a kiss to his chest and gazed up at the man who had seen the real her and loved her anyway. "I love you too, with my whole heart. And I'm not going to let you go either, but we can't pretend that whatever took place in there didn't happen."

"You *love* me!" He looked up at the sky and closed his eyes, whispering, "She *loves* me!"

Laughter bubbled out with more tears. "I *do*. I love you. I love you so much, and I'm scared to death that I'm going to mess up your life."

"No, doll. Never. The only thing you're going to mess up is our sheets, as often as you'd like."

She buried her face in his chest again, happiness and worries battling for dominance. When he lifted her chin and pressed his lips to hers, happiness trampled those worries and she kissed him back.

"I love you," she whispered. "But before you make a decision about me moving back in, I just realized that I didn't even get to say goodbye to your mother. She's going to think I'm a lunatic for running out, and then she'll hate me, too. You were right. I'm kind of chaotic."

"You're my chaos, lover girl, and I wouldn't want you any other way." He took her in a sweet, languid kiss. "I have never had second thoughts about us, and I don't now. *Our* house needs you in it."

"Even though—"

Her words were lost on the soft press of his lips.

"Even though," he whispered.

"Okay, but your mom...?"

"My mother adores you," he said calmly. "I'll call her tomorrow and explain. But right now I need to get you away from all of this negativity. It's not good for your mind." He kissed her forehead. "Your body," he said tenderly, and kissed the center of her breastbone. "Or your spirit." He pressed his lips to the area above her heart, and she felt the shattered pieces of herself working their way back into place.

Chapter Twenty-Three

THE DRIVE HOME was tense and silent. Emery kept a death grip on Dean's hand, her face turned toward the passenger window, while Dean relived the storm that had taken place with his father. He'd tried so hard to be civil for all these years, but he was done fooling around. It infuriated him to think that Emery would back away, even for a second, because of his father.

He parked in front of his cottage and cut the engine. Darkness enveloped them, save for the dusky moonlight sprinkling through the trees. He lifted Emery's hand and pressed a kiss to her knuckles. When she didn't turn to face him, his heart sank. She didn't deserve any of this nonsense, and darn it, she needed to be in his arms.

He stepped from the truck and came around to help her out, but when he opened the passenger door, she turned the other way.

"Emery?"

When she finally faced him, with tears sliding down her cheeks, every one of them slayed him anew. He gathered her in his arms and held her trembling body. "It's okay, doll. I promise you'll never have to face anything like that ever again."

Her shoulders shook. "It's not that. I want to be enough for you, but I only know how to be who I am. I'm not highly educated, or from a wealthy family, or whatever else your father wants me to be, but…"

"Shh, sweetheart." He kissed her tear-streaked cheek, all of his protective instincts surging inside him. "You are more than enough. I don't care about any of that. You're all I want. You must know that."

"I do," she cried. "But it hurts knowing your father thinks…"

He didn't know for sure what his father had planned to say before he'd cut him off, but he was fairly certain he'd read his message clearly. "He was commenting about *me* and what he wanted for me. He wants me to make a mark for myself in the medical field, and he thinks to do that I need a woman who doesn't make waves and won't distract me. Which is crazy considering my mother has always spoken her mind. He called you *intelligent*, Emery. This isn't about you not being enough. It's about you being too much."

He brushed her tears away with the pad of his thumb and kissed each damp cheek. "The important thing is that I don't want to be that person, and I've been with women who don't make waves."

"Diana?"

He nodded. "I've been honest with you from the start. You know how I feel about my relationship with her."

"*Nice enough, but boring*," she said, parroting what he'd told her before she'd moved there.

"And…?"

She sighed. "That you'd have clawed your eyes out if you'd stayed with her."

285

That brought a small smile.

"You're the only woman I want, Em. Headstrong, brilliant, willing to fight for the things you believe in, and full of energy so compelling, it radiates from your soul." He touched his forehead to hers and said, "Don't let him come between us."

"I won't."

"Promise?"

She nodded. "I just got my feelings hurt. It was very girly of me, and I didn't expect it."

"I love girly you, and I'm sorry." He guided her arms around his neck and slid a hand beneath her knees.

"You're not going to carry me," she said as he lifted her into his arms, cradling her against his chest. "Dean…"

"I think it's time you stopped talking and let me love you."

He lowered his mouth to hers and kissed her as he carried her up to the front door. He unlocked the door with one hand, kicked it open, and carried her inside.

"That was pretty impressive," she said as he used his back to push the door closed.

He was glad she was no longer crying, and tried to keep things lighthearted. "You haven't seen impressive yet."

"Mr. Masters," she said as he carried her into the bedroom. "I believe I've seen your *impressiveness* before and found it quite enjoyable."

He set her on her feet, and when she reached for him, he guided her hands to her sides. "No hands, Emery. Tonight I'm going to love you so completely, you'll never want to tell me not to love you again."

She reached for him again. "You don't have to—"

"Relinquish control and breathe, sweetheart." He guided her hands back to her sides. "Find your inner calm."

She smiled and said, "When did you become the teacher?"

"Since I became an expert on all things Emery Andrews."

Her tongue slid across her lower lip, and a flush rose on her cheeks. "I think you like me taking control." He was aware of every breath she took, the seductive darkness settling in her eyes, and the quickening of her breathing. He brushed his beard along her cheek and whispered, "Don't you?"

"Yes."

She watched him intently as he stripped off his sport coat and tossed it onto the chair, sending the cats scampering out the door. He loosened his tie and unbuttoned his collar, stepping closer, mere inches from her, and stood, unmoving and silent, letting the thrum of desire drown out the hurt of the evening. He waited a full minute, maybe more, every silent second heightening the anticipation. When she reached for him, he caught her wrist. Her eyes flamed as he lowered her hand again.

"Patience, beautiful."

He skimmed his fingers from wrist to shoulder, feeling goose bumps rise on her flesh. He did the same with his other hand as he lowered his mouth to her shoulder, tasting his way across her warm skin to the hollow of her neck. She was panting now, her chest rising against his.

"I can taste the lust in your breath," he whispered, and put his hands on her waist as he moved around her. His fingers grazed her stomach, feeling her quick inhalations as they slid over her waist to the backs of her hips. He kissed her shoulder. "I'm going to love all your hurt away."

He unzipped her dress slowly, stopping to kiss her toned, beautiful back as it was exposed. She reached behind herself, searching for him, and he grabbed her wrist again. Tighter.

He leaned forward, putting his mouth beside her ear, and

ADDISON COLE

said, "Uh-uh, sweetheart. You're not in charge right now."

Her fingers curled into a fist as he guided her hand back to her side.

He followed her gaze to the leather necklace wrapped around his wrist, the two charms dangling just above his palm.

"You're wearing it," she said with awe.

"I wanted a piece of you with me. Do you mind?"

She shook her head as a smile appeared, and love rose in her eyes. Dean's heart squeezed at the emotions looking back at him. He kissed her softly. Her fingers curled around his.

"I've got you, doll. Always."

Sometime later—an hour or three, he wasn't sure—as Emery lay sleeping in his arms, he tossed a hopeful prayer into the universe, asking for answers. Because if he knew his beautiful doll, she would carry the weight of his trouble with his father like a penance. And he wasn't sure how to help his spiritual, bighearted *whirlwind* let it go.

Chapter Twenty-Four

IF EVER THERE was a time Emery needed clarity, it was now. Dean had distracted her with his intense lovemaking last night, and she'd even managed to fall asleep afterward. But she'd woken up to pee, and her mind hadn't settled down since. Unable to lie still a second longer, she climbed out of bed before sunrise Saturday morning, found one of Dean's sweatshirts hanging in his closet, and pulled it over her head. It hung down to her knees. She glanced at Dean, sleeping soundly on his stomach with Tango and Cash curled up beside him. The sheet was bunched up around his hips. One muscular leg was bent at the knee, his arms tucked beneath the pillow. She loved him so much. She never would have imagined that she could fall in love, much less with the man who had become one of her best friends. She had to be the luckiest woman on earth. *And the unluckiest*, she thought sadly. If she'd been like Ethan and gone to college, studied hard, and become a businessperson, would Dean's father have respected her more? Or did he only respect women who were seen and not heard? She still couldn't make sense of the man she'd met last night being Rose's son or Sherry's husband. She didn't know how either of them put up with him.

That was something she might never understand, but there were things she could understand, like the realization that it was more than being surrounded by death that had turned Dean away from medicine. It was clear that he needed to be surrounded by life. He was a nurturer at heart, and he'd tried to use that to heal, which Emery thought must have been ten times harder than he'd ever let on. But after meeting his father, she knew Dean's decision to leave medicine also had to do with not wanting to end up like his father.

He'd made the right choice, but she doubted Dean could ever turn his back on those he loved. And that was why she needed to get her mind centered, so she could wrap her head around what had happened with his father last night and put it into perspective. Maybe even figure out a way to make it better.

She gathered her dress and heels and searched high and low for her underwear, but she couldn't find it anywhere. His house really was turning into the Bermuda Triangle. As she headed out of the bedroom, Dean's voice whispered through her mind, and she stopped short. *You are not going out there without underwear.*

She reached into his underwear drawer and pulled on a pair of his boxer briefs. *For you, big guy.* Something red caught her eye in the back of the drawer. She reached in and pulled it out. Like a magician with his never-ending handkerchief, a long, wide, four-foot piece of red ribbon spooled out of the drawer. She couldn't stop smiling as she reached the end of the ribbon she'd had tied around her body the night they'd met, and saw that the heart she'd drawn for him, and her phone number, were still legible. Her heart beat to a happier rhythm, knowing he'd kept it for all those months. She walked over to the side of the bed where he slept soundly, worn out from loving her so thoroughly all night long.

She didn't want to wake him, so she blew him a kiss, and as she hoisted up his briefs to keep them from falling off, she corrected her earlier thought. She didn't put them on for *him* after all. *It was for us.*

She carefully rolled up the ribbon and put it back where she found it, and tiptoed out of the bedroom. She saw two unmatched flip-flops from pairs she'd left there and searched the living room for their companions. She finally gave up and slipped her feet into them, and quietly left the house. She ran the whole way to the inn, determined to figure things out before Dean got up.

When she reached the inn, her lungs stung from the brisk air, and her dew-drenched feet were mucky with sand. She sat on the back porch and brushed them off. Back home, the grass was as thick and plush as a carpet. Here, grass and sand came hand in hand, but she didn't mind. It was part of the bayside town's charm. She tipped her chin up toward the sky, watching the sun's glow edging the dim predawn haze out over the bay. The peacefulness was completely at odds with her inner turmoil. She closed her eyes, soaking in the serenity of the morning, concentrating on the air filling her lungs as she inhaled, and tried to visualize the anxiety and heartache leaving her body with a long exhalation. She did this two, three, *four* times, and still she felt as if she were drowning in a sea of something she couldn't break through or push away.

She carried her things inside and went through the motions of washing her face and brushing her teeth, but she was too distracted and brushed well past the time the toothbrush stopped talking. It was time to pull out the big guns.

Donning her favorite yoga outfit and gathering her supplies, she headed back to Dean's house. He was still sleeping, which didn't surprise her, since they'd been up until nearly three o'clock in the morning fooling around. A shiver rippled through her with the memory of the way he'd taken control.

Okay, Emery. Stop thinking about that. That isn't going to fix your problems.

She grabbed a pot from beneath the sink and headed outside hoping for a miracle. Because while she might be able to clear her mind, the sea she was drowning in, the thing she couldn't escape, which Dean's father was using to pull them down, was herself.

DEAN AWOKE TO an empty bed and the smell of...*weed? What the heck?* He bolted upright. "Emery?" he called out.

Answered with silence, he threw himself from the bed and pulled on a pair of briefs, noticing Emery's clothes from last night were gone. His hands curled into fists. If his father scared her off, he'd never forgive him. He stormed into the living room, wincing at the stench of marijuana...or skunk. He couldn't be sure which.

There was a big black pot on the stove, and the doors to the patio were wide open. He walked around the counter and peered into the pot, which was empty save for a few inches of water. Whatever had been in it smelled a lot better than the rest of the house. He headed out to the patio, following the scent around the side of the house. He stopped short at the sight of Emery standing in the front yard with her back to him. She wore a pair of gray yoga pants with a thick blue and white tie-dyed waistband and a pink exercise bra. Her feet were bare, and her yoga mat was spread out in a patch of sunlight beside the gardens. She looked angelic standing there in the sun's ray.

She bent over and waved something around her feet, trailing smoke as she waved whatever it was around her legs and torso. She waved it around in a circle over her head, and the scent he'd smelled in the house filled his nostrils. Curious, but not wanting to interrupt her, he stepped behind the bushes and peered around them as she continued what looked like some sort of ritual. She waved the smoking bundle behind her leg, and then behind her back as best she could. Smoke chased her every move. He didn't know how long he stood there, but guessed it to be at least five or ten minutes before she held the bundle between both hands. From the back, it appeared she was holding it in a prayer position. Loopy smoke wafted above her shoulders.

From there she waved the bundle toward the porch and front door, making wide sweeping movements. Eventually she set the smoking bundle down beside her mat on what looked like a clay bowl, and she stood in the middle of her mat. He'd seen her move through her morning yoga routine enough times to recognize some of the positions. One of his favorites was the triangle pose. He loved the way her body seemed to lengthen and open up during that pose. But the thing he noticed most was the way her face relaxed, even though the rest of her body seemed almost to be in motion—her fingers reaching for the ground and sky, her legs stabilizing her core, toes pointed, and the muscles in her belly taut. He imagined her with a round belly, carrying their child, and felt himself smiling. The thought came unbidden, and yet it felt natural. He'd never imagined any woman carrying his child, but with Emery, he wanted *everything*.

She moved fluidly from one position to the next. Suddenly she sank down to the mat, her face in her hands. Was she crying? He stepped from behind the bushes at the same moment she pushed to her feet and threw her hands up toward the sky. He slipped behind the bushes again.

"What do I have to do to clear my head?" she said angrily. "*Challenge* myself?"

With a huff, she knelt on the mat and stretched her arms over her head, parallel to the ground. He knew this was child's pose. And he also knew it was what she called her go-to pose for quieting her mind and centering her attention before moving into more difficult poses. When he'd first seen her doing more complicated poses, he had made the mistake of rushing over to spot her, which not only threw her off-balance, but she explained that it defeated the purpose of mindfulness.

She repositioned into a squat, then splayed her hands on the mat, seamlessly aligning her shoulders and elbows. Dean's fingers flexed, as if by doing so he could help hold her up. She was a vision of control and grace as she leaned forward, her back rounding slightly, and drew her knees up, balancing with her legs on the outer edges of her upper arms. She remained there, holding herself up with only her hands, her feet together, heels pointed up.

Dean held his breath, his every muscle flexing in support of her. The upper-body strength and concentration it took to achieve such a pose was more than he could grasp. His legs carried him toward her without any cognitive thought. When he realized what he was doing, he stilled, fearing he might startle her. Her eyes were closed, and he was mesmerized watching this incredible woman defy gravity.

As she returned her feet to the ground and moved into

child's pose once again, his breath rushed from his lungs, and he closed the distance between them. He knelt on the edge of the mat, and she lifted her head, a loving smile on her face.

"That was incredible. I've never seen anything so beautiful in my life. Your grace and strength were so powerful, I could feel it in my own body."

"Thank you. Crow is a really hard pose, and it takes full concentration of my mind and my body. I was having such a hard time clearing my head, I needed to dig deeper." She sat up and took his hands in hers, her expression turning serious. "I'm sorry I left you sleeping, but I had to get rid of the bad mojo from last night. The house might smell a little funny."

"Just a little." He winked.

"It's white sage. I was ridding the house and everything around us from conflict and bad feelings. The sage smoke absorbs the bad energy and cleanses our energy fields. It's like a deep, metaphysical cleansing." She glanced at the sage, which was no longer lit. "We'll have to relight it, but whatever you do, never blow. Like *ever*."

"Now you've lost me."

"Breath is for life, not for extinguishing it, and fire is seen as life. Oh! I need to do you, too."

He arched a brow. "I'm liking this…"

She rolled her eyes. "I mean cleansing you from bad energy. Oh, and I picked some of your lavender. I hope you don't mind, but I made tea." She pointed to a mug on the front porch. "I can make you some if you'd like. It helps calm me down. Well, usually it does."

"I can't get over how complex you are. Seriously, doll. You talk about the five layers of being? You have so many layers I'll be learning them forever. And the fact that you did all of this for us? It means the world to me." For the millionth time since they'd come together, his chest felt full. He wondered if it were possible for a heart to overflow. He slid a hand to the nape of her neck and drew her closer. "I am so sorry for everything. I'm going to speak to my parents today."

"I don't know if that's a good idea, with your dad, I mean. And I don't know if the spiritual cleanse will be enough either, because even without the bad mojo, I'll never be who he wants me to be."

"But, baby, you are the woman I want you to be, and that's all that matters."

She shook her head. "I wish it were, but there will always be a cloud over us. I'm not giving up. I'm going to figure this out. Maybe Rose can help me find a way to get through to him."

"My grandmother can't even get along with her own son. I'm not sure her advice will be any help." He squeezed her hand and said, "We're a team. You and me. And we're only going to get stronger. Now, how about we stop thinking about the negative and move on to positive, couple-strengthening activities."

She laughed. "That was a pretty good segue into naughtiness."

"You are my dirty girl. I was thinking I'd skip my run today, and you could teach me some yoga moves."

"Mm-hm. *Yoga* moves."

He pushed up to a sitting position. "I want to immerse myself in your world. Tell me what to do."

"Really?" she asked with disbelief.

"Yes, really. Come on *dirty girl.* Teach me."

"Well, there is one yoga move I've been dying to try. I saw it in your *Yoga* magazine."

"Great! Tell me what to do."

"Okay, you need to lie on your back." She pushed to her feet and moved off the mat. "Go ahead. Put your head here."

He lay down with his body half on the mat. "This doesn't feel very strenuous."

She moved to the opposite side of the mat and knelt by his head. "Yoga isn't about strenuous. It's about the coming together of the mind, body, and soul."

She pivoted up, resting her knees on the backs of her arms as she'd done before, only this time she moved quicker, and she lowered her lips to his, kissing him through their smiles. When her lips lifted, she beamed down at him and said, "That made concentrating *so* much easier. I think I'm going to like our joint yoga sessions."

Chapter Twenty-Five

"THANK YOU SO much for inviting me to your class," Diana said to Emery Saturday morning at the end of her yoga class. "I really enjoyed it. Can I sign up for weekly classes?"

"Sure. There's a schedule on the Summer House website. You can sign up or just drop in when you feel like taking a class. I'm glad you made it out this morning."

"Me too. Thanks again." Diana waved as she headed toward the parking lot.

Emery thanked the other women and men who were rolling up their mats, and talked with a few of them before they made their way to their cars. Her class size had nearly doubled over the past week, thanks to the referrals from the resort and word of mouth. She was glad the weather had held out so she could hold the class outdoors. She saw Serena and Mira heading her way. Serena had not only sent her referrals from the resort, but she and Mira had attended this morning's class and had brought three friends with them.

"Thanks to Des, Vi, and the guys, word travels fast around here," she said to Serena. Although Violet didn't *do* yoga classes, she had referred several people over the last few weeks, and Desiree asked every new customer if they'd like to take part in

Emery's classes, maintaining a constant influx of curious tourists. "I hope your friends liked the class."

She watched their friends Jana and her sister, Harper, who were as blond as their friend Sky was brunette, roll up their mats. They were all very animated, which Emery hoped meant they had enjoyed the class.

"You might have to stop taking drop-ins," Mira suggested as the girls joined them.

"Or hold more classes," Emery said, although with the way things were going at LOCAL, she didn't want to tie herself up too much. She hoped to continue to grow that aspect of her business as well. "I'll have to see how things go. I assume a lot of these people are here on vacation and probably won't show up for more than a few classes."

"We're not tourists," Harper said. "I'll definitely be back." She pulled the elastic band from her hair and shook her head. A mass of blond tumbled past her shoulders. "I think you'd have a hard time keeping Jana and Sky away now that they've discovered your classes. They both get off on this kind of thing."

"Oh yeah, we'll be back," Jana said. "Hopefully we'll bring a few of the other girls from Seaside, too."

"Seaside?" Emery asked.

"It's a cottage community down the road, off Route 6," Mira explained. "Matt's brother Pete and his wife, Jenna, have a place there. Matt stayed there the summer we got together. I'm surprised you haven't met any of our Seaside friends yet."

"She has now," Jana pointed out. "The Seaside cottages have been owned by the same families forever. They're like one big happy family."

"I was staying there when I met Sawyer, too. I think there's something in the water that makes people fall in love. But I hear some of that magic has traveled over to Bayside. You and Dean?" Sky pointed over Emery's shoulder to Dean stepping from his truck.

"You know about me and Dean?" Emery couldn't suppress her smile as she watched Dean walking toward her with a wolfish grin. They had talked this morning, and she felt much better than she had last night. Dean was going to give his father some time to cool off before trying to reason with him, and he planned to call his mother later today, after they moved Emery's things into his house. A thrill darted through her at the realization that this wasn't a temporary stopover, or a let's-see-how-it-goes situation. They were a couple in love, and they'd made the decision to cohabitate. A truly heartfelt decision. This was their lives. Their *future*. And she couldn't be happier.

"If she didn't know before, she could have guessed by the way he's visually devouring you," Mira said.

"Actually, it was my fault," Serena said. "If it was a secret, you should have clued me in."

"It's not," she said as Dean reached for her.

"What's not a secret? That you're moving in with me?" Dean leaned in for a kiss and said, "Hey, doll. I missed you."

"Geez. You've turned into a sap," Serena teased. "You guys are moving in together for real? Like, not just because of a naked man in the kitchen?"

Dean pulled Emery against his side and said, "The only naked man in her kitchen from now on is going to be me."

"She is one lucky girl," Harper whispered too loudly to Jana.

"I can hear you," Emery said with a smile. "And I have to agree."

Harper leaned closer to Sky and said, "Maybe I need to stay at Seaside or Bayside, so I can have some of that magic work for me, too."

"You and I need to hang out together and find some hot single men," Serena said to Harper.

"Maybe you should wait until you see if you're moving first," Mira suggested. "Between you gearing up to get back into interior design, Desiree and Rick thinking more about dates for their wedding, and now you two moving in together, it feels like we're all on the cusp of changes." She placed her hand on her belly and looked hopefully at Emery, who had shown her a few fertility-boosting poses before class. "Maybe luck will be on our side and we'll get pregnant this month."

"I hope so," Serena said. "But nothing is going to change too quickly on my end. If I do get a job offer, I'll need to find someone who's really good with people, numbers, *and* can handle stepping between Drake and Rick when need be."

"I've got that last part covered," Dean assured her.

"And I can pitch in during my off hours." Mira ran Matt's father's hardware store, and she'd put together a multistate small-business co-op that was doing remarkably well.

Jana put a hand on Harper's shoulder and said, "Harper's great with people and numbers."

"I've got another screenplay on the horizon," Harper said. According to Mira, she was a very talented screenplay writer and was trying to break into larger markets with bigger scripts. "But if you get in a bind, I could probably help out."

"We'll talk." Serena winked at Harper. "But right now I have to get to work."

That sparked a flurry of hugs and goodbyes as everyone went their separate ways, Dean and Emery heading inside to gather her belongings.

Emery saw Desiree walking with Cosmos up the driveway. She and Desiree had talked before her yoga class, and Emery had told her what had happened at the dinner and about finding out that Rose was Dean's grandmother. When she'd told Desiree about Dean professing his love to her, she'd gotten choked up, and when she'd told her she was moving in with him, she'd drawn happy tears from both of them. But since they hadn't had much time together, she wanted to touch base again. "Can you give me a few minutes to talk to Des?"

"Of course. Take as long as you need." He kissed her cheek and said, "I'll go scarf down some of her leftover muffins."

Emery jogged over to greet Desiree and picked Cosmos up before he could try to climb her legs. The pooch smothered her face with kisses.

"Hi," she said to Desiree. "We're just going to grab my stuff from the house."

Desiree tucked her blond hair behind her ear and kicked at a dandelion in the grass, shifting her eyes away, but not before Emery saw tears in her eyes.

"Is it silly that I'm going to miss you, even though you're only across the yard and only moved back in for a little while?" Desiree asked.

Emery shook her head, surprised by the sting of her own tears. "No, but it's weird that we're both so emotional when we weren't like this when you moved here and I was still in Virginia."

She set Cosmos down and he sat by her feet, his tongue lolling out of his mouth, tail wagging. Emery looked at the woman who had been there for her when she got her first period, her first bra, her first *thong*. She was there for her when she lost her virginity, when she decided not to go to college, and for countless other milestones—and things that shouldn't be considered milestones, like for her first traffic ticket and holding her hair back the first time she drank so much she puked.

Emery's heart climbed into her throat. "You're the reason I'm able to be here. You offered me the chance to start over on the Cape when I was floundering at home." She reached for Desiree's hand and smiled at her sparkling engagement ring. "I think the reason we weren't this emotional when you moved was because we both knew I'd end up here eventually. I couldn't be that far from my very best friend in the whole world. But it's different now, because it's not just us anymore."

"It hasn't been just us for months," Desiree reminded her.

"I know. I'm sorry."

"Don't be, Em. I had Rick, and you and Dean were finding each other." Desiree stepped closer, speaking softly. "We grew up. We've found our happy places with Rick and Dean, *and* each other. We're going to be living walking distance away from each other, and we're working together at the inn. We're so blessed. There's nothing to be sorry about. I'm truly happy for both of you."

They fell into each other's arms, hugging as tight as they ever had.

"This is all good, right?" Emery asked as they separated.

"Better than good." She patted her leg for Cosmos to follow them as they walked toward the house. "Maybe Dean will be *so* good, you'll be inspired to learn to cook."

They shared a laugh.

"Not happening," Emery said.

When they reached the door, Emery hugged her again. "I love you, you know."

"I know. And that man in there?" She motioned toward the house. "He's crazy about you, Em. Rick said he's never seen Dean happier. That's all you, babe."

"Well, well," Violet said as she came out the kitchen door. "If it isn't the pants chaser and the morning moaner."

"Violet!" Desiree shook her head.

"What? I just call 'em like I see 'em." Violet winked at Emery. "I just saw your love slave up in your bedroom."

"Ohmygosh." Emery gave Desiree a quick hug, blew a kiss to Violet, and headed upstairs.

She found Dean standing in the middle of her bedroom at the inn, shaking his head.

"You never unpacked?"

She shrugged and began tossing clothes from the piles where they lay on the dresser and chair. "I've been so busy, I just didn't think about it."

He wrapped his arms around her from behind and kissed her cheek. "I love that about you."

"That I'm a slob?"

"No. That you don't worry about the little things. I probably worry about them enough for both of us."

She turned in his arms. "I'm a little worried about moving in together."

"Emery..." he warned.

"Oh, don't worry. I'm not backing out. But..." She reached into her hamper and pulled out his boxer briefs. "I had to resort to wearing your underwear this morning because mine was missing. I think you have gremlins living in your house."

He laughed and snagged the briefs. "You wore these? And I missed it?"

"Trust me, it wasn't sexy. They kept falling down."

"Didn't you have pants on?"

"No," she said as she plucked his sweatshirt from the closet floor. "Just this."

He groaned and tackled her to the bed. She surrendered in a fit of giggles.

"You were wearing only a sweatshirt?"

"And your underwear," she said as he grabbed her ribs, causing her to squeal. "At least I put it on! I wasn't going to, but then I knew you'd want me to!"

He pressed his lips to hers, stifling her laughter.

"Thank you for not leaving the house with that gorgeous butt of yours hanging out."

"I'm a little concerned that the gremlins in your house will leave me with nothing. I mean, they've stolen my bracelet, keys, hair bands, razor, my yoga strap, and heaven knows what else. What's going to happen when *all* my things disappear?"

He nipped at her neck. "Then you'll have to be naked and jewelryless every day."

"Not completely jewelryless." She lifted her wrist with the bracelet he'd given her. "I never take this one off."

"That's good. Then the delphinium flower charm worked."

Her brows knitted with curiosity.

"Among other meanings, like protecting you from dangers that might stand in your way, expanding your options and attracting new opportunities, that little flower also has been known to help people remain open to new emotions and feelings."

"So...You put me under your spell without me knowing?"

"Something like that." He pressed his lips to hers, and then he gazed into her eyes, silently thanking the flower gods, and said, "And seeing you naked, except for that magical bracelet, every single day sounds perfect to me."

AS DEAN PULLED the truck into his driveway, his mother's car came into focus. His stomach knotted up as he parked beside it. He was relieved to see his mother sitting alone on the front porch steps, and reached for Emery's hand. It was clammy, her eyes wide and worried.

"It's okay. It's just my mom. My father drives a black Lexus."

She nodded silently.

He climbed from the truck and called out, "Hi, Mom," as he walked around to help Emery out.

His mother pushed to her feet and met them halfway up the walkway. "Hi, baby." She embraced him and then reached for Emery. "Hi, sweetie. How are you two doing?"

"We're okay," he said at the same time Emery said, "We're good."

"I mean, me and Dean are good, as a couple," she said nervously. "But we don't feel good about what happened yesterday. I'm sorry if—"

"*We're* sorry," Dean interjected, "if we caused any embarrassment for you last night."

"Honey, you and Emery couldn't embarrass me if you stood on your heads naked in the middle of dinner. I have pretty thick skin." She slid her fingers into the pockets of her white jeans and shrugged. "We should talk about your father, though. From what little I've seen, you and Dean are too good together to let a bitter man come between you."

"We're not," Emery said softly. "I mean, it's *there*, and we need to figure out a way to make things better, but"—she reached for Dean's hand—"he won't come between us."

"Emery's moving in, Mom. We have her stuff in the car."

A smile formed on his mother's face and reached all the way up to her eyes. She threw her arms around them. "I'm so happy for you both. I knew the two of you were too strong to let anything bring doubt to the love I saw in your eyes last night." She put a hand on each of their cheeks and said, "Always follow your hearts. They'll never lead you astray."

"That's what Rose told me," Emery said, remembering she hadn't mentioned to Sherry that she was working with Rose. "I just realized last night that the woman I've been helping with her back issues at LOCAL is Dean's grandmother Rose."

"I know," his mother said.

"You *know*?" Dean asked.

"Honey, you know your grandmother and I talk every day. I wasn't sure at first because she called her *Emmie*, but how many yoga back-care specialists named Emmie are there in the area?" She smiled at Emery and said, "Thank you for all you are doing for Rose. She's a very special woman, and we are all so thankful that she is finally finding relief."

"It's my pleasure. I love working with her. She and her friends are hilarious, and she's remarkably determined to get out of that wheelchair. I wish all my clients could be so inspired." Emery squeezed Dean's hand and said, "I think I'll go inside and give you guys some time to talk."

"You don't have to," Dean said.

"I know. But I need to figure out how we're going to fit my clothes in your closet, and I think it's time I finally unpack." Emery hugged his mother again and thanked her for coming over. Then she walked inside, like she hadn't just set his whole world spinning.

His mother wrapped her fingers around his arm and lowered her voice. "Your brother is a bit angry with you."

Dean inhaled deeply, trying to switch gears. "Which one and why?"

"Doug never gets upset with you. He thinks you walk on water, and at the moment, he's not aware of what happened last night. I would imagine he'll give your father an earful, but he's so busy with his wife and his job, I didn't think I should bother him with this. But Jett's another story. He called this morning, and apparently you haven't told him how serious you and Emery are. I think he feels a bit left out that he's finding out after us."

"Yeah, well, he can deal with that. I've got bigger things on my mind. Let's go sit down." They went out back to the patio and sat at the table. "Would you like something to drink? We've got ice water with fresh lemon slices, or iced tea."

"Fresh lemon slices?" She raised her brows. "Oh yes, you are definitely smitten."

He chuckled. "That I am. Would you like a drink, Mom?"

"No, honey, but thank you. What I'd like is to talk about you and your father."

Dean leaned forward, elbows on knees, gathering the courage to finally step over a line he hadn't ever before. But after what happened last night, he needed answers. "Can I ask you something first?"

"Of course."

"Why are you still with him?" he blurted out before he could chicken out. "I mean, he's not the man he used to be, and I can't imagine you're happy."

He expected his mother to take offense, but her smile remained in place. She was quiet for a long moment. So long, he wondered if this was her way of telling him he'd overstepped his bounds.

"I'm sorry, Mom. You don't have to answer that."

"It's okay. I'm just trying to figure out how to put my thoughts into words you'll understand. I've been with your father since we were in high school."

"I know, but that's no reason to remain in an unhappy marriage."

"We're not unhappy, honey. This is the hard part to explain. Do you remember when your father left, when you were just a boy?"

"How could I forget?" He ground his back teeth together, struggling with the truth. "That was the year I saw my mother with two other men. The year I lost my brother. That was the year I grew up."

"*Oh boy.*" She sighed. "I think I could use that water now, please."

With a nod, he went inside and filled two glasses. He heard Emery humming and peeked in to see her dancing with Tango in her arms in the bedroom. *I do love you, my quirky girl.*

He carried the glasses outside and handed one to his mother, who was watching him intently.

"You know that feeling you have right this second?" she said as he sat down. "That feeling of being on top of the world because you just saw the girl you love?"

"How do you know that?"

"Oh, honey, please. I've been your mother for a long time." She sipped her water. "And more importantly, I've been in love for even longer. That feeling that you have when you see Emery? That's the feeling I have for your father. Your father is the strongest, bravest man I know, but he's also become cynical and I worry that sometimes he's unfeeling."

"What he's become is a jer—" He bit back the word "jerk" and said, "He's become cold and rude. How can you say he's strong or brave when he left us?" The hurt he'd buried so long ago clawed its way out from the dark place in which he'd buried it, twisting into his gut and burning as it infiltrated his chest and limbs.

"Yes, he's become *unpleasant*, but he's still your father."

Dean scoffed. "Please don't give me a lecture about respect, because I've given that man nothing but respect, and he's thrown it in my face."

"I won't lecture at all. But it appears that I made a mistake all those years ago. I told you boys that your father left because we weren't getting along, but that wasn't the whole truth. Little boys are supposed to see their fathers as being larger than life, with no flaws. Your father was struggling back then. And I understand why you think he's weak for leaving us, but I think he's strong for the same reason."

She took another drink and set her glass on the table, then got up and paced. "Your father spent years trying to avoid becoming the type of man your grandfather was, and during that time, your father was under a tremendous amount of pressure with the growing practice."

"Everyone's under a lot of pressure, Mom. All jobs come with it, but I do remember you fighting all the time."

"We did, because your father started giving in to your grandfather's demands to work longer hours, travel, give talks, and somehow try to maintain our family. It was a sticking point for both of us. But the truth is, your father was angrier at himself than I ever would have been for his increased schedule.

He felt like he was failing me and failing you boys. He left not because he didn't love us, but because he wanted to get control of himself so you, Doug, and Jett wouldn't grow up in the same untenable situation as he and his siblings had."

Dean felt as though he'd been punched in the chest. He moved out to help *them*? He leaned back in the chair, dragging air into his lungs.

"He worried that if he continued to take out his frustrations on me, and our marriage, then he'd lose us all," his mother explained. "He's human, Dean. He didn't know how to get control of his mounting responsibilities and the frustration that came along with them while living with us. He was becoming the type of angry man he didn't want to be. Coming home every day at nine, ten o'clock at night with patient notes to dictate and three boys who wanted his attention. I know it's hard to understand, but he didn't abandon us. He left to save us."

Dean pushed to his feet, unable to sit still any longer. "Come on, Mom. He couldn't have stayed and figured it out? That's bull."

"I know it sounds like that, but it's not. Your father spent those twelve weeks working that crazy schedule and seeing a therapist three nights a week, and he still made time to see you boys as often as he could."

"If that's true, then why did you go out with other guys? And why did you let them come to the house to pick you up?"

She smiled and shook her head. "I didn't go *out* with other guys, Dean. Your grandmother sent those two men over. We didn't want to upset her, so we never told her the truth about what was going on. She thought your father needed a reminder that I was still young enough to attract another man, which he didn't need and I never would have done. But I didn't want to get into it with Rose, because then your grandfather would have gotten involved, and it would have defeated the purpose of your father's leaving to get his head on straight."

"But you went out with those men. I *saw* you. I'm not judging you, Mom. I'm just saying. I might have been a kid, but I was there, remember?"

"I did go out with them. Twice, with each one. We had dinner, and I told them exactly what was going on and set them up with my friend Eva Chase, who was more than happy to entertain them. I added about five rag dolls to my collection that year. I'd sit in a coffee shop and make them while Eva was out having fun. I would have rather been with you boys, but we couldn't blow our cover."

He continued pacing. "It's like a frigging soap opera." His mother had been making rag dolls since she was a little girl, learning how from her own mother. He knew she treasured them because of the memories they held, and now he wondered if she treasured the dolls she'd made during that time, too. The fact that she'd kept them was all the answer he needed.

"I know. Life isn't always easy. But your father came back, and he was a wonderful, attentive father to you three until years later."

"He lost Jett just because he left. You have to tell Jett the truth."

"I already have," she said solemnly. "Unfortunately, because of the way your father is now, he's not ready to forgive him yet."

"I'm not sure I am either." Dean stopped pacing and rubbed an ache at the back of his neck. "He was good to us after he came back."

"Yes, he was."

"And then I went away to school and something changed."

"He lost his father, Dean. Years ago, he'd promised your grandfather he'd carry on the Masters name with pride. Your grandfather's shoes would have been hard for ten men to fill, and your father wasn't going to let anyone else take care of *his* father's patients. And at the same time, he wasn't going to let down his own. Suddenly the success of the practice and the name of the foundation came down to *him*. He couldn't see twice the patient load. He couldn't do it alone, but he refused to accept that and refused to give up his father's or his own patients to his partners. To him that would have felt like he was letting his father, and his patients, down."

"He's a control freak," Dean seethed.

"No. He's a perfectionist. There's a difference. He cares deeply about every patient he sees."

Dean scoffed. "It doesn't seem like it. He's all about image and income."

"I know it appears that way, but he's not. He's image conscious only because it's his image, in his father's shadow, that keeps the high standards of the foundation in place and the donations rolling in so that that foundation can help millions of families. *Millions*, Dean. Not one or two, not a hundred, or even a thousand. *Millions*. He caved under the pressure of it all, sweetheart. Don't you see that? You boys were on your way to adulthood, and he only had me at home to worry about. And I didn't mind the longer hours. I've always been self-sufficient, and I knew how important this was to him. It wasn't until months later that I realized how much he had changed. How the job had sucked all the joy out of him."

Dean sank down on the chair again, his chest constricting.

"He has partners to help him with the practice."

"Yes, he does. But they're not *Masters*."

His heart thudded against his ribs as the pieces of his father's life worked into some semblance of understanding. "But he treats people—"

"Wonderfully, *and* not so nice, depending on where he is and what he's going through."

"It's inexcusable."

"Yes. It is." She sat in the chair beside him and sighed. "Honey, he pushes you because he has always seen greatness in you. He knows you'd make an amazing doctor. You were top of your class. You never let things go. You were relentless in your pursuit to save every patient who landed on your table."

"And he called me *weak* for it." The venomous word still burned. "Grandma called me *human*."

She smiled. "Grandma is an incredible woman, and she's right. But he's lost, Dean. He got swallowed up by the business and the pressure, and he doesn't know how to get out from under it. His ability to separate what he wanted for you, and what was best for you, got buried, too."

"Well, I'm not the answer. I will never go to medical school."

"I know, honey. I'm not here to ask you to do anything. Not to apologize to him, not to change your life. I just thought it was time we talked about all of this. You probably don't know this, but when Doug decided not to remain here in the States and practice with your father, he went head-to-head with him. It wasn't pleasant, but Doug isn't Jett. He left the door open, like you always have."

"Dad thinks the world of Doug because he's a doctor."

"No, honey. Dad thinks the world of each of you because

you're his sons. He doesn't think one is more or less of a man because of their job. He just wanted more for you." She paused and stared out at the gardens. "Do you remember why you decided to be a trauma nurse?"

"Of course. How could I ever forget?" He'd been in a car accident as a teenager and in addition to broken bones, he'd suffered internal bleeding. The thing he remembered most was the calm and confident demeanor of the trauma nurse. She'd taken the overwhelming fear out of the situation, and he'd wanted to do that for others. It had been a bone of contention with his father, who had wanted him to follow in his footsteps and join the practice. That had been the tip of the skeleton that would forever haunt them.

"You were determined to be the best trauma nurse you could. You told me that you were made for the job. Remember?"

He nodded. "I do. I thought I was."

"But you learned otherwise," his mother reminded him. "Real life got the better of you."

His pulse raced with the memories of too many nights feeling as though he were in a dark tunnel with no way out. "Seeing all that death and destruction nearly killed me," he said defensively as his mother's point began sinking in. "I might be weak, but I know what I'm capable of, and that wasn't it. I chose to surround myself with life instead of death."

"You are not weak, honey. What is it with you men? You all think there's some line drawn in the sand between weak and strong, and you have to be on one side of it or another at all times. Life isn't like that. We are all weak, strong, pathetic sometimes and valiant at other times. You did the right thing for yourself by changing careers. You were stressed even when you weren't working because, like your father, you carried the emotions of the job with you on your days off, and that stress affected every aspect of your life. But it's easier when it's just you with no one else's life hanging in the balance. Don't you think it's a little wrong to judge your father for not taking that *out*, when he has so many people—families, physicians, children, researchers—relying on him? How does a man walk away from families and patients who have developed years of trust in him? Tell me, Dean. If you had been him, after practicing for decades, becoming a pillar of the community because of your dedication to medicine and to the well-being of children around the world, could you have walked away from it?"

His throat tightened with emotion, making it hard to breathe. It was all he could do to process the truth in her words.

"He may not be the same person he used to be, but, honey, I know the man I married is still in there somewhere. I get glimpses of him from time to time, and I can't walk away from that. I see the father who used to read you bedtime stories and take you fishing. The man who adores you, regardless of whether he's able to show it at the moment." She set her hand on his and said, "I know it's hard to hear the truth, but you needed to hear it even if it doesn't excuse what your father has done. What you do with all of this information is up to you."

He saw Emery walking by the window and his heart ached. "I will never be okay with the way he demeaned Emery's career or the way he treated her. I love her, Mom. She's my life now, not him."

His mother's eyes dampened and she nodded, a small smile lifting her lips. "I know, baby. It's a shame that you feel there's a choice to be made, and it's a greater shame that he can't see the light. But I have faith that one day he will. We can't always control the things we think, or do, no matter how hard we try. We're all only human."

Dean reached for his mother's hand. "Thank you for making *me* see the light. I never in a million years would have seen myself as anything like Dad. But I guess I was in denial." He shook his head, thinking of Emery again. They had even more in common than he'd thought. "I'm sorry that you're caught in the crossfire, Mom. I never wanted to hurt you."

"You didn't hurt me, baby. What hurts me is seeing my family suffer. But that's more on your father than anyone else. I have faith that we'll get past this."

"Mom, can you please just tell me one thing? Are you *happy*? Is what you have right now *enough*?"

"It has to be. I love him."

Emery peeked outside with a hesitant smile, and he waved her over. She took his hand and he pulled her down to his lap. The knots in his chest began to unravel. He felt like he could finally breathe again. He tried to imagine what it would be like if Emery's life suddenly took a stressful or tragic turn and she changed in ways that weren't pleasant. As he gazed into her eyes, he knew he'd still love her just the same.

He looked at his mother, who was watching them adoringly, and said, "I think I understand where you're coming from. Thanks, Mom."

Chapter Twenty-Six

EMERY HAD WOKEN up in Dean's arms Monday morning and they'd made slow, sweet love. Afterward, Dean had dipped his toes into learning yoga. They'd ended up kissing more than exercising, and when Dean turned onto his stomach and began doing push-ups, all his glorious muscles flexing temptingly, Emery had lain on his back. *Can you handle a few more pounds?* Dean had pumped out thirty more push-ups with ease before sweeping her beneath him and taking her in more delicious kisses. Drake and Rick had interrupted them and dragged Dean off for a run, which she knew he needed—the run, *and* the guy time. She'd taught her morning class and then found Dean putting the final touches on the flagstone patio, which was beyond gorgeous. He'd called Rose that morning, as unbeknownst to Emery, he did most mornings, and he'd told her *everything.*

Now, as Emery waited in Rose's living room while Rose got ready for their session, her nerves got the better of her.

It felt weirdly confining to meet in her room again instead of the larger one downstairs, but Magdeline and Arlin were down in the theater watching a special showing of *Gone with the Wind,* and they didn't need the extra space for their session.

Emery had offered to reschedule so Rose could watch the movie, but Rose claimed she'd *had enough Clark Gable for one lifetime.* She said she'd be happy to *plunk herself down and watch Dirty Dancing* if they ever gave her the chance.

"I'll just get the mats ready," Emery called into the bedroom, and began moving the coffee table and chairs.

"Why didn't you tell me you were dating my grandson?" Rose called out to her.

"I knew you and the other ladies knew Dean because of his work in the gardens, and I didn't want to make things weird for him. But I honestly didn't realize you were his grandmother until I met his father."

"Okay, I'll buy that," Rose said, as if she had a choice. "But what's your plan now?"

Emery huffed out a breath, thinking about the weekend. After his mother's visit, Dean had received a call from Jett, who was out of town again. They'd spoken for more than an hour, and Dean had seemed relieved when he'd finally ended the call. The rest of the weekend had passed in a strange bubble of contentment for Emery and Dean. They both thought it was odd that they could be so happy having breakfast with their friends, going swimming in the ocean, and out to dinner while the relationship between Dean and his father was in complete turmoil. But while stargazing on the patio last night, they'd realized the love they shared was exclusively *theirs.* Family would always have a hold on them on some level, and they were both determined to try to make things better with his father. But no matter what happened with his father, or in the future with any other family members, they knew it wouldn't lessen what they felt for each other.

"Emmie?" Rose called from the bedroom, pulling Emery

from her thoughts. "Silence is not always golden."

After everything Dean had told her that his mother had said to him, she wondered if maybe his father just needed extra love and understanding. "I'm going to kill him with kindness," Emery answered.

She heard Rose laughing at the same moment a knock sounded at the door.

"Want me to answer that?"

"Please. It's probably Mag and Arlin realizing that even Clark Gable gets boring after a while. We might need to head down to the larger room after all. I'm just going to use the bathroom. I'll be right out."

Emery pulled the door open, and the hair on the back of her neck stood on end. "Mr. Masters."

Surprise registered in the clenching of his jaw, and she saw a flash of Dean in that mannerism.

"Emery," he said tightly, and walked past her.

Emery closed her eyes for a second, inhaling a calming breath. It didn't help. She turned and found him standing in the center of the room, looking like a bomb ready to explode.

"Where is my mother?"

She bit back the urge to say, *She's busy being ashamed of you for your lack of manners*, straightened her spine, and reminded herself of her resolution to be extra understanding. Forcing a smile, she said, "She's in the bathroom. How are you today?"

He visibly bristled, clearly surprised by her kindness. "Late for a meeting."

"I'm sorry. I meant, how are *you*. I wasn't asking about your schedule. You had a trying time Friday night, and I apologize for my part in that." She felt herself shaking and clasped her hands in front of her, hoping he wouldn't notice.

A deep V appeared between his brows, as if he didn't understand what she'd said. "Yes, well. No apology necessary."

She had no idea if it was courage or stupidity, or why she was doing it, but her shaky legs carried her toward him. "I believe an apology is necessary. I was raised to be polite, and though I have no idea why you don't approve of my career, or my being with your son, I am sorry for whatever I've done to cause strife between the two of you."

His eyes narrowed. "It's not my job to approve or disapprove of your career."

"Darn right it's not," she said before she could check herself, but he was looking at her with a piercing stare. She'd be darned if she'd allow him of all people to spend one more second making her feel small.

"As for my son, he's capable of being a much greater man than he's achieved, and your involvement with him could hold him back."

"What on earth are you talking about?" *So much for kindness.* "Dean is twice the man you'll ever be."

He drew his shoulders back, and she swore he grew several inches taller right before her eyes. "I'm a leader in the field of pediatric neurosurgery. The head of three boards of directors. I have been invited to speak all over the world about—"

"Do you even hear yourself?" Her words tumbled out fast and accusatory. "You're spouting all those things off as if they speak to who you are. You're so messed up you don't even see the difference, and here I felt sorry for you."

He chuckled. "Young lady, I of all people do not need your pity."

"You're wrong," she said, pointing up at him. "You need it more than anyone I know, even if you're not deserving of it.

You achieved those things you mentioned at the expense of your family. What kind of man does that? What kind of man leaves his adoring wife alone so he can hobnob with the rich? What kind of man doesn't do everything within his power to make amends with his sons he left when they were teenagers? And I'm not talking about Dean." She had verbal diarrhea, and there was no hope of stopping it despite his clenching jaw and the steam pouring out his ears. "What kind of man speaks to his own mother the way you do? You should be ashamed of yourself. You act like a spoiled child who expects the world—and even worse, your *family*—to kowtow to him. And you don't care about your sons' happiness."

"What do you know about parenting?" he seethed in a voice so dead calm it sent her stepping backward.

"Douglas Masters, you hush your mouth right this second."

They both turned at the sound of Rose's voice. She stood in the bedroom doorway wearing a pair of black spandex pants and a shirt that had YOGA GRANNY emblazoned across her chest. Emery's heart swelled and ached at once. She'd made such progress, and *this* was what she was forced to endure?

"Mother, sit down." He rushed to her side, towering over Rose, and tried to usher her toward the couch. "You'll hurt yourself."

She swatted at his hands. "Douglas!"

He stilled, breathing hard.

"Do not touch me." Rose smoothed a shaky hand down her chest. "I have sat by and watched you treat other people badly for a very long time. I am ashamed of that, but I'm more ashamed of the fact that despite years of love, years of me teaching you right from wrong and supporting your endeavors, you turned out to be just like your father."

"He was a great man," he said adamantly.

"He was a pillar of strength," Rose agreed. "A great pediatric neurosurgeon, but he was *not* a great *man*." She walked over to Emery, and his jaw hung open with disbelief at the sight of her walking, unaided, standing straighter than she had in who knew how long.

"Emery Andrews did what you could not. She helped me. She listened to me when I told her that I knew I'd be able to regain my mobility, and she *believed* in me. She is a great *woman*. You could learn a thing or two from her."

"Mother—"

Rose silenced him with her palm and a glare so powerful Emery held her breath. "You are my son, but you are not omnipotent. Please do not do to your son what your father has done to you."

His angry gaze moved between Emery and Rose, and Emery swore she saw sorrow beneath the anger flaming in his eyes. But that might have been wishful thinking. She was about ready to pass out. He straightened his spine once again, lifted his chin, and stormed out the door without a word.

The air rushed from Emery's lungs, and sobs followed. She collapsed onto the couch. "I'm sorry," she cried. "Oh, Rose, I'm so sorry."

Rose sank down to the couch beside her and gently wrapped Emery in her arms. "Come to Grandma Rosie."

"I'm sorry." Emery cried on her shoulder, soaking in her comfort and feeling guilty at the same time.

"I'm not. He needed a good wallop in the patootie. You were the only one strong enough to give it to him."

"I've ruined everything. He'll never make up with Dean as long as I'm in his life."

Rose held her tighter. "I'm his mother, and this hurts me to say, but he doesn't matter, sweetheart. You and my grandson are the only two people in your relationship that matter. Don't you let his bitterness spoil your beauty."

Unable to speak past the lump in her throat, Emery stayed with Rose long after she finally stopped crying. Rose comforted her, and they talked about the changes Dean's father had gone through and how she believed he'd fought them for as long as was humanly possible. They talked about Emery's family and how she hadn't missed them as much as she'd thought she might until recently. But she knew being with Dean was where she belonged. They talked until Emery built up the courage to go home and tell Dean what had happened.

As she drove down Dean's street, she thought of the first day she'd arrived at the Cape and how her heart had leapt at the sight of Dean standing in the yard looking at her with what she knew now had been love in his eyes. She'd been so blind. But her eyes were wide open now. She had to get to him before his father made her seem out of her mind—

Oh, no.

She parked beside the shiny black Lexus, panting as if she'd just run a marathon. *No, no, no!* She might have lost her mind back there, but she'd meant every word she'd said, and she wasn't going to let him twist it into something more horrible than it was and try to poison Dean toward her.

She threw her car door open, charged up the front steps, and flew through the front door, hoping she could save their relationship. Three men pushed to their feet.

Dean, his father, and the mini-me beside him had to be Jett.

And by the look on Dean's face, she was too late.

DEAN FELT LIKE he'd been run over by a Mack truck. First his brother knocked him off-kilter by showing up out of the blue because "You needed me, bro," then his father stormed into his house unannounced, and now Emery blew in, looking like she was facing a firing squad.

Not in my house.

It sounded to him as though she'd already faced that particular nightmare.

He ate up the space between them and wrapped her trembling body in his arms. "I've got you."

"I'm sorry! I tried to be nice, but—"

"But you can't do anything but be brutally honest," Dean said in her ear. "And I adore you for that, doll." His grandmother had once told him that the woman he'd fall in love with wasn't the one who would keep him up all night doing dirty things or building up his ego. *Though she may do those things, she'll be the one you want to last forever for a million other reasons like the way she listens, and makes you think, and the way she makes you a better man. The woman you fall in love with will be the one you cherish and protect, like your mother's treasured dolls.* "You are my perfect match."

She pulled back, her eyes darting erratically from him to Jett.

Jett lifted his chin and said, "Hey, spitfire."

Her confused gaze slowed only long enough to reach his father. Her fingers curled tightly into Dean's side as the man who had dismissed her career, thought she was a distraction to his son, and had tried to use her as a weapon against Dean lowered his gaze to the floor.

Dean couldn't believe his eyes. His father never lowered his gaze. Not for anyone.

Emery pushed against Dean's side, like she needed his strength to remain erect as her shaky voice threaded from her lips. "I'm sor—"

His father stepped forward, silencing her with his mere presence. His gaze was soft and apologetic as he opened his mouth to speak, then wordlessly closed it again.

Tension hung in the air like a ghost suffocating them all.

"Dad, you owe—"

This time it was Dean his father silenced, with the lifting of his large hand. "I know, son. Give me a minute, please."

Dean tightened his grip on Emery, who seemed frozen in place.

"I am many things," his father finally said in a regretful tone Dean had never heard until his father had appeared on his doorstep an hour earlier. "And until earlier today, I thought being a strong man was at the top of my list. Now I am beginning to understand that I have been mistaken."

Emery's nails dug into Dean's waist, but she didn't move, didn't speak. Dean was pretty sure she couldn't. Things were not fixed between him and his father, and definitely not between his father and Jett. But this was a start. When his father had stormed through his front door ranting about Emery, Dean had challenged him, and his father had collapsed in a chair, shaking his head, and said, *You don't understand, son. She's right about what she said. She got under my skin. I have a lot of thinking and making up to do with too many people to count, but this is where it starts, and it's because of that doll of yours.*

"You've done great things," she conceded.

"Don't do that," his father said sternly.

Her nails dug deeper into Dean's skin. He ground his teeth together, willing to take whatever pain he needed to in order for her to get through this.

"Don't back down on your convictions," his father demanded. "I've achieved great things in my professional life, but you were right. I did so at an expense so great, I'm not sure it will ever have been worth it. But I want to try. I'm going to try. And I owe you a great deal of thanks."

Tears streamed from Emery's eyes as her hand slipped from Dean's waist and she wrapped herself around his father's chest, dwarfed by his size. His father's arms hung stiff by his sides as he stared down at the top of her head, but she didn't relent. She simply hugged him tighter.

His father's gaze met Dean's, and Dean said, "She only knows one way to be, Dad. As real as the day is long."

Emery pushed back, and his father stopped her with an awkward, but well-meaning embrace.

Sometime later, after a more-than-slightly uncomfortable conversation and promises to work on figuring things out, Dean closed the door behind his father, feeling like he could breathe for the first time in years.

"I never thought I'd see the day..." Dean pulled Emery into his arms and hugged her.

"This hasn't been a great way to get to know you," Emery said to Jett. "I didn't know you'd be here. I promise I'm really not a crazy person."

"I'm not so sure about that. Look who you're with." Jett winked at Emery. "He didn't know I was coming either. But when Mom told me what happened at the benefit dinner, I knew my brother needed backup."

Jett pointed at Tango, who was creeping under the couch

skirt with the white thong Emery had worn to the benefit dinner hanging from his mouth. "Is that…?"

"What the heck?" Dean dropped to his knees, lifted the decorative flap, and peered beneath the couch. "Holy cow. Em, you've got to see this."

She and Jett dropped to their knees on either side of him and looked under the couch at a stash of Emery's underwear, her necklace, headbands, two sets of keys—Emery's and the set for the golf cart—and one of her pink flip-flops.

"Your place isn't the Bermuda Triangle after all." She laughed as she pushed to her feet, and man, it was so good to see her smile. "You just have thieves for pets. Oh my gosh, you guys…"

They followed her gaze to Cash prancing out of the guest room dragging Emery's missing yoga strap, and they all laughed.

"*Our* place," he reminded her. "I guess there were bigger forces than me trying to keep you here." He pulled her close and glanced at Jett. "Now, if we could just get rid of this guy, maybe we can leave some more things on the floor for our kitties to steal."

Epilogue

EMERY PULLED HER legs up to her chest, her fingers tucked inside the sleeves of her sweatshirt. The temperature had dipped with the mid-September sun as all their friends gathered around the table in Desiree's yard for a late dinner. She couldn't believe she'd been at the Cape for four months already. Her brothers had come up to visit in August, and after a brief banging of chests with Dean, they realized he was just as alpha as they were, and they could trust him to take care of her. Austin continued to call Dean *Viking*. And when they were out dancing at Undercover, one look at all the cute girls and her brothers threatened to never leave. She missed them, but she was enjoying what she and Desiree had deemed as their *grown-up lives*. She knew her brothers were only a phone call away and nothing would ever come between them.

Cosmos pawed at her leg, and she lifted him into her lap. "I'm still convinced you had something to do with Tango and Cash's thievery, in some sort of animalistic matchmaking scheme." The pup cocked his head and licked her chin. She leaned down and whispered, "Thank you." The kitties had continued stealing Emery's things. Since she'd moved in with him, she and Dean had discovered another stash of items under

Dean's bed that they hadn't noticed had gone missing—pens, hair clips, underwear…

Dean's laughter drew her attention like music to her ears. He still wore her necklace around his wrist, and they'd added his elemental sign to the mix. Her strong, stable man was an earth sign. Their love even made astrological sense. While she lifted him from the confines of reality, nourishing his sillier side and showing him the intangible, magical side of things, he kept her grounded. And like the banks to a flowing creek, he supported her creativity and ideas so her dreams could flourish, while she continued believing in miracles.

And one miracle seemed to be coming true.

Things between Dean and his father weren't great yet, but they were working on it. They were talking more, and his parents had come for dinner twice since she'd moved in. His father was so blown away with Rose's progress now that she was out of her wheelchair, he'd even relented about the value of yoga back-care. Just last week, after observing one of Emery's yoga classes at LOCAL, he had proposed that his practice refer patients to her. She considered that a major milestone. But everything wasn't coming up roses on all Douglas Masters Sr. fronts. Jett wasn't as accepting of his father's apologies as Dean had been, though Emery hoped one day he would be. No man could have raised three sons as loving and remarkable as Dean, as affable as Jett, and as kind as Doug—whom she'd had the pleasure of meeting via Skype the week after she'd moved in with Dean—without possessing a large amount of kindness, patience, and tact. Their father simply needed to dig out from under years of mistakes to find and nurture those sides of himself again. But he was making strides in the right direction, and for that she was grateful. They all had a long road ahead of them, but she knew it would be worth it.

Emery snuck a piece of a corn muffin from Dean's plate, but he was too busy giving Drake and Jett a hard time about not having steady girlfriends to notice, as if he'd become the authority on the subject. Jett was down for a visit, but Dean was doing his best to convince him to stay for a few weeks.

Desiree leaned closer and said, "Rick found a plate big enough for two in one of the wedding catalogs that says HIS and HERS on opposite sides. We should get you guys a few of those."

"Why bother?" Dean said as Emery snagged another piece of muffin from his plate. "She'd eat only from my side anyway." He pressed his lips to hers. "Right, doll?"

"I didn't think you were paying attention."

"I'm always paying attention to you." He kissed her again.

"We need to get going if we're going to make it to the drive-in," she reminded him.

She'd recently enjoyed a girls' night with Rose, Magdeline, and Arlin, and they'd watched *Dirty Dancing*. Afterward, as they were discussing movies, Rose told her all about how much Dean had loved the drive-in theater as a boy, and how his mother used to make popcorn sprinkled with sugar and cinnamon for him and his brothers to eat during the movie. Emery had gone one better. With all of the hullabaloo around the benefit dinner, she'd forgotten to show Dean what she'd bought for them in the back room of Devi's Discoveries. Tonight, that edible lingerie would come in handy—and it just happened to be cinnamon flavored. After all, her man did like her *hot*. A little thrill darted through her with the thought.

"You guys are going to the drive-in?" Jett asked.

Dean nodded. "Yeah, why?"

"Because I called Mom to see if I could swing by and pick

up something from the attic, and she said she and Dad were going to the drive-in."

"I guess old dogs can learn new tricks." Dean glanced at Jett and said, "You know that land you have overlooking the bay?"

"Yeah, what about it?"

"Now that things are getting better with Dad, maybe you should consider moving back here. Build yourself a place. Get a real life again instead of living out of suitcases," Dean suggested.

Jett scoffed. "*Getting better* is not exactly good."

The sound of a car door brought Serena to her feet. "Oh good. Harper's here."

Drake pulled her down by the back of her shirt. "Why is she here?"

"I told you she was coming by to talk with me about taking over part-time while I get back into interior design." Serena swatted his hand away from her shirt and ran toward the fence, waving.

Violet came outside carrying a tray of desserts. She took one look at Drake as she handed out the bowls and said, "Careful, boy. You'll crack your jaw."

"Hey, Harp!" Serena yelled. "Over here!"

Jett whistled. "I'd like to *harp* on her for a while."

Dean glared at him.

All the girls got up to hug Harper, and Jett got in on the game, pushing between the women and embracing her.

"Jett Masters, at your service." He pulled out a chair and said, "You can sit right here, pretty lady."

"Put your tongue back in your mouth," Serena said. "She's here to talk business."

"Who says I'm not talking business?" Jett arched a brow at Harper and said, "I'm especially good at *risky* business."

"I need to give you guys a lesson in pickup lines," Violet said. "Don't use them."

Harper giggled.

Emery glanced in the bowl Violet set before her and gasped with delight. "Karamel Sutra!"

She looked at Desiree and in unison they said, "Who needs men when we have Ben?"

The girls all laughed, and the guys groaned.

"Come on, doll." Dean handed her a spoon. "Let's finish this who-needs-men nonsense, because I'm pretty sure you need me."

She gave him a chaste kiss. "You know it."

They all dug into their ice cream.

"I want that delicious core." Emery stuck her spoon right into the middle of the bowl, and it clinked against something hard. "Hey, what the…?" She dug around and uncovered a clear plastic bubble, the type toys in gum ball machines came in. She picked it out and wiped it off with a napkin. Her eyes caught on a sparkling ring inside at the same time Dean sank to the ground on one knee. Her heart skidded.

"Dean? You're not…?"

"I most definitely am," he said with a serious expression.

There was a collective gasp from everyone except Violet, who was taking pictures, and obviously in on the plan. Emery was shaking as he took the plastic container from her.

She. Couldn't. Breathe.

"Emery Andrews," he said with a slightly shaky voice, which made her heart tumble even more. "Ever since the first day I set eyes on you, you have consumed me. And every day since, you have filled me with happiness, frustration, *horniness*, and so much love. I'm not sure how I can ever love you more than I do right this second. But I know that in the next second, and the next, and for years to come, my love will continue to grow. Because you are *my perfect*. You are smart and beautiful. You're fun and inspiring. You make me think and feel and *hope…*"

He opened the plastic bubble with shaky hands, which made her heart swell even more. He put his large fingers into the little bubble and withdrew the most gorgeous ring she'd ever seen. Tears sprang from her eyes as she took in the adoring look in Dean's eyes, and the beautiful ring he held in his palm. There must have been a dozen intricately designed yellow- and rose-gold leaves, intertwined with three thin gold vines. In that ring, she saw *life*. It was perfectly Dean, simple and elegant, strong and bound in nature. And she couldn't love it more.

He took her hand in his and said, "My beautiful doll, will you do me the honor of allowing me to love, honor, cherish, and ravish you for the rest of our lives? To father your children and grow your lemons? To be your yoga partner and learn to meditate beside you on the patio we built together overlooking the bay? Sweetheart, will you marry me and let me spend the rest of my life trying to find your inner bliss?"

Tears slid down her cheeks as she nodded vehemently. "Yes. Of course, yes!" She launched herself into his arms and he tumbled to the ground, both of them laughing and kissing as everyone cheered.

"I love you so much," she said between kisses. "I can't believe you love me, but I'm so glad you do!"

He smiled and kissed her again. "Don't you ever doubt it, baby. I am yours, and you are mine."

"Forever," she said through her tears. "I was never like those little girls who dreamed of white weddings and forevers. And now I can't imagine not having forever with you."

"Aw," Desiree and Serena said in unison as Dean lifted

Emery onto his lap, his strong arms and broad chest cradling her against him.

"You've been my forever since the day I first saw you. Now," he said proudly, "for your ring."

"The ring!" Desiree exclaimed. She and Serena plopped down on either side of them. Harper peered over Emery's shoulder, and the guys watched, while Violet circled them, taking more pictures.

Dean opened his hand and pointed at the leaves on the ring. "These are oak leaves. They symbolize longevity, patience, faith, power, and endurance. They also symbolize humble beginnings, which is how I feel we started out together."

He kissed her cheek, and she couldn't do more than nod.

"It's incredible how many things they stand for," he said. "Just like you, baby. You are the embodiment of everything good and everything possible. Thank you for loving me."

More tears streaked down her cheeks as a disbelieving laugh fell from her lips. "Thank me? Thank *you*."

He slipped the ring on her finger, and with a smirk on his handsome face, he held up a sparkling gold chain she hadn't noticed was attached to the ring. "Because my girl often loses things…"

Emery couldn't stop smiling as he laid the glimmering chain over the back of her hand, wrapped it around her wrist like a bracelet, and secured it to a tiny gold hoop, creating a gold leash that ran from her ring to her wrist.

"Oh my gosh," she said just above a whisper. "You really do know me."

"Know *and* adore you, doll. And my feelings will only get stronger with every passing minute."

As he pulled her into another kiss, their friends converged on them in mass, sharing congratulations and well wishes as they passed them from one warm hug to the next. When she finally landed back in Dean's arms, she felt like she was walking on air.

"I hate to spoil the fun," Desiree said, "but you guys are going to be late for the movie."

"I had wanted to get to the drive-in early," Emery said, debating forgoing the movie so they could celebrate, but she'd finally planned the perfect date. She knew they'd be celebrating for the rest of their lives, and tonight was the last night the drive-in theater was open for the season.

"Why early, doll?"

"Because I don't want anyone to take our spot." She went up on her toes and whispered, "Rose and the girls clued me in to the best make-out spot. And I *might* have worn edible lingerie."

His eyes flamed. "Sorry, guys. We're taking off. We'll catch up tomorrow!" He took her by the hand and ran through the gate.

They laughed and kissed the whole way to his truck, and when they finally tumbled into the front seat, he came down over her, taking her in a long, sensual kiss. She came away breathless.

"Who needs the drive-in theater?" he said seductively.

"You mean you don't want to pop my drive-in-theater cherry?"

She'd never seen a man scramble into the driver's seat faster. He might be calm, and she might be chaos, but they were each other's *perfect match*.

The End

Ready for More Bayside?

Fall in love with Drake Savage and Serena Mallery as they navigate the wild waters of friends-to-lovers in search of their happily ever after.

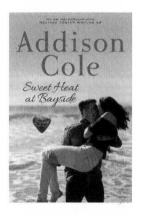

Drake Savage has always done the right thing, especially where beautiful and fiercely determined Serena Mallery is concerned—even when it means keeping his feelings for her to himself. Serena has always wanted more than what their small town of Wellfleet, Massachusetts has to offer, and Drake's roots are so deeply entrenched in the Cape, it's all he can do to watch her pack up her life and move away.

Serena has always had big dreams. As a teenager she dreamed of becoming an interior designer and marrying smart, musically inclined, sexy-as-sin Drake Savage. Now she's finally landed a killer job with a top interior design firm, but though she has spent the last four years working side by side with Drake, he's never made a move. Four years is long enough for her to accept reality, and her new job in Boston is the perfect way to move on.

A weak moment leads to sizzling, sensual kisses, opening a door through which they've both been aching to walk. But Serena's determined not to give up her shot at the career she's always dreamed of, and Drake has loved her for too many years to stand in her way. With true love at their fingertips and a world of unstoppable passion igniting between them, can the two star-crossed lovers find their way to their happily ever after?

Have you met the Seaside Summers friends?

Read, Write, Love at Seaside

The complete series is now available for your binge-reading pleasure!

Bestselling author Kurt Remington lives to write. He spends twelve hours a day in front of his computer, rarely leaving the seclusion of his beach-front property, where he's come to finish his latest thriller—that is, until free-spirited Leanna Bray nearly drowns in the ocean trying to save her dog. Kurt's best-laid plans are shot to hell when he comes to their rescue. Kurt's as irritated as he is intrigued by the sexy, hot mess of a woman who lives life on a whim, forgets everything, and doesn't even know the definition of the word organized.

Leanna's come to the Cape hoping to find a fulfilling career in the jam-making business, and until she figures out her own life, a man is not on the menu. But Leanna can't get the six-two, deliciously muscled and tragically neat Kurt out of her mind. She tells herself she's just stopping by to say thank you, but the heart-warming afternoon sparks an emotional and unexpectedly sweet ride as Kurt and Leanna test the powers of Chemistry 101: Opposites Attract.

More Books By The Author

Sweet with Heat: Seaside Summers

Read, Write, Love at Seaside
Dreaming at Seaside
Hearts at Seaside
Sunsets at Seaside
Secrets at Seaside
Nights at Seaside
Seized by Love at Seaside
Embraced at Seaside
Lovers at Seaside
Whispers at Seaside

Sweet with Heat: Bayside Summers
(Includes future publications)

Sweet Love at Bayside
Sweet Passions at Bayside
Sweet Heat at Bayside
Sweet Escape at Bayside

Stand Alone Women's Fiction Novels
by Melissa Foster (Addison Cole's steamy alter ego)
The following titles may include some harsh language

Chasing Amanda (mystery/suspense)
Come Back to Me (mystery/suspense)
Have No Shame (historical fiction/romance)
Megan's Way (literary fiction)
Traces of Kara (psychological thriller)
Where Petals Fall (suspense)

Acknowledgments

If this is your first Addison Cole novel, you have an entire world of fiercely passionate and loyal heroes and heroines waiting to meet you in my Sweet with Heat romance collection. All Sweet with Heat books are written to stand alone, and you can jump in anytime. But you might enjoy starting at the very beginning, with *Read, Write, Love at Seaside*, the book that started the Sweet with Heat sensation (free at the time of this publication). Get more information here: www.AddisonCole.com

Emery and Dean's story was so fun to write. I'd like to thank Alex van Frank, C-IAYT Certified Yoga Therapist, for her constant support and never-ending patience with my incessant questions.

If you'd like to see the cottage Dean's house was loosely based on, take a look at Firefly Cottage in Cornwall, UK. I knew it was perfect for Dean, and it became my inspiration the very first time I saw it.

As always, thank you to Lisa Filipe and Lisa Bardonski for our fun chats and headbanging. Heaps of gratitude go out to my meticulous and talented editorial team. Thank you, Kristen, Penina, Juliette, Marlene, Lynn, Justinn, and Elaini for all you do for me and for our readers. And as always, I am forever grateful to my main squeeze, Les, who allows me the time to create our wonderful worlds.

Addison Cole is the sweet alter ego of *New York Times* and *USA Today* bestselling and award-winning author Melissa Foster. Addison enjoys writing humorous, and deeply emotional, contemporary romance without explicit sex scenes or harsh language. Addison spends her summers on Cape Cod, where she dreams up wonderful love stories in her house overlooking Cape Cod Bay.

Visit Addison on her website or chat with her on social media. Addison enjoys discussing her books with book clubs and reader groups and welcomes an invitation to your event.

Addison's books are available in paperback, digital, and audio formats.

www.AddisonCole.com
www.facebook.com/AddisonColeAuthor